meli

PENELOPE NOW

ALSO BY JOHN CROSBY

An Affair of Strangers
Nightfall
The Company of Friends
Dear Judgment
Party of the Year

PENELOPE NOW

A NOVEL

JOHN CROSBY

STEIN AND DAY/*Publishers*/New York

First published in 1981
Copyright © 1981 by John Crosby
All rights reserved
Designed by Judith E. Dalzell
Printed in the United States of America
STEIN AND DAY/*Publishers*
Scarborough House
Briarcliff Manor, N.Y. 10510

Library of Congress Cataloging in Publication Data

Crosby, John, 1912-
  Penelope now.

  I. Title.
PS3553.R55P4   813'.54   80-6149
ISBN 0-8128-2793-7   AACR2

For Jimmy and Werna Kidd
who brought us our first pigs

__ BOOK __
ONE

__ CHAPTER __
ONE

SILENT IN THE spring sunshine under the biggest pear tree lay the death of a great civilization.

The way New York would look when the end came.

Where once had been the most tightly ordered discipline and high purpose. Now cobwebs, filth and decay.

The larvae of the wax moths had tunneled through the magnificent hexagons, destroying geometry, symmetry, reason. The floor of the yellow hive was littered with dead bees, the death stink rising in Jessie's nostrils like an accusation.

If I'd fed them properly . . . I'm too busy! Too alone!

Excuses.

Angry with herself.

Shaken to her very toes.

Jessie slammed down the lid of the yellow hive, hurried out of the orchard to the house. In the back kitchen she stripped off her jeans and work shirt and stepped into the downstairs shower.

To wash off her solitude, her premonitions . . .

"Anybody home?"

She could see him indistinctly through the frosted glass door. All six foot six of him, almost as wide as he was tall.

"Harry Sloane, you big baboon! You get out of here!" she said furiously.

"What you doin' takin' a shower in the middle of the day?" Full of good humor.

3

"You make a practice busting into ladies' bathrooms! I bet your wife doesn't allow that in your own home!"

"In my own home it's not so much fun," the big man said peaceably. "I come to ask you want some he'p laying that phosphate."

Jessie's indignation vanished, replaced by greater urgencies. She poked her head out the shower door: "You bring your spreader?"

"Parked right out on your front lawn."

"Hand me that towel, and then get out of here so I can get dressed."

Drying herself she thought: I don't even stay mad at him long enough. He's moving in, moving in—and I hate him. Hate his fat ass, his redneck ways. But I need the help. Laying the phosphate by hand would have taken three days. With his tractor and spreader—a couple of hours.

She rode the codpiece on the Fordall as she had ridden on her father's tractor, hands holding the iron seat on which rode the fattest ass in Altamont County, shouting advice in Harry Sloane's ear, advice he largely ignored. After all it was his tractor.

The sun blazed down from a sky blue as cornflowers, Jessie feeling the joy of it in her bones. I'm vernal as a hyacinth, she was thinking. I'm Ceres herself. Watching the white ducks as they circled the barn and making careful note of which window they went in. Later she'd have to rescue them and their duckling from the rats. Watching the geese as they waddled to the pond because later they'd be laying eggs and *they'd* have to be rescued from the foxes.

Between trips, while loading phosphate and green sand on the spreader, they squabbled. Much too amiably.

"Where you get this stuff, Jessie?" She was Jessie now where before she'd been Miz Jenkins, then Miz Jessie, now just Jessie—movin' in. "And how much you pay for it?"

"Three hundred dollars. And it's paid for." A dig at Harry Sloane who ran his huge farm altogether on bank loans.

"Three hundred dollars to fertilize this little field! You never get that back, Jessie."

"It last four, five years. Not like that chemical trash you laying on your fields, Harry Sloane." Harry Sloane used chemicals and pesticides that made Jessie sick even to think about. Between them yawned a gulf wide enough to drive the Fordall through. Jessie was New Farmer who hated pesticides, hated the use of chemical fertilizers; Harry Sloane was Modern

4

Farmer, which is to say eighty bushels of corn an acre and never mind what that did to the land.

Ideologically they were as far apart as the Catholics and Protestants in the seventeenth century, each not only convinced of the righteousness of his cause but of the wickedness of the other side.

"Which fifty million people you gone starve to death when the farmers stop using pesticides?" he inquired. This was the theology according to the Department of Agriculture which Jessie Jenkins thought had been spoon-fed to the idiot bureaucrats by the chemical companies she hated.

"They not gone to starve to death," Jessie retorted. "Those fifty million gone die of cancer you giving 'em with all those pesticides you putting in the food. And the first to go is going to be you. You realize, Harry Sloane, how much that poison you are spreading is getting into your own lungs when you throwing that stuff around with your tractor? How you feel, Harry Sloane? Now honestly?"

"Just fine."

"That's because you got such a big fat belly and such a big fat ass, you going to take a lot of killing." Even as she was saying it Jessie was uncomfortably aware that she would never use crude language like "fat ass" to her own husband. With Harry Sloane she talked redneck.

Harry Sloane's grin was a foot wide. "Where you get all these ridiculous ideas, Jessie?"

"I read, you big ape, and you should read—*New Farm, Farming Age, New Horizons.* It might broaden your own horizons."

"I'm too busy farming to read about it," Harry Sloane said. This was the catechism among farmers when Jessie tried to spread her own gospel. They were all too busy making money at farming to read about how to go broke not using pesticides, talk that drove Jessie wild. "You are going to ruin your land, and then where will we all be?" she'd shout at these fossils. Much good it did.

She and Harry Sloane continued the argument—for the sheer fun of the thing—on the tractor, shouting insults at each other over the roar of the engine. None of this interfering with the spreading, which was the important thing. Much as she loathed him, Jessie had to admit Harry Sloane was a marvelous hand on a tractor, spinning it on its tracks, getting into the hard corners.

In two hours it was done, and they were both famished. "Come in, I give

5

you some lunch." Never before had she offered any hospitality to Harry Sloane. But after all, he'd spread her phosphate. . . .

Jessie's lunch was goat's milk from her own goats, goat cheese on crackers, lettuce from her garden.

Harry Sloane stared at it with horror. "You ain't got a steak in that freezer by any chance?"

"That fat ass going to get even fatter you eat like that in the middle of the day."

She didn't have a steak, but she had hamburger. He ate a big hamburger with beans, washed down with two cans of beer—a caloric total that made Jessie dizzy to think about.

Still, it was nice to have a man to cook for. Since Derry had disappeared, there'd been no one. "What does Kitty think about you being over here all the time, helping a widow lady with her phosphate?"

"Kitty got more sense than to ask where I at? She might find out, and she wouldn't like that one bit." He laughed at his own joke, preening himself on his reputation as a ladykiller.

Jessie looked at him, cold with dislike. It didn't bother Harry Sloane. He was not renowned for sensitivity.

After a bit, he asked, "Any word?"

No need to say about what. Derry, her husband, had vanished six weeks earlier in mid-February. No one knew why or where. Including Jessie. Nobody spoke of it in Jessie's presence. It was unmentionable—except to clods like Harry Sloane.

Actually, Jessie thought wryly, she hadn't thought about her missing husband all day. Not once. Well, it was the first spring thaw. She'd had to muck out the goats and fertilize the barn field.

"You looking mighty grim all of a sudden," Harry Sloane said. Stuffing great quantities of food in his mouth.

"Yeah," Jessie said. "I got problems."

"I know. They threatening to sue."

Derry had disappeared with an eighteen-wheeler he'd rented from John Droll Rent-A-Truck in Richmond. It was not the kind of thing Derry would do, him a solid, happily married (she thought), altogether respectable landowning small farmer. Still he'd done it. Anyway vanished. There it was. Inexplicable.

"That all over town?" Jessie asked.

"Things gets around."

Jessie put down her cheese and cracker, unable to swallow any longer, the misery rising up in her.

"They gone try to grab the farm?" Harry Sloane asked.

"They can't. Derry and I own the farm jointly—in the entirety as the Virginia law says. They can't touch that, my lawyer says." Jonathan Glass was her lawyer. First Family of Virginia. Pillar of the community. Also her godfather, so he didn't charge.

"Maybe they try to grab everything else—the truck, the pigs, the horses, the goats. Clean me out."

Silence in the kitchen.

Harry Sloane had finished his huge repast and was draining his second can of beer. He picked his teeth and grimaced.

After awhile he said, "They's way of handling that."

Jessie stopped breathing. She'd been racking her brain for ways to handle that and not coming up with anything. Jonathan Glass was no good because he was, alas, too honest. He could tell her all the legal things when what she needed now was some nice crooked advice. And who knew more crooked angles than anyone else in Altamont County but this big fat slob at her kitchen table?

Why didn't I think of Harry Sloane earlier? Cause I didn't want to be any more beholden than I already am. But with livestock on the line . . .

Harry Sloane was not in a hurry. He lit a cigarette. Jessie hated cigarettes, hated the smell of them in her clean kitchen, the mess. There it was again, the difference between them yawning wide as Grand Canyon—her with her goat cheese, him with his cigarettes and beer and pesticides.

Silence in the kitchen. She had to break ground when she couldn't stand the suspense.

"Tell me how you handle these things, Harry."

Harry. First time she'd ever first-named the big ape. Always before, it was Mr. Sloane and more recently Harry Sloane. Now Harry . . .

"You gone need me do that," he said picking his teeth.

"I know I need you. Harry. I'm askin' you polite."

He smiled a great wide smile, looking like a lecherous Pan. "Politeness ain't what I'm after, Jessie Jenkins."

"I know what you're after, Harry Sloane, and you just better forget it. I'm a good ol' fashioned girl in love with her own husband, that's what I am."

Harry Sloane's smile got even wider until it split his huge face altogether. "I am greatly impressed by your virtue, Miz Jenkins," he said, rising to his feet, yawning and stretching. "It's nice to know they some virtue left in this wicked world. I'd about lost faith."

He picked up his round-visored cap, which had Pepsi-Cola written across the front.

"Thank you for lunch, Miz Jenkins. I enjoyed it."

Jessie sat there, furious, but not letting her fury interfere with her mental processes—because this was important.

He was putting it right on the line. Either she did, or he didn't. Just like that. She didn't think a man could be that crass. But, of course, Harry Sloane could be that crass. That's what got him where he was—wherever that was. He pushed people into a corner—and laughed at them. She hated him.

On the other hand . . . She thought of the sheriff loading her goats, her horses, her pigs on a cattle trailer, driving off with her precious animals!

He knew all that, too.

"A girl's virtue quite a prized possession," Jessie said, holding up a dish to the window to see it shine in its cleanliness, a sort of symbol of the innocence she was about to lose. "What I want to know, Harry Sloane, is what guarantee I got that these acquaintances of yours, this knowledge of procedure, going to save my goats. This man going to show up here with a judgment from a judge. Pretty powerful piece of paper. How you gone to combat that?"

"That would be telling, Jessie Jenkins. I tell you that, and you just kiss me on the forehead and say bye-bye."

I wouldn't even kiss him on the forehead—but the other part he's got right.

"I see your point," Jessie scrubbing her milk pail very hard to get the milkstone off it. Milkstone was a hard, almost rocklike encrusting left by milk—the curse of dairy farmers everywhere. Both of them, Harry Sloane and Jessie, knew about milkstone, him with his cows, her with her goats. They had a few things in common, thought Jessie sadly—like milkstone. "But you better see mine. If I surrender my . . ."—a little hesitation here for comedy and emphasis—". . . virtue to you, Harry Sloane, what guarantee I got these miracles of yourn gone work?"

"You just got trust me, Jessie Jenkins."

Well, I don't, Jessie said to herself. Too much a diplomat to say aloud. What she did say was, "If I trust you, will you trust me?"

Got him mousetrapped there, thought Jessie, back to him, scrubbing away at her pail.

8

A silence. Harry Sloane had smelled the mousetrap but didn't quite see what direction it was coming from. He stalled. "Course I trust you, Jessie Jenkins. Your . . . virtue is . . . unquestioned in the county."

"Mmmm," Jessie said, unable to resist the thrust. "That the only reason you want it, Harry Sloane, cause I the last piece of ass you haven't sampled."

Piece of ass. She'd never used such an expression in her life aloud. . . .

"I wouldn't go so far as to say that, Jessie Jenkins. Also, if you think your . . ."—he was using the same hesitation she had used—". . . virtue is you greatest attraction, you are quite wrong. You got others, Jessie Jenkins. You want me name 'em?"

"Yeah," Jessie said. "Name 'em. I like to know these things."

Scrubbing away, her back to him, so he couldn't see her sad smile.

"You straight back and the way you carry y'self. I like that, Jessie Jenkins. Those gray go-to-hell eyes . . ."

"Go-to-hell eyes? You *like* that, Harry Sloane?"

"Yeah I do. Also you wide lips and you thin hips and you long legs and . . . that 'bout sums it up."

Not bad, Jessie thought. He sums up a girl pretty good. "All that and my virtue too," Jessie commented dryly. "You getting quite a bargain there, Harry Sloane. Now we both agree we got to have a little trust of each other. But the big question is, who is gone trust who first."

Here she swung around and faced him square, arms folded across her chest, solemn-eyed. "And I say it's going be you. You save my animals from that sheriff, and I surrender my virtue but only after the deed is done, Harry Sloane. That's the end of it."

He'd been mousetrapped, and he didn't like it. This was the kind of maneuver Harry Sloane was renowned for pulling on others, and he didn't like it pulled on himself. He thought it over, his huge face belligerent, looking at her rocklike resolve, seeing instantly there was nothing he could do about it. It wasn't that he doubted her. He didn't like being outwitted.

He rose ponderously. "Okay, Jessie. I be in touch."

He moved to the door, big as a battleship and as authoritative.

"Don't worry about you goats. We save you goats. One thing you got to do is come in from the farm now and then and listen for the phone. When we move, we got to move very fast, and we got to be able to contact you in a hurry. When you likely be in your kitchen?"

"Noon," Jessie said. "And six o'clock. I come in during the day when I can."

9

"Come in a little oftener."

She followed him on to the porch and watched him mount his tractor like a great bear mounting a bicycle in the circus. He waved at her with his sly grin—you and me in this plot together, it seemed to say—and she waved back.

Wryly.

That night, milking Dusky, her head against her warm boney flank, she confided to the goat, "Sold my body in exchange for your freedom and well-being, and you just damn well better appreciate it and give me a full gallon tonight, Dusky goat, or I be very cross with you."

Dusky didn't give a full gallon, which was asking an awful lot of a goat on the nighttime milking, but she did give three quarters of a gallon which is pretty good going.

Supper that night was pork chops from the freezer, which contained a hundred sixty-eight pork chops from the two pigs she and Derry had butchered in December, applesauce she'd made from their own apples, potatoes she'd laid away in the fall from their own garden, goat's milk she'd milked that morning, peaches from her own trees she'd frozen the previous fall, with cream from her own goats.

But while she could feed herself out of the larder, she couldn't feed her animals. It would be six weeks before the pastures would support the horses again. The pigs needed commercial feed, and so did the chickens and goats. She got out the farm check book.

Balance $43. Enough for maybe six sacks of layena, four of pig food, maybe some Sweetena for the horses. She brought out the jam jar where she kept the egg money and counted it. Ah! $86.20. Not bad. That would flesh out the account a little bit. By stringent economy, maybe—just maybe—the eggs would bring in enough money to support the animals until farrowing. Her sows were stuffed with maybe a thousand dollars worth of pigs. If I'm lucky—and I need a lot of luck. One of the local pig farmers Jessie knew had two sows last winter who produced a total of twenty-six piglets, only two of which survived. You couldn't count on there being a thousand dollars' worth of pigs until you got them to market. After farrowing it was eight weeks to weaning, while the sows ate a lot of expensive food.

Jessie ran her fingers over her face and stroked her eyeballs, giving herself new energy.

All of this was begging the big central question that couldn't any longer

10

be ignored. Jessie took out the calendar on which were written all the significant dates, when Saturday was bred and when her foal could be expected, when each sow was bred and when her little ones could be expected, when the winter wheat had gone in and so forth. The fourth of every month was circled in red without explanation because none was needed.

The fourth of every month was the day they paid their loan on the farm. $350. Here it was the first. The money locked up in Derry's account. She got out Derry's checkbook and stared at the balance. $863.14. Only he could draw checks on it.

The image flashed across her mind—her handsome blonde innocent missing husband. Innocent? Well, she'd always thought of him that way, and it was difficult to change her mind about that, even in light of his disappearance.

If there had been no phone call, she'd have thought he was at the bottom of a river somewhere. It would take death itself to keep him from the wife he loved, the farm he cherished. But there had been the one phone call.

"I'm in Tennessee headed west, and I won't be home for a little while because of circumstances beyond my control," he had said. And hung up. Or someone else had hung up for him. Very abrupt, unloving, and uncharacteristic.

She had run the gamut. Grief. Rage. Jealousy. She'd had to invent women to be jealous of because Derry had never shown the slightest interest in any girl except Jessie. She'd known him since she was seven. He'd taken her virginity when she was sixteen, married her when she was nineteen. . . .

Jessie sat staring at the checkbook, hands clasped together, lips pursed. For the first time she thought of the bargain she had struck with Harry Sloane in relation to her husband. Up to then it had been a private deal—between her and Harry—but only then, with Derry's checkbook staring at her accusingly did she think of the deal as involving also her husband.

Adultery.

Jessie hadn't thought of that angle. It was just a deal. Unpleasant but then lots of deals were that. I'm staying alive, she argued with her absent husband. Just staying alive. Like the song said.

If you want the farm to be there when you get back—if you ever do get back—then I got to do what I got to do. So argued Jessie in the privacy of her mind.

11

All this wasn't getting the bank paid.

Jessie pulled a sheet of white bond paper out of the desk drawer and took up her pen. Across the top of it she wrote DERRY JENKINS. Not very good. It didn't look like Derry's signature at all. She pulled out the big drawer which contained the farm files and looked for a letter signed by Derry. Trouble was there weren't any. There were letters signed by everyone else—but Derry's letters had been sent. She ransacked the file and finally found a letter to Western Farm Equipment in Wisconsin, ordering a saddle that had not been sent for the simple reason they had decided they couldn't afford it—yet. So the letter had been thriftily put away for whenever they could afford it. There was Derry Jenkins' signature in full script.

Showed every bit of his character, too. Firm, righteous, resolute, romantic—a man of earth and fire that was her Derry. She burst into tears looking at it. Oh, my God, Derry where are you and what are you doing to me and to you?

This wasn't getting the bank paid.

She set about copying the signature—again and again and again on the white paper. After all, she thought, the bank is not going to question a signature when the money is being paid to themselves, is it? A check coming from this house to them, making a payment that was made every month regularly—who would question that?

After twenty minutes' practice, she felt sufficiently expert. She made out a check to the bank for $350.00, forged Derry's signature to it, put it in an envelope, addressed to the bank, and put a stamp on it.

That took care of March, When April came, she'd cross that bridge and not until. Sufficient unto the day and all that.

In the warm bed that night she pulled the covers to her chin and opened Herodotus. Antiquity was her vice, her own fairy story.

Not that Herodotus had much time for fairy stories. He was by nature a debunker—even of the Trojan War. That night Jessie read Herodotus' version of the war, very cool stuff indeed. According to Herodotus, Helen and Paris had never gone to Troy at all; their ship had instead been blown to Egypt where Helen stayed on, detained by King Proteus. When the great Greek armada arrived at Troy, the Greeks were told by the Trojans that Helen wasn't there. The Greeks didn't believe this story and laid siege for ten long years. They finally took the city, leveled it and found that Helen was indeed not there.

12

What an anticlimax! Jessie grinning with the fun of it. The Trojan War was an exercise in futility. Like most wars.

She slept and dreamed. Of Athena, the Gray-eyed Goddess. The first feminist. In full armor.

"Why you dressed like that?" Jessie asked in her dream. "You the protector of agriculture and civilization."

"First I was a Warrior Goddess," Athena said. "Ruthless."

__ CHAPTER __
TWO

SPRING EXPLODED ON the landscape, the land greening and warming in weeks. It was the wettest, the warmest, the greenest, the most vernal spring in Jessie's memory. Also, the most beautiful.

Dashing from one farm chore to another, from the milking to the mucking out, the feedings, the tilling, the fertilizing, Jessie still made time to gaze open-mouthed at the riotous yellow of the forsythia, to sniff the musky little green flowers on the lime tree, to appreciate the Japanese geometry of the dogwood, the glory of the flowering tulip poplar, the piercing fragrance of the lilac and that most fabulous of wildflower scents— the honeysuckle which in Virginia can stop a man in his tracks.

She was a country girl who inhaled every breath of fresh country air as if it were her first and lifted her face to the spring sunshine as if the sun might never shine again. This alone sustained her and goaded her on in the midst of her perplexities which got much worse as spring came in.

She was already stretched to the limit of her capacities and in spring came the long line of birthings, each of which added a new task. Still, she looked forward to each birth as if it were her own baby, planning feedings, vaccines, bedding—the date of each birth painstakingly calculated—and usually wrong because mothers went their own way in these matters.

First came Annie, her smallest and most loved goat, who gave birth to two bucks. Adorable but useless except as food. In the goat world sexism was reversed—does getting pride of position, little bucks assigned to the freezer.

15

The next day another barnyard event of some significance. The sun glared red over the henhouse from which emanated a new sound, never heard before—the crow of a cock. Not a very good crow but unmistakable. Jessie threw open the door and out strutted the black rooster, first rather than last, the white hens tumbling after, giving him respect.

He sounded again—high pitched, thin but commanding. The cock's demeanor had changed altogether. The timorous little coward who ran for the goat shed where he skulked alone all day now was a proudly erect rooster, his black chest iridescent with purple and gold shadings, his comb fleshed out bright red.

As Jessie watched, stupefied, the black rooster raped a white hen. Not at all inexpertly. The cock leaped on the hen, its talons grasping the hen's head, thrusting it into the dirt. Like all chicken rape, very brief—a second and a half. The hen then went about the most important of life's tasks—eating. The black rooster strode away, chest out, as if he'd invented fornication.

"Congratulations," Jessie said ironically. Without warning the black rooster attacked *her* viciously, sinking his spurs into Jessie's leg clear through her jeans.

"Hey," Jessie cried, in pain. "I'm your friend! Remember me! I'm the one took care of you when nobody else would speak to you."

But gratitude plays as little part in the farmyard as it does in international affairs. The black cock attacked again, flying straight at her face. Jessie fended him off with her fist. "What's the matter with you? Just because I'm white—that your problem?"

It ripened into a full-blooded unending war, the black rooster attacking her every time she came in the chicken yard, Jessie responding with fists, sticks, stones, her feet. The end of a beautiful friendship. The rooster meanwhile acquiring eight white wives whom he alternately raped and protected from other roosters.

Later that morning Jessie caught up with Amphitrite, waddling across the barn field enormous with pregnancy. Jessie squeezed one of Amphitrite's swollen teats and out came a spurt of milk, which meant the pigging should happen within twelve hours. With a tray of food, Jessie lured the big sow into the farrowing pen she'd calcimined and bedded the big pig down in fresh hay.

Back to the house where the telephone was ringing.

16

"Jessie," Jonathan Glass said, anxiety in his voice. "Are you all right? I've been trying to call for days."

"Well," Jessie said. "I'm pretty busy on the farm, without Derry. I don't get in the house much. What's up?"

"Bad news. The insurance company has been seeking a writ of attachment on your livestock. Judge Dabney is an old friend, and he told me about it. I entered an objection that as sole proprietor of Jenkins Farm, the writ would damage you, not Derry, and you are not party to the grievance."

"How far did you get with that argument?" Even to Jessie it seemed thin.

"Delay. I got three days, but the three days are now up and Judge Dabney has granted the writ. Very foolish of the insurance company because there's not going to be nearly enough to satisfy the judgment. . . ."

But more than enough to ruin Jenkins Farm, thought Jessie.

". . . Insurance companies do these things *pour décourager les autres* if you know what I mean."

"When did you hear this?" Jessie asked.

"A half hour ago. Is there any word from Derry? I could enter another objection if we had anything at all to go on."

"He's vanished from the face of the earth, Uncle Jonathan."

"Do you want me to come out there, Jessie?"

"No, Uncle Jonathan, I'd rather you didn't." Legalities hadn't helped. What she needed now were the illegalities.

She got Jonathan Glass off the phone and immediately called Harry Sloane. Kitty Sloane answered. The last person in the world Jessie wanted to talk to was Kitty, who was very hostile.

"Is Harry there, Mrs. Sloane?" Immediately conscious of the fact she was first naming Harry and last naming Kitty.

"I get him." Cold as death.

Harry came on. "How you, Jessie?"

"They got a writ, Harry, on my animals. Jonathan Glass just called."

Harry took command. "You jes' sit tight, Jessie. We handle things."

"All my animals having *babies,* Harry! That deputy sheriff be on my back in half an hour. . . ."

Harry Sloane chuckled: "That deputy not gone be there in any half hour, Jessie. That deputy gone have a lot of trouble *findin'* Jenkins Farm. I got this thing wired. Oney tell me this: how many vee-hick-les you got on the farm? Jes' the truck?"

"Just the truck," Jessie said.

"Go about your business, Jessie, and don't worry. Take a couple hours to round up the boys, but we get there long afore that deputy. He's my nephew, the one who serves the writs, and he been talked to."

Jessie hung up, stomach full of misery. He'll save my animals and take my body. Heavy-hearted she put together her birthing equipment—her black-handled scissors, her iodine spray, an old towel to wipe her hands on, a worn pillow to sit on because pig birthing was a long business.

In her farrowing pen, Amphitrite was turning her bulk round and round, pushing the hay with her nose, making a nest. Her eyes were in the other world, which meant birth was not far off. Sows take leave of their senses before and during delivery, strung out like heroin addicts. An awesome sight, a five hundred pound sow in narcolepsy. Jessie climbed into the pen and sat on the rail that keeps baby pigs from being crushed by their big mothers.

"You and me together, yet one more time," Jessie said. It was the third pigging they'd shared, the sow getting nastier with each one.

Me and Harry, Jessie was thinking, laying down her scissors, her iodine, her towel.

The sow was very restless, going round and round. Jessie leaning back, eyes half closed. Few other pig farmers stuck with their sows during delivery but Jessie always did. Amphitrite was a careless pig, frequently trampling on the tiny newborn pigs, even after they squealed. A bad mother. There were a lot of them in the animal world, just like in the human one. Jessie had never believed in the *only man is vile* bit. Lots of animals were quite as vile as man, just not quite so ingenious in their villainy.

At 2 P.M. the first piglet issued from Amphitrite's inflamed rear end—with a little plop, surrounded by the gelatinous birth coating, the little pig flailing away with his little trotters, squeaking its wonder at being alive. The miracle of birth, which ravished Jessie, always as if it were the first time.

Jessie picked up the little one, squealing its fear, and cleaned the gelatine away from its mouth, dried it on the towel, cut the umbilical cord two inches from the belly and squirted iodine spray on the navel. Admiring it. Beautiful little red Duroc with one eighth of Hampshire on its mother's side, tough, wiry little body, bright shoe-button eyes. Jessie put it down on the straw, and immediately it scrambled to one of Amphitrite's large teats and started feeding.

Amphitrite lying, eyes closed, grunting, in her private schizophrenia. The next pig, healthy and squealing, came forty-five minutes later. Ten minutes later Amphitrite heaved to a half-sitting position, scattering her two newborn into the hay, where Jessie hurriedly retrieved them and put them in her own lap as the huge sow stumbled to her feet and started to make her nest again, revolving her great body, Jessie holding up her own feet to keep from being trampled on.

"You're rotten to the core, Amphitrite," Jessie said.

Amphitrite grunting away in her nether world.

The next pig was born dead, landing like a lump of clay from its mother's womb. Jessie picked it up quickly, cleared the mucus away from the mouth, and put her own mouth to its mouth, breathing her breath into him, squeezing the flanks hard, then letting up, anything to get the life force moving. Nothing worked, and Jessie laid down the dead pig, with its long perfectly formed body, beautiful head. It had everything a baby pig should have. Except life. Too long in the birth passage.

"What a shame!" Jessie cried aloud.

"Yeah," the voice said in her ear. "But it happens."

Scaring the wits out of Jessie. She leapt up from the railing and only then noticed the barn was full of big silent men, most of whom she knew. Harry's foreman, Todd Gassett, who was even bigger than Harry—six foot eight and just as round; Humboldt Pickering, one of Harry Sloane's hunting pals who had never done a stroke of work in his whole life, lived on welfare and hunted—that was Humboldt; Jamie Goosens, another powerful, redneck ne'er-do-well who spent his life fishing in the James, sometimes acting as guide when he needed the money. Other immense men, one of them black, she didn't know.

"Humboldt," Harry Sloane commanded, "you take that quarter. Jamie over there, Todd . . ." The men climbing into the farrowing pen.

"Harry, you can't take Amphitrite *now*!" Jessie wailed. "She's having her *babies*!"

"You want that insurance man take that pig—and her babies?"

"My God, Harry, how could he? She weighs five hundred pounds. Maybe *six hundred* . . ."

Harry Sloane grinned his great Pan grin, splitting his face in half. "Okay,

19

men, one two three—heave!" The five immense men, one on each of Amphitrite's quarters, one in the middle of the back, heaved and up came the sow, still in her birthing position. Pure machismo, at its most basic. *Look at me, ma! Look how strong I am!* The terrible thing, Jessie thought, transfixed, is that I'm thrilled to the marrow by all this disgusting masculinity, all this musculature, feeling sexuality clear to her toes.

The men carrying Amphitrite out of the barn and right into the pickup truck drawn up at the door with its cattle bar sidings on. Jessie carried the two baby pigs after them.

"Jamie," Harry Sloane commanded, "you take that pig straight to old Doc Simmons. He got some he'p there to get her off—and you come right back with that truck, you hear."

"I'll go along," Jessie cried. "Amphitrite goes crazy having pigs. She kill the little one if I not there. . . ."

"You not going anywhere," Harry said brutally, lifting the little pigs out of her arms and placing them—gently, himself a farmer—with their mother. "You gone stay right here, Jessie, and learn your lines. You got to be coached so you don't make any mistakes and louse yourself up."

"Harry, I've never left Amphitrite when she piggin. . . . Oh hell!"

Submitting because she had no choice.

Outside the barn, glinting in the afternoon sunshine, was the biggest array of trucks that Jenkins Farm had ever seen—Harry's yellow pickup, Shadow Creek Farm's great cattle trailer, two red Ford pickups Jessie couldn't identify—one of them pulling a horse trailer.

"Where them other pigs with the funny names?" Harry asked.

Jessie led the men to Starvation Corners where Ariadne, Clytemnestra, Persephone, and Juno, all named by Jessie, the classics scholar, were lifted, battling every inch, into Harry Sloane's pickup and driven off by Todd Gassett.

"Where they all going, Harry?" Jessie asked anxiously.

"They in good hand," Harry said. "Where the horses?"

Wednesday and her foal, Ariel, were loaded on the cattle trailer. Saturday, who hated all trailers, trucks and mechanical contrivances of any nature, was a thousand pounds of stubbornness, refusing to budge. Each of the great men pulled and hauled, then all four together. The black man—his name was Terence Scott—stepped forward and took over. "Gimme a blindfold and some food," he murmured. With the pail of sweet feed in one hand, he crooned gently to the horse, a low song of reassurance, all the

20

while slipping the blindfold over the horse's eyes, leading her into the trailer with the pail of sweet feed just ahead of her nose, as if handling a little child.

The goats—Snowflake and Annie, Midnight and Dusky—went in Humboldt Pickering's pickup with the enclosed van which he used to conceal the deer he shot out of season. The two little goats went in the front seat with their bottles, all in a cardboard box. "You tell Everlee every four hours," Jessie said to Humboldt. Everlee was Humboldt's wife and could be trusted to have maternal feelings about little goats.

Jessie's chickens were chased down in the chicken run with long wire chicken catchers, which caught their legs—or were lifted off nesting boxes, or scooped out of their dust holes; the ducks were chased off the pond by men wading in after them—right into sacks held by men on shore. The geese fought their captors with wing and beak but were subdued and hauled off in chicken crates.

The men even took the dog and cat because you never knew how senselessly vengeful an insurance company might be.

All of it beautifully organized as if these men had done the thing before.

Them enjoying the thing to the hilt. Spitting in the face of an insurance company. Rednecks getting a little bit of their own back from the city folk who screwed them at every turn.

In forty minutes Jenkins Farm was devoid of animals, silent of cock crow, pig grunt, horse whinny, goat bleat. An awful silence. The emptiness was worse—no horse grazing, chicken pecking, pig rooting.

In the kitchen Harry Sloane taught Jessie her lines. Then he, too, pulled out in Terence Scott's pickup.

Jessie was left alone in her empty acres, waiting for the deputy and his piece of paper. She filled in the time planting a row of carrots, weeding her onions, and rototilling her lower garden for the corn planting.

That's where they found her—in the garden—and they had to yell very loud to be heard over the noise of the rototiller. When she saw them, Jessie turned off the rototiller—and waited. Let them come to her.

One of them was a sandy-haired, fresh-faced, blue-eyed young lout with a gleaming smile. "Tomlin Peters," he introduced himself. "Deputy Sheriff of Altamont County, ma'am. I'm 'fraid I have to serve you this writ of attachment on you livestock to satisfy a claim brought by the John Droll Rent-A-Truck Company of Richmond, Virginia, on its insurance company, Great Southern Insurance, as ordered by Judge Dabney in Superior Court."

All spoken in a resonant playacting voice, Tomlin Peters clearly enjoying himself.

The other man stood there, listening, sad-faced, and at the same time, ashen, as if the writ were being served on him. This was the insurance company man, Jessie guessed, and he hated his job. She knew the type well. A middle-aged man who'd had one job after another, each one of lower importance than the previous one, hating all of them, and now he'd come to this—seizing people's chickens, and he hates me, as if it's my fault he's no-account. One of life's losers, this fellow, in a threadbare jacket and white shirt and necktie—all wrong for the blazing sunshine of the country.

Jessie took the piece of paper and read it carefully as she'd been instructed to do, noting what was specified on it—chickens, horses, goats, pigs—and also what was *not* on it.

"What are you going to take these horses, goats, pigs away *in?*" Jessie asked. Not one of the lines she'd been taught but she was curious.

The sad-faced one pointed to an immense cattle trailer standing on her lawn pulled by a great International tractor, the kind of rig used for long hauls to San Diego. With driver, Jessie guessed it cost the insurance company a hundred dollars a day or more. The company was laying out quite a wad to exercise its vengeance.

"You go right ahead and take any horses, pigs, goats you can find," Jessie said sternly. "You just be quite sure you don't take anything not written down on that paper."

"I'm here to see to that," Tomlin Peters said, smiling his empty-headed smile. Giving me the eye, too, Jessie was thinking angrily, like it's open season on Jessie Jenkins with her man gone.

She went back to her rototiller and left the two men and the driver to search the empty barn, empty chickenhouse, empty goat shed, empty stables.

They were back in half an hour, and Jessie turned off the rototiller.

"Miz Jenkins," the sad-faced one said. "You are willfully concealing livestock that has been lawfully attached by order of Superior Court and in so doing you are in contempt of court." Reciting his lines.

Jessie recited hers: "That is not for you to say." Her arms folded across her chest, looking the ashen-faced one straight in the eye. "That is for the court to determine."

The ashen-faced one went on with his recitation in his sad voice: "If you have sold these animals in anticipation of this seizure, you are in violation of Section 235 of the Criminal Code and any proceeds of such sale can and will be attached. . . ."

Jessie said to the young deputy (who was still giving her the eye), "Read him the law, Mr. Peters."

"Mister Young," the deputy said, enjoying himself too much. "You and me got authorization seize some animals. Tha's all we got authorization for."

"In the absence of said animals which have been willfully concealed I order you to seize that rototiller and that red truck."

"Nothing on that piece of paper 'bout a rototiller or a truck," the deputy said.

"Whose side you on in this matter?" the ashen-faced one asked, the voice hopeless because he was beginning to see it all.

"I on the side of the law," Tomlin Peters said with his gleaming smile.

The sad-faced one took off his glasses and polished them with his handkerchief. "I will return to Judge Dabney's court tomorrow morning and get a writ for the rototiller and the truck," he said dispiritedly.

"You just do that," Jessie said. "I'll be here."

"Yeah," the insurance man said. "I bet you will." He turned his back on her and walked back to his car, defeated yet once again. When he returned with another piece of official paper, the truck would be gone and so would the rototiller—and any other objects he would have on that piece of paper. Whatever piece of paper he got from the court, she'd be forewarned and forearmed. It was very hard to bring the brunt of the law on these country people because they knew just enough law to turn it around and hit you in the face with it. It was their territory, not his territory, and the forces of law were their friends, not his. He was returning empty-handed, and he would catch hell for that from the dunderheads who sent him on these fool's errands.

He climbed into the passenger seat of the tractor-trailer, and the big rig slowly pulled round the circle and out of the drive.

Jessie sat on the steps of the porch and burst into tears.

"Hey!" said the young deputy, who had been entertaining lecherous thoughts. "No call for that! No call at all! Everything all right now!"

"I'm not used to telling lies," Jessie said, sobbing. "I was brought up strict."

"You didn't tell no lies!"

"It's all a lie! All of it! And I miss my animals."

23

"You can't bring those animals back yet, Miz Jenkins. That man not above lying in wait down there at the end of you drive, just waiting for something like that. You just better keep those animals outta sight for a few days be on the safe side."

"They're having babies—my goats, my pigs. My Amphitrite's having her babies right this minute," Jessie wailed. "Oh hell!" She dried her eyes, ashamed she'd given way in front of this young man. "Come in. I'll give you a cup of coffee."

"Thanks ma'am, but I think I better get back and report to my uncle." A minute earlier and he'd have stayed and made a pass. The tears drove that idea out of his head.

The young man drove away, and then Jessie was truly alone.

No animals.

No husband.

Derry. She felt the weight of his absence, the physical need of him, now that there was nothing to do. The animals had filled her days, and exhaustion had extinguished her at night. She sat on the porch steps and felt famished for her handsome loving husband. If he were only there . . . But then if he were there, the whole situation would never have happened.

In Tennessee headed west . . . Why west?

She'd long since exhausted the possibilities. He'd run off with another woman. Ridiculous! He'd been kidnapped. Who would kidnap a man with eight hundred dollars in the bank? He'd been killed. Why? He'd had an accident. But that phone call was no accident.

No husband.

Now no animals.

She looked at her watch. Ten after five. She'd be feeding the pigs at that moment if she had pigs to feed. After that she'd have worked the foals, breaking them in to lead ropes, getting them used to harness. After that, she'd have led the goats up from the lower pastures talking to them all the way, fondling them, laughing with them.

"I've got a little holiday," she cried to no one in particular. "I should be overjoyed. I could get in the truck and go to the movies."

No, she couldn't. She had to wait for . . . Harry.

I could weed my garden. I never have time enough for the garden. But she hadn't the strength for it. The absence of her animals drained her. *I'm Samson without his hair,* thought Jessie, looking at her calloused hands wryly. *It takes the spirit out of me.*

24

She crossed the lawn and climbed the fence into the alfalfa field where the goats had been that morning, climbed another fence into the road which led past the empty chickenhouse, trudged slowly across the empty chickenhouse, trudged slowly across the empty barn pasture and entered the barn where she climbed the aluminum ladder into the hayloft, now empty even of hay until the first cutting. She walked softly now, tiptoeing to the far corners of the cavernous loft. There under the eaves, a white duck sat on her new nest, hissing at Jessie as she sat cross-legged on the hayloft floor.

"I just had an idea they missed you," Jessie said. "And they did—all those farmers and that insurance man and that deputy."

She wanted to take the duck in her arms, but she'd get pecked, so she contented herself with looking at the last and only animal on Jenkins farm.

"You sit there and lay an egg, and I'll sit here and watch because I have absolutely nothing to do for the first time since I can't remember when."

Thinking about Derry. Her handsome, capable, reliable, *predictable* husband. Reliable? Predictable? Jessie smiled a tight smile. Couldn't rightly say that anymore. Did she really know Derry as well as she thought she did? That was the trouble with over-familiarity. When you were in each other's pockets all day every day, lay next to each other night after night, you assumed certain things that were not necessarily true. The fact is married people didn't pay that much attention to one another. Especially on a farm where there were so many other things to pay attention to. Derry could have had a woman on the side, and I'd never have known. . . . Oh, yes, I would. I would have smelled it on him.

No not a woman. But perhaps some other . . . foible? Weakness?

She never thought of her handsome husband as having any weakness at all. Some faults maybe. Not telling her things was one. Being as predictable as a metronome . . .

Couldn't say that any more, could she? Not after this.

"The funny thing is," Jessie said, aloud to the duck, "that I haven't actually thought about Derry all that much since the disappearance. I'm just too busy all the time. His disappearance has caused so many problems they take all my thoughts. . . ."

That wasn't the trouble altogether. The fact was she hadn't yet marshaled her feeling about Derry. Should I be angry? or anguished?

At that moment, she felt a gush of sheer sexual longing, stronger than anything she'd felt for Derry since . . . well, ever. After all, a girl didn't feel that sexual for a man she'd known since she was seven, and sexually known

25

since sixteen. Me having an orgasm over my own husband, thought Jessie, only 'cause he's missing.

Twilight fell, and presently Jessie heard the motor in her drive.

Harry Sloane.

In twilight, she walked across the barn field to the house. Harry sat in the kitchen, grave as a sphinx.

"How my animals?" Jessie asked.

"Awright."

"How many pigs Amphitrite have?"

"Eleven—three dead. Two she sit on."

If she'd been there she'd have rescued the two Amphitrite sat on, perhaps resuscitated one of the dead ones. She couldn't reproach Harry for that. He'd saved the whole barnyard.

"You outwit that insurance company real good, Harry. I'm very grateful."

Harry Sloane tapped his fingers on the table absently. "We had a bargain, Jessie Jenkins."

"I know. You are going to take my honor." In her clown voice cause you couldn't say *honor* without gagging it up a little bit.

Harry Sloane grinned. "You not keep a bargain, Jessie, you sure as hell lose your honor."

"Either way I lose. That's usually the way with women, Harry. It's a bum rap, being a woman."

"I don't think I'm a total misfortune, Jessie."

"You want a little food before . . ."

"I had m'supper. You ain't had supper yet?"

It was long past country supper time, which was six.

"I miss my animals so much it's took my appetite. You never been upstairs in this house, Harry. Come on, I show you." Leading him upstairs, chattering away because silence in the circumstances was upsetting. "It's a nice house, more'n a hundred years old when they put the ceilings up high because they had so much wood they didn't know what to do with it. They didn't have energy problems back then. . . ."

Up the stairs now and into the big room she and Derry shared.

"My great-grandfather was in the lumber business, and he made a fortune cutting down trees, but I don't know what he did with all that money because none of it filtered down to me."

Unbuttoning her blouse all the while.

26

"There's great-grandfather there." Pointing to a brown tinted photograph of a man with a bristly white moustache, an expression stiff as wax paper. "He owned fifteen thousand acres round here. Now we got thirty-two."

She was bare-chested now, Harry Sloane watching, discomfited.

He lay down on the bed, arms behind his head. "You mighty matter-of-fact about undressing, Jessie," he complained. "Like a whorehouse."

"Were you expecting *romance*, Harry?" She sat on the bed next to him to take off her shoes. "Just a good fuck is all you gone to get." She burst out laughing at that because she would never use that word *fuck* in front of Derry. My goodness, wouldn't Derry be scandalized!

"With the others, that's all I'm after. With you, Jessie, I'd like a little more. I admire you more'n any woman I know. That's God's truth."

Jessie stood up to slip off her panties.

"I don't think we want God's truth in here at a time like this, Harry." She stood before him quite naked now, slim as an arrow, firm muscled from years of farm toil, and looked at the great size of the man. "I don't know how we going to manage with that great belly of yours, Harry. How do you make it with Kitty? She even littler than me."

"We make it fine," Harry said. He pulled her down on his great belly and kissed her on the mouth, revulsion flooding her.

Athena, where are you when I need you?

The Gray-eyed One was there in her whitest garment, her owl in one hand, an olive branch in the other.

"Make me like it!" Jessie whispered to her favorite Goddess.

"Indifference is all I can manage," the Virgin Goddess said. "This isn't my line."

Harry Sloane was stripping off his clothes.

"You even fatter naked then you are with your clothes on, Harry," Jessie said, lying there in her cloud of indifference. "You're going to hurt me, Harry."

"We manage all right," Harry said.

And so they did. Jessie lay under the vast bulk of him, indifferent, thinking about the Greek drama she had once tried to impart into young country heads. Idly she remembered—as he pumped away on top of her—the Greek heroine who had said that wives, led into captivity by the warriors who had killed their husbands, resisted the first three days and after that embraced their captors.

27

Or was it only two days?

Harry Sloane was unsettled by this coolness.

"You hated it," he grunted afterward.

"I didn't hate it, Harry."

"You didn't like it."

"No, but I didn't hate it."

"Maybe next time," he said, wistful.

"What makes you think there be a next time," Jessie said. There wasn't going to be a next time unless he paid for it with some further service, herself feeling like a whore. But not minding, still in her cloud of indifference given her by her Goddess.

"You boast about this all over the countryside, Harry Sloane, and I'll be after you with an axe."

"I got more sense'n to talk about you, Jessie, but that not going to stop people talking. They already talking about you an' me."

Jessie: "Somebody been talking to Kitty. She mighty cool."

Just there the telephone rang.

Derry.

Jessie was psychic about phone calls. Always had been. Especially from loved ones. Knew when her mother called. Knew when it was Derry. Sure as she knew her own name. Knew even what they were going to say. When it was good news, when it was bad.

It was Derry on the other end, and the news was bad.

The telephone rang again.

"You gone answer?" Harry Sloane asked.

Jessie reached for the phone. "You make one sound, Harry Sloane, I bite your ears off." Into the phone, "Hello."

"Jessie!" Derry's voice—but with a difference. A lot of pain in the voice, but there was also distance. She didn't like the distance.

Jessie burst into tears, the last thing in the world she wanted to do. "Derry! Where are you?"

He sidestepped the question, something he'd never done. "Jessie, I love you very much. You must always remember that."

Worst thing he could have said. It meant he was going to hit her with some awful . . .

"Derry when are you coming home. People are talking. I got the farm on my neck! The mortgage!"

"I can't come home, Jessie. I can't!"

All the time Harry Sloane lying there with his fat belly and cunning eyes.

"Why not?" she whispered. With the utmost reluctance. I'm just like Kitty, Jessie thought wildly. I don't want to ask questions because I'm afraid of the answers. He's got some woman he can't tear himself away from.

There was a long pause here, and Jessie, who knew her husband's insides as well as her own, could feel him struggling to bring up the words. When it came, the answer was not what she expected. It was far worse.

"I've killed a woman, Jessie. I didn't mean to, but I did. I can't come home just yet because there are things to be done about that." A new timbre in his voice. This was not the husband she knew. He sounded older and tougher—and infinitely desirable.

"Derry, why..." The eternal why Jessie knowing she wasn't going to get an answer, knowing even as she said it, Derry didn't know why either.

"Jessie, I can't talk any more now. There are people looking for me, and I got to get out of here or I'll get killed. I love you, Jessie. Just don't make any mistake about that."

He hung up.

Jessie hung up, dry-eyed, and angry. At Derry. At fate. At the world. She rolled over on her back and stared at the ceiling with such fury in her face, Harry Sloane dared not say a word.

Killed a woman! What woman? What was she to him and he to her? Jessie was torn with jealousy and rage and frustration and desire, all mixed together.

Harry Sloane let her cool down for ten minutes before speaking up. "I think I should tell you Jessie Jenkins, I got very sensitive ears. I heard all that."

"You heard nothing!" Jessie said ferociously.

"Okay, I heard nothin' and you heard nothin'. He never made that phone call. When the sheriff comes round and starts asking questions, you never heard from Derry at all. Otherwise, they trick you into tellin' much more'n you want to. I was a deputy sheriff m'se'f, and I know them tricks."

With that, insensitive clod that he was, Harry Sloane made a great lecherous lunge at her. Jessie jumped off the bed.

"No more of that, Harry. I got problems." She slipped into her red wool bathrobe, extinguishing her nakedness. That made Harry's fat frame even more disgusting, and Jessie tossed her Piedmont quilt over him, blotting out everything but the face.

"You help me with my problems and perhaps..." Jessie said. Well, the farm was at stake so why not? And no Derry to help out.

"Ain't I always he'p you with your problems, Jessie?"

29

"I need money, Harry. Otherwise the bank is going to take this place. You are a man never had any problems raising money."

Harry's fat face looked complacent: "How you know that, Jessie?"

"Whole county knows that, Harry. You are very expert at staying afloat on somebody else's money. You are *not* widely admired for it."

The whole bed shook with his laughter. "They just envious, tha's what!"

"You got to show me how, Harry, or I go under."

"What I get out of it?"

Jessie shook her head ruefully. "You the limit, Harry. You always got to get something out of it? You never just do something for someone for the pleasure of it?"

"No, sir!" Harry laughing at his own rottenness.

Jessie smiled. "I admire your candor, Harry. Not much else about you I admire, but I must admit a girl always knows where she's at with you, which is right behind the eight ball."

"You ain't said what I get out of it."

"You get another fuck, Harry. That's what you get."

The naked word aroused him afresh, and he made a lunge—and missed. "Business first," Jessie said, not minding the whoredom of it, the cloak of indifference still protecting her.

"You never hear tell of the Farmer's Home Administration?"

"Well," Jessie said, "I know there is one. What does it do?"

Harry told her. Not a lot and by no means all of the swindles a farmer could pull on the taxpayer. Just enough to get Jessie out of her predicament. Jessie didn't give in easily. She wanted to know names—who ran the office in Folkesbury—amounts, procedures, cash balances. Harry had it all at his fingertips, and he told her, getting hornier as he got closer to payoff time.

As he told her about percentile points of grain reserve ruined by frost, reparations for, including payment of loan interest, he was wrestling with Jessie, trying to remove the red bathrobe.

"How *much* interest?" Jessie panted, still resisting.

"Three percent," Harry said, straddling her, tearing away at the buttons. "That's five and three quarters percent less than your mortgage interest and eight percent lower than the prime." He had his cock out now, erect and hunting for its quarry, but she was keeping herself an inch or so away from copulation.

"My goodness!" Jessie gasped. "You mean I could pay my eight and three quarters percent mortgage with three percent Federal money?"

30

"You ain't supposed to do that," Harry said, spreading her legs a little wider, getting his cock into the aperture, "but how is they to know?"

He rammed it in, full length, explosive as a bull.

"What time does the Farmer's Home Administration open in the morning?" Jessie asked.

He didn't answer, humping her good and proper, much longer than the first time.

Jessie, in her mantle of indifference, kept her eyes on Athena, feeding her owl an olive from the Acropolis tree she'd planted herself.

"You arranged that phone call," Jessie accused.

"I thought you ought to know so you could lay your plans," the Goddess said. "You've got to get out of this situation by yourself."

"Is he ever coming home?" Jessie asked.

"Odysseus took twenty years getting home," the Goddess said.

__ CHAPTER __
THREE

A HUNDRED YARDS from her driveway on the road to Folkesbury, a Volkswagen was parked where no car should be parked so early. The insurance man huddled miserably over his steering wheel. Jessie stopped her truck abreast of him and leveled a reproachful stare. The insurance man shriveled visibly. After a moment of this, Jessie wound down the window of the truck and asked quite loud, "Do you enjoy your work?"

She drove away, reflecting that meanness wasn't ordinarily one of her traits. Enjoyment of vengeance. A virtue in ancient Greece. No longer so considered. I am getting deplorably ancient Greek in my moral outlook. School teaching had done that. Like a lot of farm women, Jessie had done a bit of part-time school teaching, filling in when the regular teachers were sick, putting to use that two years of teachers college, trying to insert a little education into tiny minds and succeeding only in educating herself.

A farm girl like me shouldn't go messing about with ancient Greek Goddesses. I should stay in my own religious time zone. But I can't! I can't! I was never a good Baptist! I hate Christianity! Mean-spirited, evil-sniffing, small-souled religion for mean-spirited, evil-sniffing, small-souled people.

Astounded at her own heresy!

The sun molten over Altamont County's green hills, sparkling like emeralds in the dew-fresh air. I should be struck dead for blasphemy. Instead, I'm rolling along, feeling much too marvelous, considering my situation. I should be riddled with guilt about my first adultery. I'm not. Guilt was not anything the ancient Greeks wallowed in much. Certainly not over simple adultery, which they committed all the time. Shouldn't do it with your *mother*, of course, but apart from that . . .

And how about Derry? *I killed a woman.* Jessie was pierced with jealousy. A flash of divination, clear as sunlight. He was having it off with that woman! That's why he killed her.

Not just once either! Again and again.

Torn with jealousy.

Driving through the green countryside, up hill and down dale, around the many curves, to Folkesbury we go, eaten by jealousy. No guilt over my absolutely unquestioned adultery, while stabbed to the breastbone with my husband's guilt imaginary. . . .

At 8:30 Jessie waited on the doorstep of the county agent's office and was the first person in when the office opened. Just inside the door was a rack of pamphlets containing all the latest wisdom of the Department of Agriculture on egg production, fruit marketing, soil conservation, tree care, pig diseases. Jessie helped herself to every single pamphlet, something she had never done before because in her opinion the Department of Agriculture didn't know its ass from its elbow about any of those subjects. She had read USDA pamphlets before and disagreed violently with almost every line.

However, Harry Sloane had told her that deep inside these unutterably boring and frequently inaccurate dissertations, tucked so far into them that most farmers had long since quit reading out of sheer rage, despair, or boredom, was the information about government loans and grants, deliberately placed so that it would elude all but the most zealous search. Bureaucrats having their little games with the citizenry. The bureaucrats were constrained by law not to keep the loans and grants totally secret, but they did their best. The information that the government was willing to pay half your expense of fertilizing your alfalfa field or impregnating your mares or improving your cattle herd was vouchsafed only to those with the stamina to read through some of the most paralyzingly dull prose ever written by government hacks.

Watching her sourly as she plucked pamphlet after pamphlet from the rack was a dried-up husk of a woman with the flavorsome name of Oleander Pinckney, which was printed on the wooden plaque on her desk. "Those are only for the use of small farmers whose incomes fall between two thousand one hundred fifty and twenty thousand dollars a year," Miss Pinckney said sharply.

"I happen to fall into that category," Jessie said, with a wintry smile, plucking away at the pamphlets.

The beginning of open warfare.

Jessie sat on one of the hard benches that rimmed the wall and read the boring stuff from end to end, her pencil underlining the relevant bits. Miss Oleander Pinckney throwing body blocks every foot of the way.

"Where is Form Eleven forty-four? It seems to be missing," Jessie asked.

"That program is closed," Miss Pinckney said flatly.

"It says right here," Jessie said, reading from the pamphlet, "that the seed loss program does *not* close until nineteen eighty-three."

"The committee has already met and passed on those applications."

"It will meet again," Jessie said. She'd been well coached about that by Harry who was half the committee, its chairman and most active member.

Oleander Pinckney fought hard and dirty all the way, saying first that Jessie Jenkins hadn't a snowball's chance in hell of getting a grant on last winter's seed loss (until Jessie pointed out the relevant section in the Department of Agriculture pamphlet which contradicted this altogether), then saying the funds were exhausted, at which point Jessie said that she'd just talked to the chairman of the committee (Harry Sloane) who'd assured her they weren't, and finally that the application forms were long since gone, wherein Jessie threatened her with committee reprimand for dereliction of duty. Only then did Miss Pinckney produce the forms, and Jessie immediately filled them out.

She filed application for reimbursement for crop loss of $2,500 due to severe cold (actually the winter wheat was doing fine), $156 Federal assistance for half of the fertilization of her barn field, and $720 for "improvement of trees" (a phrase that amused her no end). Even God can't improve a tree, but if the Department of Agriculture thinks it can improve my trees by showering them with money, I'm not going to stand in its way.

Oleander Pinckney threw every counterpunch she knew at Jessie—and she knew a lot. She was a veteran bureaucrat of forty years in the department, and she knew that a bureaucrat's duty is to obstruct, obfuscate, infuriate. She had not only the experience but the temperament for that sort of work. She haggled over spelling, she niggled over details, heckling Jessie over amounts—"How did you arrive at one hundred fifty-six dollars for fertilizing your barn field?"—questioning her authority for some of the grants and even Jessie's identity and her residency in Altamont County.

With dazzling good humor (stemming from the fact that Harry Sloane was in her corner—to say nothing of her bed), Jessie countered each of these maneuvers, refused to take no or even maybe for an answer, and pointedly made out twin applications—each of them dated—in order, she

35

told Oleander Pinckney, to bring them to the attention of Harry Sloane, chairman of the committee, in the unlikely event she didn't have action on them within a reasonable period of time.

Oleander Pinckney fought to the end as if the money were her own and she was being robbed of it by malefactors, acting throughout with total indignation as if these grants and loans were an outrage to public decency. ("They've been passed by Congress, the *representative* of the people," Jessie pointed out.)

In two of the applications she told flagrant lies, which, Harry Sloane had assured her, would not come home to roost because he was the arbiter in these matters. Anyway everybody did it. So said Harry. Thought Jessie: My farm is at stake, and the most immoral thing a girl can do is lose her land. Next to that anything goes.

An hour later she was at the Farmers Home Administration where she made an application for a $5,000-loan at 3 percent interest to lease 100 acres of land owned by the American Lumber Products Company to plant barley in. After that she went to the Virginia National Bank and got a $1,000 loan with no more security than her own bright smile and her acquaintance with J. Fred Percy, vice president of the bank. She deposited the $1,000 (at 18 percent annual interest which she planned to pay back in a month, when the FHA loan came through) in the Jenkins Farm account and promptly paid (in the nick of time) her monthly payment on her farm loan. In the last two months, she had forged Derry's name to two checks for $350 each, bringing his bank balance down below the $350 needed for each month's payment.

That extremity—and only that—had launched Jessie into the sea of debt and prevarication in which she was now embarked. She had been brought up to view debt as a monster that would eat her alive if she so much as left a grocery bill unpaid by the end of the month. As for telling lies, it was the deadliest of the deadly sins.

But not in Attica where she now resided. Odysseus was one of the smoothest liars in the annals of prevarication—and much admired for it, not least by Athena herself.

At 10:30 A.M., Jessie rang up Harry Sloane and got a very frosty Kitty Sloane. "Harry in the field on his tractor," Kitty Sloane said, only to be immediately contradicted by Harry's rough bellow of a voice. "Yeah?" Harry said.

"Harry," Jessie said. "You call American Lumber?"

"Yeah." Very toneless, businesslike. "Man named Oscar J. Willoughby waitin' your call. He want to take you to lunch."

"Lunch?" Jessie said dismayed. "Do I have to go to lunch? I just want to lease a hundred acres of his land."

"I think," Harry Sloane said, "he got something more elaborate in mind. Something he want to talk to you about."

"What?"

"I couldn't say. I think American Lumber want to unload that whole mountainside. Maybe he wants to proposition you 'bout that."

"I don't want his mountainside," Jessie said. "You said I could lease a hundred acres."

"Jessie, why'nt you just go listen to the man? You don't have to agree to anything. Just listen and say that's very interesting. Let me think about it and I get back to you."

"Harry, I'm in *jeans*."

"For God's sake, Jessie, ain't you got a dress? Go home and put it on, and go listen to the man, what he got to say? You in agribusiness now. You got to do a bit of listening."

"I don't want to be in agribusiness," Jessie wailed.

"Jessie, I got to go disk my corn. I can't be arguin' with you all morning." He hung up, leaving Jessie with a dead phone into which she said, "I just wanted to plant a hundred acres of barley and . . . oh hell. . . ."

She drove home, annoyed at Harry for hanging up on her, for thrusting her into something she didn't want to get into—and yet, lightheaded, lighthearted. There are depths of perfidy in you, Jessie Jenkins, you don't even suspect.

At the entrace to her driveway the insurance man in his Volkswagen still lurked. Wrapped in her euphoria Jessie drove up, rolled down her window and said, "Most of those animals you are waiting for have already been eaten—and digested—and shit out into the ecology and are now making worms in the ground, and I hope that makes you very unhappy."

She rolled up her window and drove up her driveway: Why am I so mean to that poor little man!

She telephoned Oscar J. Willoughby at American Lumber Products and was duly invited to lunch at the Pendragon, an incredibly expensive restaurant she had sold eggs to for years—but never considered eating in.

"My goodness, the Pendragon," Jessie murmured. What would she wear? In her closet side by side hung the only two possibilities—her white

37

flounced organdy (much too dressy), her navy blue rayon with the white collar and cuffs (much too prim).

In the end she settled on the navy blue. Impress Oscar J. Willoughby with her sober reliability. Wearing a dress in daylight. When had she last done that? Even when she was teaching school, she wore trousers. She felt overdressed and vaguely whorish, getting all gussied up to go to lunch with some man. Had she ever had lunch with a man in her whole life? In a restaurant? She doubted it. Even Derry had never taken her to lunch. To dinner, yes. Lunch with the girls—but that was something else. Usually at the Monster Burger where they all had the salad plate and screamed with laughter over each other's misadventures with husbands and boyfriends.

The Pendragon? I hope I know how to behave, Jessie said to Jessie. What will Oscar J. Willoughby think when I show up in a pickup? But then she found three other pickups in the Pendragon parking lot. Lots of people drove around in pickups these days.

The Pendragon itself was dark and conspiratorial. Coming in from the bright sunshine, Jessie could barely make out the figure of the headwaiter who led her through labyrinthine corridors to a booth in the rear of the restaurant, past diners who were already chomping steak and crustaceans and marvelously complicated salads that looked like they had taken days to prepare. Jessie found each dish dazzling and wished she weren't rushed past them. She'd like to have lingered over each one, just looking at the parsley. She'd never seen so much parsley.

Oscar J. Willoughby sprang to his feet when she arrived, all bright smiles and enthusiasm, and bowed her into the booth with himself as if he had a little headwaiter in his bloodstream. He was a young high-pressure dude in a bright yellow sports jacket with gold buttons and white trousers so immaculately pressed that Jessie could hardly tear her eyes from the creases.

"Drink?" Oscar J. Willoughby asked while the waiter was still there.

"Daiquiri," Jessie said. She had no idea what a daiquiri tasted like but she thought it looked delicious in the ads, and she'd heard someone pronounce it—dykerie—on television—so what the hell.

"Isn't this weather marvelous?" Oscar J. Willoughby asked. He compared this spring with the previous one when it had been so dry. From there he went on to deplore the truck strike, denounce Salt II, and ask her how the daiquiri was. (She had barely dipped her tongue into it.) Everything except talk about the business at hand. Jessie had crabs because she knew all about crabs, having eaten some at Virginia Beach one summer. She threw in an occasional assent and dissent to Willoughby's wide-ranging

38

conversational ploys—and waited for him to get to the point, not knowing that business lunches rarely got to the point before coffee. Or even that people drank coffee at lunch.

However, Jessie was pretty good at playing things by ear. She found Oscar J. Willoughby amusing (though reactionary) and quite sexy with his gleaming smile and his overpowering cleanliness. There was absolutely no doubt that he was the most spotless young man she'd ever had dealings with. It stirred her.

This is the way people live, she was thinking. A whole world of people who lunch for two hours every day, eat all these delicious crabs and salads, and charge it to their expense accounts, and somebody else does the dishes.

Meanwhile listening and laughing at the right places and making the occasional tart rejoinder and disagreement to keep Oscar J. Willoughby on his toes.

Over coffee he finally got down to it. "We have three thousand acres on that mountain pretty well forested out."

"The flatland at the bottom is the only decent growing land," Jessie said, eyes on her coffee cup.

"We've been offered a good price for that strip—all two hundred fifty acres."

"You mean—to buy?" Jessie said, her heart sinking. Two hundred fifty acres was almost beyond imagination. To *buy*? She was interested in leasing some good growing land. Even a hundred acres, which had been Harry's number, her own being much more modest, had scared her. Now this bright cheery young man was talking about selling her three *thousand* acres, a figure that made her dizzy. Keep your mouth shut and listen, said Jessie to Jessie.

Aloud she said "um."

Oscar J. Willoughby was saying: "... Germans mostly but some French. They got all kinds of cash, but they're not fools. They want that bottom land, not the rest of it."

Jessie ventured: "That's going to be your problem."

The young man said: "Well, that's our position. We've got two hundred fifty acres of prime bottom growing land as a teaser to get rid of three thousand acres that's been timbered. We want to sell the whole thing as a package—five hundred an acre which is one-half the value of Virginia rural land just now."

Something's wrong, Jessie thought. Five hundred was a very low price for Virginia land. They're trying to unload something.

"You at all interested in leasing that land?"

"No," the young man said. Very firm no.

Three thousand acres at five hundred an acre equals one and a half million dollars! Heavens to Betsy!

"Mmmmm," Jessie said, and took a sip of coffee.

The young man said nothing, letting her run with it for a while.

I've got to say something exquisitely noncommittal, Jessie thought. "Before I can make any decision at all," Jessie said, "I must take a look at that land."

"The Germans don't look. Except at the numbers."

"Some of that land is straight up," Jessie said. "No good even for pasture."

The young man was paying the bill now, signing with his Visa credit card. "I'll want the same table tomorrow, Franz," he was saying to the waiter. "Hold it for me."

"Yes, sir," Franz said.

On Jessie Oscar J. Willoughby turned his bright smile. "Germans. Little by little they're buying up America. They're very interested in that three thousand acres."

"Well, they better go look at it," Jessie said. "You lumber people leave land in one hell of a mess, no good for anything."

"Except buying and selling," the young man said smoothly. "Land is always good for that. Not much of it left in the Western world."

That was the Gospel—according to Luke, John, and Peter himself. Land always went up, up and up. Great fortunes made in land alone. Nobody ever said the opposite, which was just as true, that you could lose your shirt as well as your mind in land deals.

"I'll get back to you," Jessie said. That was the great phrase promising nothing except a phone call in an indefinite future. "Thank you very much for lunch. It was delicious."

At the entrance to her driveway the insurance man still kept his vigil. Jessie rolled down her window once more. "Loitering is a misdemeanor punishable by up to thirty days in jail and a one thousand dollar fine."

The insurance man sank even lower into his shell, like a turtle, and Jessie drove up her driveway. My animals, she was thinking. I miss my animals. How long is it going on?

"Harry," she said on the telephone. "How my animals and when I going to get them back?"

40

"You animals okay. You get 'em back in a few days when that man goes away. What did Willoughby say?"

"He trying to sell me three thousand acres of his rotten land for a million and a half." She laughed.

"Offer him half that!"

"Harry, where in hell would I get seven hundred thousand dollars?"

"I not gone tell you that over the phone. Go look at the land, see if it worth anything at all."

"Must be something wrong with it, or they not try and sell at that price."

"They need cash to pay they interest," Harry said. "Go look at the land. See what you think."

Jessie drove her truck to the mountain tract, but on the way she detoured to Humboldt Pickering's farm, something she wasn't supposed to do, to see her goats. Humboldt was off shooting deer out of season as usual, so Everlee and Jessie had a good talk. "I've cut them down to three bottles a day, and I getting about half a gallon extra I feeding to my pigs for which I'm mighty thankful," Everlee said.

"I'm grateful to *you* Everlee," Jessie said. She had the two baby goats in her lap, stroking them, kissing them. "I'm starved for my animals. Who's got my horses?"

"Jamie Goosens. They all right. He gettin' a little restive about what they doing to his pasture. Eatin' him out of house and home, he says."

"I give him a little pig. That ought to make up for it."

"What you hear from Derry?"

Jessie shook her head, closing that subject, rising to her feet. "I got to go look at some land. Thanks for everything, Everlee."

The two women embraced and looked into each other's eyes to see what they could see of joy and heartbreak and love and understanding—all things more eloquent in a glance than in words among country women.

Jessie drove to the mountainside where the devastation was even worse than she'd imagined. The lumber company's saws and bulldozers had swept through the area with the fury of an act of God, leaving behind a sea of torn stumps, underbrush, and weeds. It was nothing land—neither pasture nor woodland nor field. Give it twenty years, and it would revert to timberland—and, pretty good timberland, Virginia woodland healing faster and more completely than most. But twenty years at today's interest rates!

Jessie walked through the devastation going upward ever upward, letting

41

her mind play with the possibilities. Couldn't even feed a cow the way it was, but perhaps a dozer and a plough could work the lower level into shape for barley. The less steep bits could be made into pasture with a bit of work. The very steepest bits were hopeless for anything Jessie could think of. . . .

Except skiing.

Skiing!

Jessie stood stock still and looked up the steep slope to the summit. Eight hundred feet, straight up. Well, not all that straight up or, by Rocky Mountain standards, very far up but, hell, skiing had only recently hit Virginia, and Virginia skiers were content with far lower, flatter slopes than more experienced skiers. Skiing was a license to steal the money. Twelve dollars for a ski ticket. Six for the kids.

The lumber company had done most of the work already, cutting down the trees, had even pulled out most of the stumps for paper, leaving only that steep slope, such a total liability to a farmer—unless you thought of skiers on it, when it became solid money.

She walked back to her car, her mind in turmoil. Thirty miles from Folkesbury was too far to commute but not to ski. Skiers would drive a hundred miles.

I'm out of my mind even to think about it. I'm a farmer, not a damned real estate operator. She despised the whole profession. Still, looking at the devastation wrought by the lumber company, she saw in her mind's eye what she could do to restore it to some approximation of its wildness. The slopes would be cleared but leaving wide areas of woodland where the animals could come back. The lumber company had driven out every deer, possum, coon and rabbit. She could bring all that back.

Standing by her truck, Jessie looked up and imagined the mountain buried under a foot of snow, its slopes covered with skiers on one side and tall trees on another—the two complementing each other.

Ecology.

Plus money.

Money, Jessie thought. I hate it!

Nevertheless . . .

That night in the warm bed she read *The Odyssey*. Suddenly it was all new, bristling with implication. . . .

"Thence to a beautiful wooded island, where we heard a Goddess singing in the forest. She was Circe, and she turned into swine the men I sent out; but Hermes gave me a magic root and when she struck me with her wand I defied her and she was subdued to me. . . ."

Subdued to me. What a way to put it, Jessie feeling her entrails twist with the jealousy again.

Some modern Circe has got hold of my Derry, and he's had to kill her to break loose. *I don't understand any of it,* he had said. Well, he wouldn't. Odysseus had had to go to the dark land of the Cimmerians and make sacrifice. Derry in Tennessee on his way to the dark land of the Cimmerians.

There we stayed a year, Odysseus said.

On Circe's Island.

A *year!*

I am Penelope, Jessie thought, waiting for my Odysseus—and it took him twenty years to get home. . . .

Jessie heard Harry Sloane tramping into her kitchen—already he treated the place like his own home—and thought afresh about Penelope. She'd kept her suitors at bay for twenty years. And me. Derry's been gone two months and already. . . .

Harry Sloane stood at the foot of her bed, beginning to unbutton.

"Whatever you got in mind," Jessie said, "you just forget it—until you tell me how I can lay my hands on a million and a half."

"If that what they asking," Harry said, slipping out of his jeans, "then they be happy with half that—oh maybe two thirds."

"I need development money on top that. Where I get that, Harry?"

"Federal Land Bank," Harry Sloane said, "but you got to have a proposition sounds reasonable."

"I got a proposition. Where's it at—the Federal Land Bank, and who's in charge and how much interest they want? Now cut that out Harry, till you tell me a few things. . . ."

He told her.

43

__ CHAPTER __
FOUR

JESSIE IMMERSED HERSELF in land prices because she had to know just what she was risking, even if it was Federal money (which she privately thought of as Fairy Godmother's gold, something Rumpelstiltskin spun out of straw). Land prices had gone up tenfold since World War II and in some places almost a hundredfold since the 1930s but there had been vast changes in who owned the land and why. Institutions and insurance companies and corporations like American Lumber Products, Inc., now owned much of the land that was once owned by farmers like Jessie. How an institution thought about land differed from what Jessie thought about land altogether. To the institutions it was money, it was numbers, it was percentiles and rates and return and taxes and interest. To Jessie it was earth and worms and living organisms and orchard grass, something you lived on and with.

She differed fundamentally with everything an institution thought about land, but, she argued to herself, if she had to talk to these idiots she'd have to learn their phraseology and at least understand their rotten economics. And rotten it certainly was. Land values multiplied astronomically, she discovered, when land use changed. What made her grind her teeth in rage was that the more frivolous the land use the higher the value. When land went from farm use to suburb—from the growing of life-giving food to the rearing of adolescents whose chief occupation was looking at television and juvenile delinquency—it shot up tenfold. When it became a ski resort, the ultimate in useless frivolity, it could multiply thirtyfold. No wonder Solzhenitsyn denounced Western civilization as beneath contempt.

45

But, if that was economic law, she'd have to live with it. One thing she rapidly discovered when looking into real estate was that most of the sharp operators were not all that sharp; they had stumbled accidentally into making a lot of money, and some of them stumbled accidentally into losing it all the following year. Information was everything. When word got about that a bit of land was changing from farm to suburban use, everyone got into the act—and ruined it.

Thus Jessie had to keep her ski plans secret, and among those she kept them secret from was Harry Sloane. She spent much time prying information from Harry—about loans, rates, collateral, people to see, things to say, and, above all, things *not* to say even if they were true (especially if they were true); and she applied this last lesson (with keenest pleasure) to Harry himself. Three thousand acres were a lot of acres (two thousand acres more than he owned), and Jessie told him she planned to put the lower acres into barley, hold the upper acres for restoration—all of which sounded plausible, largely because Harry Sloane was too busy with his own farm (and his own swindles) to go look at the land and see how implausible it was.

That was another thing. In applying for a loan of a million and a half, an astronomical sum to Jessie but not much to bankers, Jessie was surprised at the naïveté of the lenders. Bankers took a look at the land she coveted, but what they were looking for were buildings (or absence of buildings), distance from cities, water (which was important, but there was plenty of that in Virginia), and acreage. What they didn't pay nearly enough attention to was the condition of the land and the things that could reasonably be done with the land and, even more importantly, what could *not* be done with it.

There were a lot of people involved in her plans. She deliberately picked people busy with their own concerns. It was easier for such people to take Jessie at her word—and her word changed to whomever she spoke. To Harry she spoke glibly of putting a thousand acres into barley, the kind of thing he understood. To Jonathan Glass she confided her skiing plans (holding him to secrecy) because he'd understand that.

Jonathan Glass she needed badly from the outset. One thing Harry had taught her was that many of these government loans were swung on whom you knew and how much public trust resided in them. Jonathan Glass was a fount of trust, a member of one of Virginia's oldest families, a lawyer of almost sacred reputation. Jessie went to him immediately to use him as reference. She needed two sacrosanct references. Jonathan Glass was one,

46

testifying to her character. (Poor Uncle Jonathan has no *idea* how my character has disintegrated in the last two months.) The other was Judge Dabney whom she'd scarcely seen since childhood when he used to hunt partridge on her father's land.

The one name she carefully avoided using as reference was Harry Sloane's. Nobody trusted Harry Sloane. He was an operator, people told Jessie. Early on, in pursuing her own plans, she discovered that many of Harry's deals were shaky indeed. "His whole house of cards gone to fall in on him one day." That's what people said. With much glee. Harry had been much too successful to be popular.

Thereafter Jessie was careful to keep her name and his distinctly separate. It was one thing to have Harry in your bed, quite another to have him anywhere near your dealings.

First, she had to get hold of the land, and, following Harry's advice, she offered exactly half their price—$750,000 (over another delicious lunch at the Pendragon, to that spectacularly clean young Mr. Willoughby), which American Lumber Products, Inc., scoffed at and counter-proposed $1,200,000. While this negotiation was underway, Jessie was undertaking to get a loan of $1,500,000 from the Federal Land Bank.

The Federal Land Bank, Harry had advised her, was a U.S. government agency with a lot of money and a minimum of common sense but enough sense not to be too eager to loan $1,500,000 to a young girl with a missing husband. What Jessie did was to incorporate herself as Columbia Land Development Corporation in Delaware with $200 of her borrowed money, and the application was made on the letterhead and over the signature of Jonathan Glass, that paragon of legal respectability, which changed the complexion of the deal altogether.

The Federal Land Bank was a bunch of bureaucrats who were ostensibly interested in providing not only help for small farmers, but new jobs in hard-pressed communities. At least that's what these bureaucrats *said* they wanted, but what they really wanted was something that looked well on the forms. Actual jobs—real people doing real work, ploughing, upending stumps, that sort of thing—was beyond their comprehension. Jessie discovered early on it was dangerous to tell these people the truth about anything. It scared them.

She went from Federal agency to Federal agency—FHA, FLB, SGK, ABQ, and all the other alphabetical chairs—strewing plausible lies not only because that was the way to get these loans, according to Harry, but also, as

47

she rapidly learned, because that's what bureaucrats wanted to hear. They wanted not the truth (God forbid) but the forms filled out so they made bureaucratic sense, which was far removed from real sense.

Harry was a master at filling out these forms. Where it said "Extent to which performance data is incomplete," he unhesitatingly wrote: "Three and a half."

"What does extent to which performance data is incomplete mean?" Jessie asked.

"Never mind," Harry said.

"Three and a half *what*?" Jessie asked.

"It don't matter," Harry said. "That's the right answer."

And it was. At least it was never challenged. All this activity was made possible by the stubbornness of the insurance man who kept his untiring vigil at the end of Jessie's driveway. That meant she couldn't get her animals back and that, in turn, meant Jessie had a lot of time on her hands.

But the day came when the forms were all filled in, the applications made, the right people seen, everyone talked to who needed talking to. Now came the time when she had simply to sit back and wait for these things to be approved (the speed of Federal lending was about that of glaciers).

"Harry," Jessie said, "you got to get that man away from my driveway so I get my animals back."

They were in bed, and Harry was at least temporarily winded. A good time to pester him.

"Easiest thing in the world," Harry said. "Offer him money."

"You mean bribe him! Harry Sloane, I'm shocked!"

Harry guffawed. "Didn't think it possible shock you any longer, Jessie Jenkins."

"Harry, I can't bribe anybody! I wouldn't know how! You really mean he'd . . ."

"Gimme fifty dollars—and you got that much in you egg money jar downstairs—and I guarantee I get rid of him in five minutes. But first . . ."

"Oh, Harry!"

The lechery commenced, Jessie making only token protests by now. There was no denying he was a mighty insatiable lecher, and the terrible thing is I'm beginning to like it.

Half an hour later, Jessie stood in the bushes at the foot of her drive, concealed from the insurance man, and watched Harry Sloane as he approached the man's car. She insisted on making Harry wait until she reached this vantage point because she wanted to see with her own eyes. She simply didn't believe such a thing went on. In *Virginia*! North Carolina, maybe. Certainly not Virginia!

It did, though. Money changed hands, and there seemed to be a lot of conversation. Harry Sloane was grinning and laughing, leaning his huge body against the man's Volkswagen familiarly, as if they were old friends. The insurance man's sour face had even creased into a sour smile as he listened to Harry's jokes. It went on for quite a while before the Volkswagen was driven away.

"What on earth did you two talk about?" Jessie asked.

"You!" Harry said, braying with laughter.

"Harry Sloane, you talked about *me* to that worm! What did you say?"

"We both agreed you the meanest, nastiest, most bad-tempered female on the face of this earth."

"*Harry*!" Jessie surprised at how hurt she was.

"Well, you wanted to git rid of the man, didn't you? Tha's the way to do it. You stand there and agree with him about what a bitch you are and tell him what a tough job he got and how you 'preciate that and maybe this little bit of cash might he'p out and have you heard what the traveling salesman said to the whore—and five minutes later he's gone."

"You mean I could have give him fifty dollars to start out with and avoid all this?"

Harry shook his huge head: "No, you could not. At the beginning he had his job to do, and he would got very mad you offer anything as small as fifty dollars. But, he been here for a week, and he about to give up anyway. He just needed a little push—and that fifty dollars is a mighty little push.

"Ah had to say a few bad things about you, Jessie, because after all you been insulting the poor man, hurting his pride for a week now. He needed to get a little of that hurt pride smoothed over. You got to understand people."

"Yeah," Jessie said. She recognized the sense of it, but didn't like it. I get back at you, Harry Sloane, she was saying to herself.

She did. The next day.

She had been seeing quite a lot of Oscar J. Willoughby during these negotiations, if only to see he didn't sell the land to someone else. Not telling him too much. They'd had two lunches at the Pendragon, and the next day was the third. Perhaps, with the memory of Harry using her as joke material, she opened her eyes a little wider than usual, laughed a little more invitingly, opened herself up a little more than was absolutely necessary for business.

Whatever it was that caused it, when they got to the coffee instead of the usual business, he propositioned her. "Let's go to bed," he said with his gleaming Pepsodent smile on his well-scrubbed face.

Jessie found herself, to her very great surprise, saying, "Where?"

He knew a motel not ten minutes away, and there they were half an hour later, Jessie still in a state of bemused astonishment. I'm just getting back at Harry, she said to herself, while slipping out of her clothes. That thought stopped her in mid-button. She was being unfaithful to Harry, her lover, not to Derry, her husband! How very peculiar!

"Hurry up," said Oscar J. Willoughby, who was already naked and, my goodness, so *clean*!

"I've never been in a motel before," Jessie said. She was entranced with the fittings, opening the drawers in the bureau, trying out the gleaming faucets, turning on the color television—herself quite naked now—going from object to object.

"We didn't really come here to look at color television did we?"

Jessie laughed like a child. "It adds a little something to the wickedness!" Wickedness was what it was. Pure wickedness. She sat next to him—the TV set on to a soap opera but with no sound—and full of mischief, said, "Tell me about your wife, Oscar."

Oscar looked as if she'd hit him. "Why?"

"Because it adds to the wickedness," Jessie said, wide-eyed. She kissed him, their first kiss, putting her tongue in his mouth, pushing him down on the bed, and grappling with his nakedness with great glee—the TV set looking at them as if a voyeur. She was fully aroused by her own abandon now, pushing his erection into her, herself on top.

"Perhaps your wife is in bed with some other man in some other motel at this very moment, Oscar. How do you know?"

"Oh, for God's sake, Jessie!"

She closed his mouth with kisses giving herself over to it. Take that, Harry Sloane, she was saying to herself, and that and that until the bliss came to her and she had no thoughts at all.

Afterward, they watched color TV for a while, actually turning the sound on and listening to the drivel. "People actually watch this stuff?" Jessie asked.

50

"By the millions. One of them, my wife. She knows all these characters by heart and all their problems."

"I don't want to talk about your wife," Jessie said grimly.

"You did before!" Oscar said, flabbergasted.

"That was pure sex," Jessie said. "Now it's different." She got off the bed and started to put on her clothes.

"Why?" Oscar asked.

She wasn't going to tell him that. The truth was, she had been turned on by this young man (who was actually younger than she was) and his slim clean body, and she hated herself for it. He had no mind to speak of, and what there was, was pure reactionary Republican. He stood for everything she despised—suburbanism, cocktail parties, big business, consumerism—and yet she lusted after those gleaming flanks so badly it hurt. It was despicable, but there it was. She just wanted him to take her in his arms and fuck her into insensibility.

Some of this must have showed in her face because he did exactly that. He leaped from the bed and pushed her down on it, himself naked, herself in her navy blue dress thrust up to her hips—and gave it to her good.

Afterward, she caressed his shiny brown hair and groaned, "As if I didn't have enough problems, now I got you."

It was not for nothing, this passage at arms. Soon he was telling her, "I shouldn't be saying this, but you're in danger of losing the deal."

She was instantly alert. "To who?"

"Some big outfit from Cleveland. Now for God's sake, Jessie, you must never never tell this to anyone. You'd get me fired. An outfit called Anderson Chemical. They got clout in Washington."

It's better to have clout here in Altamont County, Jessie thought, and kept the thought to herself. "What do they want the land for?"

"Some big plastic factory, but they're keeping that dark. First they want to own the land. Then they'll go ahead changing land use."

This was precisely Jessie's strategy. Get the land, then tell the county what you planned to do with the land. That's the way the game was played in modern times. You had to tell lies or at least conceal the truth because there was always some government agency interested in forbidding whatever you had in mind.

"Thanks, Oscar." She kissed him absently and leaped off the bed. "I've got to go."

She had him drop her off at Jonathan Glass's office and, as always, Uncle

51

Jonathan made time for her. "Who do you know at the Environmental Protection Agency?" she asked.

By happenstance (which happened all too often in the South), one of his best friend's nephews worked over there, full of high purpose and environmental zeal and before the hour was out, Jessie was across the desk from this nephew of Jonathan Glass. "We don't want a plastics factory disfiguring the skyline of the Blue Ridge Mountains, do we?"

The difficulty was she wasn't supposed to know about this, and therefore some strategy had to be devised to tell Anderson Chemical to go climb a tree without actually doing just that. Between them they composed a letter to American Lumber Products, Inc., which said that it had come to the attention of the Environmental Protection Agency that three thousand acres of land of great scenic and environmental value was being offered for sale and the agency must warn prospective purchasers that the land could not be despoiled by industrial waste, the air polluted by industrial smoke, the landscape fouled by the industrial process.

Then came the clincher, invented by Jessie herself: "This letter must be shown to any prospective purchaser so that he cannot claim innocence of its contents after purchase. The agency will hold the American Lumber Products, Inc., responsible for informing all prospective purchasers of the contents of this letter."

"I'm not sure we've got authority to do that," said the young man, whose name was Freddie Mountjoy, a tremendously idealistic young man with blue eyes and gold-rimmed spectacles and a beard.

"It's your *duty*!" Jessie said. Law was one thing, duty quite another. This was the kind of young man to whom duty was everything.

The young man thought about it. "Yes, it is our duty to see that these things are known. Yes, I see what you mean."

He wrote the letter, and Jessie drove home in the pickup thinking about Oscar J. Willoughby and how on earth she was going to fit him into her already overcrowded life along with Harry Sloane (who still had his uses) and her company.

On her driveway, she encountered Jamie Goosens in his pickup hauling his huge trailer. She pulled off the driveway to let him by, shouting at him. "My horses! You bring back my horses?"

"They in the big field," Jamie shouted and waved.

The horses were grazing near the barn field gate—Wednesday, Saturday, the foal Ariel—and Jessie flung her arms around each equine neck, kissed

52

their noses, and looked into their beautiful eyes, murmuring endearments. Ariel was frisky and shy with her, clearly hadn't been handled while she'd been away, but she seemed to be all right. Saturday and Wednesday she examined from head to tail, their eyes, teeth, hooves, cunts, tails for evidence of damage. There was none, but they looked a little thin.

Out of the corner of her eye she caught a glimpse of Amphitrite, the big sow waddling along at the head of a line of little pigs. "Amphitrite," Jessie cried, and tore across the barn field swooping up two of the baby pigs, ignoring the mud which smeared her navy blue dress in order to get a good feel of body weight, firmness, strength, liveliness.

Only then did she notice Harry Sloane with three of his chums—Humboldt Pickering, Todd Gassett, and Terence Scott—who had paused in their task of unloading chickens to watch her fondling the baby pigs.

"You gone ruin your pretty dress," Harry shouted. "You the only woman in the world *kisses* pigs!"

"Where my goats?" Jessie shouted.

"In the goat yard. They all right," Humboldt Pickering said.

Jessie vaulted the fence between the barn field and the goat yard, the skirt riding high up her thigh in the process, and sank to her knees before Annie's two little kids. "Oh, my God, I've missed my babies. How are you? Did Everlee give you lots of love and kisses?" Fondling them, caressing, laughing over them—dangerously close to tears. Smelling the marvelous goat smell she'd so missed, feeling Annie's udder, and admiring it for its fullness and beautiful shape.

Midnight and Dusky were kissed and fondled in their turn. Finally Snowflake who stood a little apart perfectly huge with kid. "Heavens, Snowflake," Jessie said. "You look ready to have it right now." She squeezed a teat and got a spurt of milk. "You're ready all right," Jessie said and led the goat up the hill to the stable where she could get a little peace and quiet. She bedded her down with straw and a pail of water and then returned to the chicken yard where the men were unloading crates of chickens.

Jessie walked up to each of the men in turn—Humboldt Pickering, Todd Gassett, Terence Scott, and thrust out her hand and said "Thank you. I deeply 'preciate what you did for me."

Embarrassing them almost to the point of physical anguish. Nevertheless it had to be done. The men didn't want to be thanked, but they'd have liked not being thanked even less.

To Harry Sloane who'd organized the whole operation and to whom she'd been deplorably unfaithful that very afternoon, she said, "Harry, without you, I'd been at the bottom of the well long ago."

"Jessie," Harry said. "You better change you clothes. You not dressed for the barnyard."

"Yeah," Jessie said. "Guess I better."

It was going to be a long night.

All the signs were there. Snowflake was one of those animals who had no gift for maternity. It wasn't supposed to happen, but it did happen. Nature occasionally goes haywire and throws up a thoroughly emancipated goat like Snowflake who thinks motherhood is a drag, wants no part of it—or of sex either—and left to her own devices would not conceive. But, thought Jessie grimly, I didn't leave her to her own devices. I pushed it down her throat (or more accurately up her cunt), and we both got to abide by it.

Jessie went to her kitchen, made herself a cheese sandwich, poured herself a glass of milk, and picked up her copy of *The Odyssey*. In the stable she made herself comfortable in the straw, leaning against the stable door where the light was best. She ate the sandwich, drank the milk, and read. Snowflake was restless as a squirrel. The goat lay down, got up again, made a nest in the straw, moved away from it to a different part of the stable, made another.

By fading daylight, Jessie read about Odysseus' trip to Hades, where he asks one of the ghosts whether his wife had been faithful to him. "With enduring heart, she waits for you," the shade said. "In your own palace and always with her the wretched nights and the days also waste her away with weeping." It smote Jessie, that sentence. I've wept for you, Derry, but I'm too damned busy to weep all day. Penelope has all those slaves to do the work so she can lie around weeping, I got my animals to take care of.

Jessie read Agamemnon's advice to Odysseus about how to handle Penelope when he got home: "Do not be too easy even with your wife. Nor give her an account of all you are sure of. Tell her part, but let the rest be hidden in silence."

It wouldn't be hard for Odysseus to tell Penelope a few lies about Circe and the other girls he'd screwed. Odysseus was a famous liar—his "thievish tales" the talk of the fireside all around the Mediterranean. "So devious," as Athena proudly related. "Never weary of tricks." Back when tricks were widely admired. After all, it was Odysseus who invented the Trojan horse, a very devious trick indeed.

54

Am I going to tell Derry everything that happened while he was gone? About Harry Sloane? About Oscar Willoughby? No. Sleep obliterated her.

She awoke in broad daylight. Snowflake uttering a squeal never before heard from the throat of a goat. Pure terror. On her knees, Jessie scrambled to the side of the goat.

A small black hoof stuck out from the uterus.

A breech birth—and where was I? Asleep!

What had the manual said about breech births? Reach in the uterus and turn the baby goat around. Very easy said the manual—but only if you did it early on. Clearly this breech was well along and desperate. Jessie forced her hand into the aperture—already much too full of large baby goat—instantly found out what the problem was. The second leg was doubled up, blocking the birth passage—the hoof stuck tight into the uterus wall—and getting tighter every minute from the sheer force of the birth contractions.

"Oh, Snowflake," Jessie whispered. "I should have been awake! And I would have been awake if I hadn't got myself all tuckered out fucking in a motel room all afternoon! I'm sorry! I'm sorry! I'm *sorry!*"

Pushing hard as she could to back the baby goat down the birth passage to free that leg, Snowflake's bleat rising in pitch and intensity, mixing with Jessie's "*I'm sorry! I'm sorry! I'm sorry!*," playing counterpoint to her wails.

"Hold on, old girl! We're almost there!" Jessie straining her mightiest.

The little leg came free and popped out of the rear end of Snowflake. Easily. Much too easily. Blood from the ripped uterus poured from the aperture, drenching Jessie's knees and lower legs. The baby goat now slid altogether from the mother's womb—a beautiful big velvety doe. Quite dead.

Snowflake gave up. Jessie could feel the muscles of the abdomen which had been taut as bridge cables go limp as macaroni. The body became indifferent as if its functions were none of its concern any longer. Head and neck which had been arched in muscular tension over the body now unbent, dissolved. Snowflake's head lay in the straw, her one visible eye remote and lost.

It took the goat five minutes to die—a long five minutes—but she died without protest, without any of the anguished bleating that had gone before, as if she'd lost all interest even in her own death throes. Jessie holding her tight in her arms, tears cascading out of her as the blood poured out of Snowflake, the two fluids mingling in the straw.

55

Derry's favorite goat, the one that was to have been mother of her purebred herd. Their one and only prizewinner. Mother and daughter, deceased. Jessie picked up the baby doe and examined it morbidly to see what might have been. Fawn colored, beautifully muscled and shaped. It would have been her most beautiful.

At seven A.M., the sun making red streaks on the green hills, Jessie carried Snowflake and the daughter she hadn't wanted across the barn field and buried them at the highest point of land where woods met pasture in a grave four feet deep because she didn't want the dogs digging up the bodies.

__ CHAPTER __
FIVE

SHE WAS DIVING into something she knew nothing about, something she didn't approve of, something she didn't *do*. She'd hardly even seen a skier except in the movies (Robert Redford in some movie or other), so she read everything she could find in the library, consulted Jonathan Glass about what the law required her to do in the matter of safety and regulations and building codes. Evenings she wrote contractors and builders.

Meanwhile running her farm again full time, milking goats, feeding chickens, thrusting calf manna in the beautiful new filly Saturday had presented her with. She couldn't go on with that load and she knew it. If the loan came through, she had to have help, and she'd already hired a young couple named Jane and Warren Widdy. They were as country as she was. He'd been driving tractors at Gun Metal Farm for a slave-driving German and was anxious for a change. Jane was pregnant with her first child and had been to school with Jessie. She could do anything Jessie could do—milk goats, muck out stables, tend chickens and pigs. She knew the hard work, the heartbreak, and the laughter of farming from birth. Like Jessie.

Jessie put them in the front room, the sitting room in which no one sat. Jessie used it as her guest room on the rare occasions when she had guests. The plan was that when prosperity struck, the Widdys would have their own house somewhere on the farm. Meanwhile it was nice having someone to talk to at meals. To say nothing of having someone to prepare them. Jessie paid them scale wages, which was more than she could afford.

A gamble based entirely on the premise her loan would come through. In the old days she'd have waited until she had money in hand. Not any more.

She was gambling because she had nothing to lose. If she didn't gamble, she'd go under. The only way to play was to gamble—and win. No other alternative.

She needed the Widdys—not only to talk to, to mend fences, and milk goats but to keep Harry Sloane off her back.

As long as they were in residence, Harry couldn't be, though, God knows, he tried. The very first night they moved in Harry Sloane appeared, uninvited, in the kitchen doorway all ready for love.

Instead he got the Widdys.

"Jane and Warren," Jessie explained, "are going to he'p out with the chores and until we find them a place, they'll be staying in the front parlor." All in a rush before Harry put his big foot in his mouth.

Harry's eyebrows shot up, and he scowled a great scowl.

"Like to talk to ya 'bout harvesting you winter wheat if you'd just step outside," Harry said.

"Sit down," Jessie said with a great smile. "We got no secrets here."

Harry tried hints, and winks, and everything short of hand wrestling to get her out into the yellow truck. Jessie willfully misunderstood all these signals and stayed glued to her kitchen chair until Harry gave up and went home. Furious. Jessie could tell by the savagery with which he spun the wheels in her driveway.

Two days after this encounter, Jessie sped off to Folkesbury for some long-delayed adultery with that deliciously clean young Mr. Willoughby at the motel where the affair had begun. Oscar offered lunch at the usual place but Jessie waved it aside as a waste of time. She was in too much of a rush to get into the motel room, turn on "As the World Turns," and fondle her young man in the air conditioning. What marvelous fun, she was thinking, nibbling on him, kissing him, all but undressing him.

"Hey," Oscar complained. "I'm supposed to be undressing *you!*"

Jessie curbed herself sharply. Let Oscar do the running. Lay there, eyes demurely closed. Submitting. Thinking furiously. Here I am running away from that huge masterful Harry to a younger man I can hoodwink, clambering all over him. What does this mean? Before sex overwhelmed her, and she stopped thinking about things altogether.

Later they talked about business. Mildly disturbing talk.

"We got a letter from the Environmental Protection Agency," Oscar Willoughby said. "You didn't have anything to do with *that*, Jessie?"

"Environmental *what?*" Jessie asked.

"Don't know how they got into this unless you told them something," Oscar said. "If my company finds out I told you about the Chemical offer, it's my neck. You know that, Jessie.

Snuggled up, Jessie said, "I wouldn't want anything to happen to your pretty neck, darling." She kissed it, the thought flashing through her mind: I can *use* that neck. Big operator, me! I haven't even got a deal yet, and already I'm picking out vice-presidents.

What she said aloud was, "Couldn't we have a little more love before we get down to brass tacks?"

"Love?" Oscar asked with a rising inflection.

"Lust," Jessie amended.

"Love," Oscar said with greater resonance.

Damn, thought Jessie, putting her tongue in his mouth, anything to get his mind off *love*. I don't want him to fall in *love* with me. Romance is the last thing I want. What I want is . . .

What she wanted, was a nice pneumatic sex toy. She was mad about the boy in the way she was mad about her baby goats, a furry object to fondle. Oscar was a sex object, one of those things the feminists so strenuously disapproved of.

An *educational* toy. Jessie was learning a lot about business from him in addition to engaging in all those sexual calisthenics.

Nevertheless, a new light shone in Oscar's eye as he looked over Jessie's long, lean, naked frame. He's comparing me with that TV-watching wife of his, and she's coming out badly.

To cool his brain, she queried him about her last offer, where negotiations had got stuck. What else was new?

"We've had a couple of nibbles," Oscar said. "When are you going to get your loan?"

"Government loans take forever," Jessie said. "They got to go through committee."

Harry Sloane was the committee, and he was mad at her.

"If somebody comes along with a better offer, we can move very fast—so you better hurry them along. Your Uncle Jonathan must know a few legislators in Richmond."

"What?" Jessie asked, snapping to full attention.

"Some muscle in the capitol. Doesn't he know a few wheeler-dealers in the state house?"

"He knows them all," said Jessie, sitting bolt upright. "Is that how. . . ?"

59

"They can swing things with a phone call."

"But it's Federal," Jessie cried. "It's not state."

"Makes no difference. Most Federal farm programs are run by the local people. The state crowd has got a lot to say about who gets the loans. . . ."

"Let's get dressed," Jessie said.

Half an hour later, she was in Uncle Jonathan's office.

"Well, I know the Governor, of course," dear Uncle Jonathan said, "but then everyone knows the Governor."

"No, darling," Jessie corrected. "Everyone doesn't." (Although in Uncle Jonathan's world, of course, everyone did. Everyone in Jonathan's world was a very small group.)

"You just get on the phone to the Governor right now and see if he can't speed this loan up. Otherwise I'll lose the deal and my farm and my livelihood."

Uncle Jonathan was not instantly persuaded. Jessie had to call on all her reserves of tact and sex appeal, plus information, argument, and moral suasion. "What I'm doing, Uncle Jonathan, is to preserve the best of the land from ruthless industrialization."

Telling the *truth*! First time all day!

"He's a busy man," Uncle Jonathan said.

"It's what he's for—to serve the people. I'm preserving three thousand acres of beautiful historic Virginia from despoiling by vicious polluting mobsters."

"I had no idea you were such a high-powered operative, Jessie," Uncle Jonathan said.

She leaned across her godfather's ornate eighteenth-century desk, afire with resolve. "I'll tell you this, my company will never do anything that will hurt the land it uses. We will protect and nurture the forests with the money we make out of the slopes, so help me God. And just to be sure we do all that and keep us all honest, I'm going to make you chairman of the board."

"Jessie, that's sweet of you. But I'm already chairman of too many boards. I haven't time. . . ."

"It won't take any of your time. I'll do all the work. We need your respectability to frighten off the weasels, the chiselers, the bad people. . . ."

What she needed was Jonathan Glass's name on the letterhead of the stationery in order to get another loan—a quite different ordinary bank

60

loan for Columbia Land Development Corporation, and even as she talked she could see that letterhead in pale blue—Jonathan Glass, Chairman! Jessie Jenkins, President, and, just possibly, Oscar Willoughby, Vice President.

In the end he called the Governor, not because he was persuaded of the superior morality of Jessie's Land Development Corporation but because he was fond of her and it was late in the afternoon when his powers of rejection burned low—which is how a great many deals are made in the South.

That night, as she and Jane Widdy sat shelling peas and gossiping about the village of Dobbsville—who was having babies and who was having trouble—Harry Sloane loomed in the doorway of the kitchen. Jessie had never seen Harry quite so threatening before—huge, dark-browed, solemn as a church.

Without preamble or invitation, he sat at the kitchen table with the two women, helped himself to a handful of the newly shucked peas and gobbled them down. "Y'got that Land Bank Loan," Harry said, chewing the peas viciously. "Come through in big hurry. The Guvnor hisself 'spressed interest."

"Isn't that nice?" Jessie murmured, shelling peas. "You been sitting on that loan, Harry Sloane?"

"You know better'n 'at, Jessie. I 'proved that loan day it got to me. It's the Feds been sittin' on that loan, the bureaucrats. They suppose check it out, but they never check nothin' out 'cept the spellin'. They just delay—until a Guvnor calls, and then they git off their fat ass. . . ."

"Look who's talkin' about a fat ass." Jessie said.

". . . an' do some processin' they shoulda done weeks ago. If I'd known you knew the Guvnor, Jessie. . . ."

"I don't know the Governor," Jessie said. "I have no idea how he got into this. Maybe . . ."

"You a liar, Jessie Jenkins."

"Don't you go calling her a liar!" Jane said furiously.

The trouble is I am, Jessie thought, shelling peas.

Nobody said anything after that for the longest time. After a while Jessie couldn't withstand the curiosity any more and looked up from her pea-shelling, directly into Harry Sloane's intense gaze. A very different gaze it was. He's looking at me as if I were an adversary, someone to be feared or, at very least, respected.

61

She moved instantly to mollify. "I should think you'd be pleased, Harry. This whole thing's your idea. I owe it all to you, and I'm very grateful. I do something for you sometime, Harry."

"How 'bout right now?"

She gave him a look at that, both arch and exasperated, indicating Jane with her eyebrows. He tried to outsit Jane Widdy, but he couldn't do it. One reason was that the two women presently plunged back into their chatter.

"Easy havin' terrible trouble with her meringues. I tell her you got to use the *oldest* egg white. Otherwise they not dry properly, and whole thing git gluey. . . ."

"I use typing paper put 'em on because it stays so flat."

"Trouble is Easy *hurries* her meringues, and you can't *hurry* meringues. You got to beat the egg white till it's stiff as cardboard. Oney then . . ."

Harry Sloane put up with a full hour of this which showed the extent of his desire before giving up and leaving, sending his pickup out the driveway in a great shower of gravel.

At 10 P.M. Jessie went to bed and lay there between sleeping and waking—waiting for the Goddess she'd not seen for quite a while. Tonight she'd be back. Jessie couldn't explain how she knew this, but she did.

When she appeared, ten feet tall, eyes flashing fire, dressed in soft raiment of yellow pastel, the Goddess was smiling.

"I admired the way you handled your Uncle Jonathan," the Gray-eyed One laughed. "Odysseus himself couldn't have been more devious."

"Can you make me admire myself for my deviousness?" asked Jessie.

"No," the Goddess said, "I can grant only forgetfulness."

Athena scattered forgetfulness on Jessie's eyelids, and Jessie slept deeply and dreamed of childhood.

She was swimming in the James River, which her mother had told her again and again she must not do. She would be swept downstream, and sure enough she *is* swept downstream—the bank flashing past her eyes faster and faster. Presently she is drifting through a city dark and sinister, the riverbank lined with people looking at her as she bobs along, naked. Naked among strangers, and how am I to get home? Jessie awoke in panic, sun streaming through the windows. Now what did that dream mean? Because sure as she was alive, it *meant* something. Athena didn't plant dreams like that in a girl's head that had no meaning. Look out! But for what? That was the trouble with the ancient Gods. They treat us like performing dogs—betting on the result.

*   *   *

Jessie looked at herself in the full-length mirror, stark naked, seething with possibilities. With a million and a half dollars, I can afford a new dress. Must have one to talk to bankers.

She went to Miramar's, the most expensive shop in Folkesbury, and bought a dress in pastel yellow that was exactly the color of Athena's tunic—impractical, expensive, and pure in design, and with it shoes and a handbag of brown leather, simple and again expensive. When she put all these things on and looked at herself in the mirror, she thought: I need a haircut, and I know exactly how I want it. Short and curly, shaped around my skull like Apollo.

An hour later she was in a chair at Ladbroke's, the most expensive beauty salon in Folkesbury, pointing to a picture in a child's book on mythology. "I want to look like that," pointing to Apollo's ringlets, as he drove the chariot through the sky—amazing Leah (the name printed on the operative's blouse).

While Leah was cutting and shaping her hair, Jessie called Oscar Willoughby at American Lumber Products and did something that had never before been seen in Folkesbury outside of the movies—talking business from a chair in a beauty salon. Attracting intense attention from the other customers as well as manicurists, hair stylists, and cutters.

What they heard was largely incomprehensible numbers.

"We're prepared to go at three hundred seventy-five dollars," Oscar said.

"Mmmm," Jessie said and did her arithmetic on a yellow scratch pad. Three hundred seventy-five times three thousand. No, it was actually 2,930, and she didn't want two hundred of that so the figure was 2,730. Jessie did her sums—one million, oh two three, seven five oh—too much.

"Three fifteen," Jessie said. They wouldn't accept that, but they'd counter with something a little more human than three seven five. (Jessie's head swimming with the excitement.)

"I'll set up a conference call," Oscar said.

"Beautiful," Jessie said to Leah.

"What!" Oscar said.

"Not you," Jessie said. "Though of course, you are." (Not on a conference call, she told herself severely.)

"Three fifteen," Oscar was telling two vice-presidents of American Lumber—all of them on the telephone line at once.

"Out of the question," one vice-president said. "Three seven five."

63

"Unacceptable," Jessie said. (A new word she'd learned from Oscar.) To Leah. "Not you, dear."

A buzz of conversation on the line from which came "Three six oh," from one of the vice-presidents.

So it went until the numbers got stuck at three four five (Jessie's number), and one of the vice-presidents said "Cash?"

"Cash," Jessie said.

"Okay," the man said.

"My lawyer is Jonathan Glass," Jessie said. She could feel them being impressed clear over the telephone. "Send the agreement to him." She was doing the numbers on her pad, and they were doing it on a calculator and came up with a figure sooner.

"Wrong," Jessie said crisply. Just guessing. "Two hundred acres I don't want so the acreage we're talking about is two seven three oh, not three thousand."

"Sorry," the vice-president said—and recalculated: $831,950.

Quite a climbdown from a million and a half. I've saved myself six hundred thousand dollars, my goodness. Three forty-five an acre was a very low price for Virginia land but a high price for land that had no agricultural value, had been lumbered over, and couldn't be lumbered again for twenty years. Only for skiing was this a bargain—and no one knew about that except herself and Jonathan Glass.

"Lunch?" Oscar asked hopefully.

"I've got to see bankers," Jessie said. Sex had nothing like the attraction of a million and a half dollars—and possession of three thousand acres. (Well, 2,730.)

Jesse took a deep breath and looked at herself in the mirror. Straight in the eye. Her and her new classically ringleted hair. I look a little like the gray-eyed Goddess herself. I can do anything.

An hour later she was in the waiting room outside J. Fred Percy's office at the First National Bank of Folkesbury when the door opened.

Harry Sloane came out of J. Fred Percy's office, scowling, bedraggled, rumpled. First time Jessie had ever seen him look scared.

"You can go in now, Mrs. Jenkins," the receptionist said.

Instead she went to Harry Sloane. "Harry! Is something the matter?"

He was looking her up and down—the new togs, new haircut. "What ya done to y'hair, Jessie. It ain't feminine."

That made her laugh. "Always the soul of charm, aren't you, Harry?"

64

He stood in front of her, massive as a bear, shaking his head. "At ain't you!"

"You better get used to it. You going to see a lot of it."

In J. Fred Percy's office she said: "What have you done to poor old Harry? Slam down the window?"

J. Fred Percy was too much a banker to tell her anything about another client.

Instead he said, "We've received notice of your authorization." Very neutral tones. He had the papers in his hands, shuffling them from hand to hand, reverently. "If you'll just sign here and here and here and *here.*"

It gave her keenest pleasure to say, "I think I'll just take them home and read them first, Mr. Percy." They'd made her wait. Now let them wait. "What I came for is something else. I want a straight commercial loan of another million and a half."

She didn't need that much now that she'd bargained American Lumber Products down, but she needed half that. Anyway they wouldn't give her all she asked. Might as well shoot for the moon.

She showed him her designs of ski slopes, figures of profit of the nearest ski resort, and how much business they had had to turn away because they had no place to park cars and no room on the slopes for the skiers. She flourished estimates of how much it would cost to build Ski Village (as it was to be called), how much to operate, and how much profit to expect. The last was formidable. The big expense in ski places is building. Operation cost is so minimal that sometimes gross and net income are almost the same thing. Skiing in Virginia was a growth business, and business had always outstripped the wildest of predictions.

J. Fred Percy listened, pursing his lips. Finally he said, "Two things I don't like. You can't get the Environmental Protection Agency to side with you on land use. . . ."

"Oh, yes, we can," Jessie said.

"And you can't get it built before snow flies."

"Want to bet?" Jessie asked.

The Gray-eyed Goddess was back in her corner, wasn't she?

She hoped.

65

__ CHAPTER __
SIX

THEY WERE CASTRATING pigs—Warren with his oak face wielding the razor, Jessie holding, hating the whole business, but if she had to be part of it preferring the holding to the cutting.

The eight-week-old pig was on its back screeching in the upper registers, Jessie astride it, the pig's snout in her crotch, her two hands holding the hind legs spread wide and pulled back toward her. Warren was on his knees next to her, his head bowed as if at the altar. With finger and thumb of his left hand, he found the tiny testicle and squeezed it firm under the flesh. The single-bladed razor in his right hand sliced a neat straight line down the haunch, and out popped the small vitality in its wrapping of silver flesh. Warren sliced through the outer casing, and posterity itself was exposed— silver and purple with its tracery of red veins, attached with streamers of arteries. Warren cut the little grape-sized object free and threw it on the pile.

The little pig had uttered a high squeal accompanied by a mighty jerk at the first thrust of the razor, but now it was silent and still, paralyzed by the enormity of what was being inflicted on it. Some little pigs died under the razor, a form of protest, and Jessie, astride the little animal, never could banish the fear that sometime she'd find a little dead pig under her. Still the terrible deed had to be done, or the meat would taste awful and would be rejected at the livestock market. Torment to Jessie, all of it. Watching Warren with his razor, she thought, that it was men who were the natural castrators, not women, as the idiot Freudians would have it. Men loved cutting flesh. Was there a single woman surgeon in the whole world? Or butcher?

67

Jessie sloshed the wound with Mercurochrome diluted with water and pulled the little pig into her arms, cradling it and crooning over it for a moment before returning him to his castrated companions. The little pig stood still for a moment, testing out life without balls, and then trotted away and crouched down in the straw to protect the wounds from flies. By morning the wounds would have healed, and the little pig would be full of appetite and mischief. At that moment, he felt low.

Jessie climbed into the pen and chased down the last of fifteen clamorous male pigs. The other little pigs crowded around her bare legs trying to protect their little companion. The clamor reached the big sows outside the barn, and they added their enormous protest to those in the barn. Pigs truly cared about what happened to their fellow pigs and screamed their anger with the solidarity of an anti-nuclear group lying down in front of the bulldozers—and with the same futility.

Jessie held the last pig by its rear legs, turned it on its back, and sat on it, and Warren went to work with his razor. As always, the caterwauling not only from the pig under her but from all the others inside and outside the barn rose to an inferno of noise (a grown pig at full scream reaches two decibels higher than that permitted the *Concorde* taking off) and then, as always, silence fell on the barnyard. In that silence, came a new roar—this one machine-made.

Jessie looked at Warren, and Warren looked at Jessie, two country people as sensitive to noises as forest animals. Warren made a little grimace and finished off the last little pig's castration. Jessie sloshed the cuts with Mercurochrome and returned the pig to its pen.

The two of them left the pile of testicles (which Warren would slice up and feed to the dogs) and went out of the barn into the brilliant hot July sunshine.

The Gleaner was lumbering down Jessie's driveway, like a two-story house, brushing aside the branches on her Norway maples when not tearing them out by the roots.

"Heavens to Betsy!" Jessie said and ran toward it.

The Gleaner had halted now near the wheat field, its sixteen gleaming aluminum snouts sniffing the ground like a pig looking for acorns. A surrealist pig in a nightmare of farm machinery.

"Sixty-two thousand dollars for one of those machines!" Jessie shouted up to Harry Sloane in the cab, two stories above her. "You out of you mind, Harry Sloane!"

"I didn't buy it new!" Harry Sloane screamed with his great Pan grin. "Only twenty-two thousand! Burn damage on the paint—so I got it for one third list. Real bargain!"

Twenty-two thousand, Jessie thought—and bankruptcy closing over his head!

"I got to charge ya fifty-three dollar an hour, Jessie, cause it cost that much to operate this monster. I'd do it for nothing, but things being as they are, I just can't."

"Fifty-three . . ." Jessie choked it off. Hell, she could afford it, money flowing out of her ears these days. "Okay! Okay! Wait, I come along."

"Ain't room up here for two!" Harry Sloane shouted.

"I'll find room!" Jessie said and climbed up the steel ladder past the sign which read: NO ONE BUT THE OPERATOR MUST BE ON THE BRIDGE OR IN THE CAB WHEN THE GLEANER IS IN MOTION. The Gleaner puffed diesel smoke into the pure air and turned into the wheat field, Jessie clinging to the steel railing on the bridge.

The winter wheat, golden and lovely, was waist high and should have been harvested weeks earlier, but Jessie hadn't been able to find anyone who owned a machine that would harvest eight acres of wheat. Nobody was making little harvesters any more—just these brontosauruses, designed for harvesting whole prairies. Like using the *Queen Mary* as a rowboat, Jessie thought, looking down from her ridiculous altitude at the golden grain vanishing into the monster where it was separated, the straw spewing out the rear. For sixty-two thousand dollars, Jessie thought furiously, you'd think it could bind up the straw into bales, but no one thought about straw any more. Left it in the field to rot, which was why a bale of straw cost three dollars. Small farmers in America going broke at the rate of eight hundred a month because they couldn't afford these locomotives.

Jessie thinking all this, her new short haircut blowing in the wind. She took a look at Harry Sloane, massive as a tree trunk, running the huge machine with savage concentration, loving the racket it made, the bigness of it. Macho! Macho! Macho! Jessie thought—but with deep pity because Harry Sloane was going under. The word was all over the countryside. The money men were going to get him is what everyone was saying—but not to Harry.

Harry himself driving his huge farm trucks, his tractors, his new Gleaner, his farm hands—with furious intensity that summer—while the rumors whirled about his massive head.

In the blazing sunshine—90 degrees in the shade, 105 in the sun—the great machine devoured the eight acres of winter wheat in under three quarters of an hour and disgorged it all through its aluminum blower into the small silo.

Jessie clambered down the iron ladder carefully, off the Gleaner's bridge, which resembled that of a small cruiser, her eyes darting about, the monster machinery with its baffles, its pistons, its plates. Harry was ahead of her down the ladder and with a screwdriver was removing a panel which contained the words in bright red: THIS PANEL MUST NOT BE REMOVED EXCEPT AT THE FACTORY. That was Harry. Always disregarding the warnings.

"Makin' a funny noise," Harry said. He peered in the aperture and reached his hand in cautiously. The hand came out a moment later clutching a small egg-shaped bit of copper. Bits of copper chain clung to it.

Printed across the egg-shaped copper was the single word DERRY.

Jessie stopped breathing.

Derry. She hadn't thought about him for weeks. Well, she was *busy*! Trying to extricate herself from the mess his absence had caused!

Harry staring at her curiously.

She took the egg-shaped copper object from his hand and looked at it.

"You seen it before?" Harry asked.

She nodded, wordless. Derry had got it at the state fair, the same state fair at which Snowflake had won her prize. Had had it stamped out and wore it on his wrist. Never took it off. Good luck talisman. He said. It had never brought much.

"Where you buy this Gleaner, Harry?" Jessie whispered.

"It fell off the back of a truck, ya know what I mean."

"I know what you mean."

Stolen. A lot of farm theft going around, and Harry would be the one who would know where to buy it at one-third the market price. (He couldn't afford even that.)

Derry! Stealing!

Inconceivable.

Later they sat in Jessie's kitchen and drank ice-cold lemonade, Harry rubbing the sweat out of his eyes, while Jessie wrote out the check. Fifty-three dollars. Much good that would do him. He owed over a million, the rumor was.

Harry Sloane took the check with a snort of derision: "S'prise you c'n write a check for so *small* an amount, Jessie Jenkins. Big operator like you! I hear they lend you five million at the bank. . . ."

"Where you hear that, Harry?" Jessie asked. He was bleeding inside. She could tell from the fierce grimace on him. "Where you hear things like that?"

"Down at the Gulf station they sayin' it."

"You know better than to pay attention those people, Harry," Jessie said softly. You should hear what those people down at the Gulf station saying about *you*, Harry Sloane, she was thinking.

"Jessie a big wheel now—too big fer you, Harry Sloane, that's what they sayin'."

"Come *on*, Harry," Jessie said. "Always have time for you. You saved my bacon, you know that."

"You ain't had time for me this whole last month."

Jessie drew a deep breath and took the plunge because it had to be said sometime and they were alone in the kitchen. "Harry, I don't want to go to bed with you any more, and that's the truth of it. I never wanted to. You forced my hand, and that's the end of it. But as for having *time* for you, Harry. I'll always have . . . Oh, my God!"

She'd caught a glimpse of the clock. ". . . I'm late."

She tore for the shower behind the kitchen, tearing off her blouse. "Harry, my dress is hanging out there in the front hall closet. Bring it back here, will ya, please!"

She peeled off her jeans and stepped into the shower, keeping her short hair out of the stream, washing pig blood, pig shit, pig smell off ankles, hands, arms and face. Through the glass door, she could see Harry Sloane bringing in the dress, hanging it on the hook behind the bathroom door.

He won't stop there because he's not the kind that stops, not Harry, Jessie thought. He didn't. Through the glass door she saw him coming toward the shower door. She anticipated him, turning off the water and stepping out of the shower, stark naked and dripping wet.

"I ain't got time for rape, Harry Sloane," she snarled at him, and brushed past to snatch a towel from the rack.

"You ain't got time for anything but bankers, Jessie Jenkins. You worshippin' the golden calf, that's what you doin'."

Jessie toweling away furiously. Rubbing the water out of her eyes, looking at him. Him mighty calm, drawling his words.

"Rape! You not a fit object for rape, Jessie Jenkins."

Jessie wriggling into her underpants, her new smart white cotton dress, her mocassins.

"You got about as much sex appeal as my tractor. Maybe a little less."

Jessie running her hands through her short hair in lieu of a comb because she was in one hell of a hurry.

He followed her now as she ran past him down the corridor, through the kitchen, the front hall—picking up handbag, plans, briefcase—Harry bellowing his gibes at her.

"You not a *woman* any more. You a machine—like that harvester—chewin' up money like that Gleaner chews up wheat. . . ."

Jessie ran across her porch down the front steps into her brand new Triumph sports car, Harry still shouting his diatribe. "I be turned on by my pigs quicker'n by you, Jessie Jenkins. . . ."

She couldn't hear any more, flying down the driveway in her car, but she could see Harry Sloane in her side mirror voicing his insults. Well out of sight of the house, she stopped the car and took a look at herself in the mirror—gray eyes, short blonde hair, anxious face. *As much sex appeal as my tractor!*

She continued on down the driveway, feeling the onslaught as if it were physical.

One thing you had to say about Harry. He was going down with all guns firing.

Derry. That copper plate. Derry loved to have his name on things. Couldn't resist gadgets that stamped his identity on bits of copper. Jessie had put that bit of metal around his wrist and he had never taken it off, not even in the shower.

Where are you, my husband, when I need you!

But she didn't.

72

__ CHAPTER __
SEVEN

JESSIE DROVE PAST the fourteen-foot sign that bore the words SKI VILLAGE in antique lettering, past the bulldozers on the lower slope to the construction hut on the summit. There she ran straight into controversy. Oscar Willoughby arguing furiously with Jorvald Dench, the Danish ski instructor. Jessie's ski slope designer.

"Look at it," Jorvald shouted, blue eyes blazing. "Exactly right for instructors, that slope. Two hundred meters wide. Gentle. At the entrance where it should be. Exactly right for baby slopes. You can park cars anywhere."

"You can't," Oscar said. "That's what got Winterhaven into all the trouble. They put the cars up the hill, and when it snows they can't get up there so you don't make any money. This is the place to park cars—at the *foot* of the hill. *We'll* take the skiers up the mountain on a cable car and charge them a dollar and a half."

Art versus commerce.

"Jorvald," Jessie said, smiling into the Dane's beautiful angry face. "You are absolutely right in everything you say, but your art must give way to commerce because in Virginia the parking problem is infinitely more important than ski slope design. This isn't Aspen. The skiers around here are *terrible*. They will accept any kind of ski slope, anything that goes downhill they find marvelous. But Virginians know all about parking cars, and if you make it too hard for them to get there, they won't come."

"What am I *doing* here?" Jorvald Dench asked.

"You are helping us avoid serious mistakes," Jessie said. "Already you've been worth your weight in gold."

73

"Gold!" the ski instructor muttered. "That's all you think about, Jessie."

Second time today, Jessie thought.

She drove the little Triumph down the ridge to the lodge that would house the cafeteria and the lounge for non-skiers where Jessie planned to sell food, drink and magazines to non-skiing wives waiting for their skiing husbands—at the moment surrounded by a mass of scaffolding.

Jessie walked up wooden steps to the balcony where, leaning against the balustrade, stood J. Fred Percy, the banker, looking at his watch.

"I'm sorry," Jessie said crisply. "I've had to referee a fight over what to do with the lower slopes."

Keeping J. Fred Percy waiting now. He used to keep her waiting. Outside *his* office. Now he was on *her* turf.

Unrolling the plans for the condominiums. A new wrinkle.

"I want sixteen of them, side by side, on that slope over there," Jessie said. "And sixteen more on that ridge, opposite. With connecting roads, and sewage, and electricity, I'll need seventeen million dollars. But I don't want a loan this time. I want to issue bonds, and the only way I can do that is to incorporate Ski Village as a municipality, and that's where I need a banker's help. . . ."

"You'll never get state approval," J. Fred Percy said.

Jessie sighed. "You always say things like that, don't you? Want to bet?"

After the banker had gone, taking her plans and his discretion and his cold heart, Jessie leaned against the balustrade, gazing out at her three thousand acres, feeling her wounds. They were not a pretty sight, her three thousand acres. A woodland slum. It would take twenty years for this flotsam to grow into a respectable forest again, but some day hardwood trees would tower all the way to the horizon. So spake Jessie to herself. This was her inner fire, this the moral thrust that justified the lies, the commerce, the ass-kissing, the whole rotten business.

Oscar was nuzzling at her neck now, and she moved away, annoyed.

"Not *here*, Oscar!"

The slopes crawled with bulldozers, the building with carpenters.

"We haven't been to bed together for weeks," he complained.

"Darling, it's so difficult with the Widdys in the house and so many meetings. Tonight there's the highway department meeting on the access roads." Jessie was trying to persuade the county to widen Highway 28 to four lanes at *their* expense to take two thousand cars an hour at peak load.

74

"You might come to the meeting with me, Oscar. I need your help with these people. And afterward, perhaps . . ."

"Afterward," Oscar said bitterly. "You'll say you're too tired."

"Well, I *do* get tired, Oscar! Today I've had four meetings, and I helped castrate fifteen pigs. . . ."

Her hand flew to her mouth. Wishing she hadn't . . . castrated fifteen. . . . Oscar pointedly *not* saying anything, *not* jumping on it, just looking at her with that ironical twist of his cleanly shaved mouth, which was comment enough.

Looking out over her three thousand acres. My life is a series of thinly painted impressions. Full of color and dash.

No depth.

She became conscious of Oscar saying: ". . . many more of these late nights, and she says she's going to leave me."

Oscar was talking about his wife. Jessie snapped at it. "Oscar, we can't have that! I'm asking for favorable decisions from the Environment people, the planning commission, the banks, one government agency after another. I can't get involved in a sex scandal. It just *sounds* irresponsible. . . ."

"*Sounds* irresponsible," Oscar said bitterly. "You don't mind *being* irresponsible. Just sounding that way. You're getting very cold-blooded, Jessie."

"Oscar!" She was appalled and hurt. "If I were cold-blooded I wouldn't be involved with you in the first place. I'm too warm-blooded is my problem!"

"Yeah," Oscar said with his gleaming, Pepsodent, skeptical smile. "But the banks and the planning commission and the rest of them are more important than I am in your life."

"I'm fighting for survival," Jessie cried. "If I go under, you go under too. Oh, Oscar, for heaven's sake, must we talk like this *now*! With so much to be done!"

"You don't want to talk about it ever," Oscar said wearily.

"When things settle down," Jessie said softly, trying to placate.

"Things will never settle down with you, Jessie," Oscar said wearily. "Never! You're not the kind lets things settle down."

With that, he walked out of the building, something he'd never done before. Always she'd ended the scenes. Now Oscar did. That meant he wouldn't go to the Planning Commission meeting with her that night. She'd have to handle it—as she'd handled so many others—alone.

In all my life I have never been so surrounded by so many people—and I've never been so alone.

Late that afternoon she stopped at the Gulf station to fill up the little Triumph. The Gulf station was at the corner of Main and Water Street, the heart of downtown Dobbsville (Pop. 342)—Dobbsville's Rialto. Here the good citizens and the no-good citizens gathered in complete equality and heard the gossip, voiced their suspicions, and gave tongue to their deprecations (of themselves as well as everyone else). Dobbsville's Greek chorus, these idlers and buffoons. Jessie's first appearance with little Triumph had brought forth a shower of pretty good country repartee at which she wasn't at all bad. And enjoyed very much.

This would be the first time the Greek chorus would see her in a white dress—and that should bring forth some pretty smart country raillery. Jessie was all ready with her rejoinders.

Instead she got silence.

She reached for the gas nozzle as she had so often done in the past, but Jerry Harper, whose station it was, took it from her and filled her tank. That was his gibe at her white dress—and it was pointed indeed.

The Greek chorus lounged around the tire rack, silent as wraiths.

"How things with you, Jerry?" Jessie asked, to get things going.

"Middlin'."

"Martha had her baby yet?"

"Last week."

"Oh, my goodness." Everyone else must have known. "What was it?"

" 'Nother boy."

"How many boys that make—four?"

He just nodded, wordless, when not monosyllabic. The Greek chorus should have been right in there tossing out repartee because Jerry Harper and his stream of boy children was good solid joke material.

Jessie looked at the full circle of idlers—Humboldt Pickering, Abner Caldwell, Jamie Goosens, Todd Gassett. She'd known them all since childhood. Yet the air was full of chill. Not hostility so much as derision. Jessie Jenkins getting too big for her britches.

Which is what they had said about Harry Sloane.

Once.

Jessie, among them.

Jessie scrabbled in her handbag for her credit card. That, too, would excite scorn, probably already had. She'd always laid out cash. Now . . . Well, she'd got a credit card in the name of Columbia Land Development only because it made the expense deductible. She could make a nice joke about that. If they were speaking to her.

They weren't.

They were saving the talk for after she left, as she'd seen them do (in fact, done herself) with others who had gone up the greasy pole a little too fast.

As she drew out of the gas station, she kept her eye on the Greek chorus in the mirror. Sure enough, she had barely pulled into the main street when the jokes started to fly. Abner Caldwell with his lizard eyes said something, and the whole crowd broke into tight smiles. Jerry Harper made rejoinder. That really broke them up.

Jessie wished she'd heard the jokes. She could use a few laughs.

Ski Village was growing, fleshing out, becoming a reality taking all her time now, Jessie dazzled by her own creation, going from room to room, overseeing every last detail, making a great nuisance of herself to architects, builders, carpenters, plumbers, electricians, with criticisms, questions, suggestions. She had to know why every last wire went where it went, the set of every last brick, the tone of every last color. . . .

"I'm terribly sorry but would you mind explaining why that chandelier has to be quite so low?" "Wouldn't it be more sensible to put that stove on *that* wall, instead of this. . . . I realize that means rewiring the kitchen but. . . ."

Smiling, throwing the charm around—but turning into cold-rolled steel when the charm didn't work. The carpenters and architects and builders would go their own way when the thing was finished, and she'd be stuck with their mistakes. So she would not let them make any. . . .

In her mind, the corridors were already full of skiers, and she was controlling the flow—from the toilets to the cafeteria to the rental shops to the slopes—anticipating all the problems.

It was changing her nature, toughening her—not always liking this process.

On her knees at night to the Gray-eyed Goddess, she said, "You were pretty blood-stained yourself in the early years, my Divinity, yet you became in later life the protector of civilization, the embodiment of reason and wisdom."

"I was always the same person," Athena said. "The poets saw in me what they wanted to see."

77

"Take care of my Derry, and bring him back to me," Jessie prayed on her knees.

"He'll be back—when the time is ripe," the Gray-eyed One said.

She saw her animals hardly at all any more because she had no time. Except in the very early hours when sometimes she went riding.

Riding at full gallop that morning on Saturday, Derry's horse, because Jorvald was riding hers, Jessie went full tilt around the big bend of woods, past the half-harvested corn, toward the stand of Norway maples just turning red gold, her muscles protesting all the way. She and Derry had ridden every day in good weather (when it wasn't too hot or too cold). Since his disappearance she'd ridden hardly at all because riding alone was not very much fun.

She pulled up at the fence beyond which Harry Sloane's Black Angus grazed and looked back at Jorvald bouncing along awkwardly on Wednesday. How could anyone bounce like that on Wednesday whose stride was smooth as cream? Marvelous as he was on skis, Jorvald was pretty dreadful on a horse.

He arrived at her side, disheveled and angry at losing the race. "You have the best horse," he said sulkily. "It's not fair."

"I'm getting a little revenge for what you did to me last night," Jessie said—and laughed.

She had gone to bed with Jorvald—a situation that had been building for some time—and Jessie's articulation of this event was that she had been seduced rather than the other way around. Jorvald wanted to believe this image of himself as masterful seducer—and so she played along. Actually, Jessie had arranged to bring him home, had cleared the decks, and had all but taken his clothes off.

Looking up at the beautiful, angry Nordic face, she mentally lined up all her adulteries. The differences were excoriating. In the first case she'd been blackmailed into it; the second time she'd been propositioned and consented largely to revenge herself on Harry Sloane; this time, the whole affair was her idea, from start to finish.

As a lover Jorvald was beautifully muscled and untiring but much too full of himself. Jessie was already bored with having to smooth his feathers. The speed of satiety! I'll be getting bored with them before I get my clothes off. . . .

Cantering back to the farm, she thought about Derry who rode a horse as if it were part of him and he were a minotaur.

Come back, my handsome husband, and rescue me from my suitors. If you'd been here, none of this would have happened. Anyway, I've only had three suitors. Penelope had a hundred and eight. Theoretically she didn't go to bed with any of them, but I simply don't *believe* that. At what point did I *stop* believing that? Because once I did, but now I don't, which is a mark of my descent down the slippery slope. Homer was pulling the wool over our eyes. Or perhaps Penelope pulled it over his.

After all, when Odysseus got back after twenty years, he killed all one hundred and eight suitors (with a little help from his friend and mine, Athena). Now why else would he do that? Admittedly, they'd been nuisances. They'd eaten too many of his pigs and sheep and messed up his house. But *kill* them!

For messing up the house?

Jessie doubted all of it, especially twenty years of fidelity. Homer simply didn't understand women. Penelope had been to bed with all one hundred eight (hardly more than a new man every couple of months to while away the twenty years), and that's why Odysseus had slaughtered them all. Why didn't he slaughter her, too? Well, the Greeks didn't do that to unfaithful wives much. After all, Helen, who had caused the Trojan War by running away with Paris, simply went back to Menelaus after the fall of Troy and became a good wife and hostess, playing hostess to, among others, Odysseus on his way home.

"What are you grinning about so evilly?" Jorvald asked.

"I find life unexpected," Jessie said.

"I hate the unexpected," Jorvald said.

Oh, dear Goddess! Which brought to mind what the Gray-eyed One had said: "I was always the same person. Poets saw in me what they wanted to see."

Change is in the eye of the beholder.

Back at the farmhouse, Jane Widdy served them eggs and bacon. Jane enjoying Jessie's love life as if it were her own, Jessie showing off Jorvald and his muscles. She who had used the Widdys as excuse to fend off Harry Sloane and Oscar. Now *parading* this conquest. . . .

How contemptible! How delightful!

The telephone rang.

79

Bad news. Jessie psychic about phone calls.

"Jessie, I want to see you. When can you come in?"

Jonathan Glass. Icy as a winter storm.

An hour later she was across the desk from an angry Jonathan Glass across the street from the courthouse where Thomas Jefferson had once argued cases. He tossed it to her—a Xerox of a long letter, *her* letter but signed by Jonathan Glass, to the Planning Commission with its technical details. Underlined in red—a paragraph devoted to taking half an acre out of agricultural use to build four houses for agricultural workers.

"I've just seen the plan for Ski Village," her Uncle Jonathan said. "Those homes for agricultural workers are now labeled ski repair shop, cafeteria, and recreation hall. What is going on Jessie?"

"Where did you get this?" Jessie asked.

Jonathan Glass leaned across the eighteenth-century desk, icy with disapproval. "Did you ever have any intention of building homes for agricultural workers?"

"Oh, for heaven's sake, Uncle Jonathan. This is done all the time when you're trying to get something out of the Planning Commission. Those bureaucrats don't want to hear the truth and wouldn't know how to handle it if they did. They just want the conventions observed so that they can get the application out of their in-basket into somebody else's. . . ."

Then repeating her question because that loomed much larger in her mind, "Where did this Xerox come from, Uncle Jonathan?"

"It came anonymously in my mail."

And in how many other people's mail? "Somebody is rummaging through the files of the Planning Commission, getting my applications. . . ."

"Jessie," Uncle Jonathan said. "This is beside the point."

"No," the alarmed Jessie said; "this *is* the point. . . ."

"How many lies did you tell the Planning Commission to win their approval?"

"Lies," Jessie cried, angry now. "They're *not* lies! They're figures of speech. They're metaphors forced on us poor civilians by you damned lawyers. Every one of those ridiculous questions on that ridiculous application form was framed by some lawyer. You've made this legal swampland in which truth founders. You've made crooks of us all—rewarding the liars and penalizing the truth-tellers. You!"

Jonathan Glass was ice-cold aristocracy now, the gaunt face and thin lips masklike with integrity. He bore in, lawyer that he was. "Were you ever

80

under the impression you were telling the truth in this application, or was it falsehood from the very outset?"

The language was eighteenth-century as was the logic.

"Is it falsehood to rescue three thousand acres of forest that had been devastated by one rotten industry from another rotten industry? Is that what you call falsehood, Uncle Jonathan? I was far more truthful in my application than Anderson Chemical was in theirs."

"Who is Anderson Chemical? And what have they to do with this?"

Jessie had forgotten how good a lawyer Jonathan Glass was, how expert at cross-examination.

She rubbed her eyes with the tips of her fingers. Buying time.

"They were trying to buy the land, too," she admitted finally. "To despoil it. I outwitted them, Uncle Jonathan."

"By getting my signature on your lies."

"They're *not* lies!" Jessie cried. "They're word play!"

Jessie afire with her own integrity, her own resolve. Winning was itself a moral objective against so contemptible and vicious a competitor as Anderson Chemical, who would pollute her earth, her skies. This was the germ, the inner heart, of her moral posture, and she flamed with righteousness as certain in her own heart as was Jonathan Glass. Between them, she realized, yawned generations. When Jonathan Glass was her age, there was no Planning Commission, no Environmental Protection Agency, hardly any bureaucrats at all. So the two of them, loving each other, but in this matter close to hating, went at it hammer and tongs in their separate and totally conflicting rectitudes, getting nowhere.

"Anderson Chemical would poison our bodies, our minds and our souls if we'd let them," Jessie cried. "The ultimate truth in that kind of conflict, Uncle Jonathan, is winning. If we lose, the earth perishes. There is no higher morality than victory."

Athena putting the words in her skull because they certainly hadn't been there before.

"Jessie, I can't accept any of this. I got into this with extreme reluctance only because you are my goddaughter and you were in trouble. I am resigning here and now as chairman of the Columbia Land Development Board."

Jessie didn't change expression, letting these fateful words fall into a pool of silence. The situation called for stratagem, and she knew precisely the one but she hated to pull it on dear Uncle Jonathan whom she loved.

81

Who loved her.

Once.

"You can't resign from that signature, Uncle Jonathan."

Entangling him in his own integrity.

A dirty trick.

Jonathan Glass's aristocratic countenance was etched with a fine distaste. For her method and for her lack of scruple. A terrible moment for both.

"How many lies have you persuaded me to sign, Jessie?"

But she would not get back into that semantic quagmire. "I'll not ask you to sign any more letters, Uncle Jonathan. I just ask you not to resign just now because that is what they are after. Getting you out of the way to get at me."

"You don't even know who they are," her godfather said quietly.

No, Jessie thought, I don't. But I read them pretty well, their motives, their character. Somebody bold enough, unscrupulous enough, and ingenious enough to go rummaging through the files of the Planning Commission, whether legally or illegally, somebody rotten enough to resort to anonymous letters.

I have an enemy, Jessie thought. I have come up in the world. I have attained the eminence of enmity, a long stride past the simple hostility at the Gulf gas pump. My own real live *enemy*! How interesting!

That was a Thursday. The following Monday, another shot across her bow.

It came during her daily walk in the woods. Every day, after the bruising battles with carpenters and plumbers and builders, as balm, as moral refreshment, she took a walk in her woods—where a different battle was going on. There the debris left by American Lumber Products was being cleared up. The slopes had been reseeded with orchard grass. In the areas outside the ski slopes, the forest was being replanted with hardwood trees, and Jessie had bullied the Forest Service into providing both the trees and the manpower to plant them. There every day she walked in glorious autumn sunshine, basking in her vision of a restored forest, feeling her spirits lift.

Propelling herself up the steep slopes to give her legs a little exercise, breathing the scented sunshine, feeling at peace. That day she saw ahead of her three Forestry Service men in their green uniforms, planting small oaks.

With them was a man Jessie had never seen before.

82

A dark-faced man, with an excess of tan on his face. He'd worked on that tan—lain for hours by a swimming pool. Or under a sun lamp. An activity, or rather inactivity, she despised. The man had a chunky muscular body, and Jessie was willing to bet he'd worked on *that*, too. With barbells and rowing machines. Or other obscenities. She hated the man almost before she'd had a good look at him.

"Hel-lo," Jessie said, hitting the last syllable the way the English do. Meaning, "What the hell are you doing here?" Not a greeting at all.

The stranger turned his heavy glance at her, eyes as murky as dark glasses.

"Hello," the stranger said, throwing it right back at her.

"Hi, Roger," Jessie said to the Forest Service boss. "This one of your gang?" Indicating the stranger.

"No, Ma'm," Roger said. "I thought he one of your gang. He asking us a lot of questions."

"What kind of questions?" Jessie asked.

"What we doing here and why?"

The stranger during this flashing a huge smile—all white teeth over that phony tan.

"What are *you* doing here, stranger—and why?" Jessie asked.

"I'm a taxpayer," the stranger said, with his shark-toothed smile. "I like to know how the money's spent." Not a bit abashed. Enjoying himself.

"You're trespassing on my land and on these men's work-time."

Without apology or any sound at all, the man turned his back on her and walked down the hill toward the highway with a kind of jaunty rudeness.

"Act like it's *his* woods, don't he?" Roger said.

Jessie ran after the man, lightly, swiftly, making no sound. By the time he reached the highway, she was only twenty feet behind him. She watched him climb into his car, a blue Mercury with the license plate "Virginia KXB 919." She filed the number away in her mind.

It ended her walk, ruined her daily shot of moral uplift.

Ten minutes later she was in Oscar's office, asking, "Who do you know in the sheriff's office?"

"Your friend Harry Sloane knows everybody," Oscar said. "They're all his cousins."

She couldn't ask anything of Harry, things being as they were. "How about your pal in the police department at Folkesbury? Ask him if he can find out who owns a Mercury with a license plate KXB 919."

A rented car, it turned out. Intercity Rental.

"I'd like to find out who rented it. Name and address," Jessie said.

"My pal's likely to ask me why I want to know. He's not supposed to do this."

"Trespassing in my woods," Jessie said. "Wait! I'll call your friend myself."

"You want to make a charge?" asked the cop, whose name was Charlie Samuelson.

"No," Jessie said in her throaty sexy voice, "but I'd be ever so grateful if you'd stretch the rules a little bit. I'll do something for you sometime, Charlie."

"You're *stroking* that man," Oscar muttered. "On the *phone*."

The stranger's name was Milton Ford, a name that struck a bell somewhere in the recesses of Jessie's mind. She got on the phone to her cousin Agatha who worked at *The Folkesbury Advance* and who had the gossip on everybody. "Yeah," said Agatha, "it strikes a bell in me, too, Jessie. But he's not local. I think he's Richmond. I'll look him up in the morgue and call you back."

Milton Ford, it developed, was a Richmond lawyer. Young. Brassy. Not at all the Jonathan Glass-type lawyer. A shark—like his teeth.

"Very rough and ruthless and not very ethical is the message I get from these clippings. Don't tangle with him, Jessie!" Agatha said.

"I'm not tangling with him. He's tangling with me. Who does he represent?"

"Only know when they make the papers," Agatha said, "but Milton Ford makes the papers pretty regular. He's one of those *litigious* lawyers, you know what I mean."

Agatha read off the list—a pretty fancy list—United Brass and Foundry, Ferrous Metal, Inc., Jensen's Wax, Teenie Tiny Toys, Anderson Chemical. . . ."

"Whoa," said Jessie. "Who's that again?"

"Anderson Chemical," Agatha said. "They make all the things you *hate*, Jessie—pesticides, plastics, poisons. . . ."

"Yeah," Jessie said. Anderson Chemical.

Agatha still talking: ". . . they got no soul, Jessie, and even that they don't own. They're owned by a big conglomerate in Cleveland named Galaxie Industries which owns *everything*—banks, cement companies, shipping, you name it they got it, including Anderson Chemical."

After hanging up, Jessie had sat very still at her desk, elbows planted, chin in her hands, thinking it out. Suppose I were a big conglomerate like Galaxie Industries, Inc., which wanted to pick up a nice Ski Village somebody else had conceived and sweated out. How would I go about elbowing out Jessie Jenkins and taking over?

First, hire a shark-like lawyer named Milton Ford to look for chinks in the legal armor. . . .

Twilight crept over the mountain, and then darkness fell. Oscar loomed unexpectedly in the doorway of her office.

"Jessie?" Oscar said.

She shook violently as if he'd wakened her from sleep. "Oscar," she murmured. "You scared me."

"You're working late, Jessie. Something bothering you?"

"Yeah," Jessie said.

He was nuzzling her, wanting affection, and she was giving in to him, absently, from habit, because she was fond of Oscar and because she couldn't keep asking favors of him if she didn't grant any; and so presently they were stretched out on the office sofa, but not before Jessie had asked anxiously, "You sure everyone's gone, Oscar? The carpenters, the plumbers . . ."

"All of them," Oscar said.

"Jorvald . . ."

"He left an hour ago."

Gone to Jenkins Farm, thought Jessie wearily, where he'll be wanting the same thing when I get home. So she gave herself to Oscar fully clothed, her mind on her problem, caressing the back of his head (Oscar's hair always so *beautifully* cut!) and only after passion had been satisfied, followed by a decent interval of tenderness, did she spring it:

"Darling, I want you to go to Washington tomorrow. I need a private investigator."

"They're expensive, Jessie. What for?"

"I want to investigate a crooked lawyer named Milton Ford—and that's a very big secret, Oscar Willoughby. Nobody's to know about that but you and me. You ever hire a private investigator, Oscar?"

"American Lumber Products did. Twice. You've got to watch them, Jessie. The other side is likely to give them money to give you a phony report. Big outfits are likely to be the most honest."

"Yeah, but Milton Ford probably knows all about big outfits, maybe uses them himself. I want somebody not known in Richmond, not known too well even in private investigation. What I need is a disbarred lawyer. Maybe one who just quit because he didn't like the profession. Anyway, somebody who knows all the tricks of the trade, especially the crooked ones."

The first two investigators Oscar produced Jessie smiled at and showed out the door, not telling them a single thing, especially what she wanted them for. "They'd sell me out in ten minutes if they knew who to sell me to," she explained to Oscar. "Try harder."

It was three weeks before he showed up with one she approved of and, above all, liked and trusted. He was an amiable, rubicund, white-haired Jew of seventy-five, named Jake Levin, who was not a lawyer but an expert on libel. He'd worked with lawyers for years, defending libel cases for one of the big defunct New York newspapers. His task had been to get something on the people who were suing the newspaper in order to make them drop the libel suit—and he never failed. "They've all done something," he said cheerfully. "Every man in the world has got a little something in the closet he doesn't want known. Every last one."

Far from making him cynical his immense knowledge of man's weak-- nesses and folly amused him no end. He howled with laughter at their foolishness and forgave their viciousness because, like Christ, he thought they knew not what they did. "I'm close enough to the villains to know what idiots they all are," he said to Jessie with his great round smile.

After an hour of searching questions, she trusted him absolutely and turned him loose on Milton Ford—but without telling him why she wanted what she wanted.

Three days later he was back with a sheaf of information: "Just prelimi- nary research," Jake Levin said with his gentle Jewish smile, "much of it boring, but you should read every scrap. Know your enemy! It helps in the clinches."

Jessie took the huge bundle, making a little face. "Let's get to the core of the matter, Jake. What makes him go?"

Jake Levin leaned back and smiled at the ceiling. "He's married to a very rich and very social shiksa named Patterson. Now why would a Jew change his name from Raskin to Ford and marry a rich social gentile?"

"*I'm* not going to say it," Jessie said. "You're the investigator."

"So he doesn't want to be Jewish. Still, that's no crime. Lots of people like that—Bill Paley, to name one—who hang around goys and marry shiksas and act like goys. Everyone knows they're Jewish. No harm. Everyone knows Ford is a Jew who likes goys so you haven't got a weapon there, but what we have is a clue. He wants a certain kind of what he thinks of as respectability. Above all, above *all* . . ." here his eyes grew positively lyrical with fun and laughter, "he wants to be something he *isn't*. That gives us a little edge. Not much. But a little. He wants respectability."

"We all do," Jessie said.

"He wants it a little more. That gives us that little edge. On the *other* hand, we mustn't forget that behind that goy façade, bolstered up by all that goy money and shiksa social prestige, lies a Jewish brain. It's not going to be easy to plant something on him. He's got too much to lose. He's a very clever fellow."

"We know why he married her," Jessie said. "Why'd she marry him?"

That provoked an even huger grin from the rubicund Mr. Levin. "You're thinking like a Jew now. Why indeed? If she were a liberal, intelligent, activist, feminist, forward-looking woman—or any combination of those— she might very well marry an ambitious, clever Jewish lawyer. She isn't. She's chairman of the Women's National Republican Club, a member of the Birch Society, a fervent supporter of Anita Bryant, an Episcopalian anti-abortionist, a member of the First Families of Virginia and the Daughters of the American Revolution."

"Poor Milton!" Jessie said.

"*Why* would she marry Milton Ford?" Jake Levin asked. "For only one reason on earth! He got into her pants, and she liked it. Jews are very good at that—the best—at getting into their pants and making them like it."

"And she'd hate it if he got into somebody else's," Jessie said. "Is he?"

"There is a total absence of any gossip or even speculation of that nature," Jake Levin said. "Total! Theirs is the perfect marriage—so everyone says. And *that,* considering the equation—arrogant, intelligent, ambitious Jewish boy, rich stupid social shiksa girl—is strictly ridiculous. He *must* be getting it somewhere else. He *must* be unfaithful. If he weren't, it would violate my complete lack of faith in human nature! It would destroy everything I stood for! I cannot believe that man is faithful to his wife. How could such a thing be! It's against nature. Next thing you know I'd be believing in God and other superstitions too primeval for intelligent man to contemplate!"

__ CHAPTER __
EIGHT

THE DAYS WERE blue and gold, drenched with sunshine, the nights velvety, starlit, chilly. The lower field had yielded its third crop of sweet-smelling alfalfa. The sows were in the woods eating the black walnuts, sidling up to the horses who were nibbling chestnuts, the horses moving disdainfully away, snobs that they were.

That week Jessie had wrung the necks and chopped the heads off seventy-five chickens. That day it was ducks—Jessie cutting their heads off and handing them to Jane Widdy who dipped the headless bodies in the steaming iron cauldron, the two girls then settling down to the plucking.

They were working on a big oak table in the shed. It would have been easier to do all this in the kitchen, but Jessie wouldn't allow killing in the kitchen. "I can smell death. It spoils my appetite."

Her arm almost up to the elbow, pulling the guts out of a duck. Blood smeared from forearm to wrist.

"You don't have to do this anymore," Jane Widdy said. "With all your money, you could *buy* the food."

An old argument: like a lot of modern farm girls, Jane Widdy wanted to put it all behind her—the hard work, the killing. Watch the soap operas in the afternoon and heat up a TV dinner—like everyone else.

Jessie hosing out the inside of a duck was saying, "I know everything these ducks ate. I raised these ducks from eggs. I knew their mothers and what they ate. Supermarket ducks are stuffed with antibiotics to protect them from diseases my ducks never got because the supermarket ducks are

89

raised in such close confinement in such numbers they catch everything—like city people. They drink chlorinated water, breath air poisoned by pesticides."

Jessie brushed the hair out of her eyes with a bloody hand. "Everyone talking about a population explosion. I tell you, Jane, we going to have the opposite—a population *collapse*. People just going to stop having children because of something their grandparents ate. We're ruining the gene pool with poisons. Every tomato in the supermarket been sprayed *seven* times. You think you're not getting some of that poison in you!"

A speech Jane had heard many times. Jessie's latest distress. "You don't have to worry," Jessie said. "You eating *my* food. There hasn't been a poison on this farm since . . . My goodness, Jake, where you come from?"

The rubicund face on the plump body had appeared at the end of the oak table.

"*Jessie?*" Jake asked. Hardly believing this bloody apparition was indeed herself.

"Come on, Jake," Jessie said. "You never seen a farm girl before?"

"I was brought up in Brooklyn," Jake said. "I never found out about cows until I was twenty-two. I couldn't get you on the phone. I had to come out. It's important."

They walked up the road under the Norway maples, now bereft of their red and gold leaves, Jake staring at the barn field in stupefaction.

"You must have seen a horse before," Jessie said.

"Only on television," Jake said. "Where would I see a horse? In Municipal Court? You must realize Jessie, this kind of scenery"—here he spread his hands out very theatrical, very New York—"is very unusual. Even on the television. The only time I ever see anything like this is on the Waltons—and you know I never believed the Waltons. I thought they made it all up."

"They did," Jessie said. "How old are you, Jake?"

"Seventy-five," Jake said. "Old enough to be your grandfather."

"And never saw a horse," Jessie said. "My God!"

They were in the kitchen now, Jessie pouring him lemonade. "What's up, Jake?"

"Nothing's up," Jake said softly. "That's the trouble. I think I should take myself out of this, Jessie. I'm costing you lots of money, and I'm coming up with nothing."

"Jake, you can't do that. You have no idea how I depend on you." She'd grown tremendously fond of this immensely cynical very human man who was to Jessie as unlikely as horses were to him. She'd never known anyone quite like the quick-witted Jake. "What's the problem?"

"I can't get anything on that man. He's too clever for me—anyway too careful—because I'm sure there's something to be got."

Jessie sat at the kitchen table and sipped her lemonade. After a bit she said: "Okay, we can't get anything on him. For the time being. What he getting on *me,* Jake?"

"What's there to be got, Jessie?"

Jessie thought about that. She'd played her cards very close to her face up to now. But she trusted Jake Levin absolutely because you had to trust someone. "I cut some corners. I had to. What's he doing?"

"I can only guess, Jessie. He's preparing a case. I have friends in the Court of Records. He is asking for everything about you and about Columbia Land Development he can get his hands on *legally.* I've got a suspicion he's getting his hands on everything he can find illegally too. A lot of those records are not open to his legal inspection, but there are ways of getting at them because I've done it myself. What I don't understand is—he is not *moving.* He's dead in the water. Months go by. Why?"

"He is waiting for me to fall on my face. If there is no snow ... if I run out of money ... if this, if that—he can pick up Ski Village on the first bounce. But if I *don't* fall flat on my ass, then . . . he'll move. How does he move, Jake?"

"Tie you up in court. A million ways. What have you done to him, Jessie?"

She didn't tell him, still playing her cards close. But there was that letter from that nice young Environmental man Freddie Mountjoy. "I don't know that we have the power," Mountjoy had said, and she'd overridden him. Could a clever lawyer seize on that?

"He's representing Anderson Chemical. They tried to buy my land. They're owned by some big conglomerate from Cleveland, Galaxie Industries."

"They play very rough—Galaxie Industries," Jake said. "Very rough. If they want something bad enough they get it, a lot of mob money in Galaxie Industries."

"I don't think they want Ski Village all that bad until they see how it's going to do," Jessie said. "That's not until snow falls—or *not* falls, as the

91

case might be. So we got a bit of time. In the meantime, we have to try something. If we can't surprise Milton Ford in bed with somebody, are you above *planting* somebody in bed with him? How scrupulous are you?"

"Not very—but cautious," Jake said carefully. "He's a very bright man, this Milton Ford. You can't plant any whore on him. He'd be miles ahead of you."

"I wasn't thinking of any whore," Jessie said.

"Who then?" Jake asked.

"Me," Jessie said.

"You!" Jake said, round-eyed.

"I'm not so bad," Jessie said. "When I wash the blood out of my hair."

"Jessie, no! I can't let you do that to yourself."

He was horrified. The little wry mouth was round with astonishment, the brown eyes liquid with revulsion. And compassion. He was a very compassionate man. "You and that . . . monster, Jessie. There are limits!"

"There are no limits when you are saving your farm," rang Jessie's voice like a bell.

"Jessie! Jessie! Jessie! What's a farm? Possessions! Blah! We are talking about your immortal soul, Jessie. You can damage your self-esteem beyond redemption."

The old man, pleading with her with his eyes, his eloquent hands and eyes, and all his mind. Jessie felt a gush of love for Jake Levin for caring so much, not only for her, but for the conventions.

Again—the generation gap. To her, sex was a weapon like any other. Beyond *redemption,* my goodness. "Jake," Jessie said softly, "it's just *sex!* Think of it as an exercise—like beating a man at tennis. I'm outwitting the man with my body. That's all!"

Jake rose to his feet, all five foot four of him agonized. "No, Jessie. It's *not* all! You don't know what you're saying! There are depths of perfidy beyond which mortal man should not go. Nor mortal woman! Because there is no returning! This is the wisdom of the ages, Jessie. All religions say it in one form or another. One draws a line. Beyond that point you don't go, no matter what! You are going beyond that line."

Silence. Jessie looked at the man, towering in his moral principles, looked at her feet, and wrestled with herself. Finally, she said, "Jake, it's either you with the camera and the flashgun and the witness—or it will be someone else. I have my own high resolve and, though you may not believe it, my own high principles. I'm embarked on a mission, Jake, and I can countenance anything—including going to bed with that man—anything at all—except failure. That I can't face. Are you with me, Jake? Because if you're not it will have to be somebody else."

In the end that was the determinant. Opposed as he was to this enterprise, Jake was even more opposed to the idea of some other man breaking into the hotel room and taking pictures of a naked Jessie and a naked Milton Ford. In winning the argument, Jessie lost a bit of herself. She hated the beaten look on Jake's face when he came round to her wishes. But it had to be done.

And more.

Because she wasn't finished yet.

"Jake," Jessie said, "I've got to know what he's getting on me. Are you above a little breaking and entering?"

Jake sighed and closed his eyes and when he opened them he looked not at Jessie but at his own toes. "Yes, Jessie, I'm above it. I'm too old and too wise to get into trouble with the police. However, I know some people who are *not* above it." He looked at her now with a sad smile.

"Just remember one thing, Jessie. I will have had nothing to do with this breaking and entering. The Xeroxes will arrive by magic in your post box. But don't thank me, thank God, because it will be He not me that did this wondrous illegal thing."

Jessie smiled at him, full of love. "Let me tell you something, Jake Levin, I don't go down on my knees to any of your male gods. I pray—and I have never told this to anyone but you, Jake—to a Goddess. Athena, the Gray-eyed One. She's my Deity. She's been . . . helping me out in the clutches."

Jake Levin rubbed his nose. "She better be good, this Goddess. Galaxie Industries is very tough and very crooked."

Ski Village was inching to completion at a speed rarely seen in Virginia, which is to say about half the speed found anywhere else. There were infuriating days when whole teams of carpenters failed to show up because—as they explained when they finally showed up—cousin Henry's pigs got out and they had to go help round them up and fence them in properly. When this happened, Jessie kept her two men—Oscar and Jorvald—securely tethered, and she herself greeted the tardy workmen with commiseration and sympathy rather than outrage. She was a pig girl herself and knew these things must be done. By her sympathy she won a bit of loyalty, and they tried to make up the lost time. Not killing themselves, but doing a little better than usual.

Cafeteria and restaurant and lounges were now in the last stages of completion, their wiring and pipes in place—the toilets not yet installed, but the bowls and urinals and the rest of it all on the premises. Kitchens were wired up waiting for the stoves, while shelving, counters, coffee urns, stainless steel cocoa dispensers were already in place.

Every day Jessie walked through the place, room by room, checking and rejoicing at each new completion. Adding up the sums in her head of the uncompleted. Exhausting but fulfilling.

On the slopes the great steel towers were going up one by one. On that day, after her tour of the buildings, Jessie walked up the slope called Big Chestnut—all five slopes had names now—to see how things were going with the topmost tower where the cable would go round its great steel wheel and send the chairs down again.

On the summit were Jorvald and Oscar standing together, laughing. Jessie grimaced. Those two had started out mortal enemies and were becoming—by reasons of some mysterious masculine alchemy totally incomprehensible to Jessie—very good friends. Jessie didn't like it. Would they compare notes, these two? Jessie was still bedding both of them. Infrequently now, especially Oscar, but technically both were still her lovers, largely because she couldn't summon up the emotional resolve to call it quits. She delayed and threw roadblocks and other tricks. Still, she didn't quite *end* it—with either of them. Both of them thinking he was the one and only. Unless they were comparing notes.

Me telling my lies, thought Jessie. Or perhaps lies was too strong a word. I'm reserving information, giving to each man what I think he's entitled to. Perhaps they're doing the same to me. Does anyone know everything about anyone else—husband, lover, friend. No, they don't, and it's well they don't. I can hardly cope with what I know about men—and sometimes I think there are areas of me I know nothing about. How much hypocrite am I? How much, for example, did she really love her missing husband?

After all, she had functioned very well without him; there'd been months when she'd barely thought of him at all, because—she told herself—she'd been too busy, her back to the wall, but now, with her lust for both Jorvald and Oscar ebbing, she thought of Derry much of the time when her mind wasn't occupied by other things, which wasn't very often. Not only thought

94

about him but yearned for her handsome, slim, muscular, quick-witted husband.

Was he all those things? Walking up the slope through the dry autumn leaves that crackled and rustled around her feet, she thought, I'm romanticizing him; I'm putting in things that aren't there. Why am I doing that? Because, if the truth must be told, I've *forgotten* the real man and I'm filling in with schoolgirl dreams. About my own *husband*!

These thoughts skittered through her mind as she approached her two lovers who fell silent as she approached and immediately she began wondering about that. What had they fallen silent *about*? Her?

"Nice day," Jessie said, glancing from one to the other.

The two men were very quiet, looking at her, then at each other, then away at the mountain.

"You tell her, Jorvald," Oscar muttered.

"We have big problem, Jessie," Jorvald said in his monotonous Norwegian accent. "No cable."

He handed her the letter. American Cable and Wire Products. "... due to production difficulties connected with the Metal Workers strike last spring, we are unable to fulfill our contracts ... six months' delay."

Six months! The ski season ran from December to March! Six *months*!

"Oscar, weren't there penalty clauses in that contract?"

"Yeah," Oscar said. "A thousand a week. Six months' delay would cost them twenty-six thousand dollars."

Twenty-six thousand dollars—to ruin her. Cheap at the price. Jessie was looking at the letterhead. American Cable and Wire Products, Inc. A Galaxie Industry.

"When did this arrive?" Jessie asked.

"This morning."

"And that strike was last spring. Long time for them to find out...." Her mind racing ahead, shutting off her mouth because it was none of their business. Play the cards close to the vest. "When did we order the cable, Oscar?"

"May twenty-third."

"Mmmm," Jessie said, telling them nothing. Not even feeling panic, just excitement. Galaxie Industries "very tough and very crooked," Jake Levin had said.

"Oscar, what else *haven't* we got? I mean what else *vital*? What else that could stop us opening?"

95

Oscar thought about it and shook his head. "Nothing I can think of. The towers aren't all up, but they're *here*. Some nuts and bolts here and there. Nothing else *vital*. But the cable *is* vital. We got no cable, we can't get the skiers up the slopes. We're cooked."

Jessie asked a question whose answer she already knew, but she had to ask to make sure. "Aren't there any other cable manufacturers?"

"Sure, but you can't get cable that fast. This is high quality cable, very expensive, with very high standards to meet the safety requirements. You can't order it up like popcorn. It was almost the first thing we ordered last spring."

Jessie remembered it well. She had personally involved herself in that, as in every other detail, and she remembered going over the whole cable situation. She remembered something else.

"Jorvald, carry on here, as if nothing has happened. *Don't* tell anyone here anything about this. You understand! It's vital to morale that no one know anything about this. How many know about it now?"

"The three of us," Oscar said. "No more."

"Keep it that way. Come on Oscar."

Back in her office she outlined her plan born of desperation. Brilliant improvisation made possible only by all her meticulous research on ski cables last May. "Nobody's to know," Jessie snapped. "Not even your wife. Nor Jorvald. Not anybody. You and me, Oscar. These people play tough and rotten, so mind now."

"Jessie," Oscar protested. "I'm not at all sure that cable will pass the safety inspectors."

"We'll cross that bridge when we come to it. We're gambling. What else can we do? We need cable in a hurry. I want you on that plane this afternoon, Oscar. And top *secret*!"

Oscar saluted. Sardonically. He didn't like being ordered around, and Jessie quickly put her arms around his neck and looked deep into his eyes. "Darling, it's my ass! Do you understand? It's the whole ball game. I haven't time to be nice." She kissed him passionately and hugged him hard. "It's *important*," she whispered. "And it's just as important that no one know. If they do, Galaxie Industries will think of some way to stop it. Nobody must know I got this up my sleeve, Oscar. Nobody! Don't even tell yourself."

That was the nub of the plan—to look as if Ski Village had its back to the wall. After Oscar left for the airport, Jessie dictated letters to two other cable companies pleading for ski cable for five ski lifts needed immediately, etc., etc. Impossible to get it fast, but she wanted those letters to go out where whoever was gathering all that material about her would know she was screaming with pain.

An hour later she was in Jonathan Glass's office. A sticky meeting. Relations had been strained for months now. Jessie had avoided her beloved Uncle Jonathan, hoping time would heal the wound. It hadn't.

"Jessie," Uncle Jonathan said, the voice sad and distant. "You promised to let me alone. I have not resigned because I know how much harm that would do to you. But I don't propose to associate myself with Columbia Land Development to any further degree, and I think you know why."

There was quite a lot more about legal ethics and morality. Jessie let him talk himself out, sitting there, the picture of submissiveness, hands folded in lap, eyes fully on him, dripping contrition. When he'd finally fallen silent—and he spoke for fully half an hour, all very high quality ethics, some of those splendid phrases Jessie squirreled away to use herself when the opportunity arose—she let the whole argument lay there, replying to none of it, striking out in wholly new territory as if nothing at all had been said.

"Conspiracy," she said. "You're the greatest specialist on conspiracy in the Virginia legal establishment. I want to file a ten million dollar suit naming Galaxie Industries, Anderson Chemical, American Cable and Wire Products, Inc., and Milton Ford, attorney for Anderson Chemical *and* American Cable and Wire Products."

"Ten million dollars!" The aristocratic old lawyer was dazzled by the sum and—as Jessie knew he would be—by conspiracy. His special love—or perhaps hate.

Jessie outlined the complaint. She'd ordered the cable last May. American Cable and Wire Products, Inc., held the letter saying they couldn't produce the cable until November when they knew she couldn't find any other cable in time to open her ski resort. Anderson Chemical had tried to buy the land, and she'd outmaneuvered them. Galaxie Industries controlled both American Cable and Wire Products and Anderson Chemical—and Milton Ford was attorney for both of them. Milton Ford had been observed skulking about her Ski Village in a very suspicious manner, and she had witnesses. Etc., etc., etc.

"Very thin, Jessie. We need proof." But his eyes were shining. Conspiracy turned him on like cocaine. Jessie could feel it.

"I'll get you proof. Uncle Jonathan, but that's not the point. I want headlines and ten million dollars is a very nice headline. They've got Mob connections. Galaxie won't like headlines. I want to make the papers—even if it never makes court, I've got to make them back off, Uncle Jonathan."

All this was true as far as it went. That was precisely what she wanted—to make Galaxie aware *she* was aware of their plans and planned to fight them.

The most important point of this lawsuit she didn't tell Uncle Jonathan. That was to smoke out Milton Ford. If she were going to seduce him, she had to lure him out into the mainstream—and what better way to stir up a fellow's interest than to sue him for ten million dollars. At least it would give them something to talk about—and it always helped to have something to talk about when boy meets girl.

__ CHAPTER __
NINE

BRILLIANT DECEMBER SUNSHINE warmed the open spaces of Harry Sloane's barnyard, but it was cold in the black shadows of the huge silos. The sale had attracted every farmer in miles. Harry was not widely loved and his downfall was not greatly mourned, but there were some that did. One of them, Jessie.

Jessie hugged the shadows of the silo because the thing was too painful. The auctioneer—old Josiah Sims, with the white hair and shrill voice—was shouting, "This here a nineteen seventy-six Gleaner. Hardly been used. One of the finest, most versatile farm implements ever made by man! Do I hear thirty thousand?" No, he didn't hear thirty thousand. Or twenty-five. Or twenty. Humboldt Pickering bought it finally for ten thousand. Where would Humboldt get ten thousand dollars? Borrowed probably.

Jessie kept her eyes on Harry Sloane who leaned against his yellow truck—it wasn't in the sale catalogue—huge and glowering. "You'd think he'd have the decency to stay away," Aimee Law had whispered in Jessie's presence before the sale started. But Harry Sloane was not celebrated for nicety of feeling. He went where the action was, and right now it was in his barnyard. So he leaned against his yellow truck in a great pool of emptiness, nobody getting anywhere near that powerful body, as if it might explode.

The small farm implements had gone first, rakes, hoes, spreaders, small tractors. There was one small tractor—the very one she'd ridden that day when they'd spread the fertilizer on the barn field—that Jessie wanted very much for herself. Just the size for her. Or Jane. But she couldn't buy Harry's things. She just couldn't. Instead she skulked in the shadow of the silo

99

watching Harry as *he* watched his possessions being auctioned off—the tractors he'd not only bought but drove, the cultivators, the plows—every one of which he'd used himself and repaired and oiled and, above all, *possessed.*

The fury in his eyes.

Jessie couldn't stand it. She walked across to him. "Harry, take it easy! You going to blow sky high in a minute!"

He didn't look at her. His eyes were on a cattle truck that would hold twenty-five head going for two thousand. "Why you ain't bidding, Jessie?"

"I can't buy your things, Harry. It wouldn't be right."

"You missing some bargains. That cattle truck worth ten thousand. They *stealing* the stuff!"

"They's a recession, Harry. You know that."

Anyway, Harry should talk. He'd been a great one for picking up cattle trucks at one half their value; he'd been the hardest bargainer of all. He couldn't rightly complain now that somebody was driving hard bargains in his backyard.

"What you going to do, Harry?"

That brought forth nothing at all. Harry burned with his inner fires and said nothing.

"You need some money, Harry, you got it. You know that."

He just sneered, eyes on the auctioneer. Yeah, he needed money. A million or more is what he needed. Jessie knew this. He didn't need to say it and didn't say it.

"For heaven's sake, Harry, that's what friends are for! You need anything—anything at all—you know where I'm at."

That got him. "*Anything* at all?" His huge face broke into its great Pan grin. "Anything!"

"Oh, Harry Sloane, can't you get your mind outta the haystack for one minute," Jessie said—and burst out laughing. Harry burst out laughing, too, both shouting with laughter there beside the truck while the farmers at the sale and their wives—especially their wives—wondered what on earth there was for Harry Sloane to laugh about while the possessions of a lifetime were being sold out from under him.

Jessie got into her Triumph and drove to the Municipal Court annex where the depositions were being taken. She didn't have to be there, Jonathan Glass had said, but it would help him if she were. Anyway she wanted to be there because that was the day Milton Ford was being deposed. She had dressed very carefully for this meeting. Not too flashy and *not* too innocent. Her red wool dress, very simply cut out of a color that drew the eye. *Not* a dress for the witness stand. But then she wasn't going to be on the witness stand. He was.

The deposition was being taken around a long heavy table—Jonathan Glass on one side with his briefcase and papers. On the other side—Milton Ford and his attorney, a little ferret of a man named Skopnik. At the end of the table, the court reporter—Mary Furth, a motherly old soul, whom Jessie had known since childhood.

Jonathan Glass was questioning Milton Ford about the day he'd been in the woods asking questions of the foresters who were planting oaks in Jessie's woods. Milton Ford was beautifully dressed in a dark blue wool suit with brass buttons that fitted him like skin. Only a man with a sculptured body would dare wear anything quite that tight fitting.

Milton Ford sat easily in his chair and fielded Jonathan Glass's questions amiably and effortlessly.

As Jessie slipped into the chair next to Jonathan Glass, Milton Ford was saying, "I am a member of the advisory board of the State Forestry Commission. I am also a member of the Sierra Club, and counsel for the Society for the Improvement of Virginia Forests. Naturally, I'm interested in anything to do with forest land."

Jonathan Glass asked, "That day—September thirteenth—were you there by accident—or design?"

"By design. I don't do many things by accident."

I'll bet, thought Jessie. Looking him over. Not bad. Not at all bad. I wouldn't trust the son of a bitch around the block, but it's his cock, not his character, I'm interested in.

Jonathan Glass was asking, "What was your design that day? What were you in Mrs. Jenkins' woods for exactly?"

"It had come to my attention that major construction was taking place there. As advisor to the State Forestry Commission I have to keep abreast of what's going on in the woods."

"Were you aware the Forestry Commission had been advised of this construction well in advance?"

"Oh, yes."

"You made no objection then, did you?"

"I make no objection now. My purpose was to see whether the reforestation promised in the application for change of land use was being carried out in the proper manner."

Almost as smooth a liar as I am, Jessie thought, her gaze straight at him.

101

Jonathan Glass went into Milton Ford's questions to the foresters, knowing just what he'd asked and asking why this question, why that. Milton Ford's own eyes were on Jonathan Glass, his tone polite and just a shade contemptuous. One lawyer's opinion of another who was as different from him as satin from shit.

Jonathan Glass was boring into him from another direction. Wasn't Mr. Ford attorney for Anderson Chemical? Wasn't it true that Anderson Chemical had made a bid for this land? Was Mr. Ford aware of that bid? Had Mr. Ford advised them to make a bid? Or advised them against it?

What Jonathan Glass didn't ask was far more important than what he did. There were no questions about how ruinous Anderson Chemical would be to the forest land. Nothing about the ecological impact of putting a chemical company in wilderness. All that would come before a jury (if the suit ever came to trial). All Jonathan Glass was interested in were facts, thousands of little facts that he'd later hold Milton Ford to when the cross-questioning started, facts that he would use as abrasives in relation to other questions such as: How can a man with such a professed interest in ecology reconcile it with being counsel to such despoilers as Anderson Chemical? Trouble was that Milton Ford was himself a lawyer skilled (and vicious) in cross-questioning, and he must see these pitfalls ahead and have some answers. He was, as Jake Levin had warned, very bright.

All afternoon, the questioning went on and on, Jessie having difficulty keeping her mind on it, so innocuous, almost inane, some of the questions were, all designed to lure Milton Ford off guard which, as far as she could see, it never did. He remained alert, sharp, just a bit contemptuous, for all the long session. All through this she was sizing him up. How was she going to crack this nut—this bright contemptuous shark with the Mob connections and the overpowering self-confidence?

Not once did he even glance at her.

It wasn't going to be easy.

It was dark when they left the courthouse, and the air was cold. Just outside the revolving door, she paused to ask Jonathan Glass, "How's it going?"

"It's very early. This is just groundwork. Will you be here tomorrow?"

"Do you want me to be?"

"Yes."

Jessie sighed. Another day listening to those boring questions and even more boring answers. "If you think I'm useful, I'll be here, Uncle Jonathan."

102

"You're very useful."

"Why?"

"You're unsettling him."

"Oh, come *on*! I never saw such serene self-confidence. An earthquake couldn't unsettle that man!"

Jonathan Glass smiled his wintry smile. "He doesn't like your being there, himself on the witness stand. He doesn't like it a bit. I can tell, Jessie, believe me. I'm an old hand at this."

Just then Milton Ford came out of the revolving door and gave them both a polite smile. "Good evening," Milton Ford said as if they were all friends. Jessie watched him go to his car, unlock it, and get in.

"I'll see you tomorrow, Uncle Jonathan," Jessie said and planted a kiss on his waxen cheek.

She walked down the courthouse steps to her own car, parked just three cars away from Milton Ford who hadn't yet started his. He was just sitting in it, arranging his briefcase, doing mysterious things with his hands. Jessie unlocked the door of the Triumph, and she was just about to step into it when she glanced back at Milton Ford. He was looking directly at her. A dark unsmiling look. The two looks locked just for an instant.

Sexual electricity crackled.

That was quite enough for one session, Jessie decided. She drove home.

The deposition of Milton Ford went on for three days, ranging far and wide—his career, his education, his beliefs, his interlocking directorships, his actions in law, community, ecology. Jessie came every day in the same dress, kept her eyes on his face, during the questioning, as he resolutely avoided her eyes. Every day they left the courthouse within moments of each other, walked down the courthouse steps—not together but not exactly apart. The two cars were never parked very far from each other, and the two of them fumbled in unison for car keys, unlocked car doors, in lock step.

Then would come The Glance—each to the other, as if on signal. Both of them imperturbable. But not altogether. Always the sexual electricity. Jessie not daring quite to smile—this was too complicated a fellow for open and shut come-hither—not actually relaxing the facial muscles into anything resembling a smile but *thinking* an erotic note, a very high note, one only bats could hear.

After all, he was a subtle character.

Herself a subtle woman.

103

Not entirely at ease with the operation. Jake had unsettled her more than she'd realized. Night after night she went down on her knees to seek—what was that word the Christians were so fond of—absolution.

Athena found the concept mildly comic. "Right and *wrong!*" the Gray-eyed One said as if she could hardly believe her ears. "We have never worried about that on Olympus. You know better than that, Jessie."

All religions Jake had said. Was he mistaken?

"I seek only vengeance and the annihilation of my enemies," Jessie said on her knees.

"All quite proper," the Goddess said. She added a qualification, as the Ancient Ones usually did, just to make compliance not easy. "In the spirit of the Divine Law."

Anomie, Jessie thought. Both the word and the concept were Greek. Descent into nameless sensation. Quite a lot of that going around.

"Guide my hand, my Goddess," Jessie said.

"I can guide your hand. Not your heart."

"My heart is pure, my Goddess."

"We shall soon see," Athena said.

That was not very comforting.

The game went on in the parking lot—the two antagonists eyeing one another daily, their looks growing longer, bolder, *not* softer because he was not a soft man nor she a soft woman, but quickening in sexual voltage.

"I'm here for the taking," Jessie said in the privacy of her mind, fumbling with car keys—wondering if there was anything in thought transference.

What thought transference was she getting back? Something there, all right. No doubt about it. He is thinking about me. I can smell it.

She was in no doubt about what she was thinking about *him.* He turned her on if only because he was such a son-of-a-bitch. A dangerous son-of-a-bitch. Him and his Mob connections. There was eroticism in the *danger* of him.

What on earth did Milton Ford do with his evenings? He was staying at the Fraser Hotel, a ramshackle structure in the heart of Folkesbury, in order to avoid having to go back to Richmond every night. There were whispers it was Mob-owned, or controlled.

All the time—the sexual current getting stronger—on his part as well as hers.

After a week, the roles were reversed. Jessie was on the stand, and the

104

questioner was Milton Ford. Right from the outset she detected the effortless skill of him. The questions were wrapped in velvet, underneath which lay sharp rocks she'd not find out about until the trial itself. Tell the truth, Uncle Jonathan advised. If you can't remember, say so. If you want any documentation to refresh your memory, say that. It's all here, and if it isn't, we'll get it.

So the questions started—her education, background, farm life, reasons for acquiring her three thousand acres, ecological interests, plans for ski village, etc., etc., etc.—hours of question and answer. Now it was a whole new ball game. Now their gaze was locked together for hours on end, facing each other, their faces sometimes not more than a foot and a half apart.

She had to keep her wits about her while struggling with sex desires that were overwhelmingly complicated. She'd started this whole business by thinking about seducing him and succeeded largely in seducing herself. At least she had planted thoughts in her head that had, through proximity, grown and flourished and now . . . it was an erotic avalanche. The only bright spot was that he was as engulfed in the avalanche as she was.

She was sure of that. She could smell it and taste it. So could he. She was sure of that, too. She only hoped it wasn't glaringly obvious to everyone else in the room—Uncle Jonathan, Mary Furth, Skopnik.

When it came, it had the inevitability of a thunderstorm that had gathered on the horizon hours earlier and gradually moved overhead.

She had parked her car that morning deliberately next to his. The two cars had edged closer day by day, but this day was the first on which they adjoined.

That day, too, they had both delayed a bit, putting papers in briefcases, picking up topcoats because the weather had turned chilly that last day so that, when they went down the steps, the others—Jonathan Glass, Skopnik, Mary Furth—were already in their cars. Again there was the fumbling of car keys during which the others pulled out so the two adversaries were left alone and actually touching, the two cars being that close together. As he leaned down to put key to lock Jessie felt his rump against hers—first time they'd ever touched—and the electric shock of it almost made her gasp.

She turned toward him, blindly, instinctually, and he turned toward her—then they were kissing voraciously because this sexual tease had gone on for almost ten days.

"Your place or mine?" he asked, as if asking street directions.

"Yours is closest!" Jessie whispered.

105

They took both cars because it wouldn't do to leave a car conspicuously in the courthouse parking lot, which emptied of cars every night. As she turned into Tite Street out of the parking lot, Jessie caught sight of Jake Levin's car—not of Jake himself because he was too clever to allow himself to be seen—and that brought her back to her senses. This wasn't sex, it was realpolitik she was playing—and she wished she weren't. She would have given anything to be able to stop the plot. Oh, dear Heaven! Jake and his camera and his *witness*!

She couldn't stop her car and talk to Jake with Milton Ford looking at her in his rearview mirror. How could she explain? Of course, she could give the whole thing up—all these thoughts while tailing Milton Ford's car down Tite Street, turning there into Main Street where his hotel was—and drive home. That would be the sensible thing. It took no account of the sexual voltage she'd built up to trap Milton Ford. She *had* trapped Milton Ford! Also Jessie Jenkins.

Behind her, she saw Jake Levin's car doing a U-turn and following hers to the large ramshackle hotel.

When she parked Milton Ford had already gone into the hotel. Through the glass of the revolving door, Jessie could see him buying an evening paper. She paused. Could she wave at Jake Levin? Go away. No, she couldn't. Milton Ford had bought his paper and was looking at her. She came into the hotel lobby and went swiftly to the elevator which was already half full. Milton Ford entered the elevator and punched fifteen.

Neither of them looked at the other. At the fifteenth floor, the other riders had gone, and they were alone. In silence they walked down the corridor to Milton Ford's room, Jessie in a state of sexual bewilderment. I hate this man. What am I doing here?

She had turned herself on, and she couldn't turn herself off. How was Jake going to do this? He couldn't go popping in with his camera *now* could he? It was only seven o'clock—the hotel full of people.

It wasn't a room; it was a suite—sitting room, dining room, little kitchen. Jessie stood in the center of the sitting room, revolving slowly, taking it all in. Panic writ large all over her—I'm out of my depth. For the first time in my whole life, I've overstepped the bounds of rational humanity. All this in her eyes, her posture. She was on the very brink of busting right out of there, when Milton Ford who had said nothing, nothing at all, who must have seen it in her face, took her in his arms, and then the sex compulsion was on her again like a force of nature.

She forgot Jake Levin.

It was very peculiar sex. Neither of them spoke or had any urge to speak. Quite the opposite. For the life of her, Jessie wouldn't have known what to say.

Stark naked in bed with a man she loathed and feared, and he turned her on because of her fear and loathing. She had no idea what he thought of her. There was, in the way he took her, the same courteous contempt he showed toward Jonathan Glass. As she had suspected, his was a body that had had the most meticulous care and feeding. Every muscle firm and full, not an ounce of fat, and during the sex she brushed against all those muscles many times. Jessie had never been one for the wilder shores of sexual calisthenics, but here she found herself engaged in gyrations—shunts and double shunts and tricks not known to common cunts, as the song said—one after another, all non-verbal, unsmiling, unquestioning, the force of nature roaring on with its force-twelve winds.

In the intervals they would fall into exhausted sleep. Waking, the sex ballet would resume with fresh exertions in new untried positions.

It was during one of these jousts—Jessie on her knees, Milton Ford entering her from the rear, a Japanese position of grotesque delicacy—that Jake Levin, whose existence she'd forgotten, burst in with his camera and his witness, catching them with his flashbulb and his Leica in this oriental extravagance: Jessie with her mouth open, which, according to the Japanese prints, it should never be, at least not in this particular contortion.

So elaborate was their physical intertwining in the Japanese position that Jake Levin had time to take three shots of them in various stages of unwinding. When they had become unwound, Jake and his witness, an elderly gentleman who watched it all unmoved, had withdrawn and slammed the door shut behind them.

After that Jessie's world exploded in her face.

Milton Ford was *laughing*. Jessie lying flat on her back on the bed altogether amazed. She'd never seen Milton Ford laugh. Not once. Smile that sharkish smile, yes, but never anything so relaxed as a laugh. What was there to laugh *at*? Being photographed in the Japanese position? That was *funny*? Jessie lying on her back looking at this muscular saturnine revolting frightening man who'd had her in twenty-two muscular frightening revolting positions—*laughing* at what should have scared him witless.

Meanwhile, getting dressed. Laughing his wild and frightening laugh—

Jessie had never seen anyone laugh quite like that, a hyena laugh with teeth—while slipping on his shorts and trousers and shirt.

Then came the shots. One. Two. Three. Not loud, clearly silenced but unmistakable. Shots in the still night. Nothing else made a noise like that. Jessie on her knees now on the bed, her face screaming with fear. Who would be shooting who? Not Jake. Oh, my God!

Milton Ford had stopped laughing but his mouth was wide open in glee, the eyes wild. He'd put on his jacket, slung his necktie around his neck and then . . . and then . . .

"What are you doing, you bastard?" Jessie screamed.

What he was doing was picking up *her* clothes—her red wool dress, her shoes, her pants, her stockings—all the time with that great sharkish grin on his face—her handbag, everything she owned in that room. Jessie hurled herself at him as he was going out the door and he lifted one foot in some sort of karate kick which hit her full in the stomach, sending her sprawling on the floor with the wind knocked out of her, her head hitting the floor so hard it almost knocked her cold.

It was minutes before she could sit up, fighting the nausea, her head screaming with shock and pain.

Naked in a hotel room without her clothes or handbag.

Jake.

She crawled on hands and knees, all she could manage in her weakness, out the hotel room door, but before going out the door—despite exhaustion and nausea and fear, still, on hands and knees, propping a chair against that door so she wouldn't lock herself out of that room. On all fours stark naked, weak, and sick to death, she groped down the corridor to where through a myopia of fear she saw what she saw and wished it were not true.

Jake Levin was on his back, his brown eyes fixed on the ceiling, two round holes in his forehead, small holes of the kind made by a silenced .22. Just down the corridor, face down, was the witness, shot in the back of the head.

Kneeling, Jessie cradled Jake in her arms not hoping any more because there was no hope: "Oh, Jake! Jake! Jake!" she whispered.

Jake who had pleaded with her not to do this thing, who had wanted no part of this enterprise, who had got into it only because he loved her too much to let her attempt it without him. She'd got him killed.

Jessie was beyond terror, beyond even remorse, on a high plateau of rage. "He'll pay, Jake! He'll pay!" Jessie whispered to the dead man.

I'll pay, too, Jessie thought.

Disregard of the Divine Law. Again and again.

Naked in a hotel corridor with two dead men. At 2 A.M. No clothes, no ...

She saw the silenced .22 lying there on the carpet.

The murder weapon.

Were they trying to plant it on her? Or suggesting she use it on herself?

Clearly Milton Ford didn't know her very well.

Herself kneeling, Jake's beautiful head in her arms. She kissed the dead lips. "Goodbye, Jake."

She picked up the gun and, fighting the nausea with all her might, made her way blindly back to the hotel room, closing the door behind her. In the bathroom, she threw up violently, again and again. When it was over, she was lightheaded. Clearheaded. Calm in her fury, in the eye of the storm, where all was peace. For the moment.

Naked in a hotel room. Without money or car keys which had gone with her purse.

Two dead bodies outside her room. The gun in her hand.

Outwitted at every turn.

By that contemptuous son-of-a-bitch.

Even while he was fucking me inside out, he was aware his killers were outside, aware I was trying to plant something on him, aware. . . .

I wasn't aware. I was enjoying. . . .

In disregard . . .

Jake's camera! Where was Jake's camera? Gone. They'd taken it with the pictures of me in the Japanese position. What would they do with that?

Shrouded in the calm of her fury.

She looked at her watch, the only thing he'd left her. 2:10 A.M. No sound in the corridor. No movement.

The gun in her hand. Got to get that out of here. A plant. Somewhere there's a faked document showing I bought this thing. Got to get rid of the gun.

Clothes. Got to improvise.

Sheets. Flower-patterned. A sari, of course.

She pulled off the top sheet and draped it around her, around the arms, over the shoulder, fastening the ends around her waist. Hardly the costume for a December night, but she was warmed by her fury.

How was she going to get home? Twenty-five miles. No money. No car keys.

On her knees, she prayed: "Gray-eyed one. My life is at stake! My soul! My reason!"

Nothing happened.

Nothing was vouchsafed to a girl who had disregarded the Divine Law.

Jessie on her knees thought of Derry and the many times he'd tried to teach her how to hot-wire a car. Derry who knew all those things so well. There'd come a time, he'd said, again and again, when you will have lost your keys or forgotten them and you will need to know how to start a car without a key. Always she had laughed and said she was non-mechanical. Anyway, she'd said she had him, Derry, to do it for her. Always she had refused to listen, to be shown.

Right there on her knees she *was* shown. Derry showed her. Jessie recalling something that had never taken place. Derry lifting the hood, showing just where this wire went, where that one went—how to make the starter work from inside the hood—the whole bit she'd always refused to watch.

"Thank you, Goddess," Jessie whispered. Why was Athena helping her?

At the door she listened. No sound. Opened the door a crack. Looking for killer, for anyone. After a minute and a half, she slipped swiftly out the door, down the corridor—not looking at the bodies—to the staircase, the elevator too risky, too attention-getting. In her improvised sari, the gun in her hand, she crept down fifteen flights of stairs clear to the basement, walked through the boiler room to the rear end of the hotel where she let herself out the service door.

The Triumph was where she had left it on the hotel parking lot. Had she locked the doors? No, she hadn't. Too much of a hurry. She opened the hood and under the streetlight saw the engine in all its mystery. Except now it was no longer all that mysterious.

I'll need a bit of wire.

Again Derry instructed her—as she was absolutely sure he had never instructed her—that you could always snip a bit of wire off the taillight— there was always too much wire there—and go home on one taillight.

Snip it off with what?

There were tools in the Triumph. Pliers and a screwdriver in the glove compartment because she'd put them there herself. For emergencies!

She snipped off a bit of taillight wire which was indeed much too long, fastened it sure-handedly, there and there, as if she'd done it all her life, and then pulled the starter rod to make the car turn over.

It didn't start.

After a bit she dropped the starter rod, put her head inside the driver's seat, and pulled out the choke.

110

The car started immediately.

Jessie drove home, pausing only once on the high bridge over the James River, into which she threw the revolver.

__ CHAPTER __
TEN

SUNNY AND COLD, the air piercing. Just right for pig killing.

Jamie Goosens sharpening his knives, ten of them. First the whetstone. Shower of red sparks in the cold air, then the worn gray stone, finally the bright steel. Clisp closp. Clisp closp. Jamie's eyes lazy with the bliss of it. He loved sharpening knives. Loved even more the using. . . .

Todd Gassett at the fire under the scalding tub, boiler plate steel, enormous, for the enormous hogs. Humboldt Pickering and Jessie setting up the hanging pole trussed to crossed cedars, lashed together by chain, stout enough for ten hanging pigs—one of them seven hundred pounds.

Air of expectancy sharpening the moment.

Even the pigs feeling the tension, moving restlessly in their pen, not liking it.

Pig jokes, salty with age. Jokes about their age, parentage, demeanor.

Everyone smiles.

Except Jessie.

Jessie in the bright solitude of terror. Bereft of friend, Goddess, husband. Soul unraveled.

Everlee Pickering in the big sitting room of the house, never used except for times like this, setting the table for the big lunch. Ten pig stickers with hearty appetites. "Jessie in a trance." Thus Everlee to Amanda Goosens. "Never see her like this before. She unstrung."

On a rise near the wood, the pig killing ground. Warren Widdy taking the temperature of the water in the scalding tub: 145 degrees.

113

Pigs moving restlessly.

Humboldt Pickering, best shot in the crowd, sights down the .22 bolt-action. Inch above, midway between the eyes.

Cr-r-ack!

Todd Gassett and Humboldt, moving in swiftly before he starts kicking, flip the beast on his back. Jamie Goosens slips the sharp knife into the throat, thrusting and lifting, severing large branching vein, the artery.

Blood pumping out, a fountain of it, red as raspberries.

Jessie white as paper. Hand at her throat.

Swiftly, into the house.

All eyes on her.

Not like Jessie.

"She not well," Jane said, fiercely protective.

Following.

Jessie in the john on her knees. Trying to throw up.

Nothing to throw up.

No vomit. No tears. No anything.

Empty of purpose.

"Jessie!" Jane on her knees beside her.

Jessie grasping Jane's hand, clawlike, hissing, "Don't tell anyone what time I got in last night. No one. Not even Warren."

She didn't have to worry about Warren. Warren never told anyone anything. Not ever.

The two women back now at the killing ground, Jessie white as a skull.

First pig in the scalding tub now, men swarming over it with the hog scrapers. Jerry Harper cleaning the ears. Best ear man around. Jamie Goosens working over the feet, getting them ready for the brine.

The jokes flying. Camaraderie of slaughter.

Man's true vocation—killing.

Women at the hanging pole. Everlee Pickering, Amanda Goosens, Jane Widdy, Easy Perkins . . .

Jessie Jenkins.

"You okay, Jessie?" from Jane Widdy.

Unexpectedly, a gleam, blistering in its brightness. *They'd killed a pig when Odysseus returned.*

A gleam of sunlight in the very bottom of her.

The lines ringing like bells.

He hit the beast with a split of oak that he had lying by him.
The breath went out of the pig; then they slaughtered him and
singed him,
Gave Odysseus in honor the long cuts of the chine portion of the
white-toothed pig.

Jessie's hand to her throat.

Cr-r-r-ack!

Second pig down.

In the cold air to get the heat out of the body.

Jessie's testing one of Jamie Goosens' sharp knives on her thumb.

First pig hanging, butcher white, from the cedar pole.

Humboldt Pickering, Jamie Goosens and Todd Gassett heave the two hundred fifty pound second pig upwards, muscles straining, Jerry Harper astride the pole, fixes it there with a hickory split through ankle tendons.

Jessie's mind three thousand years away. I am Penelope and my liege lord is returning today because it's got to be today, tomorrow is too late.

The snout hanging an inch from the ground.

Jessie slipping the sharp blade into Jamie Goosen's incision in the neck, arms straining upward.

Blade hits the rib cage.

Easy Perkins hands her the saw.

Sawing through the breastbone.

Got to be today, Athena, tomorrow is too late.

Jessie straining upward, cutting through the rib cage of the big pig, twenty-five times the size of the pigs in Odysseus' day.

Three thousand years ago.

Jane Widdy huge with child holding the beast to keep it from swinging.

Athena, the Gray-eyed One, had said to Odysseus, "I am a God, and through it all I keep watch over you. You will soon be out of your troubles." That's what she'd said.

On another occasion. Much like this one.

Cr-r-r-ack! Another pig down.

Jessie's hand to her throat.

"You okay, Jessie."

"I okay."

Jessie cutting around the asshole of the second pig. Steaming entrails in

115

her left hand. Right hand cutting away from the carcass with the sharp knife, dropping the mess in the big galvanized tub.

Cutting the liver away from the offal. Handing to Jane Widdy to wash.

Expectancy hanging in the air. Palpable.

Even the pigs feeling it.

Jessie cutting the heart out of the pig. Handing it to Everlee to clean and trim.

Guts steaming and stinking in the cold air.

It's got to be today, Athena, tomorrow's too late!

Jessie, sweating in the icy air, pulls the leaf lard out with both hands and puts it in the iron cauldron.

Jessie with no sleep, spectral. . . .

Lunch. . . .

Ten hungry pig stickers around the big table in the sitting room eating ravenously—roast chicken, turkey, ham, roast potatoes, mashed potatoes, candied sweet potatoes, peas, green beans, sliced tomatoes, fried onions, chocolate cake. . . .

Jessie saw it first.

Through the big window facing the driveway.

A dark shadow on the ground, under the Norway maples.

Two men.

One black.

The other.

Bearded. He who had never been bearded!

Slender.

Loose-limbed.

The stride unmistakable.

Jessie flew out of the sitting room.

Out of the house.

Down the drive.

Everlee with a chicken bone in her hand, half gnawed. Jamie Goosens' mouth full of ham hock. Jerry Harper chomping turkey. Amanda Goosens buttering her bread.

All in stop motion. Frozen.

The wonder of it.

Halfway down the drive, Jessie stopped. After all this time, it was not up to her.

The bearded man came on in his long loose-limbed stride.

116

Took Jessie by the hand and led her up the drive.

Toward the house.

Jessie shook her head, whispering in his ear.

They changed course then, turning into the barn field.

Into the barn.

In the sitting room there was so much to say, no one said anything.

Except Martha Harper who said, "Ask the black man in, Jerry."

Jerry brought him in.

"Name's Hector," the black man said.

"Sit right here," Amanda Goosens said, putting him in Jessie's place. And served him up.

"How you with a saw?" Humboldt Pickering asked.

"Not bad," the black man said.

"Ten pigs to cut up by nightfall."

The pair in the barn not mentioned.

All that long afternoon, they sawed the carcasses into shoulders and hams and sides of bacon, the women boiling the lard, grinding up the scraps into sausage, slicing the rib cage into pork chops.

The pair in the barn never reappeared.

Darkness came early, and the men and the women climbed into their pickups with their butchered pigs wrapped in cloth and carried in galvanized washtubs.

To carry the story far and wide.

That Derry Jenkins was home again.

Bearded and much changed.

__ BOOK __
TWO

__ CHAPTER __
ELEVEN __

DERRY FIRST NOTICED her leaning against one of the posts along the covered walkway that ran the full length of the stable. A thin figure in blue jeans and a filthy white T-shirt bearing the legend *Screw You* across her flat chest. She was lounging against the post, one leg crossed over the other, giving him the eye. Not a friendly eye. Like a mare that offers her behind to the stallion just before kicking his face in.

"That your rig, mister?"

Derry was at the back of the trailer feeding bales of alfalfa down the steel rollers that carried them into the feed room. A black man named Hector Larrabee was helping.

"Mr. Mancuso not gone to like you takin' you ease like that, Mickie," the black man said.

The girl paid no attention, eyes fixed on Derry's slender body, naked to the waist in the sharp February sunshine.

"Virginia," the girl said, reading the license plates. "You going back to Virginia in that rig, mister?"

In the stall directly opposite the lounging girl, a thoroughbred put her chestnut nose against the steel bars of her stall and whinnied low, deep inside her throat.

"Whyn't you give that horse her dinner?" Derry asked. "She's hungry."

A pail of sweet feed hung on the stable door just out of reach of the velvet nose. Other pails of feed hung on each of the thirty stalls on this side of the

121

stable, each stall containing a thoroughbred, some worth a hundred thousand dollars.

"She git her dinner in due course," the girl said. "With the others."

The girl flaunting her bony body. Lot of sexual voltage there, and Derry couldn't understand why. She wasn't a very pretty girl, sullen face, much too white for his country taste, the body too skinny, that *Screw You* message an affront. He didn't like her.

"Here come Mr. Mancuso now," Hector said softly. "You better git hustling, Mickie."

Mr. Mancuso was a squat figure, bald as an apple, who was scuttling crablike down the line of stalls looking into each stall briefly, scowling. The girl heaved her skinny bottom away from the post, took the pail of sweet feed off its hook, slid open the stall door, emptied the pail into the feedbox, slammed the door shut, and shot the bolt.

Each movement, a statement. Delineating her disagreement with the world and its arrangements. Very editorial, the message getting to both Derry and Hector who exchanged amused glances.

The girl walked down the line of stalls, emptying feed pails into each one, and disappeared around the edge of the stable without once glancing at Mancuso.

Mancuso peering into one stall after another, eyeing each thoroughbred unhappily, though they were beautiful horses.

When he reached the eighteen-wheeler, he thrust his hand out in the general direction of Derry, his gaze meanwhile directed into the stall.

"You Jenkins?" he asked.

The hand outthrust, asking to be shaken. Instead Derry put the invoice into it. If a man wanted to shake hands he ought to look at you.

Mancuso stared balefully at the bill. "Five dollars a bale," he muttered.

"It's getting here costs so much," Derry said, not at all apologetic. Man had a million dollars' worth of horseflesh in the barns complaining about a twenty-four hundred dollar bill. "Your pastures be back in shape in another week," Derry said. "You won't need any more."

"Come into the office," Mancuso said.

The office was polished pine, covered floor to ceiling with photographs of racehorses, some of them posing beside their stalls, with their names and pedigrees, some shown crossing the finish line first. No one hung a picture of a horse crossing the finish line anything but first. "Point of Order taking Man O' War Stakes at Belmont. 2 minutes 10 2/5."

One wall lined with books containing stud records of every thoroughbred in Christendom. In one corner stood a glass case containing silver cups won by horses foaled at Meadowland. A very hushed aristocratic room in every respect except one.

Mancuso.

He didn't look as if he belonged there or should even be allowed in. The sport of kings was full of riffraff now.

Mancuso had pulled out a fat wallet and was counting out hundred dollar bills, twenty-four of them. He thrust the wad at Derry who didn't take it.

"I was expecting a check, Mr. Mancuso," he said.

"Money's better," Mancuso said. This time he pushed the money straight into Derry's hand and closed the fingers around it. "I don't care to carry that much cash in the rig," Derry said.

Mancuso's face wrinkled with scorn. "That ain't much cash. Not these days." He sat down at the rolltop desk where again he looked very out of place, turning his leaden glance on a stack of papers.

Derry looking at the wad of bills in his hand, not liking it. It wasn't customary for a bill that size to be paid in cash, and Mancuso knew it as well as he did. It smelled of larceny, money being laundered, illegality. It meant there was no record of the transaction, and why shouldn't there be?

Something very funny about this deal.

Back at the rig, the last of the alfalfa had gone down the steel chute into the feed room. Two black men were carrying away the steel chute. Hector had his hand on the thimble-bolt of the trailer, ready to lock it. "You want I should sweep the trailer? Only take a minute."

Derry shook his head. "I want to get to Monroe before the night's out." He shook hands with the black man, smiling. Not much about Meadowland he liked, but he did like Hector.

"You off home now?" Hector asked.

"Yeah."

"I be gittin' off home mese'f pretty quick," Hector said. "No more to do here."

"Where's home?"

"Tennessee. Kinkajou, Tennessee." Hector laughed. "Kinkajou 'bout the size of fifteen cents, but mighty pretty in the spring."

Derry climbed into the cab, ten feet off the ground, and did his paperwork. They were sticklers for paperwork in Florida even on empties. In his logbook he entered the time for leaving Ocala—5 P.M. Before that he wrote down his rest period, as the rules required. (Some rest, unloading two hundred bales of alfalfa.)

Hector squinted up at him through the late afternoon sunlight. "You ever in Tennessee, you come look me up in Kinkajou," he shouted over the roar of the diesel.

"Don't work too hard, Hector," Derry shouted.

"I am not about to do that," Hector said gravely.

Derry shifted to first gear with a screech of metal on metal. After ten yards he shifted to second, double clutching. He eased it into third and in that gear went down the two-mile driveway, all of it planted with young live oak not more than a year ago. The whole farm reeked of newness and money, shady money. In the past decade or so Ocala had become a rival of Kentucky in the breeding of racehorses. It had its share of Vanderbilts, but it also attracted the Mancusos who came from the urban swamps of Brooklyn, men whose bankrolls had no limits and no origins.

Meadowland was part of the empire of Galaxie Industries, an immense conglomerate, Derry had heard, based in Cleveland.

Driving through the soft opalescence of Florida twilight, beautiful but unreal, a stage set. Some day someone would come along and take it all down and store it away. Listening to Linda Ronstadt singing "Back in the USA." Florida wasn't USA—it was Never-never Land.

Darkness blotted out the countryside, foreshortening the landscape to a few sinister pines in the headlights, the eighteen-wheeler roaring through the purple starlight in chilly solitude.

At 2 A.M., he crept carefully into the truck park at Monroe, the cornbinder sneaking in past bulldogs, reefers, Kittyhoppers, and a few other cornbinders—a great jam of eighteen-wheelers, some headed south to Miami, most of them empties headed out to Cedar Rapids, San Diego, Chicago, Boston.

The bed lay behind the seat, protected by a curtain of fake leather. Derry rolled up the curtain and switched on the little top light, swinging his legs around to get into the bunk bed.

Only then did he see her, the girl called Mickie, crouched in a ball at the foot of the bed, eyes large as plates. The eyes didn't fit the rest of her was his first thought.

"Sorry," the girl said. She didn't look sorry. "I had to get outta there in one helluva hurry, and you was the oney one leaving."

Derry said nothing. ("He's the quietest man in the whole world when he doesn't like something," Jessie had said of him.)

The silence upset the girl. "I just wanted to hitch a lift," she whined. "I had to get away from that man."

"What man?" Derry asked.

"Mancuso."

"Why?"

"He tryin' to get between my legs that's why."

That sexual voltage again. Derry could understand Mancuso wanting to have the girl. He simply didn't believe that was why she ran away.

"Hitchhikers against ICC regulations," Derry said. "They're very tough on that in Florida. I'm sorry but you got to get out."

The girl looked forlorn. "2 A.M. in a truck park. You throw me out here, I get raped. I damned tired getting raped in truck parks."

"How many times you been raped in a truck park?" Derry asked.

"I stopped countin.'"

Unreal, all of it. Derry had the country boy's feel for the real and the unreal. This girl was way out in fantasy land. Still... 2 A.M. in a truck park. He couldn't do that to her.

"Come on," he said. Derry clambered down the ladder and led the way. He unlocked the big steel door of the trailer and hoisted her up into the cavernous interior, still smelling of alfalfa.

"You ain't gone lock the door, are you? I can't take being locked up. I been locked up enough."

Derry shrugged and walked away, leaving her to close her own door. Or not close it, if she saw fit. You could work that door from either side.

Back in his bunk bed, he could hear her moving about, closing the big steel door from the inside. Feeling a stirring of desire for that dirty sullen girl. Five minutes later he was asleep.

Derry snapped awake. 4 A.M. Her face was next to his, terror in her eyes. "Sssh!" Terror in her voice. "Listen!"

Derry could hear the sound of a car in low gear driving slowly. Very peculiar—a *car* in that truck park at that hour. He could see the headlights way to the left and to the rear of his tractor.

"They come after me," the girl said. "We got to get out of here."

"This is ridiculous," Derry said. Then he saw the gun in her hand. A .25 caliber. Not many of those around.

She jabbed him with it. "Get out that bed. We gotta get going. They find

125

me they kill me. They kill you, too, because they think you in on it."

"Look," Derry said. "I couldn't even start this thing. Do you know how hard it is to start a cold cornbinder. . . ."

"I have driv' cornbinders," the girl hissed. Eyes crazy with fear. "I know all about these rigs. You get up on top and pour a little ether down the stack. I start your engine, mister."

Headlights from the car had stopped now. In his side mirrors, Derry saw a man get out of the car.

"Searching for *us*," Mickie said. "Get up on that roof."

Derry thought about making a quick grab for the weapon but the girl's eyes were too crazy. The safety on the gun was off. Steady, Derry thought.

He slid out of the berth and reached for the ether can. In his stocking feet, he climbed the steel ladder of the roof and poured a pint of ether down the stack.

The car with the headlights had moved on to another part of the truck park and again stopped. The man on the ground was reading the license plates. Derry could see him in the headlights.

Mickie had turned the tractor key and the big diesel with the pint of ether in its guts roared to life. Derry scrambled back down the ladder. The girl leveled the gun at his head. "Let's get out of here fast and without lights," she said. "They hear the noise, they don't know where we are."

Derry didn't argue. He couldn't with that gun pointed at him. Besides it was very good advice. The truck park was loaded with eighteen-wheelers, maybe fifty of them, and without headlights, it would be hard to tell which one had started up. He put the big rig into the first of its thirteen gears and pulled down the line of trucks.

"There's an exit right over there," the girl said. "Turn right on it."

Behind him in his side mirror, Derry saw the car's headlights going sidewise, at ninety degrees from him, searching for the truck making the racket. Not finding it. Did he want it to find him? No, he didn't. He didn't like Mancuso. If that was Mancuso.

On first gear he crept out of the truck park and turned right. Now they were on a feeder road, not the main highway, crawling through darkness lit only by the stars. No moon. If there were anything else on that road, he'd slam right into it, or it'd slam into him. But there wasn't. He crawled two hundred yards along the road, feeling his way by looking at the stars through the breaks between the trees. Sharp curve now, and he slowed way down to make it. Ninety-degree turn. The headlights of the other car had disappeared.

"Put on your lights," the girl commanded. "And give us a little speed."

Derry turned on his headlights, which showed a dreary expanse of pine and canebrake. He moved the truck up—first, second, third, fourth, fifth— till he hit fifty. "I am not going to drive it any faster on a little road like this," he said firmly.

"All right, don't." The voice came out of the blackness beside him and startled him because it wasn't . . . the same voice. Different timbre altogether—softer, gentler. Gentleness was not a quality he had associated with Mickie.

He stole a quick glance sideward. There is no seat for passengers in a cornbinder so she was seated on the floor next to the CB equipment. Cross-legged. Face uplifted. He couldn't see much in the gloom but what he saw was startling. The outlines were softer, rounder. The bony look had vanished. Looked like a different girl.

"What did you do to them to get chased two hundred miles?" Derry asked.

"It wasn't me," the girl said softly. "It was Mickie who did it."

Dear God, Derry thought. What in the world have I got myself into? Another quick glance. When driving eighteen-wheelers in the dark, a quick glance is all a driver dares take.

Uplifted face, mouth half open in a little *O*, picture of innocence.

"It's *Mickie* got us into this?" Derry asked.

"Yes, it was," the girl said. Not *yeah*. *Yes*—with the *S* on it.

"What's your name?" Derry stole another quick glance. The gun had disappeared. Only the round innocent face looked back at him.

"Sarah."

"Tell me about yourself, Sarah." Should he brake the rig, turn around. No, he didn't want to run into Mancuso and his crowd. He didn't know where he was. Sooner or later there must be a crossroad with a sign.

Meanwhile the girl was talking.

"You want the story of my life? It's unbelievably boring. I was born and brought up in Cleveland, and you can't get any more boring than that. I went to St. Thomas Episcopal Academy and sang in the choir and played field hockey. I hope I'm not putting you to sleep."

The syntax prim as a school teacher's.

Ahead of him a road sign proclaimed I-75. East to the right. West to the left. Derry throttled down and shifted from fifth down to second and started to turn right.

He felt rather than saw the commotion on the floor of the truck. The girl was standing beside him, eyes blazing.

She had the gun in her hand again, pressed against his temple. With her other hand she turned the key in the lock shutting off the engine.

"Where ya think ya goin', mister?"

The personality change was shattering.

Derry rolled his eyeballs to the corner of their sockets to look at the catch on the gun. It was off.

"Virginia," he said dryly.

"We ain't goin' to Virginia, mister. They be lookin' for you and me in Virginia because they saw your license plates just like me. You start this rig and back up and head west on I-75. You and me going to Georgia."

Derry sat rigid, the gun at his temple. "Look, Mickie, this rig is leased. Seventy-five dollars a day. It's due back in Richmond tomorrow. . . . No, tonight."

"I'm sorry! Real sorry!"

"When it doesn't show up, they'll start looking for this truck on the road."

"I said I was sorry. Now get moving."

Derry kept his face rigidly calm: "They'll send out an eight-state alarm—description of truck, license plates. We'll be picked up in a couple of hours."

She jabbed the muzzle into his temple painfully. "Start ya engine, mister."

"Suppose I just say 'screw you.' " It wasn't Derry's choice of phrase. He read it off her T-shirt.

"Then I just shoot you through your pretty head and drive the rig myse'f. I have driv' a cornbinder before."

Derry started the truck and backed it away from the east entrance.

An hour later, he turned off I-75 on to 90 and in another hour the rig was in Georgia proceeding cautiously down state road number 119, which was much too small for eighteen-wheelers, past swamp oak, brush pine and unpainted wooden shanties that looked like settings for *Porgy and Bess,* their wooden boards gone silver from sun and rain, their porches sprawling like drunken sailors. Overhead the spanish moss hung from the live oaks like a canopy, shutting out the world.

At seven o'clock the sun rose blinding red, steam rising in the chill. On both sides of the truck stretched swampland, the narrow macadam road rising high over the water table so that the cab rode parallel with the tops of the mangrove trees whose tangle of foliage roots were dense, dark and scabrous. The water stank of old age and rottenness.

The country people, all black, stared owl-eyed at the vast truck going through their untraveled country. After a bit the land rose. Mangroves were succeeded by live oak, and the ground was dry and firm, the smells sweet and woodland.

They passed through a hamlet that consisted of one unpainted store with sagging porch and four wooden shacks, set well back from the road under huge live oaks. From the porch of one of them stared two black children. A moment later, they were out of the hamlet in a thick forest of live oak hung with moss. Here Mickie directed him to pull off the road into a glade shaded by huge trees. With her left hand, she shut off the engine and stuffed the keys into the pockets of her jeans, the right hand holding the gun.

She leaped out of the cab to the red earth. Swaggering now, playing Bonnie and Clyde with the gun, legs spread wide, bony body upthrust defiantly.

"Come on out of there," she commanded.

The eyes crazy.

Derry jumped out. The gun was a powerful persuader. That and the craziness. She prodded him toward the rear of the trailer, making him unlock the spindle and open the big metal door.

"Jump in," she commanded. Gun at the ready.

Derry went into the black maw of the trailer, hating her, hating himself for giving way. Still if he were going to get back alive to Jessie and his farm. . . .

The steel door slammed shut.

She was gone only half an hour, but it did a lot of damage. When she came back, Derry was a different person.

Unforgiving.

He heard the proof lock shoot back. The big metal door creaked open, flooding the interior with cold sunshine that made him blink.

She was smiling. Another of her personality changes, this one so swift and total it threw him off balance. "Come on out," she said, smiling like a cigarette advertisement. "I've got our breakfast."

She held a paper bag in each hand, the .25 nowhere to be seen. Now would be the time to rush the girl, her hands full of paper bags.

129

He didn't, his will sapped by a half hour of fury in the blackness. "Where did you get the food?" he asked.

"That store back there. I got each of us a fried egg sandwich the black lady made herself." Turning her back on him and seating herself under the spreading live oak as if it were a church supper. Chatting away in her Shaker Heights accent. "I hope you like your eggs firm because that's the way they're cooked. The coffee has cream and sugar. I hope you don't mind."

Derry saying nothing. Eating voraciously, drinking the coffee.

Laying plans.

The girl chattering on. "When I was a little girl in Cleveland our cook used to make cucumber sandwiches of very thinly sliced white bread and mayonnaise and salt and pepper. They were so delicious I have never eaten cucumber sandwiches again because I feared I would be disappointed."

The most ridiculous speech he'd ever heard in his life. Especially from a girl who said, "I have driv' cornbinders," as if it were English.

"What's your real name?" Derry asked.

"Sarah."

"Why did they call you Mickie back at the horse farm?"

That brought it on.

The girl's mouth twisted downward, the eyes smouldered. The body changed outline becoming bonier, scalier, more reptilian. Derry felt his loins stirring with desire.

"None you damn business," she snapped.

"Why is Mancuso chasing you, Mickie? Why does he want to kill you?"

"Because I kicked him in the nuts," Mickie said viciously. "Son bitch tried to rape me. I give it to him good. I tell that Sicilian shitheel he come on one more time like that I gonna tell the big boys how he's creamin' off the top."

"He's *what*?"

"Stealin' " the girl said. "It's Mob money. You think Mancuso owns that spread. He got two points. That's all. Two points."

"How do you know all this?"

"I know a lot, mister. I been on the road since I was sixteen, and what the hell you think I was doin' all that time?"

She'd moved to him, thrust her face into his, arrogant, vicious, demeaning.

He threw the hot coffee in her face.

And leaped.

130

A one-armed, ill-considered leap. He had to push himself one-armed, off the ground, the other hand encumbered with the coffee container. It slowed him and, in his moment of awkwardness, she kicked him with devastating accuracy in the crotch. Derry doubled over in agony, his head going forward and down. The next moment his skull rang like twenty-six gongs—and that was the last of it.

Except for the dreams of childhood humiliations, long ago, excruciating.

Consciousness came back slowly through a veil of pain. Rumbling in the ears, smell of alfalfa in the nostrils, blood in the mouth, pain in the head.

The rig was in motion, going along at maybe sixty on a pretty good road, better than the one they'd been on.

"I have driv' a cornbinder," she had said.

Why hadn't she left him there in that glade? Because he'd call the police. If the police weren't alerted, it would be days before the eight-state went out.

What had she hit him with? The gun? Base of the skull. Knew just what she was doing all right.

How had that little bonestick of a girl got him into the truck? One hundred seventy-five pounds of him?

He hated her.

I'd like to fuck her and then strangle her.

A thought so alarming it made him laugh out loud.

If Jessie ever knew I'd entertained such an idea, she'd. . . .

Jessie.

Lying in the blackness he thought of his thin, coltish, capable wife. Back on the farm. Coping. Should have called her. Now, God knows when. . . .

Where are we? What time is it?

Hour after hour, the tractor-trailer rumbling along, Derry dozing, one moment devoured by tenderness toward Jessie, the next consumed by lust for that damned woman!

The feeling so violent it wore him out, and he fell asleep.

He awoke in bright daylight, late afternoon sun pouring into the back of the trailer. What woke him was the shroud lines she was fastening around his wrists. The moment he came aware, he heaved his shoulders, hitched up his knees, strained. But it was too late for that, the straining only making the slip knots bite harder.

Mickie was laughing at his efforts, eyes crazy.

He gave it up and lay there on his back, panting. She threw a bowline

131

around his wrists and tied him to the center ringbolts. Derry screamed with fury, body thrashing from side to side.

That made her laugh even more.

Eventually he stopped the screaming because it did no good.

He lay there, listening. No sound. From where he lay he could see only sky and the leaves of oak.

"We're in the woods of northern Georgia, baby," whispered the girl, eyes bright as moonstones. "Loneliest spot on earth! Ain't *nobody* gone mind you howling." She yawned. "I'm a mighty tired little old gal. I been drivin' eight solid hours and I need my sleep, but I thought I better tie you in knots or you would do me harm."

She ran her fingers around his jawline, bending over him, eyes bright, crooning low, "I'm truly sorry I got to truss you up like that."

Her lips pressed his softly, and her tongue slipped into his mouth, quick as lightning. And out again.

He snapped at her like a hungry bass at a fly, but she was too quick as if she expected that.

"No bitin' mister. There's some likes it but not little Mickie. I likes to do my own bitin'."

She was slipping off her shirt now, revealing the thin body and almost total absence of breasts. Little immature buds was all. She wrapped the T-shirt with the *Screw You* message around the lower half of his face, first twisting it into a rope so that if he bit, he bit cloth.

Talking a blue streak.

"When you rob a bank, you got to do this to the bank guards, so they don't go makin' a fuss. That was always my job, trussin' up those bank dicks like Christmas turkeys while the boys had all the fun pawin' the money.

"Nothin' more fun than pawin' money except maybe what you and me are about to do. You turn me on with those big blue sexy eyes, mister. You did that to me minute I see you."

She'd slipped out of her filthy sneakers, and now she took off the jeans which left her naked as a hawk, all bones and lust—the lust emanating out of her in waves.

Now she was untying his shoelaces, slipping off his shoes, then his trousers, presently lying next to him, eyes glittering with lust and hatred, the one feeding the other. Derry hated her back in full measure and desired her more than any woman he'd ever known, certainly more than he'd ever desired his beloved Jessie.

Her hands fingering his cock now which hardened at the first touch. Humiliating how she was controlling the action, but, dear God, the pleasure of it! She was on top of him now, his cock inside her, the sweetness of it overwhelming him, her warm breath on his cheek.

She began to moan—that, too, intensely erotic—and after an eternity of moans, she gave a gasp of bottomless bliss and cam⌐ and so did he. Derry taking as much pleasure in her orgasm as in his own. First time he'd ever felt a woman's pleasure like his own.

For a very long time, they lay side by side, eyes not two inches apart, looking at each other with bottomless curiosity. Presently she rolled away from him. "I got to get some sleep," she said absently, stepping into her jeans. Her shirt was still wrapped around his lower face, so she slipped on a sweater over her naked torso.

His trousers lay in a tangle of hay and she picked them up and smoothed them out. In doing this, the wad of hundred-dollar bills attracted her attention. She fished them out of his pocket and gazed at them sullenly.

"Mancuso washin' his filthy money on your clean alfalfa. The pig!" She stuffed the wad of hundreds into her own jean's pocket.

Derry went wild. "Thack gorge oney" he screamed. Or tried to scream through the gag in his mouth. That twenty-four hundred dollars, he was attempting to say, was feed and mortgage money; it had to feed four sows, two horses, a hundred chickens, and four goats to say nothing of himself and Jessie until the spring farrowing. When she paid no attention to those gurglings, he lashed out at her with his feet as best he could.

She skipped out of the way of the thrashing feet which were limited in range by the shroud lines.

"My! My!" she said in admiration. "You have the prettiest legs I ever did see, especially when they wavin' about like that."

She was on her knees now, staring at his penis. "I am the greatest cocksucker in the whole wide world, mister. You don't believe that, do you, you little shitheel, but, by God, I'll make you!"

His cock slipped into her mouth as if it belonged there.

Derry had never been sucked off in his whole life. He'd heard tell of such goings-on but never really believed women did such things. (Certainly not Jessie.)

Now here . . .

She was indubitably expert and very patient. It took great patience to arouse him again, but she persisted, her whole body bent double over his, an attitude of abnegation much like worship, her arms clasped behind her back, as if drinking at the sacred spring.

This was the time to thrash out with his knees. If he caught her right, he could knock her cold.

He didn't.

Instead, he lay back, overcome with the bliss of it, and gave himself up to her. He was all body, all cock, not a person at all.

Presently he came in her mouth as if yielding up his manhood.

She looked down at him, sullenly, hating him for her act.

Without a word, she jumped out of the trailer, slammed the big metal door, and locked it. He could hear her climbing into his bed in the cab of the truck. After that, silence and blackness, hour after hour. The pain in his wrists from the tight knots was excruciating. In his nakedness, he shivered from cold. It wore him out, the pain and shivering. Eventually he slipped into a sort of coma, a doze of forgetfulness, the dreams shattering.

When he awoke, the rig was on its way again. Hours passed.

He slept again.

She shook him awake as she was untying the shroud lines, the gun in her teeth. Taking the gun out of her mouth, she said, "Get dressed."

He put on the trousers, grateful for the warmth, buttoned up his shirt, and hunched into his jacket.

"Come on!"

She jumped out of the trailer and he followed her, still half-asleep. Starlight outside and very dark. Derry glanced at his watch. Two-fifteen. The big rig was parked in a clearing before a grocery store, all locked up and deserted, a white night-light illuminating the area. At one side of it, stood a glass telephone booth, brightly lit.

"This rig already late at the garage," Mickie said. "I want you should call and tell 'em you gone be a little late back. Two three days late because you got messed up, something like that. You must got some number to call."

Holding the .25 in her fist, pointing at his midsection.

"Yeah," Derry said. He dialed the collect signal 0 and then dialed his own home number. The operator came on. "I want to make a collect call to anyone," Derry said. "This is Derry Jenkins." He read off the callbox number. Looking at the metal road stanchion at the side of the highway. Tennessee, it read, 158 W.

Tennessee! What happened to Georgia?

"A collect call to anyone from Derry Jenkins," the operator was saying. "Will you accept charges?"

"Yes," Jessie said, his wife's voice sounding in his ear like an accusation.

"Jessie," Derry said. "I can't talk much so you got to get this straight the first time."

"What!" Jessie said, alarmed.

"I'm in Tennessee headed west, and I won't be home for a little while because of circumstances beyond my control. . . ."

A stupid way to put it. He should have said he was kidnapped but when he thought of it, it was too late.

Mickie had pulled down the receiver arm, cutting off the call.

__ CHAPTER __
TWELVE __

THE BIG TRAILER was pitching and yawing like a ship in a typhoon, tossing Derry from side to side, the cords on his wrists cutting sharply into him. *Any minute she is going to get this rig stuck,* Derry was thinking. Clearly on a dirt road, not even a very good dirt road, and it seemed to be climbing.

They'd been on the move for hours. Six? Eight? There'd been several stops after the telephone stop and at least one stop before the telephone stop when Derry in his troubled sleep heard the roar of traffic, even voices.

She'd let him put on trousers and sweater at the telephone stop so he was no longer quite so cold. That left him with his thoughts, which were not comfortable. Enjoyment of rape. What was worse he enjoyed it *after* the event. Still enjoyed it. Retrospective adultery. Infidelity to Jessie who was pure as mountain spring water, a paragon of unassailable sexual virtues. Shameful, his conduct, even if unwitting.

The truck was creeping along now, dead slow, was turning painfully a full circle. The engine idled and was switched off.

Silence.

Almost. Derry could hear Mickie's faint scrabblings in the cab of the truck, the creak of the bedsprings. That brought a flood of imaginings of a deliciously desirable Mickie in his bed. . . .

After that, forest silence unbroken even by insect or frog—too early in the year for that, not even the small scratchings and nibblings of rabbit or mice.

After an eternity of silence, a presence brushed the truck light as the wings of a moth. Deer? No other forest creature was tall enough to touch the truck. Some curious deer nuzzling the trailer with its nose. Derry let his mind toy with animal images (so much more restful than thinking of a naked Mickie). He conjured up a mental picture of his horse Wednesday with her delicate foal Ariel, scampering about the barn field happy and free. . . .

Free.

Himself trussed to the ringbolts.

Jessie.

The thought of his wife swam before him, full-faced—intelligent, kind, humorous, loving, virtuous.

Virtue incarnate.

Mickie was vice incarnate.

Which of the two did he want at the moment, which one struck fire in his loins? Oh hell.

Hours passed. Hours of boredom, spiced with guilt and tumescence, finally simple hunger. It was the hunger that drove him to action. He pounded with his heels on the metal floor of the trailer—thump, thump, thump—a fearful racket in the forest calm.

It took a long time.

When the great rear door opened, flooding the interior with sunshine, the girl bounded in full of smiles and apology. "I'm so very sorry," she said. "It was shameful of me to oversleep like that, but sometimes one can't help it."

Now who was she? Not Sarah. Not Mickie. *Sometimes one can't help it.* That wasn't Shaker Heights.

The girl was babbling on. "It's a glorious morning! So fresh, the air! Ordinarily I'm not terribly fond of evergreen, but in the dreary stretches of winter, one turns to it for comfort, don't you agree?"

Hitting the consonants very hard as the British do. Very British. Like someone he'd seen in the movies.

She was unfastening the shroud lines from the center strut but not untying his wrists. No sign of the gun. This might be the right time to make a leap. Even with his hands tied behind him, he could give it to her in the kidneys with his knees.

He didn't, remembering all too vividly what happened the last time he leaped. He no longer underestimated Mickie.

"Come stretch your legs," she invited him now in that preposterous British accent. "So good for the muscles after that long ride, don't y'know. I find a long ride so *enervating! Mind stopping!* Isn't it a gorgeous view?"

The truck was in a forest clearing on top of an oak and pine covered hill. They were on the treeless crest of the hill which plunged sharply on several slopes. As far as the eye could see in any direction, there was nothing but forest, no roads, community, or farm.

"Tennessee National Park," she said gaily. "A thousand square miles with hardly a soul in it. Actually, we shouldn't be here. Anyway the truck shouldn't. This bit of forest is designated forever wild. Doesn't that sound perennial—forever wild?" She tinkled with British laughter. "It was very naughty of Mickie to drive the truck past all those signs forbidding any form of wheeled transport except pony cart. . . ."

Very naughty of Mickie to drive the truck? As if she had nothing to do with it.

The road was scarcely more than a track. Certainly not meant for a cornbinder, which was pulled up on the grass, as out of place as a grand piano in a henhouse.

"Should we have some breakfast? Mickie bought us lots of lovely food." She had opened the cab of the truck and Derry saw brown paper sacks, at least a dozen. All bought, he supposed, with his twenty-four hundred dollars.

She brought down a bag and kneeled on the grass with it. "We've delicious Danish pastry."

Derry sank to his knees next to her. "You'll have to untie my wrists."

She laughed, a lilting British laugh, looking into his eyes, guileless as a newborn child. "Oh, I'd love to! I really would—but Mickie would *kill* me if I did anything like that. I'm to feed you with my own hands. That's what she said."

Derry gave a great sigh and sat cross-legged to think that one over. Kneeling, she fed him bite by bite of the Danish pastry, alternated with sips of coffee from his own thermos which had been filled to its two-gallon brim—was she also buying fuel with his money? The cornbinder soaked up 240 gallons of diesel fuel, each fill-up costing $168. How many fill-ups to get them through Georgia?

She was feeding him some sort of brown taffy with a spicy taste. Meanwhile *singing* in a voice clear as crystal, high pitched, entirely differ-

139

ent from Mickie's throaty rasp, something about the merry month of May. He knew that tune. It came from a movie he'd seen with Jessie. What movie?

Camelot.

He'd seen it on television. And she was being . . .

"Vanessa," Derry said.

"Oh, you recognize me. How simply too bad! I *hate* being recognized! It spoils everything." Frowning sadly as if she wished she could retreat into anonymity.

Derry's head was expanding like a balloon. Very odd.

"Would you like to see me dance?" the girl asked, solemn now. "I'm *quite* good."

She put down the Danish pastry, stood on tiptoe, and skipped nimbly across the grass in a sort of forest nymph ballet. After a bit of this, she returned to him, kneeling on the grass again. "I should have been a dancer, not an actress. An actress has to speak such a lot of rubbish."

Derry's head was full of bright colors. "This isn't some damned movie," he managed—surprised at his own vehemence. "You could get thirty years in jail for kidnapping."

She stared at him, delicate as a flower. "I wouldn't do a thing like that! Mickie did it. She does terrible things—and I always get blamed. It's not fair."

She started to cry, tears rolling down her cheeks. Meanwhile nibbling at the taffy. She'd been eating it right along, Derry noticed, giving him a bite, then herself. Still talking in her British accent, "Mickie kidnapped me, too, and now she's abandoned us in this trackless wilderness." Taking another bite of candy. Her mood changed like lightning. "Marvelous stuff, isn't it? From Morocco, the very best." Smiling shyly and sexily at him.

Derry felt his body float right off the ground. He grabbed wildly at coherence. "What is in that candy?"

Her eyes the size of saucers, full of moonbeams. "*Kif,*" she whispered.

"Wha-a- . . ." He couldn't round off the word, his tongue stuck on top of his mouth.

"*Kif.*" There were three of her now, all deliciously nubile. "That's the Arab word for marijuana." She took another bite, all three of her.

"You don't eat mari. . . ." That's as far as he could go with that word.

"*Much* better that way," the girl said. "Five times as strong as when you smoke it—and this is the most powerful stuff there is." She was unbutton-

140

ing her blouse now. "It makes sex absolutely *mah*-vellous." The British accent going right off the charts. "Do take your clothes off. It's better with your clothes off, don't you think?"

A tinkle of laughter.

"Oh heavens, I'd forgotten. You're tied up, aren't you. Let me untie you."

She undid the knots, taking hours. It didn't matter. Time had slowed to a dead stop. There was no past, no future. Only a tremendously thrilling present.

She was altogether naked now, helping him with his buttons which were very difficult, both of them laughing about the difficulty. "I know you've had sex with Mickie," Vanessa said tenderly. "And I hear she's very good. But I'm very good, too—just as sexy as Mickie and just as depraved but in a more *civilized* way. . . ."

They both laughed at that, both naked now in the forest greenery under the hot sun. As she had said, the *kif* made sex truly marvelous—liberating, explosive, above all endless—going on and on and on and on.

Afterwards they slept the sleep of sexual exhaustion.

He awoke in late afternoon, the sun sinking behind the pines, casting long morose shadows. He was lying under a blanket, body naked, hands unbound, mood unspeakable. Derry had never smoked marijuana—or anything—in his whole life. Not a single puff. The marijuana he'd *eaten,* five times as strong as the smoke, cast him into a depression black as sea bottom.

Sex with Mickie had been bad enough, especially the *enjoyment* of it, but that had been forced (though, of course, the *enjoyment* was self-inflicted).

Sex with Vanessa was quite another matter—entered into voluntarily, eagerly, unbound—and again and again and again. The two of them *laughing!* And what had they *laughed* at? Mickie! How angry she'd be if she knew Vanessa was having her man, eating her *kif,* what a joke! It was Mickie he was being unfaithful to, not Jessie (who in his drug-induced euphoria never crossed his mind—not once).

No end to his despair, no bottom, no forgiveness anywhere on heaven or earth.

Clarity of design. For the first time in his captivity, he perceived himself not as victim but as dunce.

She was carving her initials on him at will, whether as Mickie or Sarah or Vanessa. As if he were a tree.

He could hear her, doing something or other to the truck. Cautiously, he

141

opened one eye, the upper eye as he lay on his side still feigning sleep. Her back was toward him, crouched down at the front of the truck, doing something with a screwdriver. Screwing on a license plate. An Oklahoma plate. Where had she got that? He remembered again they'd made some stops in the night.

Stolen some plates.

Thirty feet away from him, gun in her belt. That meant she was Mickie. Sarah used the gun, but she didn't thrust it in her belt that way. She was much more ladylike than Mickie. Vanessa wouldn't use a gun at all, not Vanessa.

He rolled over, casting the blanket aside, and took off like a sprinter, noiseless in the pine needles. It didn't work. He'd not taken two steps when she whirled—she must have been watching in the reflection of the bumper—gun already in her fist, teeth bared in a wildcat grin, eyes manic, legs spread in a sort of Japanese wrestler's squat.

This was Mickie all right. Vanessa had disappeared altogether. The lines of the face were totally different—sharp, malicious, evil, all snarl and viciousness—where Vanessa had been all curves and softness.

The same woman.

He stood there, naked as a bread knife, appreciating the viciousness of her, the ferocity, as if he could taste it.

"The minute I turn my back," Mickie snarled, "you're humpin' that stuck-up British cunt, the very first *minute*. Ah oughta shoot you like a dog."

"She doesn't like you either," Derry said.

He sank to the ground, legs crossed under him, and pulled out a blade of grass and sucked it. "Why did you go off and leave us that way?" he asked. "You might have known she'd make a pass."

This threw her off course. She straightened, pulling herself out of the Japanese wrestler's pose, now looking just awkward and schoolgirlish. The eyes clouded.

"Why'nt you get dressed," she whined. "Middle of the day like this."

"Yeah," Derry said, the thing beginning to take shape in his skull. "Where's m' clothes."

"Right there where you took 'em off to fuck that British cunt." Mickie pointing with the .25.

"I didn't take 'em off. She took 'em off me," Derry said. A flat lie. He'd undressed himself (which made it all so unforgivable). He was trying out the lie to see how much she knew about her own alter ego.

142

"She took ya pants off?" Incredulity in her voice. Not disbelief. Just incredulity.

He slipped into his trousers, face kept carefully blank before her gun and her gaze. Buttoning his shirt, avoiding her eye, keeping the face blank.

Country boy caught in a city situation.

He smiled feeling like Judas. "What you want me to do? Say I'm sorry?" Smiling at her, his hands outstretched, penitent. "You want me to say you're a better fuck than Vanessa. Okay, you are. No question of it. You're the best fuck there is."

First time in his whole life he'd ever used the word *fuck* in front of a girl. Almost never had he uttered the word aloud before anyone.

Smiling right into her sullen eyes. This time he wasn't lying. She was the best fuck he'd ever had and without doubt the best fuck he'd *ever* have. He knew that with a despairing certainty, to the bottom of his soul. Knew it and hated it, but that didn't end the desire. If anything, it sharpened it.

"Yeah?" Mickie was saying, smiling a little secret sullen inward-turning smile. "You're just saying' that cause I got a gun."

"No," Derry said. "You really are. A great fuck. The greatest."

"Aw," Mickie said. "You not so bad either. You know a trick or two." She shifted her feet now, taking a little of the aggressiveness out of her body. "If I such a great fuck, why you jumpin' on that English cunt so fast?"

"She jumped on me." Another flat lie. "You shouldn't have gone off and left us alone." He tried a new exploration. "Where did you go?"

A terrible question, but Derry had to know the answer. Where did these alter egos go in the interval? Where was Vanessa right now? Or Sarah?

Truculence returned in a rush to both the stance and the tone. "Ya ask too many questions. What's it to you? None ya business."

He'd struck a nerve all right.

"Okay. Okay. Just askin."

But it told him something. There were areas she didn't understand in this role playing, areas that scared her and consequently made her angry. Derry knew animal psychology as well as anyone, and this was pure animal. When she was scared, she was dangerous. And angry.

He smiled to reduce the tension. "What we do now—talk or fuck?"

"Talk," Mickie said immediately. "You all fucked out with that British cunt, so let's you an' me just talk a bit."

Derry sat on the grass and put on his socks and shoes. Casually he asked, "Where'd you get them Oklahoma plates?"

"Junkyard. I got more sense 'n to steal live plates. Them are dead plates.

Nobody gone report them plates stolen cause that car been dead since '69."

"Got '79 on the upper right-hand corner," Derry said.

"I took the '79 off the truck plates and transferred them to the Oklahoma plates like it's an up-to-date license."

"Very clever," Derry said.

And dismaying.

What have I got on my side she hasn't got? I know all these girls are just one girl, and she doesn't. That's a weapon. The British girl detests Mickie, and Mickie hates and fears the British girl. Must be some usefulness in that.

He pulled out another blade of grass and chewed on it. "This rig is going to be reported stolen or missing very soon. I was due in Richmond yesterday evening. They'll be calling my home to find out where I am. Asking my wife."

"Yeah, and she won't know, will she? So what they do next—call the insurance company."

"The insurance company gets in touch with police, and police start looking on the roads."

"And not findin'," Mickie said. "Because we up here in the National Forest of Tennessee where nobody look for an eighteen-wheeler and the campers don't start coming till school's out in June, and we got lots of food so we just hide out here a little while and get to know one another."

Derry took another deep breath, keeping his face impassive and his voice steady. "Till *June?*" he asked. It was February. June was three months away.

"Why not?" Mickie asked.

Derry chewed a blade of grass to keep from grinding his teeth. "Then what do we do, Mickie, in the month of June? Get married?"

"We goin' to Cleveland, you and me."

Cleveland. That was where Sarah came from. A convergence of Mickie and Sarah that jarred him. Something wrong there somehow.

"They's a man in Cleveland I got to see," Mickie was saying. "A bad man."

"Why do you want to see him?"

"I'm going to kill him," Mickie said.

__ CHAPTER __ THIRTEEN

SURVIVAL, NOT HEROICS.

Derry had to keep reminding himself because it is not an easy lesson to learn for a man of twenty-six, especially for one who had always *done* things—ploughed fields, hewed wood, drawn water. He had no gift for *not* doing, for restraint, for holding back. This was not his game, but it was the only game in town.

This crazy could pull the trigger on that little gun just once—and that would be the end of it. When rage choked him, he had to remind himself forcibly again and again that the object of the exercise was to get back, alive and sane, to his farm—and to Jessie. (Jessie wouldn't much like that order of preference.)

Mickie watched over him with cunning that verged, to Derry's astonishment, on hatred. There was hate in the eyes, hate in every movement of the bony body, hate in the very intensity of her surveillance. As if *he* were responsible for whatever had twisted her inside out and made her into the crazy that she was. She hated him worse than he hated her, which was odd.

She watched, catlike, gun always in her hand or nearby, suspecting everything, hostile, vicious, whenever he was free of bondage, which was quite a lot of the time. She made him a beast of burden. It was his task to walk down the mountain trail to the brook at the foot and bring up water in two pails, Mickie slouching along behind, gun in hand, to see he didn't get any ideas. He had to collect the wood and make the fires, Mickie always a good twenty-five feet away while he did these things.

They took their meals separated by about twenty feet on opposite sides of the fire. Canned beans, canned stew, canned vegetables. She'd got a lot of canned goods at whatever all-night supermarket she'd stopped at, enough to last quite a while.

Meals were by no means silent.

"Tell me about yourself," Derry would say, eyes on his beans, eating with good appetite on the cold ground, hunched up as close to the fire as he could get because it turned sharply cold when the sun went down. "Where you born?"

Out would come the lies. Or fabrications. Or dementia. "I was born in a whorehouse, mister, which ain't sech a bad place to be born cause I had twenty-six mothers where most oney has one. Ev'y single whore in that whorehouse claim I was her child, all of 'em and to this day I don't know which one was tellin' the truth or if none of 'em was but all of 'em love me like I was her child. What you think about that?"

Derry thought it was hogwash, every word, but he had more sense than to say it. What he said was, "Twenty-six whores is a lot of whores. Must have been a pretty big whorehouse."

"Biggest in Memphis. Not the best but the biggest. They train me good, my mothers. Had me suckin' cock when I was five, but they was very strict about my gettin' laid. None of that, they tell me. You got time enough for that later."

"How much later?"

"Not until I was twelve. Oh, they was very proper."

Without a spark of humor as if she had no inkling how comic some of this story was. Very peculiar because Vanessa had great humor.

"Sounds like a nice life," Derry said, falling into the spirit of this fairy tale. "Why did you leave?"

"Girl can't spend her life in a whorehouse or a nunnery—tha's what my mothers said. Girl got to get out into the real world. They toss me out on my ass when I fourteen. Been on the road ever since, getting pushed around by one Goddam man after 'nother."

"That man in Cleveland you're going to kill. He one of them?"

"N'mind 'bout him."

She'd shut him up fast when he tried to open her up on that subject. Who was he? And what to her? And why did she want to kill him? All he got were snarls, hatred blazing out of her like molten lava.

The hate turned him on, and it turned her on, too. Once the hate started, conversation ceased as if by mutual agreement.

146

They'd finish their meal in silence, and she'd order him into the back of the truck, leaving the dirty dishes on the ground. She'd make him lie flat on his stomach, legs outstretched, arms behind his back, and she'd truss him up, expertly. Then would come the sex in tremendous varieties. She had him with her hands, her cunt, her tits, her mouth, her buttocks, in ways and styles and positions he'd never heard of. There was no getting around the fact that he submitted to all this much too easily and enjoyed it much too much. Once the bonds were on, he could submit without having to worry that this act or these acts were in any way his idea or of his volition.

Total sexual irresponsibility.

Until it was over—then remorse tore him apart. But as the days went on, even remorse became almost a ritual, something to be endured while it lasted—and each bout of remorse seemed to get not only shorter but less severe—as if he were recovering from an illness.

The terrible thing about this was that she seemed to know this as well as himself and to taunt him with it. "I got ya number, mister!" she jeered at him. "I can make that cock do what I like when I like better'n anybody. Better'n your wife. Better'n that English cunt."

She never got over her jealousy of Vanessa. It occurred to Derry that one reason for this was that she feared Vanessa might return. Nobody else could get at them in their forest retreat in February. They seemed to be miles from any human visitor, and even forest rangers wouldn't be in that area in midwinter.

But Vanessa might.

Whenever Vanessa cropped up in her talk—and she did quite a lot— Derry would toss out a query, trying to see how Mickie would handle it. "Where you think Vanessa's gone?" he'd ask, watching Mickie closely.

"How the hell I know what that English cunt's up to and where she at? I jess wish she leave me alone."

"She says the same thing about you," Derry said, trying to stir up something.

"You soft on that cunt, ain't you?" Mickie would blaze out.

"No! No!" Derry would say—not to soothe her but to see how she'd take it—"you're my girl. You're the best fuck I ever had in my life." Which was true.

"Yeah," Mickie baring her teeth maliciously. "That's cause you never had that many. I can tell. But you had her, and I'm a better lay than that one."

Derry tried a little something here. "Yeah, except for one thing. She and

147

I did it without the ropes. That made it awful good. Why'nt you and me try it without the ropes just once?"

She hooted her derision. "Yeah, you'd like that, wouldn't ya? You'd tear my head off. You think I don't know? Ya hate my guts, ya just like to fuck me. I got your number, mister, all the way."

She did, too.

Derry waited for Vanessa—or Sarah—to reappear. Especially Vanessa. He could play on Vanessa's hatred of Mickie. Anyway Vanessa had unbound him (and he couldn't forgive or understand why he hadn't taken advantage of that), and she might well do it again. (This time he would not miss the opportunity.)

It was six days before Vanessa reappeared.

In the middle of the night.

Supper that night had been lamb stew, canned, like everything else, and Mickie had heated it herself over the fire in their lone pan, stirring it briskly to keep it from burning, the handgun stuck in her belt. Derry sat on the ground twelve feet away, planning his dinner colloquy. Tonight he was going to ask her about her career as bank robber. He'd get a lot of malarkey, as always, but in all these flights of fancy Derry could find kernels of hard knowledge that sounded authentic, which stuck out distinctly from the soft core of bathos surrounding it.

Mickie's twenty-six mothers was pure nonsense, but the fact that she even fantasized twenty-six mothers told him something about her. Who would *want* twenty-six mothers unless she'd never had even one. One mother was almost more than most girls could survive. Twenty-six?

Some of the mothers in that whorehouse had sounded painfully real, as if drawn from Mickie's friends or enemies or acquaintances. The details of life in a whorehouse sounded real too. Derry had no way of knowing about that since he'd never been in a whorehouse in his life. But Derry knew people and their longings and their frustrations and their shortcomings well enough to recognize the real personalities in Mickie's fantasies, and out of these nuggets of information and personality he was piecing together something of her past life.

She knew too much about whoring not to have done a bit of it. Or perhaps to have known one. On the other hand she also knew enough of Shaker Heights (Derry had never been there, but bits of *that* sounded awfully real) to suggest she'd experienced that too. Vanessa, on the other hand, was pure cinema, plucked whole from the silver screen. Very well

148

done, just the same, and that told him quite a lot about the whole woman. Mickie in the entirety, if you could put it that way.

Or, more accurately, Sarah in the entirety. Derry had a strong hunch that Sarah was closer to reality than any of the others. Sarah was the point of origin. Of that he was sure. He wished she would reappear because he wanted very much to ask her some questions. She was the nicest, the most human, in many ways the most interesting. He was obsessed with Sarah.

And with the others?

For Mickie he felt a mixture of lust and simple uncomplicated hate. Blaming her altogether for his predicament while absolving Sarah and Vanessa. It didn't make much sense, he realized. The three were all in this together. No, there was only one girl.

He tried to cling to this essential truth, but there were many times when it eluded him—when the three identities were quite separate people in his mind. Captivity changed the nature of reality; fantasy took over. Daydreams were all a captive had to fill the long hours.

A man had to have a little comfort and his comfort was . . . Vanessa. Vanessa was insubstantial as a moonbeam, the stuff of dreams. He was infatuated with Vanessa, which was ridiculous because she was the least real of the three personalities.

In the ordinary light of day he'd prefer Jessie, but then there was little daylight in his situation and Jessie was far away. The fact was he didn't *want* to think about Jessie. It brought up his infidelities—if you could call them that. It wasn't guilt he was feeling—what had he to be guilty about?—but reciprocity. If one could play at this, couldn't the other? He didn't want to think about Jessie being unfaithful. Even the thought of such a deviance in his pure sweet paragon of a wife seemed to him worse disloyalty than infidelity. Still the thought crept in from time to time, and so Derry avoided thinking about Jessie when he could. One way to do this was to relax into the dreamlike arms of Vanessa, that fantasy creature from the silver screen.

That night, around the fire, he asked Mickie about bank robbery, not quite sure how much this was wishful thinking on her part. His question was deceptively simple because Mickie was very shrewd about detecting his motives.

"When you were robbing banks," Derry said, laying sticks on the fire, "how did you go about picking which bank to rob?"

"Stay away from the big ones," Mickie said promptly. (That was one of his ways of testing the truth in Mickie's replies, by the quickness of her answers. If she reeled it right off, it sounded fairly authentic.) "Too many dicks, too many customers, too many tellers in the big banks. The little banks got money. Not a lot but enough." She sounded wistful. "We was never very good at it, y'know. Ten thousand was the most we ever got, and that had to be split six ways. I oney got eight hundred, which ain't fair, but then they never treat me fair, them people."

Eight hundred dollars sounded real, neither too much nor too little.

"Eight hundred dollars is not bad," Derry said, thinking that was more than he'd got at the last feeder pig sale. "Why did you give up bank robbery?"

She snarled at that, suspicious as always of his motives. "You always asking things like that? Why I give up whoring? Why I give up bank robbery? Why you want to know?"

Derry putting another stick on the fire, not looking at her. "What else we got to talk about?"

She answered him then, sullen as always. "You want to do the same thing your whole life?"

"Yeah, I do," Derry said honestly. "I like farming. I don't want to do anything else."

It was an answer he was to think about many times in later life when things changed altogether. When he said it, it was the truth, all of it.

Mickie had put Derry's food down at a good safe distance from him—and then retreated to the opposite side of the fire. He got up and got it.

She was still thinking about his question, and after a bit, she said, "I didn't always have much to say about changin' my life. They toss me out of the whorehouse when I fourteen for something I didn't do. I didn't steal the locket! Who needs a locket?"

She was changing her story. Earlier she'd been thrown out of the whorehouse to experience life on the outside. Now it was a stolen locket, and Derry didn't believe in that much either. Lockets were something you stole in grandmother's time. Not now.

His head was beginning to swim.

She was saying, "If you must know, I got out of bank robbin' because they catched them all—except me. Because they was stupid. They got drunk. They talked. They flashed money around. And they got catched. Just plain stupid. They don't catch me because I don't drink and shoot my mouth off. I just beat it—all the way to Florida. . . ."

Derry's head was blowing up like a balloon. Too late he recognized that sweet sharp taste in the stew. He put the plate down carefully (noticing that half the stew was eaten which meant he'd ingested quite a lot). "What you put in that *stew?*" Barely getting the words out.

"Nothin in that stew but stew," Mickie said. "What's matter with you?"

Derry had risen shakily to his feet and was advancing on her drunkenly. "You spike that food. *Kif!*"

Alarmed, Mickie had pulled out the handgun from her belt. "You crazy, mister. You stop right there. Right there or I blow your little face off. Go on. Stop!"

Derry stopped, the threat in the voice penetrating the drug.

"Get in the trailer," Mickie commanded furiously. "No games now! Get in there!"

Brandishing the weapon.

Weaving drunkenly Derry crawled into the back of the trailer, through the cavernous door, which the girl slammed on him the moment he was inside.

Inside he rocked on his heels, his head still expanding, light waves beating against his eyeballs in the darkness, feeling light as air, a hydrogen balloon floating three inches off the ground.

Presently he slept. Or something like sleep, a sort of extinguishment that was interrupted when Vanessa opened the rear trailer door and stole in beside him.

"We must be very quiet," Vanessa whispered, "because Mickie is sleeping just there—and she'd kill us both in a minute—if she caught us at it."

Something very funny about that statement, but for the life of him Derry couldn't figure out what it was. His clothes were being gently removed, and he participated in this absently, full of languor and desire, while dimly aware that he hadn't planned this escapade, that it ran counter to his well-being in some way.

He was in a state of mist where the world—and their two bodies, nude now—were two-dimensional as if drawn in pencil on paper, writhing in the alfalfa hay. She was laughing now softly, telling him what a lark it was to outwit Mickie yet once again. Very British in its intonations and statement.

Derry hadn't said a word because he couldn't. Words stuck in his throat—even if he knew any, and he didn't. Still, life in the alfalfa was very pleasant, and he was overjoyed to have Vanessa back. He was in love with Vanessa, no question about that. She was the most fantastic woman in his life. After a while, the only woman in his life and after that the only woman in the whole world.

No point in actually saying this because clearly she already knew it. Never were two people so together as they in body and mind and soul. This was what paradise would be like if paradise just knew what it was doing.

It ended abruptly, calamitously, when Mickie caught them in the very act.

Clearly impossible. But that's how it was.

In his drug-induced stupor, Derry was dim about the details. One moment, he was in a paroxysm of bliss with the love of his life (Jessie had disappeared from the face of the earth), and the next he was locked in combat with a biting, kicking, kneeing, gouging, foul-mouthed ferocity. With the drug in him, he was no match for Mickie who was very strong, wiry, and furious.

Now was the time to take charge—but he couldn't do it. When he aimed a fist at Mickie's hate-filled face, it never got there. Time itself had slowed to a halt, and his fists didn't do his bidding—what bidding there was and there wasn't much. He was too *kif*-astonished for decision, much less action.

She trussed him on the ringbolts, hands behind his back, as if he were an animal—and not much of an animal. Then Mickie cursed him—and Vanessa—with an elaboration of vituperation the like of which he'd never heard—obscenities, indecencies, insults so degrading they glowed in the dark like green fire.

Endless, like everything else that evening.

Stark naked against the ringbolts, he was bitter cold, his teeth chattering, while this nightmare woman, her face an inch and a half from his, showered him in spit and malevolence.

"Cold!" he managed the single word, his first word in a long time.

"Freeze!" she hissed.

After a bit he passed out. Too much *kif*. Too much love. Too much hatred. Too much everything.

When he came to, daylight flooded through the skylight of the trailer. He felt appalling, head hammering, nerves screeching, stomach nauseous.

You had to pay for the irresponsibility, he was thinking in his screeching head. You pay dear for all that sexual bliss.

Eyes still closed, he came aware that certain conditions had changed. He was clothed in pants and shirt and a blanket had been thrown over him.

He opened his eyes.

The girl sat cross-legged a few feet away, contemplating him gravely.

"Good morning," she said politely. "How is your head?"

"Awful," Derry said, eyeing her gloomily. She'd changed personality again. This wasn't either Mickie or Vanessa.

"That awful girl had you all tied up and stark naked. I persuaded her to put some clothes on you."

"Very kind of you," Derry said huskily. "You're—uh—Sarah?"

"Yes." She said it like "Yuss"—a sort of upper-class noise mastered only by debutantes. "Good of you to remember. I'm a very *boring* person, actually. Easily the most forgottable character in all Cleveland." She brayed with upper-class laughter.

"Sarah," Derry said, "These ropes are cutting into me. Could you . . . ?"

"Oh, of course, you poor boy. How dull of me not to notice." She moved over to him and started picking at the ropes delicately with her fingers.

Minutes passed, Derry keeping his hopes in check. It couldn't be this easy. It wasn't.

"Mickie has tied these knots terribly tight," Sarah said. "She's very strong, you know." She emitted a small deprecating laugh. "Unlike me. I haven't the strength of a butterfly."

That was going to be the play. She was too weak to untie him. After a while, she gave up. "I'm afraid I just can't do it. You'll have to wait for Mickie."

"There's knives in the luggage compartment at the side of the truck." He was not about to give up on Sarah just yet.

"Oh, yes," Sarah said vaguely. "Well, I don't know that I should go delving into Mickie's luggage."

"It isn't Mickie's. It's mine. It's right beside the door in the tractor."

It took a heap of persuading, but she finally went out to search for the knife.

To no avail, as he'd expected.

"It's locked," she announced, blank faced.

"There's one on the other side."

"That's locked too. I tried them both. I don't know where the keys are. I looked all over."

Derry closed his eyes and tried to think with his splitting head. How to find his way out of this maze. When Vanessa appeared, he was drugged to the eyeballs, unable to function. When Sarah showed up he was tied up, and she couldn't undo the knots. Much too neat.

Sarah knew Mickie. Vanessa knew Mickie. Did Sarah know Vanessa? He tried it on for size. "Do you know Vanessa, Sarah?"

"Who?"

"Mmmmm." Somehow, there was a controlling intelligence here that saw to it that he was either drugged or incapacitated. Consciously or unconsciously, these three personalities were not going to let him go.

That left one area unexplored and what had he to lose? He tried it out, twisting his body so as to be able to watch her closely and see the effect it had.

"You're all the same girl," Derry said. "You and Mickie and Vanessa. You're all one person. You know that, don't you?"

__ CHAPTER __
FOURTEEN

THE GIRL STARED back at him as if he were insane. She held herself erect, this Sarah personality, her cheekbones flaring out in much different fashion from, say, Mickie's, her very outline different from Mickie's or, for that matter Vanessa's. It was consummate acting—only it wasn't acting.

"I'm afraid I don't understand what you're trying to say. I'm a very dull person, you know. It's hard for me to grasp these things."

He sighed and closed his eyes to think things over. After a while, he tried a new tack. "Sarah, I'm in love with Vanessa. Did you know that?"

"I wish you every happiness." Throwing this out with a sort of vague good will, as if barely able to concentrate on what she was saying. "I don't know Vanessa, I told you."

"I *hate* Mickie.

Sarah laughed her upper-class laugh. "I think she hates you, too. She told me she did—but I don't always believe Mickie. She's such a liar."

What was he to make of that?

He threw her another curve to see how she'd swing on this.

"Vanessa hates Mickie, too."

"Well, Mickie riles a lot of people because she's so *crude!*"

Derry threw a high hard one. "Do you hate Mickie?"

She went all dreamy. "Oh, *no!* Me hate Mickie! I love Mickie! She taught me everything I know—what little that is. With Mickie, I lose all my inhibitions and, oh Gawd, have I got inhibitions!"

Mickie could roam where Sarah didn't dare go. It was all becoming almost too clear. Except for one thing. "How do you explain Mickie—all that ferocity? What is she so furious *about*?"

Sarah laughed her empty-headed laugh. "Oh, the same old thing that drives so many girls wild. She hates her father!"

"She told me she never knew her father."

"She's lying. She's the most awful liar."

Derry thought about it for a long time. He didn't want to provoke another explosion or a personality change. In the end, he couldn't resist. "How about you, Sarah? Do you hate your father?"

"Oh, no! I love my father! He's the dearest man in the whole world. And the world has not been kind to him. Not kind at all!"

Derry closed his eyes to rest his weary brain.

There was nothing Sarah wouldn't do for him if she could. She fed him; she brought him water. She tried again and again to untie the knots on his wrists. "I've always been very weak," she'd explain in her colorless upper-class throwaway voice.

They had long talks.

"Tell me about Cleveland," Derry said. He was convinced that in Cleveland lay the answer to the riddle. Cleveland was truth; everything else was fantasy.

"Oh, *Cleveland*!" Sarah would laugh, dismissively, her hands making a vague parabola in the air. "What is one to say about—*Cleveland*! It's American civilization at its most iridescent *awful*. Luminous with decay! The downtown area . . ."—here she gave her fluttery laugh, Sarah's most significant personality trait, expressive of total ineffectuality—". . . looks as if it had been under enemy occupation for about forty years. It needs a bath, downtown Cleveland. Then we should tear it down stone by stone and throw it into Lake Erie which stinks to the heavens of rottenness and corruption. Imagine a *corrupt* lake! Corrupted by the materialism and cynicism of our modern civilization until it hardly contains water any more. Imagine that."

Brilliant anathema, no question. Sarah had a brain underneath all that self-deprecation, but what struck Derry was the despair that lay underneath all that ineffectuality. Where Mickie was angry, Sarah was cold and hopeless, at the bottom of the pit. It chilled his heart, this relentless dislike of the world and of herself.

156

"Cleveland," Sarah was saying with one of her light, self-wounding laughs, "has made me what I am—I'm so passive I should be against the law. I just lie there and let people walk over me. Mickie does whatever *she* wants, never what I want—oh, no. . . ."

Derry tried to imagine Mickie working her will on herself—the multiple uses of selfhood, simultaneously.

"She's very promiscuous," Sarah was saying, "with you, with everyone, male or female, even animals. She horrifies me, and yet I love her. Isn't that *disgusting?*"

Derry fought the pit because he was in a situation that couldn't afford it. He said, "Why don't you run away from her, Sarah?"

"I do run away! Again and again! She always comes after me. She must love me, or she wouldn't come searching for me, wouldn't you say?"

Fantasizing the wild Mickie to help her in her own self-destruction, to be crueler to Sarah than Sarah could be to herself.

And Vanessa?

Derry couldn't fit Vanessa into the psychological tangle. What purpose Vanessa filled in Sarah's emotional desert was beyond him.

"Tell me about your father," Derry said.

"Oh, *father!* He loved my mother who left him for another man—in fact, for a dozen other men—and yet he still loves her, and out of this great unrequited love sprang *me*—a triumph of unfulfillment." Sarah laughed her fluttery laugh. "What a disappointment! *Me!*"

Heartbreaking if Derry had had time for heartbreak. Instead he asked, "Is your father rich?"

"Oh, they're *stinking* rich, both father and mother. *Disgustingly* rich without any of the redeeming features."

"What *sort* of redeeming features do they lack?" Redemption of the rich was not anything he'd spent much time on.

"Some rich people give paintings to the Cleveland Museum of Fine Arts which is a very fine museum. Or they give money to the orphanage. Or they join the Peace Corps or sail around the world singlehanded or do something *creative* or wild and free. You should use money to free yourself not to imprison yourself. . . ."

She cried awkwardly as if she didn't know how, as if shamed, dabbing at her eyes, trying to conceal the whole thing. Presently babbling deprecation again, this time about her home.

157

"In Cleveland, they call it The Fortress. The walls are ten feet thick! Stone, *awful* stone! Gray and nondescript and *awful*! My grandfather spent about a million dollars—back when that was a lot of money for a house—making the place *unassailable*! I don't know why grandfather wanted a house like that. Six-inch shells would bounce right off those walls. That house'll be standing there when the world ends! Why?"

"Maybe he was afraid?" Derry suggested.

"He wasn't afraid of anything, my grandfather. *I'm* afraid. I'm afraid of everything and especially of that house. Imagine being scared of a house! But I was."

Running herself down again.

Clearly she was well educated; yet she denied having any education at all. "Educated? *Me*?" Laughing her self-wounding laugh. "Why I couldn't stay in a school more than two weeks before they'd get wise to how dumb I was and throw me out. One school after another."

"You're not dumb, Sarah," Derry said. "Whatever else you are, you're not stupid. There must have been some other reason."

Sarah wore a look of paralyzing stupidity as if she were trying but failing to comprehend. Incomprehension was her trick, whether subconscious or not, for keeping him tied to that ringbolt. It might be a way out of this.

Her stupidity or pretended stupidity—plus her immense desire to please.

That night as she was spooning bread into his mouth, he said, "This bread is so hard it almost breaks my teeth. If you spread a little ketchup on it, it would soften it."

"Oh, would you like that?" Sarah's plain face breaking into a timid smile. "Wait! I'll get some."

She jumped out of the trailer, and he could hear her scrambling about inside the tractor. Derry kept his hopes in check. There were lots of ways to spread ketchup on bread—but a knife is what leaped to mind. Would she produce one? She'd said again and again she couldn't find a knife to cut him loose. But by putting knife into another context—ketchup spreading—perhaps. . . .

She was back in a few minutes brandishing the ketchup in one hand. In the other a knife—his knife, an ordinary table knife he'd brought along for use for picnic meats but it had a serrated edge that just might. . . .

Sarah was happily using it to spread ketchup on the stale bread.

"I could use that knife, Sarah," Derry said softly, "to cut the ropes."

She turned her dull gaze on him, mouth half open, the knife in her right hand. Clearly this possibility hadn't entered her mind.

"It's just a kitchen knife," she said, staring at it timorously.

"Just put the knife in my hand," Derry said, casually, not bearing down on it. "I'll see what I can do."

Now! he was thinking. *Now!*

It had to be done quickly or it wouldn't be done at all. Behind that dull gaze lay the sharp intelligence and total viciousness of Mickie. How fast did these personality changes occur? Sometimes, very rapidly. Sometimes quite slowly.

"Just put the knife in my right hand, Sarah."

While she was still Sarah.

Sarah gazed at him vacantly—her tremendous desire to please him at war with something deep within her. Slowly, she placed the knife in Derry's right hand.

Derry began sawing away, hard as he could with his unused muscles, on the rope on his left wrist. His eyes on Sarah's bland stupid face where the chemistry of change was already beginning.

The blank eyes started to light up. The lines of the face, soft and flabby as Sarah, were starting to firm. As Derry sawed away frantically at his left wrist, a ferment of upheaval was taking place inside the girl, a torment of change, not easy or quick or voluntary, something she appeared to have no control over. Anguish tore her face apart, the lips contorted, the body thrashing in physical pain.

The girl was changing before his eyes from the bland Sarah into the violent Mickie, a cataclysm of such intensity that it allowed for nothing else. She was so self-occupied that Derry had a few precious moments to free himself and he sawed away at the nylon, feeling the rope come apart strand by strand.

Sarah was now altogether Mickie, the face a snarl, but Derry still had a moment or two because she was exhausted and dazed, taking deep shuddery breaths. She was staring at Derry with her angry eyes, as if she didn't know where she was or who he was.

In those few seconds, the last strand parted and Derry's left hand was free. Just in time. Mickie had figured out not only who he was but what he was up to, and she leaped at him, screeching, fingers like claws. Derry gave her a short jab with his free hand, putting his shoulder into it. The punch sent her backward in a sprawl of arms and legs.

159

For precious seconds she lay on the metal floor, dazed. When she wobbled to her knees, she was swaying from side to side, hand feeling the jaw, eyes wild.

Derry used the moment to saw away at his right hand so viciously he cut into his wrist. But the rope parted. She was on him then with another rush—kicking, scratching, clawing, biting, Derry's legs still tied to the ringbolts. His hands were free, but he had no room for punches. Instead he used elbows and knees—elbows on her face, knees into the stomach.

Hands clinging to her. At all costs he must not let her get free to get her gun. Mickie biting his knuckles like a wild animal.

At some point she got the idea that getting away was smarter than fighting. She almost got free with a knee kick that tore his hand away. She scrambled away on all fours, but he hauled her back with one arm—an arm accustomed to throwing around hundred-pound feed sacks.

She came back, flailing with open hands, murderous nails raking his cheek, missing his eyes by inches. He was jabbing now with his right hand, holding her with his left, brutal punches to the jaw, to the eyes, to the head.

She lay quiet finally, the thin body bent into a fetal crouch, one bloodied eye gazing at him savagely.

Unbeaten, that eye.

Derry licked his knuckles, winded and heartsick. First time in his life he'd ever hit a woman.

Never taking his eyes off her, still distrusting, Derry untied his legs from the ringbolt and stood up in the trailer. He stepped around her carefully and then came down hard on her shoulders, rolling her onto her stomach, his knee in her back.

There was no resistance. The body rolled over limp as a sack of wheat.

With the ropes he'd taken off his own legs, he bound her arms in a series of double hitches, the knot he used on fractious horses, and tied her to the very ringbolts he'd just got loose from. With another rope he tied her legs and fastened them to another ringbolt.

Overkill, the second tying, but he did it anyway, so fiercely did he distrust her. After the deed was done, Derry sat cross-legged contemplating the pulpy face. This girl who'd fucked him, kidnapped him, sneered at him, lusted with him, drugged him. The gamut.

He'd looked forward to freedom for months, and now that he had it, he was demoralized. Sitting there, cross-legged, chin cupped in his hand, eyeing the fetal body, trying to understand.

And to forgive.

Not her viciousness. His.

After a bit, he roused himself to search the girl; his hands running over every inch of that body that he'd had sex with so many times and in so many ways. No gun and no keys. Not anything here but Mickie's skinny bones and bruised flesh. Her unbeaten eye closed now.

Derry left the trailer and went to the cab.

Twilight veiled the landscape, freshening the air and bringing out the smells of pine and winter earth. Derry inhaled his liberation now like oxygen, his muscles loosening, brain working again.

Jessie.

She'd hardly crossed his mind, so obsessed was he with Mickie-Sarah-Vanessa. After Jessie, the farm. He thought of his animals—two by two—as if he were Noah—horses, pigs, chickens, ducks, goats.

Money! Where was the twenty-four hundred dollars? Or what was left of it? He'd searched Mickie from crotch to gizzard. She hadn't a quarter.

He went through the cab, which had little place for concealment. In the glove compartment, he found the keys Sarah said she couldn't find, road maps, including one of Tennessee that Mickie must have acquired, and a flashlight. In a white paper sack, he found a brown powder with a sharp smell. He tasted it. Hashish exploded in his mouth. He spit quickly, again and again, and scattered the brown drug over the grass. .

With the keys he unlocked the luggage compartment on the driver's side of the tractor. There was his canvas bag with his shirts, his extra socks. Nothing missing.

Except the money.

The luggage compartment on the other side of the tractor contained the tractor's tools, the wrenches, hose lines, special ratchets designed for the tractor. The only other object was a TWA flight bag Derry had never seen before. He emptied the bag on the ground—stockings, three pairs of panties (Mickie never wore them) and a cotton dress. Brown with white cuffs.

Underneath the collar lay a label. . . .

Made for Sarah Framingham by Caldwalder of Cleveland.

Derry held up the dress in the twilight. It expressed Sarah at her most nondescript, the brown as close to colorlessness as a color could get.

Framingham? Framingham of Cleveland? Derry dimly recollected the name. They owned all the cement in Cleveland. Or in the Western world.

Something like that. Old wealth, dating from the 1880s. If a Framingham was missing, wouldn't there be an uproar in the papers?

No money anywhere in the cab or on the girl. Not a penny.

The gun was missing, too.

Derry took the flashlight and searched under both tractor and trailer, then the engine cavities which lay behind the cab. He climbed on the roof and searched that. Nothing.

The forest? There was miles of it but why should she? . . .

Why did Mickie-Sarah-Vanessa do any of the things Mickie-Sarah-Vanessa did?

He started back to the trailer and stopped before he'd taken three steps. She was singing. *Singing!*

We are poor little lambs who have gone astray.
Baa! Baaa! Baaaa!

In a pure, sweet childlike voice.

Sarah's voice.

Derry crept back into the vast trailer and looked down at her as she sang, oblivious:

Gentlemen songsters off on a spree
Damned from here to eternity.

The words pouring out of the battered lips, drenched in innocence. The face was ghastly. One eye was closed altogether, the other half shut. Both lips were split, huge purple bruises disfigured the cheeks. The jaw was swollen to twice its size on one side, and cut on the other. The eyes were blackened.

Derry went on his knees: "Sarah, I didn't mean to hit *you*! It was Mickie. . . ."

She paid no attention. Singing her song like Ophelia in *Hamlet*—her epilogue.

After a while she fell silent.

Derry on his knees: "Sarah, where is the money? It's important. It's the money for the mortgage. Money to pay the bills. I could lose my farm if I don't pay."

She stared with her one eye as if she hadn't heard.

Presently she started singing again:

162

There's a long long trail a-winding
Into the land of my dreams
Where the nightingale is singing
And the pale moon beams.

Derry crept out of the trailer and back to the tractor. Night had fallen moonless, black as ink. Inside the cab, Derry went over his gauges. Gas tanks half full—maybe 120 gallons. There seemed to be plenty of oil and the batteries were okay.

He opened a can of beans and ate them cold.

It occurred to him that Sarah might be hungry, and he clambered back into the trailer to ask. She was still singing old songs, sad songs:

Where have all the flowers gone?

"Would you like something to eat, Sarah?"

She who had fed him when he was tied up.

She sang away, paying no heed.

He had to try to explain anyway. "Sarah, I hate to leave you tied up like this, but I don't dare let you loose. You'd turn into Mickie again, and we've both had enough of that. I'm sorry."

A lunatic apology, considering how she'd had him tied up for months. He felt better having made it.

He stretched out in the bed behind the wheel in the cab of the tractor. She was still singing:

Nobody's sweetheart now.
It all seems wrong somehow.
Painted lips, painted eyes.
Dressed in a gown of paradise. . . ."

She knew a lot of old songs.

At first light, he searched the woods, looking for newly turned earth, examining the crotches of trees, feeling his way through the underbrush.

No money.

Eight o'clock now, the sun blazing.

Inside the trailer, the girl lay silent, eyes closed. Again Derry asked her if she'd like food. Or water. When she didn't answer he tried to get a little

163

water in her mouth, but it gushed to the metal floor of the trailer, wetting her sweater on the way.

Once again he asked her about the money. She said nothing, off in her private hell, beyond his reach.

From the five-gallon can, Derry poured a gallon of pure ether down the huge stainless steel smokestack. The engine turned over sluggishly, indifferent from disuse and cold. For thirty seconds, Derry bore down on the starter, getting only a single cough. He climbed back on to the roof of the cab with his ether can and poured another two gallons down the smoke stack. If the battery ran down, that would be the end of it. . . .

Again he turned the key in the lock. This time the diesel engine roared for twenty seconds—and died. Three gallons of ether left. Derry clambered back onto the roof and poured two gallons of the precious stuff down the stack.

This time it caught and held in a continuing roar.

Derry warmed the engine for ten minutes, not taking any chances of it dying on him again. Meanwhile he studied the map of Tennessee. The only clue he had was that highway sign 158 W. They were in mountains. National Park, she'd said. Not too many of those in Tennessee.

Highway 158 W led out of Remsville right up the Cumberland Mountains with part of it covered by a troll symbol, which meant National Park. Tracing the road with his finger, his eye caught . . .

Kinkajou.

"Kinkajou 'bout the size of fifteen cents," Hector Larrabee had said. "Poor as an orphan child but mighty pretty in spring."

There it was in the Cumberlands, not far from Remsville.

It took two hours to drive down the mountain down the hard-packed red dirt road, never meant for anything as big as the cornbinder. Derry's right foot rode the tractor brake; his right hand never left the trailer brake rod, the big rig making hairpin turns, threatening to jackknife at every moment. Some of the turns were too much for the cornbinder and Derry simply left the track and sent the great beast plunging through the undergrowth uprooting what lay in its path by brute strength.

Twice he stopped and climbed into the trailer to see how Sarah was, seeking reassurance. Finding none. None at all. Sarah was as empty of presence as an unoccupied grave. He felt her forehead which was clammy, her pulse which was faint. What little of the face was not purple or red with bruises was ashen.

164

Terrible moments, the most terrible moments of his whole life.

What have I done?

In Remsville, a small crossroads town, Derry drove past Southern Store, Pinker's Cafe which had a Teem sign over it, Wrench's Ladies Fashions, and the post office, from which a pay phone hung. Derry stopped the big truck and tried to make a call home. He hadn't even a dime to call the operator—and anyway the phone was out of order. So that was that.

Twenty minutes later he turned off A 38 where a sign pointed to Kinkajou. An ancient black man with a wooly thatch of snow-white hair sat on a rock at the turn, looking at the huge truck with astonished eyes.

Derry stopped. "You going to Kinkajou? Climb in."

The old man stared back, silent and hostile. It took a very long time, but eventually he rose to his feet, painfully, the feet wide apart as if the old man were unsure of his balance, supporting his bent body on a bamboo cane. With immense dignity he walked, wide spraddled, to the truck. Derry leaned out of the cab to help him up. The ancient acted as if he didn't want to but he had no choice.

Derry slipped the big truck into first gear. "You know Hector Larrabee?"

The old man's mouth fell open, his eyes widened. He frowned; he snuffed; he moved his feet. Excessive reaction to so harmless a question.

Derry waited.

They were driving through a landscape of towering live oaks, lining the green fields that looked as if they had been untilled since the Civil War. Now and then they passed unpainted wooded houses, porches clinging to them like moths to a branch.

The old man taking his time, white eyebrows beetling. Finally, he said, "Ev'body asking aftah Hector."

They passed a goat tethered to an oak. Derry said, "Hector and I are good friends."

Trying to thaw the old man out a bit. After a while, he added, "Who else been asking after Hector?"

The old man took his time, looking over Derry narrowly.

"Three white men," he said finally. "They give him a bad time."

Derry didn't like any of it.

Kinkajou sprawled across the road with exhausted dignity, traces of white paint still on its few buildings. At its center stood what was once a hotel, its wide verandah sagging in the middle, upper stories boarded up. The lower story had been transformed into Miranda's store, which sold

165

nails, Coca Cola, processed meats, and toothpaste—and was also the post office. Opposite Miranda's were four once-white houses, on a steep hill almost concealed by great trees. That was Kinkajou. Fifteen cents about covered it.

"I get off heah," the ancient said firmly. "Hector live right ovah theah." Pointing to the last of the four white houses up the hill. With that he scrambled down, bamboo cane in hand, and with his wide-spraddled walk disappeared into Miranda's store.

Derry left the engine idling, not wanting to wrestle with a cold diesel engine again, crossed the road and climbed the wooden steps leading up the steep hill to Hector's front porch. Kinkajou lay in eerie silence. No village should be that silent at 10 A.M. Something was wrong.

It was a nice house, more recently painted than anything else in Kinkajou, its two windows covered in glass that had been washed within living memory, its verandah swept. The door stood open, and Derry stepped inside a room in deep shade from the towering trees around it. The room contained a bare table, a threadbare sofa, two badly worn upholstered chairs—Hector seated in one of them.

The black man rose, unsmiling, and confronted Derry. There was no welcome in his gaze.

"You been a long time coming," he said in neutral tones. "And I won't pretend I'm happy to see you, Mr. Jenkins."

Derry frowned and moved his shoulder. "Somebody give you a bad time, Hector. Mancuso?"

"And his bully boys." Hector rolled up his sleeve. The arm was just one long red welt, from wrist to elbow. An old wound, still healing. "They do that with boiling water," Hector said gravely.

"Why?" Derry cried.

"He asking me where you is. Where that girl is. I tell him I don't know. Again and again."

Hector had crossed the room and peered out the door into the sunshine, the big rig puffing diesel smoke into the air.

"Where is she, Mr. Jenkins? Where Mickie?"

"In the back of the rig," Derry whispered. "It's a long story."

"Ain't got time for long stories. Mancuso scattered money round this village. If you show up—or if *she* showed up—give him a ring and they be more money. They only six phones in all Kinkajou, and right this very minute, all six of 'em is trying to call Mancuso—or his men. You got to get that rig out this town."

166

"You better come along," Derry said. "Unless you want some more of that boiling water."

Hector nodded, the black face expressionless. Five minutes later the big rig left Kinkajou, in low gear, climbing up and down the hills of Tennessee, and within the hour they were back on A 38.

Derry told him the story of Mickie-Sarah. Leaving out Vanessa who was pretty hard to explain.

"Mickie tell you a lot of lies," Hector said. "Mancuso didn't try to rape her. Other way around. She try to get into his pants, and he fire her. She stole his gun and his money. Oney it weren't his money. It were Mob money. The Mob don't like having they money stolen. *They* steal. The rest of us not supposed to."

"How much?"

"Mr. Mancuso not about to tell us that. A lot."

"She took my money too," Derry said.

Two miles outside Remsville, Derry pulled into a grove of trees, and the two men climbed into the trailer.

The girl lay still, eyes closed. Derry felt the pulse, faint and distant. Hector put his hands at the base of the girl's neck where the cords stood out much too far.

Neither man said anything till they were outside the trailer. "We've got to get her to the hospital," Derry said.

"Yeah," the black man said. "You gone take that battered girl to the hospital—and tell them what?"

"The truth."

Hector smiled. For the first time. A gentle smile. "Mistah Jenkins, I done you wrong. You is a truth-tellin' man. And a good man. But this is not a time for truth-tellin'. You go to that hospital and tell 'em that little slip of a girl tied *you* up, kidnapped *you*? You think they believe that? Or the police either?"

Derry was silent.

"They's a hospital in Andersonville," the black man said. "When we get there, I do the talking. We find that girl by the side of the road, all beat up. We no idea who she is."

Derry nodded. The black man was a more creative liar, no question of it. Truth-telling was a luxury of the white races. A southern black man must lie to survive.

Hector was saying, "They gone to ask for you driver license. You Social Security card. You got another driver's license?"

Derry couldn't comprehend, Hector had taken out his wallet and was shuffling through a mass of cards. "There you is."

Hector Larabee, Homer Lamb. Same initials.

"Beside the police lookin' for you, they is the little matter of Mancuso and his friends lookin' for you. We don't want any record of Derry Jenkins in this area."

Derry stared at the card with his new identity.

Hector still talking, slowly, persuasively, taking charge. "First thing we gone do, Mistah Jenkins, is unloose that girl from those ropes. She no threat to you now. Not the way she is."

The two men climbed back into the trailer.

The mouth hung open now. So did one eye. Staring at nothing.

Derry felt for the pulse, knowing it was no use, going through the motions, devastated.

He closed the one eye, squeezed shut the bruised lips, cupped the bruised face he had known so intimately one last time in both hands. Mourning each of her separately—Mickie, Vanessa, Sarah.

Most of all, Sarah.

__ CHAPTER __
FIFTEEN

A YELLOW MOON hung over the towering sycamore like the flame of a candle, smoky in the mist. Derry was digging with the trenching tool, which was entirely inadequate. Hector sat at graveside, unhappy about the sycamore.

The sycamore had been Derry's idea. The tallest tree in the forest, only sycamore in miles. His requiem for Sarah. "In case we ever want to find her again," he explained.

"Don't want nobody to find that girl. Ever," Hector said.

"She's going to haunt me, Hector."

"Only if you let her," Hector said. "Gimme that tool. You take a rest."

Derry climbed out of the hole and walked over to the cornbinder parked in the same glade where he and Mickie and Sarah and Vanessa had spent months. Hector's idea. "Money up there somewhere because where else it at. You got to find that money if you ever gone be free of Mancuso and his bully boys."

So Derry drove the cornbinder back up the mountain through all those hairpin turns under a yellow moon that glared like an accusation.

The girl lay on her back, hands folded across her chest, a figure on a medieval sarcophagus. Derry had folded the hands, brushed the hair, smoothed the bruised face. In death she was Sarah Framingham. No trace of Mickie or Vanessa. It was a face that had suffered much, the suffering nakedly exposed.

On his knees before the dead girl. Derry leaned down and kissed the lips. Expiation.

On his knees, he said, "It's not over, is it, Sarah?"

"I'm sorry," Sarah said. "I wish it were."

"You must stop apologizing," Derry said. "Now that you're dead."

Derry went back to the grave site and sat on a log. "How did Mickie arrive at Ocala?" he asked. "I got to know."

The black man looked pained. He didn't want to talk about Mickie, and Derry didn't want to talk about anything else. "She come on foot. Walked all the way from Ocala to the stud farm—eleven mile. Nobody walk in Florida, but *she* walk cause that's way she was."

Hector stopped digging and faced the white man to see how he was taking this. The white man was in a state of enchantment. Hector knew the signs, knew all there was to know about enchantment—especially the fact that you couldn't hurry it. You had to play it slow.

"She carry a little flight bag over her shoulder on a stick, and she tell Mancuso—I heard her, I was there—she know horses. She can muck out, she can exercise."

"She *rode?*"

"Good rider. Strong hands, good seat."

Derry listened, entranced.

Hector hated that entrancement. But you couldn't hurry it, or it would turn into something worse.

"She'd gallop twelve horses on good days. On her bad days, she weren't worth spit. She'd hang around stables making eyes at the grooms. She slept with 'em all. Every last one."

Eye on Derry to see what that did. Derry looked as if he'd been stabbed in the heart. The white man leaped into the hole and took the trenching tool. "My turn," he said and started to turn earth savagely, Hector leaping out of the way in the nick of time.

Derry spaded the earth passionately. Hector sat on the fresh earth and looked at the moon. After awhile, Derry slowed a bit and said, "Why'd she steal Mancuso's money? The one thing that would make him come after her!"

The black man rubbed his face with his long tapering fingers. "She steal Mancuso's money because that the worst thing could happen to Mancuso. You take away that man's money, you ain't got much left. She knew how to get at him, and she *got* at him. She laid a curse on that man, and you got to live with that curse, Derry. You better understand that."

Derry was in a hole now, almost to his shoulders. It was to be a proper

170

grave. He changed the subject. "I read about this man who had eleven different personalities. None of his personalities was aware of any of the others. One of his eleven personalities committed a whole series of murders the other ten didn't even know about. Do you understand, Hector? Mickie was the guilty one. Sarah can't be held responsible for what Mickie did."

Hector was not about to contradict a man in enchantment. Instead he said, "We all do it, *Mistah Lamb.*" Bearing down heavy on the *Mistah Lamb*, the name on that faked Social Security card, to jar Derry into realizing he was not above assuming a new identity either. "These bad times, Mistah Lamb. Man got to shed his skin like a snake sometime two three time a year or they be on you, pinning you to the wall."

They buried Mickie by the last rays of the pale yellow moon before it sank behind the pines. The next morning they obliterated all traces. They tamped down the red earth they had dug up. Over it they laid strips of turf studded with violet and fern, which would flourish after the first rain.

Headstone for three girls. Violet for Vanessa, fern for Mickie, with towering sycamore for Sarah.

After that they searched for the money in ever-widening circles, starting with the truck and going down the hill through thicket and gully, under leaf and pine needle.

Meanwhile threshing a few things out.

"Why did Mancuso come after you, Hector? Why not me? Why not Jenkins Farm?"

"He don't know where you live, Derry."

"He should have known my address. I wrote him letters. He got my invoice."

"Mickie took those too, along with the money."

"Why, for heaven's sake?"

Hector leaned against a tree and wiped his face with his sleeve. White people could be very dense sometimes. "She getting at you, Derry. You don't pay her no mind, and she don't like that. What worse thing she kin do to you? Git Mancuso and his bully boys on the trail, and way to do that is to steal his money and go off with you. She make very sure ev'body knows she go off with you because you the only thing that leave the stud farm that evenin'. She couldn't get off the farm any other way. Mancuso come after me because he think you and me good friends, and I know where you is. But I don't."

171

*　　*　　*

It was Hector who found it, what was left of it, beside the pond where they'd drawn water. From the little pile, the two men fished unburned fragments of Benjamin Franklin's rotund face, little bits of U. S. Grant, traces of Andrew Jackson and his spit curl. It was quite a large pile of ashes.

"How many hundred-dollar bills make pile of ashes that size, you reckon?" Hector asked.

Derry shook his head.

Derry drove the cornbinder down the mountain again, plunging through the underbrush recklessly where before he'd tiptoed, the big truck careening from side to side. Hector clung to his side of the cab by the handle of the door, his face set in a frown of concentration, eyes on Derry whose own eyes were far away.

Hector tried to get him back to earth. "You out of it now. Take this veehickle back to the people and say you sorry, pay the penalty, go home. It's over."

"It's not over," Derry raged. "It's just begun."

The dead girl tried. "There's nothing you can do, Derry," Sarah said. "Not any more."

"I killed you," Derry said as if that were explanation. There was just no way of getting round that.

When they got off the mountain back on A 38, Hector had had enough. "Just let me out here. I git home okay."

Hector pointed to the map; the road back to Dobbsville, Virginia, lay that way—the shortest route. He, Hector, could hitch a lift.

"I brought you here. I'll take you home," Derry said.

"Mancuso already in Kinkajou. You in *trouble,* Derry. Whyn't you just pay *attention!*"

Going down A 38 now at seventy miles an hour. Past all those fields that had not been tilled for generations.

"You ever married, Hector?"

"Once."

"What happened?"

"She too big a gal for Kinkajou. She went off to Nashville where she still at. Living with my cousin. We still friends."

At Remsville, Hector tried again to get out of the truck, but Derry insisted on taking him a little closer to Kinkajou.

172

A mistake.

Derry planned to let Hector out where A 38 met the little road to Kinkajou. A ninety-degree right turn. Right at the junction, seated on a stone was the white-thatched black man Derry had earlier given a lift to.

His black face set in a scowl of pure thunder. Something very funny about that.

"Mistah Pippin!" Hector said, surprised.

The old man saw them as soon as Derry saw him, and the white-thatched head began to shake from side to side, eyes so wide they could see the fury in him a hundred yards away.

"He tryin' to tell us somethin'!" Hector cried. "Don't you go making that turn, Derry! Don't even slow down!"

Derry gunned it, and the huge truck leaped forward, screaming.

Somebody else got the black man's message. The two in the truck heard the shot through the obscuring noise of their own truck's roar—a sort of pop, small but unmistakably evil. The white-thatched man toppled over backward from his stone, his short wide-spraddled legs pointing skyward.

The great truck shot past the intersection just as Mr. Pippin fell backward, Derry catching a last glimpse of the old fellow, eyes staring with great dignity at nothing, a small round hole in his forehead.

A very good shot, Derry thought. Professional.

He shifted from ninth to tenth to eleventh, picking up speed. Eye on the rearview mirror.

No pursuit at first. The ambush hadn't worked. Clearly they weren't prepared for pursuit.

Derry shifted from eleventh to twelfth and finally to thirteenth, gaining speed. "They'll be after us in something faster than this rig," he said to Hector. "We got to get off, you know that."

"Mile up this road. An open field. On the othah side is woods. If you kin make it."

"I'll try."

The rig going as fast as he could push it, which was now ninety-five—too fast for cornbinders or anything with eighteen wheels.

The curse of Mickie costing the old black man his life.

At the crest of the next hill, Derry glanced at his rearview mirror, and there it was—a black car that looked very fast—certainly faster than a cornbinder. Almost a mile back.

"We got to hit that field and git out of sight before they catch us," Hector said, very calm.

173

"I'll try," Derry said. Exultant. I know no fear! he said to himself.

Roaring along at a hundred miles an hour in an eighteen-wheeler, pursued by professional gunmen.

This was the life!

Derry grinning savagely. The glee was not lost on Hector who clung to the latch, eyes on Derry, shaking his head. No good would come of this enjoyment!

"The field right up theah. You bettah start brakin' this cornbinder."

"Hang on," Derry said.

He pushed the air brake and slammed forward on the wheel, Hector almost going through the windshield, as the great truck came down from a hundred to forty, to thirty, to twenty, to ten—then swung off the big road through the yawning aperture into the open field grown over with weeds and brambles, unplowed, untilled, untended for a generation—the great wheels jolting in agony.

"Keep it movin'," Hector prayed to Derry. To God. To both oif them at once.

If the truck once stopped, there's be nothing to hope for.

Over ruts, over brush, over stumps the huge truck hopped and skipped like an elephant going through a field of mice. But it kept on, even gaining speed, getting its footing. Ahead of them loomed woods thick as night.

"You got to just git into 'em somehow so they close around us," Hector said.

"She's doing the best she can," Derry said, gunning it.

Hanging on to the wheel with all his strength.

At thirty miles an hour, it struck underbrush, Derry steering it away from the bigger trees, toppling the smaller ones, the trailer yawing wildly behind.

For forty yards the cornbinder plowed through trees and underbrush until it came up against a steep rise, Derry just managing to steer it between two oaks. There it slammed against a maple that was too big to argue with; the engine gave up the fight and died, the trailer tipping against three big trees which left it at a forty-five degree angle.

After the roar of engine and wind, it was eerily quiet. Derry looked out his sideview mirror. He could see nothing but underbrush. Which meant, he hoped, that no one could see him. They waited quietly. They could hear the black car screaming along at what must have been better than a hundred

174

even from where they lay two hundred yards from the road. Heard it approach and heard it dwindle in the distance.

"Now what do we do?" Derry asked, feeling again that terrible exultance that had so gripped him during the chase.

"Walk," Hector said.

__ CHAPTER __
SIXTEEN

"JESSIE!" DERRY SAID into the phone.

In a little village called Watercress, Tennessee, at ten o'clock at night. The grocery store had long since closed, and the phone booth that stood near the gas pump was the first one they'd found that was not vandalized and broken.

Across the wire he heard the sobbing outcry. Jessie who almost never cried. "Derry! Where are you?"

He'd planned the answer—which wasn't an answer—long in advance. He couldn't explain because there were no words for his situation. "Jessie, I love you very much. You must always remember that."

It was not at all what she wanted to hear. He knew that.

The wail of her voice tore at him. "Derry when are you coming *home*? I got the farm on my neck! The mortgage! . . ."

"I can't come home, Jessie. I can't."

"Why not?"

Derry couldn't even answer that to himself. It was what Hector was asking: why not?

A long pause before he said it. "I've killed a woman, Jessie. I didn't mean to but I did. I can't come home just yet because there are things to be done about that."

"Derry why . . ."

As if he knew. He wanted to get her off now because he couldn't explain. There were no explanations. Just obsession.

177

"Jessie, I can't talk any more now. There are people looking for me, and I got to get out of here or I'll get killed. I love you, Jessie. Just don't make any mistake about that."

That last bit was aimed at himself more than at her. Reassuring himself that when it was all over everything would be again just as it was before it began, knowing that it wouldn't be, but hoping.

Killed a woman. What would Jessie think about that? His proper prim angelic schoolteacher wife? Would she have him back after that?

Derry strode out of the phone booth and down the country road, not paying any attention to Hector, who followed, disapproving.

The road sign said Nashville 15. Pointing west.

Hector a step and a half back of him, not liking any of it. "Ain't nobody after you now, Derry. And you didn't have to tell her. Who knows 'bout you killing that girl 'cept me. You could go home."

"I can't go home yet." Derry striding down the road, face black as thunder. He didn't want to talk about it because he couldn't explain it to Hector any more than he could to Jessie.

Even Sarah disapproved. "There's nothing you can do for me now," Sarah said. "You should go home."

He couldn't talk about it to Sarah because she was at the heart of it. Why did Mickie want to kill her father (who was also Sarah's father)? But you could hardly tell this to Sarah who loved her father. What he said was, "You're a very important person, Sarah. You're all of us wrapped up in one tidy bundle, and I want to understand—and since you're dead, I'll have to go to Cleveland for the answers because where else would I get them?"

"You won't like Cleveland," Sarah said. "Not you."

Hector following along a step and a half back, a wry look on his black face. He, too, homeless. Couldn't go back to Kinkajou till the spell was broken, whenever that was.

Three hours later they were in Nashville, walking through the peeling streets, under the sodium lights.

"They seem to be pulling the place down," Derry said.

"You a country boy," Hector said. "You don' realize they tear down the cities ev'y few years as a form of penance faw they sins. It keep ev'body busy and broke, which is the bes' way to keep the people quiet."

It was certainly quiet in the sleeping city, their footfalls on the hard pavement making the only sound.

They were looking for Hector's cousin's house, and presently they found it. A brick building with a fading advertisement for Dr. Pepper on its wall,

178

the windows devoid of glass or even boards, looking under the glare of the sodium street lamp like a stage set for *West Side Story*.

"People has moved," Hector said.

The pair crossed the street under the brilliant white light, mounted the stone steps whose balustrades had disappeared along with windows and doors.

"It was never a very good neighborhood even when cousin lived here."

"The neighborhood seems to have moved away," Derry said.

"You ever live in a city, Derry?"

"Never."

"Ah didn't think so. Come upstairs. I show you where my cousin used to sleep with my wife."

"Ex-wife."

"I don't think we divorced. I just don't know."

They climbed the stairs through the fallen plaster and mouse droppings, the steps rickety and insubstantial under their tread.

"This your cousin's room?" Derry asked.

It was filled with cardboard boxes full of moldy shoes. Several boxes contained books whose covers were falling off. The lone window looked out on an asphalt parking lot that contained no cars.

"They was going to improve this part of town. They got this far, and then they went away and forgot."

Derry leaned against the wall and let his legs lower him to a sitting position on the floor. He took off his shoes and caressed his weary feet, soothing each toe as if it were a recalcitrant child.

"Where you suppose your cousin is now?" he asked.

"Nashville someplace," Hector said. "He very ambitious, my cousin. He has bettered himself, you can count on that. My cousin believe in helpin' himself."

To Hector's wife, among other things.

Hector had subsided to the floor, his back against the wall, opposite to Derry. He reached into his pocket and fetched out a Milky Way candy bar, which he divided carefully in half. He threw one half to Derry and bit into the other half.

"Tha's all the food till mawnin'," he said.

"Thanks," Derry said, and chewed on his half. "How far's Cleveland?"

" 'Bout a thousand miles."

"I got to get to Cleveland."

Hector rubbed the crumbs of candy bar from his lips. "Not tonight."

179

__ CHAPTER __
SEVENTEEN

DERRY WAS THE only white person there. He felt the stares on the back of his white neck, the heat of hostility toughening his hide. Everything about Nashville did that to him.

The girl was finishing her set in what sounded like a scream of rage:

> *Get away from me man, get away, get away!*
> *I'm an all-alone girl, in an all-alone whirl*
> *It's better that way, that way, that way!*

Hector's wife.

She was a real shouter, imposing her authority all over that noisy, smoky room, which was packed to the walls. A second-story room over a grocery store, tucked behind a big electric sign advertising Marlboro cigarettes— from which it stole all its electricity. Derry could see the wire leading in through the window, connecting all the lamps on the tables, the lamps just wine bottles with electric sockets in their necks. The tables were tiny, covered with red-and-white checked cloths.

Derry and Hector sat with Julius, Hector's cousin, at one little table, barely big enough for two. Each with a glass of red wine.

"We got to grab some scam," Hector was saying over the tumult.

Hector's personality, his language, his appearance, had changed in the city. He swam in the urban sea effortlessly as a fish, speaking the vernacular, looking the part.

Julius was scowling and shaking his head. He was a very young skinny black with a large Adam's apple. He wore skin-tight green trousers, an orange shirt unbuttoned almost to his navel, with a gold chain around his neck from which hung a medallion in which a snake embraced a lizard.

"Not much sting around except street sales."

"I won't handle smack," Hector said. "I disapprove."

"Smack's out. It's glitter now. Whitey got the bad habit now, not us." Julius smiled like an otter, all teeth and playfulness, as if it were all a game. A dangerous one.

Hector nodded toward Derry. "He can't mix with that."

"Why not?" Derry asked. He was learning the new words very fast.

"Because you white on the outside and white on the inside that's why not," Hector said. "Anyway they's other things. Street ain't the only place to turn a dollar. They's the road."

The singer, whose name was Cassandra, made her way to the table and sat down. "How'd you get a name like Cassandra?" Derry asked.

"My dear mom," Cassandra said. "She said I bad news." Eyeing Derry flagrantly. "You stick out here like a clam on a birthday cake. You know that, don't you?"

"Maybe I should black up," Derry said.

The girl laughed a hoot. "You be mighty tasty."

"Come! Come! Come!" Julius said scowling.

"I've been known to do that," the girl said. "What's this whitey's name?"

"We in the process of changing it," Hector said. "We changing every-thing 'bout him 'cept his color."

"Don't change his shape," Cassandra said. "He got a nice shape."

Cassandra's last set was at 1 A.M. She sang a lot of smoke songs against the beat, rocking the dancers back on their heels. Then it was 2 A.M., and they shifted to Julius' apartment on Terence Street, which looked like a furniture store. Much too much furniture, all of it spanking-new, unsat-on, factory clean. Cassandra made them bacon and eggs in the Teflon stick-proof fry pan while Derry roamed the kitchen inspecting the microwave ovens, the frost-free automatic refrigerator with the illuminated freezer that showed where everything was and that made ice cubes right in front of your eyes, the cerise telephone that remembered telephone numbers, the glass-topped table that had an aquarium built into it with fish swimming about just under the food.

"It fell off a truck, all this stuff," Cassandra explained. "Right in front of the house. Only thing is it didn't fall upstairs. We had to carry it up those steep stairs."

"Life's unfair," Derry commented and wandered into the bedrooms to see what he could see. They were unbelievably neat, bedspreads on every bed, not a speck of dust anywhere, curtains drawn, everything new and gleaming, having fallen off the same truck.

"Looks like a demonstration bedroom at the World of Tomorrow," Derry said.

Hector tried to explain urban life to the country boy. "Julius is on welfare again. He made the mistake of working a straight job for a while. It lowered his standard of living sumpin fierce. He never make *that* mistake again."

Derry and Hector and Cassandra ate the scrambled eggs on the glass-topped table over the fish tank while Julius was on the phone. "Cool and *very* sharp," Julius was saying into the phone. "He mah cousin." He did a lot of listening, interspersed with *mmms* and *yeahs*, scribbling with a pencil on a scratch pad. Afterward he ate his scrambled eggs and said nothing until he finished. "Delivery job," he said then. "To Chicago. It's not Cleveland, but it's closer than Nashville."

"Deliver what?" Derry asked.

"Farm combines. Weight twelve tons apiece, and they do all the things the farmer used to do—pick the carrots, clean 'em weigh 'em and bag 'em—everything but eat 'em. Oney ninety thousand dollars apiece."

"They fall off a truck, too?" Derry asked.

Everyone went very quiet. Julius said, "These people ain't got much sense of humor. Just do what the man says. No jokes."

Derry didn't answer back. He had to get to Cleveland.

"You both gone need papers, but you got a week. You get a little juice up front so you can buy a pair of trousers." They were both still in blue jeans. To Derry, Julius said, "I think you better grow a little hair on your face before you get your picture took."

Derry rubbed his hairless chin, feeling his identity slipping away. He'd been Homer Lamb, for twenty-four hours, and it had already subtly modified his character, even his manner of speaking. Now he was going to change his appearance itself, and he could feel the stirrings of a new personality taking root. *You're all of us wrapped up in a single strand,* he had said to Sarah. Multiple Sarah with a different personality for each raging need.

Much later Cassandra crawled into Derry's bed. "I wanted to feel your muscles, farm boy," she whispered.

Hector was sleeping in a twin bed not two feet away.

"Risky," Derry muttered.

183

"The best things always are," Cassandra whispered, kissing him on the lips, pressing her naked body against his, without losing the thread. "I got to tell you that delivery job no picnic. They catch you you git ten years."

Derry's new name was Gerald Moore. That way Hector could call him Jerry, which was close enough to Derry for both of them to be at ease with it. The Social Security card in the name of Gerald Moore was very high-quality work.

They waited for the beard to grow, blond, curly, ragged, before they got the pictures taken for the driver's license. Hector got the Class A license, logbooks, invoices, tonnage permits from Tennessee to Illinois—all the documentation needed to go from here to there, all of it forgery, very good stuff.

Meanwhile living in Julius' flat where nothing was what it seemed. Julius was out of work, but his every moment was occupied. He was in and out of the apartment all day, on mysterious errands after brief laconic telephone conversations. Derry would watch him, through the glass curtains, as he'd drive away in a Mercury cabriolet, new and gleaming like everything else in Julius' life. An hour later—or two—or three he'd be back, driving a Cadillac. Or a Lincoln. Anyway something else.

When Derry looked out, the Cadillac would have disappeared, and in its place would be a Dodge truck. Brand new. It too would then be driven off never to be seen again.

Objects flowed through the apartment—color TV sets, computers, matched sets of golf clubs, sterling silver, china, mirrors, glassware—coming up the steep stairs, Derry carrying some of it up himself to keep in trim—and then flow out again a day or so later. Derry would help load it on quite proper-looking trucks bearing the names of the merchants who bought the stuff. All in broad daylight.

"Doesn't he ever get tagged?" Derry asked.

"All the time," Hector said wryly. "Julius not very smart. He got twenty-six indictments against him right now, but these things never come to trial. The lawyers delay. The witnesses disappear. Documents get lost. You know."

Derry didn't. But he was learning.

Hector, whose new name was Harold Crampton, and Derry ventured out only at night usually to watch Cassandra sing wherever she was singing.

Every night without fail she showed up in his bed—each night with a new warning. "You could get hijacked just as easy, and don't you go offering any resistance. Just put your pretty hands over your pretty head."

Another night, "Them combines gone be overweight for Illinois road. You got to be mighty careful."

Still another night, "They's big insurance on them two combines and it might suit the man to torch 'em with you in 'em—so watch it."

"They don't call you Cassandra for nothing," Derry whispered.

Everything between them in whispers, including the sex which was gentle and dreamy.

Hector sleeping two feet away.

One night she whispered, "I'll meet you in Chicago. I got friends."

"Not Chicago," Derry said.

"Cleveland then."

"Not Cleveland either."

"We gone meet someplace, white man," she whispered. "It's in the deck."

"Why're you asking me, then? You're the Cassandra here. Not me."

The black girl laughed her soft laugh and bit his ear.

Fifteen minutes later she was gone back to her own bed. And Julius'.

Derry would be left alone with his conscience, in which Jessie loomed large. My wife. My girl. The central fact of my existence. Jessie is flesh and bone and high purpose. She is what gives my life meaning. So he kept telling himself.

But he didn't go home.

The days slipped by.

"What're we waiting for?" Derry asked.

"They haven't stolen the stuff yet," Hector said. "These things done on order. Customer want a particular brand of goods, and he specify exactly what he want. Then you got to go find it, and get it exactly right. Takes a little while."

Modern thievery was custom-built, Derry was finding out, highly organized and impersonal.

One day the combines appeared, freshly painted with new serial numbers as false as Derry's new papers. Derry, farm boy that he was, clambered all over the monsters which were two stories high, their front tires higher than a man's head. Inside the cab he stared wryly at the

185

gleaming dials and pressure gauges and instruments—all this to pick corn, barley, wheat, carrots—the whole thing as far removed from the harvester Derry was used to as a steam locomotive from a 747.

Painted over the cab was the name THE GLEANER, named after *The Gleaners,* Millet's famous painting of French farm women. The gleaners were so poor they lived by the leavings of other peasants, themselves poverty stricken by any modern standard. What a name—the Gleaner—for a machine that cost ninety thousand dollars, a machine so heavy it could crush all the earthworms to death, compacting the soil so badly future generations would have trouble tilling it at all.

So thought Derry, running his fingers over the control panel, itching to run the monster just once. Right into the ocean. "How overweight are we?" Derry asked.

" 'Bout twelve thousand pound," Hector said. "Stop caressing that thing. We got to make smoke."

They slipped out of Nashville at 1 A.M. when the city was asleep or as asleep as Nashville ever got, Hector driving lead, Derry behind. Once out of the city on I 24 they kicked the big tractor trailers to seventy-five and in an hour they were over the state line into Kentucky where the weight stations slumbered till dawn, and they swept past with their overweight loads.

In just under three hours they crossed the Ohio into Illinois and ran through broad flat wheatland, now on I 57 where they pushed hard to take advantage of the darkness. It was daylight when they pulled off the big highway, just the other side of the Little Wabash, and drove down a little macadam side road to the pretty little farmhouse which looked like something out of a Disney movie.

A tree trunk of a white woman met them at the door.

"Gerald Moore," Derry said, introducing himself. "This here's Harold Crampton."

"Put 'em in the barn," the tree trunk barked. "And close the big door. The bulls got helicopters now, and they gettin' nosy. My son give you a hand. *George!*" Bellowing like a moose.

George was the size of a tractor. He guided them into the big red barn and closed the huge sliding doors behind them. The barn was full of sophisticated farm machinery, all new, all stolen.

"Ma got breakfast for ya," George said.

The dining room was half full of silent men, eating Ma's pancakes and sausage and eggs, in the pleasant, tree-shaded, white clapboard farmhouse—the kind they're tearing down all over the Midwest to make room

186

for more corn to ship to Japan. It had no farm atmosphere at all, no rubber boots in the hall, overalls on the hook, farm gloves on the table, none of the feel of earth and hard work. It was an underground way station, and it smelled sourly of suspicion and ill will.

"Stay inside," Ma said, shoveling pancakes, sausage, and eggs on their plates. "Your bedroom first on the left upstairs. No telephone calls."

Derry smiled wryly at Hector who said, "We not in the South no mo'. We in the No'thland, and it ain't got no manners."

It was a farm bedroom—light, airy, with twin beds of brass. Very pleasant.

"Been here before?" Derry asked.

"Not this one. Another one just like it near here."

"What happened to that house?"

"Got tore down. This place too. They don't keep 'em long. The bulls come nosin' around, and they got to be paid off. Cheaper to tear 'em down and move on."

Derry lay on the bed and looked at the ceiling. Beautifully built with hand-crafted nails in, Derry guessed, about 1880, surrounded by trees that had been planted the same year to shade the house. They'd tear the whole place down and uproot the trees in order to add a few acres of sick soil in which to plant wheat to sell to the underdeveloped nations that had lost the knack of raising their own food.

Derry pointed out at the flat plains extending clear to the horizon. "Who owns all that land?"

"Some big corporation with a name like Twentieth Century Products, Inc."

"Galaxie?" Derry asked.

"Maybe Galaxie. They own ev'thing else. Don't fight it."

"Just asking questions."

"You not s'posed to ask questions in this business."

"You must have asked some questions yourself, or you wouldn't know the answers, Hector."

The black man lay on the bed next to Derry, eyes on the ceiling. "I don't know where my answers come from. I got 'em, but I don't get 'em askin' questions. Where's an owl find out all it knows? That's where I get my information—same place as the owl."

"God, maybe?"

"God ain't got time for a poor black man, Derry. He too busy takin' care of the rich white folk."

187

"He doesn't take very good care of them either. I think He's gone fishin', Hector. We got to look out for ourselves."

Something he never would have said four months earlier.

Derry rolled over on his side and within thirty seconds he was asleep. The dreams were continuous, ominous, brightly colored. Cassandra appeared, seductive, sibilant. "Pay attention," she said. "Or you gone get smoked."

She was followed by Sarah wearing her brown cotton dress with the white collar and cuffs, looking—as always—apologetic. The bruises had disappeared. "I hate to bother you, but it's behind a plate on the lower left side, way down low."

Derry woke up abruptly in afternoon sunshine, the silence in the house so thick you could hear it. He rose and padded down the corridor in his stocking feet, to the big window at the end of the corridor which looked out on the red barn.

He waited there, listening to the silence.

It was twenty minutes before big George came out of the barn, the wire clippers in his hand, crossed the backyard and entered the house under Derry's feet. Derry went back to the bedroom and put on his shoes.

He woke Hector and, when the black man had collected his wits, put it to him. "If they want to burn us, why didn't they do it in Tennessee?" Derry asked. "Save gasoline."

Hector shook his head: "Git it out of one jurisdiction into another. Cross state lines where the bulls is different and dumber or crookeder. Insure it in one state, burn it in another. It makes confusion."

"Get dressed," Derry said.

Taking charge.

Always before, he had laid back, listened to Hector or Julius, gone with the flow. Here he was setting the new direction.

Hector was full of grumbles, but he dressed while making them. "They gone be trouble. The man not gone let us go without some messin' about."

They went down the back stairs without running into anyone and got safely into the barn. There they ran into the problem of starting two cold diesel engines, which can't be done quietly. Hector had just got his diesel firing, gunning it to warm it, when big George appeared at the open door of his rig, yelling at him.

"Still daylight!" big George yelled. "It ain't time to leave."

Hector pretended not to hear, gunning the big engine and smiling at George as if he were saying hello.

188

"Turn that engine off," big George howled, "and git outta that cab!"

Hector smile some more. "Did you say something?" he asked.

Big George pulled out a .38 special which in his huge fist looked like a child's water pistol.

"Turn that engine off," he yelled, pointing the gun at Hector's head.

"What say?" Hector asked.

By this time Derry was in position. He hit big George with the locking wrench behind the right ear, not quite hard enough to kill him. Big George toppled like a tree in the forest.

Hector pulled out his handkerchief and swabbed the back of his neck. "What you tryin' to do—make Eagle Scout?"

Derry picked up the .38 and stuffed it in his waistband. He'd never had a handgun in his life. Changing from victim to . . .

Hector still grumbling: "That hero bit gone out of style. Anti-hero is the big thing. Just stayin' alive."

"I'm an old-fashioned man," Derry said.

He slid open the huge barn doors.

"I'll lead," he said.

They drove out swiftly, down the driveway, up the little feeder road and back to I 57, staying in touch through the CB's.

"Pull in! Pull in!" Derry commanded, leading the way into the first layby he could find, ten miles down I 57.

"Not gone be easy to find it in a piece of machinery this big," Hector said. "We could be here for hours."

Behind a plate on the lower left side, way down low. That's what Sarah had said. There Derry found a plate bearing the words: DANGER. THIS PLATE MUST NOT BE REMOVED EXCEPT AT THE FACTORY. He removed it and there it was, ticking away, the timer set for 3:20 when they would have been nearing Kankakee. Carefully Derry reset it for 5:30 A.M. For good measure Derry took out four of the five magnesium sticks. One stick would just blister a little paint.

A similar bomb was found in the same place on the Gleaner on Hector's rig. Derry gave it the same treatment.

"You suppose George is going to call ahead and make trouble for us in Chicago?" Derry asked.

Hector still grumbling: "That hero bit gone out of style. Anti-hero is the big thing. Just stayin' alive."

"He is going to look pretty bad when these things go off and don't burn anything much," Derry said. He was reaching into the aperture realigning

189

the bomb, taping the bomb to the upper crossbar where it would do the least damage, well away from the gas tank it was supposed to ignite. He felt a sharp tug at his wrist while he was aligning the bomb, but it wasn't till days later that he found out he'd broken the chain on his wrist band, carrying the copper disc, the one with the word DERRY engraved on it.

They drove at sixty, not kicking the big rigs up any higher because the Illinois highway police had a nasty reputation. By 4:20 A.M. they were in south Chicago, which was once described as "civilization with its pants down," driving through the endless dreary streets of the City That Works.

At 5 A.M. they arrived at the warehouse where the big overweight combines were much too big to get through the doors. A guard directed them to a parking lot in the rear of the yard, which chewed up a little more of their small reservoir of time before those timers went off. By the time they'd parked and jumped out it was 5:10 A.M. Twenty minutes left.

"Office is up front," a guard said. "Follow the green line."

It was painted on the floor and led them through a maze of corridors and warehouse floors jammed with crates containing farm machinery, tools, dies, engines, auto parts—theft of such magnitude, variety, ingenuity and complexity that it took Derry's breath away.

The door bore a sign, OFFICE, and inside a ferret of a man with gold teeth and bad breath took their invoices without comment and paid them off in hundred dollar bills, twenty hundreds in all.

Nobody signed anything.

The two men were outside, walking fast up South Jervis Street, when Derry looked at his watch. It was 5:30 A.M. The magnesium would be going off at that very moment, blistering the paint but doing no other damage except to George's reputation as a torch.

Ten blocks later they found a taxicab and climbed in.

"The bus station," Derry said.

"We couldn't find a hotel and grab a little sleep," complained Hector.

"I got a mission," Derry said.

__ CHAPTER __
EIGHTEEN

THE LOBBY WAS cavernous, full of walnut chairs of Tudor design whose needlepoint upholstery had long been worn through and never replaced. Near the lobby entrance was a reflecting pool, which had once been full of goldfish and lily pads, its bronze nymphs and dryads once spewing water from urns held on their shoulders. Back in days of glory, long gone. There had been no water in the fountain for years, and the bronze nymphs were black with dirt.

Everyone had fled the Stanhope except a few alcoholic old ladies, some of whom had lived there for decades. They sat in the vast lobby, day after day, hating one another from old habit, examining each newcomer with a beady intensity that approached insanity. Hector and Derry attracted attention because they were new, because they were far younger than anyone usually seen at the Stanhope, because Hector was black and Derry was white. The two of them together, my goodness!

On his second day at the Stanhope, as Derry was buying a newspaper at the stand, one of the old ladies approached him and said, "I don't know what you're seeking here, young man. But you won't find it. The Stanhope is the Sargasso Sea of dead hopes."

Derry stared at the old girl boldly. His beard was now blonde and thick and curly, and Derry found bold stares easy, as if he were staring out from behind the protection of a hedge. The woman wore a black lace dress over an undergarment which showed through the lace, a parody of seductiveness. Ridiculous but expensive.

"Have you lived here long?"

191

"Since Warren G. Harding was in the White House," she cackled.

"You'd better sit down, Mrs. Kasten, before you fall down," the bellhop said jovially. He took her arm, as if escorting the Queen of Sheba, and led her back to her accustomed chair and sat her in it.

The Stanhope had its own ornate livery for its bellhops, wine-colored with elegant page boy caps, and the bellhops, all of them black, wore them jauntily, as if they were characters in a movie. They were perpetually high on pot, which they smoked openly, the little bellhop caps worn tipsily over one eye, some of them walking along, snapping their fingers, and high-stepping to music in their heads. To the geriatric guests, they adopted a tone of roguish familiarity. The contempt was friendly because if it weren't, there'd be no tip.

"Waldo," the old lady in black lace cackled, "if you would be so kind, I would like a dry martini."

"Mrs. Kasten," Waldo said with immense good nature, "we know the bar doesn't open till noon now, don't we?"

"When it does open, Waldo, would you be so kind? Very dry with real lemon peel." She snorted spitefully. "The Stanhope hasn't had a real lemon on the premises since the Depression."

Derry sat in the chair next to the old lady at a ninety degree angle from her at one side of a big square pillar. "Have you lived in Cleveland long?"

"All my life, boy," she said softly. "And don't let anyone tell you life is short. It's *interminable.*"

A statement of tragic implication. Derry looked at the old woman with a new appreciation.

From across the lobby another of the Stanhope's ancient ladies, who wore white gloves and leaned heavily on a stick, spoke up spitefully. "Don't waste your breath on her, young man. She was cast out by society in 1929, and no one who is anyone has spoken to her since."

This was old warfare. Mrs. Kasten shrugged it off with humor. "Cast out by society!" she mocked. "Nobody has used that phrase in forty years, Rosalind Trimble." To Derry she said. "Rosalind suffers from delusions of fallen grandeur." All the time looking at Derry with the ravening curiosity of the old.

Derry said, "Did you ever know a girl called Sarah Framingham?"

Everyone's mouth fell open—Mrs. Kasten's, Rosalind Trimble's, the bellhop's.

"Goodness, me!" Mrs. Kasten said. "Sarah Framingham." Dwelling on each of its many syllables with a resonance that rang through the lobby. She struggled to rise but couldn't manage it until Waldo, the bellhop, sprang to her aid. "I think I shall go to my room, Waldo, until the bar opens."

Waldo helped her to the elevator, a great open cage of wrought iron and brass and polished mahogany that came down on long cables in the very center of the lobby. Derry watched her go, thinking that's the end of that. But it wasn't. Mrs. Kasten looked over her shoulder at him and jerked her head in open invitation to come along. He leaped after her.

"Will you do the honors, Waldo," Mrs. Kasten was saying softly. To Derry she said, "Elevators make me nervous."

"Mrs. Kasten, you have been going up and down this elevator for forty years. It shouldn't make you nervous any more."

Waldo pushed the proper button. "If you would be so kind as to close the door, when you leave, Mrs. Kasten. We're too busy to have to run up the stairs and close elevator doors you folks have forgot to close."

The antique iron cage was beginning to move upward at the speed of an inchworm, Mrs. Kasten rapping out through the iron lacework, "Busy doing *what*, Waldo?"

The cage had got about as high as Waldo's head here and he looked up and said, "Takin' care you, Mrs. Kasten," with a soft laugh.

Through the wrought iron, Derry saw the whole immense lobby with its old ladies, its somnolent desk clerk, its empty fountains and faded Persian carpets on chipped marble floor, its huge potted bay trees whose leaves had run wild through sheer neglect.

At close range, Mrs. Kasten's face was quite beautiful, with a finely molded chin and cheek under the network of wrinkles, and an air of perpetual youth, as if the personality had got stuck in about 1917.

The elevator stopped with a great jerk at the fifth floor. Mrs. Kasten came out from her trance abruptly. "We must get out before it starts down again," she bleeped, tearing at the filigreed door, scuttling into the corridor. Derry carefully closed the two elevator doors and followed her down the corridor, a relic of the days when America had nothing but space. It was as wide as most modern hotel lobbies, and the ceiling was sixteen feet high. The fading wallpaper was of gold with peacocks spreading their tails on ancient green lawns peopled by nineteenth-century figures of men with forked beards and women in crinolines and bustles, all talking away to one another as if their century had none of the problems of communication that so troubled our own. All these people seemed to have purpose and confidence long absent from the inhabitants of the Stanhope.

Mrs. Kasten's room was immense and high ceilinged, its walls covered with a faded purple cloth, very old and dusty. The curtains were of velours, thick and heavy as was everything else in that room. There was much too much furniture, as was the nineteenth-century custom, oak chairs and oak tables, standing cupboards with glass fronts, packed with china and silver, walnut bookcases filled with leather-covered books that looked as if no one had ever read them. The lamps were bronze and huge with naked ladies—one could scarcely call them women, they were so ladylike—supporting lampshades with electric light bulbs sprouting from their bronze flowing curls. The lampshades were of purple velvet with gold tassels.

The old lady pointed to an overstuffed chair. "Sit down, young man." Derry sat while Mrs. Kasten bustled about. Into two tiny purple glasses she poured thimblefuls of satiny liquid. She handed one glass to Derry, took the other one herself. "Southern Comfort," she said. "It might more properly be called old ladies comfort. There isn't an old lady in this hotel hasn't got a bottle of it somewhere." She tossed hers down expertly in one gulp.

Derry took a sip to be polite. Drinking at eleven in the morning was not one of his enthusiasms.

Mrs. Kasten sat now on a big footstool and looked up at Derry, mouth stern. "You can get into terrible trouble throwing the Framingham name around in hotel lobbies. They owned this town once. That bit the Rockefellers didn't own."

"Who owns it now?" Derry asked.

"I wish I knew. The rumors are fairly horrifying, but they're just rumors." She was speaking in a powdery voice with great poise and precision, much different from her earlier cackle and wheeze.

"What did you do to be cast out, Mrs. Kasten?" The beard gave Derry boldness to ask impertinent questions.

Mrs. Kasten gave a powdery laugh. "Cast out, my foot! You mustn't pay attention to that silly woman. Nothing that dramatic ever happened. The money just dribbled away, that's all. There were no great tragedies in Cleveland, young man. Old ladies invent these scandals—Rosalind Trimble is especially fanciful—to amuse themselves, through the long days. None of us here at the Stanhope is of tragic stature. We are just forgotten, and we don't like it."

She fingered the black lace of her dress absently. "What are you doing in Cleveland, young man, mooning about Sarah Framingham?"

194

Derry answered with a question of his own, "Did you know Sarah Framingham?"

"I knew her father, Billy Framingham, when he was a little boy. Sarah..." She shrugged. "I've been out of touch for a great many years.... I know the rumors. We live on rumor here. The wine of imbecility!" She gave one of her cracked laughs. "Beaudelaire's phrase, don't y'know."

Derry waited. The old lady had subsided into one of her fogs.

After a while, she resumed in a trancelike voice, "Billy Framingham still lives in that monstrosity of a house his grandfather built. Cost a million dollars—that house—back in 1888 when a million dollars was a lot of money."

"Twenty-six bathrooms," Derry said.

"I never counted them." The old lady was back among the living again, her eyes bright and roguish. She was at the bookcase going through leather volumes, spilling them on the floor. "I have a picture here someplace." She brought the volume to Derry, ruffling through the pages until she found it—a fading sepia print of an immense crenellated structure with round towers and parapets and towering eaves and immense stone carriage entrances on both sides all in bleak gray stone.

"All the other old horrors have long since been torn down—or they're headquarters of tax-exempt charities. No one lives in houses like that any more—except Billy Framingham. Everyone fled that house—first his wife—twenty-five years ago. Then Sarah—after the scandal."

"What scandal?"

Silence in the musty room which smelled of solitude like incense. The old lady had a set stern look as if he were treading on sacred ground.

"We're not in the lobby now, Mrs. Kasten," Derry said.

The ancient eyes grew ironic. "Sarah tried to burn down the house." Mrs. Kasten uttered a mirthless bleat. "You couldn't burn down that place with a blowtorch."

From somewhere in the profusion of furniture in that room a clock started striking—cling cling cling. Madness returned to the old lady. "Noon," she cackled. "The bar is open." She trotted out the door to the corridor. Over her shoulder she commanded: "Turn out the lights if you please."

Derry had trouble finding the switches, and it was a few minutes before he could follow.

The old lady was already in the wrought iron elevator, and the elevator with stately slowness was starting down. Derry pursued on the staircase

195

which circled the elevator peppering Mrs. Kasten with questions, "When did Sarah leave?" he cried, running down the stairs.

"You're wasting your time, young man," Mrs. Kasten said. "Sarah's dead. *Officially* dead. Billy Framingham had her declared officially dead after she'd been gone seven years so he could grab her money—a very great deal of money left her by her grandfather. Not a very nice thing to do, but then Billy is not a very nice man."

Sophy Kasten sank out of sight, lips pursed.

__ CHAPTER __
NINETEEN

WHILE DERRY WORKED the lobby, Hector worked the street, doing what had to be done.

He was back early that afternoon, sitting on the bed in their room on the eighth floor of the Stanhope, handing Derry his documentation. Derry's new name was James Meriweather, a florid name to go with his beard..His third identity. It occurred to him that he now had as many as Sarah. Not as various, perhaps, but each one definitely different. James Merriweather was not at all like Derry Jenkins. A man of leaping imagination, something Derry Jenkins wasn't.

It was the beard did it. Derry staring hard at his new Ohio driver's license with his picture. He put it in his wallet along with his Social Security card, his American Express executive card (to be used only in severe emergencies). If you had these pieces of paper, you existed. If not, you were a non-person.

Hector was relaying the street gossip: ". . . girl disappeared ten years ago. Big scandal in nineteen-seventy. Almost forgotten now. Ev'body think she dead. You sure dat's Mickie? Don't sound like Mickie."

"Mickie didn't always sound like Mickie either," Derry said. "What did you pick up on the house? Why does he live there?"

"Cause his daddy did and his granddaddy, tha's why." Hector shook his head. " 'Bout this place you c'n hear anything you want to on the street. It's got spooks. It's got dead bodies. It's got a secret room. . . ."

"Secret room?" Derry asked. "Where? Why?"

"Nobody know where or why. Tha's what make it interesting. Folks talk more about that secret room than anything else."

197

"What about Billy Framingham?"

"Nobody call him Billy," Hector said.

"Sophy Kasten does."

"On the street he called *William* Framingham. Very rich, very peculiar."

"*How* peculiar?"

Hector laughed: "People jes' shakes dey head you mention William Framingham. Last of the line. Got all this money, live up in that big house. Wife leave him. Daughter run away. He just gits more and *more* peculiar. Runs his company from that big house, nobody ever 'lowed in."

"We are going to get in," Derry said.

"How?"

Derry told him.

Hector shook his black head sorrowfully. The spell was still on and while it lasted . . .

Sarah came that night and sat on the end of Derry's bed, dressed in her brown cotton dress. The bruises had disappeared. She looked forlorn. "Why did you bring me back here?" she cried.

"I've got to find out why it happened."

"I could give you all the answers. Anything you want to know."

"You're going to be the last to find out, Sarah. You've hidden things from yourself."

"I'm so unhappy here."

"Sarah," Derry said. "You're unhappy everywhere. Even in death."

She smiled her wan, self-deprecatory smile at that, forgiving him. After a while, she said: "I like you in that beard. It makes you masterful. Did you know that? I like masterful men."

A clue, thought Derry.

It wasn't easy, and it took three weeks during which Derry produced beautifully forged references. One of them on blue notepaper with engraved white initials: ". . . Mr. Merriweather was my gardener for six years during which I found him painstaking, hard-working, and skillful with all manner of plants . . ." etc. etc.

James Merriweather composed these flowing lines, which clearly were beyond the ken of Derry Jenkins, farmer.

Merriweather also wrote the references for Harry Vance, as Hector now called himself, this on violet notepaper which Hector picked up somewhere. ". . . Mr. Vance is an excellent chauffeur, sober, reliable." All those reassuring adjectives which mount to the heavens like prayers.

So it came to pass, three weeks later, that Derry was on his knees in the

198

north border of the great house on the bluff, replanting the gladioli from the greenhouse in ordered rows under the great drawing room window with its panes of colored glass that looked out over the vast polluted lake.

The great house rising behind him like a fortress, hushed and menacing. The head gardener, Mozzi, watched him, ferocious with dislike.

After a while Mozzi drifted away, and Derry went into the immense kitchen for a glass of water.

Victoria handed it to him. Victoria was black, enormous, and sympathetic. She, too, came from Virginia, and she and Derry were on the same wavelength. "Mozzi giving you hard time?"

"No worse than usual."

"He don't like you cause you not Italian."

Or for deeper reasons, Derry thought. Keeping it to himself. Aloud he said, "How long he been here?"

"Only four months. He tryin' get me fired too, me what's been here ten years."

All very sinister.

"Did you know Sarah Framingham?" Derry asked. Casually.

The black woman's eyes went wide with fright. "You bettah not bandy that name round."

Derry sighed. It wasn't going to be easy.

Hector came into the kitchen in his chauffeur's cap, his tight leggings. The costume was a joke, something out of 1915.

"I got night duty," Hector said. "Paddy says I can take you along to help."

Paddy Malone was the butler, rock hard. Too hard to be a butler. The staff was scared to death of him.

The two men went out through the dining room. They were supposed to use the back stairs, but no one would be in the dining room at that hour. A massive room full of suits of armor of beautifully embossed steel with gold joints, dress armor of the late thirteenth century which had not seen much fighting.

Great Tudor windows ran from ceiling to the window seat—all in red and purple glass, which admitted dim red and purple light and couldn't be seen through. The walls were paneled in heavy oak and hung with oil paintings of English sixteenth-century gentlemen in doublet and hose.

There were more of these on the staircase, which was of massive oak construction, the bannisters a foot wide, the supporting pillars carved into twisted columns nine inches thick, the staircase heavily carpeted in red.

They weren't supposed to use the front stairs either, but no one would be around. Paddy would be in the library getting his orders from William Framingham.

The two men glided down the second floor corridors, past the bedrooms which were clean and bright, without any of the colored glass that made the downstairs light so oppressive. At the end of the corridor was a heavy oak door, leading to the servants' staircase, and this they took because the third floor was entirely servants' rooms—a rabbit warren of them, mostly unoccupied.

Hector and Derry had separate rooms. They went to Hector's where Derry flung himself on the bed while Hector stripped off his tight chauffeur's uniform.

"Where's it at tonight?" Derry asked.

Hector put the chauffeur's cap on the dresser and sat down to untie his leggings. "We takin' the stuff from one warehouse to another warehouse."

"We make out invoices?"

"Somebody else do that. We just the hired help." Hector slipped off the tight trousers and put on a pair of blue jeans. "It don't hardly seem worth it. Petty stuff like that."

"It adds up," Derry said.

The house stood on a great bluff overlooking the lake. The bluff itself was honeycombed with elevator shafts, garages, playrooms, offices that had been built by Framinghams over a period of almost a hundred years. That night the two men took the stairway to one of the cellars, which contained an elaborate period barroom which one of the Framingham's had had built fifty years earlier for parties. No one had used it for decades. The two men walked around the dusty room and took an elevator which led to the foot of the bluff and a great garage that had once held twenty-two cars—and now contained three, one of them a pickup truck.

Hector backed the pickup out of its slot and spun it around. Derry opened the huge garage door and, after Hector had driven out the pickup, closed it behind him. He climbed into the truck, and they started off. After a while Hector said, "He don't own the house any more. The bank owns the house."

"But he owns the bank?"

"I wouldn't know 'bout that. I can't ask questions. They don't like questions."

"Don't ask questions. Just listen."

"What you find out?"

200

Derry had been exploring the house—when Paddy's back was turned.

"There's a room in the tower that's got two locks on the outside, not even connected to the inside. Bars on the windows even though it's forty feet up. I think that's where she got out."

Hector was driving through the streets that looked as if they had been under enemy occupation. The buildings were grimy and the signs on the buildings were faded as if the messages had lost all meaning, as if the wares they advertised had long ceased to exist and the companies gone out of business.

"Why anybody do that to they daughter?"

"She tried to burn down the house," Derry said.

They were going through the rotting inner core of an immensely rich city that had no money.

The area they were driving through had once housed huge industries that made immense machines that in turn made bridges and skyscrapers. For tax reasons and space these industries had long since moved to the countryside, wrecking it. They left behind a vacuum of immense empty buildings, railroad sidings on which no railroads ran, a tangle of roads and buildings without purpose. Into this vacuum moved the poor and the wicked, the drifters, the unwashed and the crooks, the venturesome and the helpless.

Framingham Cement had not moved to the country, had stayed in the same buildings it had occupied since the 1880s, because it needed the docks and the ships.

"What good all this information do us," grumbled Hector, who still had no idea what they were doing in Cleveland.

"We'll be much wiser," Derry said.

"That be nice," said Hector.

He drove the pickup to the gate of the chain-link fence that encircled the great warehouse. Derry opened the padlock with the key he'd been given, and the truck went in. They stopped at the loading platform. Inside was the night watchman, who led them to the right stack and even helped them load the stuff. Sophisticated computer circuitry. Boxes and boxes of it.

The invoices were handed over by the night watchman—all three copies, which meant there would be no record there of the stuff having been received.

Hector drove the pickup up a blind alley and there Derry took out the

201

Minox he'd bought and photographed the invoices, all of them. "What for you doin' that?" Hector asked.

"Knowledge is power," Derry said. "You ever hear that?"

"Just now," Hector said.

"Don't you forget it."

Hector was driving the pickup through more rotting inner core, including a hotel that had ceased being a hotel and was now full of half-baked enterprises—antique shops, health food stores, thrift shops, junk shops. Hector drove his truck around the rear of the ex-hotel to a loading platform. A chunky Hispanic met them there and took the invoices, carefully counting to be sure he had all three, while Derry and Hector unloaded the circuitry on the floor of what had once been the kitchen where it joined a lot of other crates.

"How you doin', Emmanuelle?" Hector asked the Hispanic.

"Pretty good," Emmanuelle said. "This all you got?" He was affixing the false invoices to the tops of the crates."

"We got to go back for the rest of it. That all we could carry. You going to give us a receipt?"

Big joke. Nobody ever gave receipts for that kind of night work. "You git you receipt in heaven," Emmanuelle said.

"Back in half an hour," Hector said.

So it went. By two A.M. they'd brought over the second load, and then they headed back to the garage under the bluff.

"Stealing from hisself," Hector complained. "I don't understand why a man want to do such a thing."

"Framingham Cement doesn't belong to him anymore," Derry said. "It's been bought up by a conglomerate—Galaxie Industries. Very big, Galaxie. Shipping companies, electronic companies, fast-food chains. You name it—they got it. Even a movie picture company."

"Big rich man stealing a few boxes."

"Hundred ten thousand dollars worth, it said on those invoices."

"He got millions, that man. What he want more for?"

"When I find that out, I'll let you know first," Derry said.

He was in his own bed in his own small room when Mickie swaggered in with her sexy walk. Throwing it around, as she always did. Sullen scowl. "Thought you shut of me," she sneered.

"No," Derry said. "I didn't think any such thing." He certainly wasn't rid of her. Not a bit. "Come on to bed. We'll talk it over."

"No more of that." She sat on the bed, the gun in her right hand, all but forgotten. Nobody could be as negligent with a gun as Mickie. With her a gun was a throwaway line.

"What's it like—where you are?" Derry whispered.

"Horrible—like everywhere else." Scowling. Picking her teeth, driving Derry sex wild. "I always hated this house."

"You tried to burn it down."

"Not me."

"Sarah then?"

"Who's Sarah?"

Even dead, she denied Sarah. Very peculiar.

"Where's the secret room?" Derry asked. "If anyone would know, you would."

"Why should I tell you anything?" Mickie snarled, her face an inch from his. "After what you did."

He lunged for her then they fought, her tough wiry body turning him on as always. She was better than he was—quicker and stronger and more ruthless—and she tied him into knots on that bed—until he woke, panting and exhausted.

The next night it was Vanessa, and she had no qualms about sex after death, slipping into bed with him, performing magical things with hands and tits, while talking a blue streak in her British accent: "Sex after death is most *peculiar* because, you see, it is non-cellular, orgasmic without organs, *if* you catch my meaning. There's nothing one can get one's *teeth* into."

"Where's the room?" Derry whispered into her shining hair.

"Dear boy, *I* don't know," Vanessa said. "I was always just a guest here."

Derry would awaken and have to confront Jessie, who remained safely in his mind. None of these people exist, he would explain to Jessie. Not any more. You have nothing to fear from these wraiths, these figments. Jessie herself was changing into a figment, becoming less substantial, more dreamlike. It was harder to see her face any more. She loomed large in his conscience but the lineaments of the face were dimming.

All this took his eye off the ball to such a degree he caught a severe tongue lashing from Paddy Malone. He was cleaning the drains on the fountain

203

which lay at the extreme lower end of the great garden, directly over the bluff. Far below the great lake, phosphorescent with its own rottenness, stretched to the horizon.

The fountain Derry was working on was full of immense bronze sea serpents, horses with fish scales and tails, mermaids, all in convulsive movement, muscles tensed, outsized faces alarmed or furious or in pain. No water had flowed in that fountain for decades but the order had been passed: put it in order.

Paddy Malone had come personally to see how the thing was coming on and found Derry, his wire brushes and wrenches and cleaning rags stretched out on the grass, elbows on the stone parapet—itself an artwork of intricate design and superb craftsmanship—gazing out at the lake, still full of moonbeams.

Paddy Malone had exploded with Irish wrath: "Ye haven't even started the work, have ye, ye dithering fool?"

Derry kept his temper bottled up: "It's difficult to know where to start."

"At the beginning, ye idjut."

Derry should have said, "And where is that?" but he didn't. Instead, because he was still full of moonbeams, he blurted out, "If we get it going again, who's to look at it?" which was none of his business.

It was a mistake, but like many mistakes it brought its unexpected twist of fate. From behind the laburnum hedge, which he and Mozzi kept beautifully trimmed (for the scrutiny of absolutely no one), there stepped William Framingham. Derry had never laid eyes on him before, but he recognized him instantly. For one thing he'd seen photographs. For another—and far more importantly—he recognized the Framingham look, which so pervaded Sarah she carried it after death.

It was the look of unhappiness so deep as to be almost a genetic defect, something passed from generation to generation like the hemophilia of the Tsars. It smote him in the heart, this look, because Sarah had imprinted it there.

"I'm sorry, sir," Derry cried. He had to make his peace with this man for many reasons.

William Framingham was looking him over with his unhappy intelligent eyes (just like Sarah's) as if his mind had already leaped far past the offense to its implications. "Nobody will see it?" William Framingham said. "You think that's what this fountain is for?" He said it musingly, as if he was working out the thing in his own mind. "Well, people *said* that's why my grandfather put it there. To show off, that's what they said, but they were quite wrong. He didn't give a damn what anyone thought. He had this fountain brought over from France because he *wanted* it here on this bluff overlooking Lake Erie. He thought it a more fitting setting than the French chateau where he found it. Grandfather didn't care if anyone saw it or admired it here, including even himself. He put it here because he thought it should be here."

A long speech from this singularly unappealing man, homely as a mud fence. He spoke almost as if addressing himself, the way lonely people so frequently do, listening to his own prose. "It was a form of self-gratification, this fountain, common in the late nineteenth century among men of his type. But now, you see, the function of this fountain has changed. It has outlived grandfather's personal feelings and become its own self-justification. It doesn't need onlookers. It's enough that it exists but it must not exist in this state of insufficiency. A fountain without water is an abomination, a degradation. It *must* have water and, once the fountains play again, I shall know that the water flows whether I come and look at it or not. This fountain will have meaning and purpose. It doesn't need anyone to admire it. Come along, Mr. Malone."

Off they went, William Framingham in the lead, the butler trailing respectfully, just as if the twentieth century had not intervened in the master-servant relationship.

Derry was left along the bluff, his back to the great lake, his mind agape.

That night Sarah was the visitant, and Derry tried to explain her father to her: "He's trying to live up to his grandfather, and he'll never manage."

Sarah sitting at the foot of the bed, as sexually uninteresting as always, disagreed. "He's a monster of selfishness, my dear Papa. You must not forgive him by bringing in Great-grandfather as motivation."

Daughters are the worst sources of enlightenment, Derry thought, about fathers. What little they knew was colored by pain and therefore hopelessly unreliable.

"You know what my father said to me once?" Sarah laughed her self-deprecating laugh. "He said, 'Oh, you don't know what it's like to be the most unattractive member of an unattractive family.' Imagine saying that to his own daughter, having passed it on to me."

So it went, this conversation, high toned as all his conversations with Sarah were. Derry never fully realized how much he cared for this girl until after she went, and then he was full of mourning that he had not used his time with her more feelingly, that he had not attempted to alleviate her unhappiness if only for a little while because clearly he was very important to her. Not sexually—he was as inert sexually to her as she was to him—but as a friend, as an asexual lover.

Instead he took advantage of her special knowledge, and it was shameful but necessary. If he were ever to get home, he had to lay her ghost once and for all. "Where is the secret room?" he asked.

She looked disappointed. "Oh, they all ask that. When I lived here, that's all anyone wanted of me—to show them the room. I'm fed up with that room."

"Couldn't you show me where it is?"

She looked intensely unhappy. "You're not ready."

She faded away into small lines of abstraction.

The next day he worked with fiendish concentration and intense dedication on the drains, cleaning out a half-century of foul, stinking sludge. By four o'clock he'd finished, and he turned the great petcock, itself of imperishable bronze. For three minutes, an agony of time, he waited. Then water gushed from the mouth of the great leaping horse with the fish scale body, from the shell clasped by the mermaid, spilling all over her naked breasts, from the gaping mouths of leaping sea serpents and playful fishes, swirling and gushing and cascading over the round basin of red-veined marble, transforming the entire landscape, bringing the nineteenth century to life again.

Derry leaned against the stone parapet on the bluff over the great lake and watched the fountain play its intricate water games, feeling the power and splendor of the nineteenth century upon him. Far up the manicured and unused lawn, a quarter-mile away, stood the great fortress of a house, and presently from the French window a figure emerged and came toward Derry.

William Framingham. Dressed in coat and collar and tie. An awesome figure in that heat. He approached the fountain slowly, eyes fixed on the swirling, leaping water, lips pursed in their perpetual unhappiness. He came all the way to the rim of the fountain and leaned against it, gazing at the splashing water. He looked disappointed. Finally, he turned his back and went back toward the house.

"Shall I turn them off, sir?" Derry asked.

"Not until nightfall."

That night Mickie came back and tied him to the bed with her ropes and

206

raped him again and again, sullen as always. "I don't know what you think you're doing here," she muttered between these sexual excesses. "It won't do any good. What's done is done."

"Lady Macbeth," Derry said.

"Who?" Mickie asked, and went after him again with furious sexuality, as if driven by the unlocked energy of the universe.

As chauffeur, Hector was getting closer to the center of things. William Framingham rarely went to his office in the city although he maintained an elaborate and huge office in Galaxie Industries. Lawyers and bankers and executives came to him when confrontation could no longer be avoided. Hector drove them up the bluff to the great house, picking them up in the city and driving them up for lunch, and then returning them.

A glass partition separated the chauffeur's compartment from the upholstered rear seat. Hector wasn't supposed to listen, but he did. Derry wired the listening devices himself independently of the speaking tube. Hector reported the conversations verbatim—and he had a phenomenal memory. Derry put it together like a crossword puzzle.

"The Tristar Credit Bank is based in Geneva," Hector said at one point. "That's who owns the house. Who owns the Tristar Credit Bank I couldn't say, and I know these gentlemen don't know either cause I hear them wondering about that."

He heard a lot, all of it confusing. "Tristar a *con-dwee* for hot money. That's what the man said. *Con-dwee* like that. What a *con-dwee?*"

"Never mind," Derry said. "Hot money is the key phrase there. What else?"

"Currency smuggling. All kinds."

A few days later, Hector brought in a fresh conversation. "Asset stripping, what the lawyer man say—three times. What asset stripping?"

"Stealing," Derry said. "Highbrow stealing."

That night Sarah reproached him, "It took me years to get out of this house. Now you've got me back here."

"Where's the room?" Derry asked.

"Oh, you and that room. It won't do any good, you know."

"Why did you try to burn the house down, Sarah?"

Sarah laughed her lighthearted laugh. "Are they still talking about *that*? It's just a story, you know. Not an ounce of truth in it."

207

"Why did he lock you in the tower?"

"To keep me from leaving, of course. He didn't want that."

After a bit she said in her disappointed voice, "You don't believe me any more than the others."

"What others?"

"Oh, all of them. Doctors, psychiatrists, lawyers, my father, my mother. None of them believed me. I didn't do it. I swear."

She really believed she hadn't.

"Tell me about your mother, Sarah."

"Oh, mother." With her lighthearted *la-dee-da* laugh. "Let me tell you a story, a true story, about a very chic lady at Deauville. She was taking a walk on the beach with her lover and she saw some children at play. 'Oh, what *beautiful* children!' said the chic lady to the nanny who was taking care of them, 'Whose children are they?' 'Yours, madame,' the nanny replied. You know who told me that story? My dear mother—and she laughed and laughed. But I didn't laugh. I cried."

Sarah faded away discreetly, politely, apologetically.

There was more nightwork that night, Derry driving the pickup through the dreary back streets of this ill-kempt city, which smouldered by the great polluted lake. From the very beginning this journey was different, marked by the urgency in Paddy Malone's manner and by the meticulousness of the instruction. "Ye got to do it tonight, and ye got to keep a record of what ye moved in yer own handwritin'. I want to see it, and *he* wants to see it."

"Wha's that mean?" Hector asked as they drove through the dirty enemy-occupied streets at three in the morning.

"I don't know," Derry said, "but I have a suspicion there's a falling out among thieves." He was looking at the rearview mirror. "There's a car following us."

"Anyone we know?"

"Let's find out, shall we?" Derry stopped the truck at the curb. The car in his rearview mirror stopped too—half a block away.

Derry walked back to it and stuck his head through the window. "You're up late, Mr. Malone."

"I had to be sure it wasn't you," the Irishman cried truculently.

"I wouldn't know where to hide the stuff," Derry said mildly.

"Carry on with it, before I belt you one," Paddy Malone said, trying to keep his voice down.

Derry climbed back into the pickup. "Amateur!" Derry said between his teeth.

"Paddy?" asked Hector.

"William Framingham," Derry said.

They had drawn behind the hotel that was no longer a hotel up to the loading platform.

"Oh, oh," Hector said. "*He* no amateur."

They both recognized the crablike walk far, far down the loading platform.

"What we gone do?" Hector asked.

"I'll handle it," Derry said. "I got this beard to hide behind."

Hector gave him a long, searching look. "You do look a different man."

"That's because I *am* a different man," Derry said. "You stay out of sight. Get on the floor if he comes anywhere near this truck."

Derry got out of the truck and went into the former kitchen of the no-longer hotel, passing three feet from the man. Mancuso didn't even look in his direction.

__ CHAPTER __
TWENTY

THE NEXT NIGHT he slipped out of his room and down the servants' stairs to the second floor where the master bedrooms were. His face blacked up. Three A.M., the wide corridor black as the second level of Hell.

Even in the blackness he knew where the place was, was beginning to know the vast improbable house very well, every crevice memorized, was beginning to love the huge nineteenth-century architectural atrocity as if he'd been brought up in it.

The old nursery was at the very end of a second corridor cut off from the main element of the second floor by an oak door. A whole self-contained living quarter where no one had lived for a decade or more. Derry tried his flashlight here. The beam lit up the corridor in its eerie selective way, picking out the faded wallpaper for its specialized scrutiny. Nursery wallpaper but of a very unusual sort. There were the bears, the witches, the gingerbread houses, the clowns, the pines, all the usual images of nursery wallpapers but this wallpaper never repeated, not once. Derry examined it from beginning to end. It ran the gamut—*Winnie the Pooh, The Wind in the Willows, Black Beauty,* all the child's classics without any repetition. How could that be? But there it was. Nothing money couldn't buy after all, even non-repeating wallpaper. Anything to keep a child amused. And out of the way.

Derry's flashlight found the kitchen. Child's kitchen painted red and yellow, child's colors. The cupboard full of a child's dishes—covered with pictures of dancing harlequins and elves. Stove. Refrigerator. Derry looked into the refrigerator and found even the inside of that laced with smiling

211

lions, smiling squirrels, smiling bluebirds. No food in the refrigerator. Just smiling animals which looked, under his flashlight beam, surrealistic.

There was also a table and chair. Well, two chairs. One big, one small, Sarah had had a companion then, some nanny or other who'd fed her from one of those dishes with the elves on them. God in heaven!

Derry went down the hall examining each room—bathroom walls covered with colored stars, moons, sailboats and butterflies, closets, whose coat hooks were conveniently close to the ground (making Sarah hang up her own coat like a good little girl), finally the nursery itself.

Huge like everything about that house.

The whimsy had been curbed here. Taken a different direction, anyway. In place of elves there were palaces. But not fairy palaces. Real ones. There was Versailles with its courtiers and its fountains and gardens; on another wall, the Taj Mahal gleaming in its perpetual moonlight, on still another one of mad Ludwig's Bohemian fancies—all in photomontage, very real, very big. But then it was an enormous room. Covered in dust and outgrown childhood. The flashlight fell now on the shelves of books. Floor to ceiling—masses of the books of childhood, all of them, from Rapunzel to *The Bobbsy Twins on a Houseboat*. And beyond. *The Sword in the Stone, The Hobbit, The Lord of the Flies*. Advanced stuff. Sarah's reading from four to . . . where? Sixteen? Seventeen? How long before she'd flown? Or rather been transferred to the room in the tower?

Derry pulled out the books one by one, looking for evidence of childhood, marks, scribbles, scrawls, drawings of little girls or—anything. Nothing. She'd read them—but left no marks. Good little girl that she was.

The flashlight traveled on. A piano in red and gold. Did she play? Lessons she hated? The window seat was covered in tan corduroy, worn almost through. She'd sat there, all right. Day after long day.

The cupboards were at the far end of the room farthest from the entrance and here were the toys. The rocking horse was a marvel. Very big with hooves covered in fanciful hair caught in the very act of prancing. The saddle was out of the Arabian Nights and the colors were out of the rainbow. When it rocked, it activated a music box which played Dubussy on a harpsichord, filling the room with music. Derry's hands flew over the toy trying to stop the noise that rang through the silent room—not finding anything. It had to play itself out until the very end, the big rocking horse rocking away far beyond his own original push. Rock. Rock. Debussy tinkling endlessly.

212

Unnerving.

Derry turned off the flashlight and sat in the darkness until the rocking horse stopped in midphrase. Glink. Just like that.

When he turned the light back on again, it was pointed straight at a doll's house. Big. Like everything else.

It was a moment or two before Derry realized it was a replica of the house he was in—carriage entrances, Gothic towers, hideous gray stone, all of it. Eight feet tall.

He walked over to it, flashlight concentrating on the front entrance hall. There was the great staircase with its red carpet and the sixteenth century paintings of noblemen in doublet and hose—four inches tall—the dining room with its suits of armor—six inches tall—behind them the windows in red and purple glass, there the great kitchen where black Victoria gave him lemonade.

The flashlight traveled up to the third floor and picked out his tiny room and Hector's room and the big one down the hall where Paddy slept. (Derry hoped he slept well.) He walked round the big dollhouse now to the rear end where the cliffside itself was cut out with its tunnels and its game room built for big parties in 1915, the long winding steps that led down to the garage at the foot of the cliff. There it was with a separate set of steps for Sarah to walk down to the lower levels while playing with this thing.

A plaything? It was too monstrous, too faithful to the real house, which Sarah had hated.

The flashlight journeyed on, probing the long winding cliff staircase because there was something there Derry had never seen before. An opening to the left midway down the bluff leading to an oval room that contained nothing at all. Every other room in the doll's house was furnished with what looked like exact replicas of real furniture. The oval room in the bluff was empty. Derry put his face close to the empty room, nose almost touching its oak-paneled curved walls (quite a trick that, paneling curved oak walls in miniature), trying to fathom just where on the long descending staircase that room was and how you got into it.

The flashlight was slowly probing every inch of the cliffside staircase, Derry's eyes inches from the model, when across his right hand which held the light he felt, light as a moth's wing, the caress of fingertips.

Scaring him almost out of his mind.

Derry jerked the flashlight left, fear choking him.

Sarah stood there inches away with her sad smile.

213

"It's only me," she said with her deprecating wave of hand. "*Dead*! I wasn't even very important *alive*. Dead I'm *hopelessly* insignificant."

Derry frozen with terror, nevertheless. He'd been in his bed before. Asleep. This wasn't. . . .

She looked spectral, the complexion ashen, the line of her sad mouth gray and insubstantial.

"I was never happy in this room. But of course I didn't know that because a child doesn't know happiness from unhappiness. Life is what happens, and one must bear it. Only in retrospect—death has certain advantages in that respect—do I realize what a miserable child I was. How unneeded, unwanted, and unloved."

She laughed her light feathertip laugh. Sarah always laughed at the most inappropriate times, thought Derry. As a spirit she was not fearsome but piteous.

"How do you get into the damn room, Sarah?" he muttered. "Show me."

"I'll have to, won't I? Or I'll never get out of here," Sarah said in her light voice (not even taking her own piteousness as seriously as it ought to be taken). She took his hand in her own dead fingers and pulled it down to the point near the floor of the cliffside staircase to the right of the door. Nothing at all to mark it, no protuberance or button or anything. Just a space an inch from the floor, an inch from the staircase corner. Sarah pushed the empty space and a four-inch square of wall slid into the floor.

"If you want to close it again, you'll find a button on the inside—quite conspicuous. Right there." She showed him and the little square slid shut again. She smiled her spectral smile. "What are you trying to do to my poor father, Derry?"

"He's doing it to himself, Sarah. He is mixed up with some very bad people."

"He's using them—as he uses everyone. My mama. Me."

"They're using *him*, Sarah. He's pretty close to the end of the line."

"Oh, poor Papa!" Sarah murmured.

"Did you really love your father, Sarah?"

"Oh, yes," Sarah said, the voice far away. "One must love one's papa. It's one of the requirements of civilized society."

She was gone as if she'd never been there.

I'm losing my mind, Derry thought. I'm around the bend.

His fingers felt for a bit of wall, an inch from the floor, an inch from the staircase corner, and pushed. Immediately the four-inch square of wall sank

214

into the floor. He pushed the button on the inside wall. The four-inch square slid shut.

It scared the living hell out of him. He pinched himself. It hurt, and he didn't wake up. He just stood there, the flashlight in his hand, swinging wildly around the old nursery—to the piano, the window seat, the bookcase, the rocking horse, the doll's house replica of the house he lived in.

After a while, he crept back to bed.

He thought of Jessie. I'm sorry! I'm sorry! he muttered to his absent wife. I've been under a spell. But, of course, she'd never accept that. Sensible earth mother Jessie didn't believe in spells or magic.

He summoned up a mental picture of distant Jessie in her jeans, milking the goats in far-off Virginia, and it soothed his nerves so that sleep came.

"You must get the generations straight in your head, young man. I was a contemporary of Billy Framingham's *grandfather*. Not his father. His father wasn't much. A rich dilettante who collected suits of armor to conceal the absence of steel in his own nature. But Billy's grandfather . . . Oh, his *grandfather!*"

Sophy Kasten's face broke out in a dazzling smile as if she were a girl again. Marvelous to behold. They were in her overstuffed room, the lights turned on unnecessarily. Eleven A.M. of a Sunday. That was the best hour to catch Sophy Kasten, Waldo the bellhop had told him. She was compos mentis at eleven A.M. After the bar opened—one P.M. on Sunday—she was gone, but in these two hours between eleven and one, the mind was sharp.

Sophy Kasten was sitting straight as a carved figure in the Restoration oak chair, her face lit with ancient memory. "I remember when he brought those fountains from France. He threw a party for five hundred people up there on the bluff and he showed off his fountains under the colored lights. Champagne and colored lights on the water and three orchestras."

"When?" Derry asked.

"Nineteen fifteen," Sophy Kasten said. "Great year nineteen fifteen. Also nineteen sixteen and seventeen. After that the world collapsed."

"Sarah's mother was a light lady. Is that right?"

"Very expensive, I'm told. Two hundred dollars a night. Quite a lot of money for those times."

"Why did he marry her?"

"Dear boy, I can only tell you common gossip."

"Tell me the common gossip."

"She got pregnant, perhaps deliberately. He wanted a son. It never occurred to him it might be a girl. She tarried only long enough for the girl to be born. Then she departed with a great deal of Billy's money."

Sarah had said both her father and mother were rich.

"Why didn't she take Sarah with her?"

"Billy wouldn't let her. He didn't want the child, but he didn't want his wife to have her either. I told you he was a monster. Why are you so interested in Sarah? She's dead."

"Not quite," Derry said.

Hector was crying the blues, as usual.

"Suppose he ask me to drive Mancuso up here for one of those lunches?"

"Mancuso's not the lunch type. He'd send somebody else," Derry said.

"Just suppose he does."

"Let's wait till it happens," Derry said sensibly. "Meantime what you got?"

Hector played the tape which was faint and scratchy. A conversation from the back of the limousine." . . . *Merry Widow* . . ." one voice said. "Portuguese. We're not claiming for the ship. Just the cargo."

"Philippine cement!" the other voice said in tones of incredulity.

"Not as good as American but thirty percent cheaper," the first voice said. "The ship never arrived in New York."

There was lots more. ". . . Costa Rican letter of credit . . . Federal Banque Suisse paid a million three . . . bill of lading . . ."

"This mean anything to you," Hector asked.

"No," Derry said. "We just keep listening."

Twice more he'd seen Mancuso, each time at close quarters and Mancuso had not so much as glanced at him. What was he doing in Cleveland? Always at night. Around the warehouses where freight moved out and bills of lading moved in. The warehouses were getting empty of everything but paper.

Mob crime, getting very sophisticated, Derry thought, his head aching with it. He was piecing it together bit by bit. Ships that left Manila and never arrived. Or possibly never were in Manila at all. Changed their names at sea. All insured, all fraudulent. Collecting from Swiss banks on forged documents for cement that never existed and then collecting again on insurance for lost cargo that never was on shadowy ships that existed only in somebody's filing cabinet.

216

Much of this Derry got from the paperman Hector had found the moment he got to Cleveland. Hector was very good at finding papermen wherever he went. These were the men who produced the bits of paper—Social Security cards, birth certificates, driver's licenses—without which a man could not live. A cheerful open-faced black man who was very good at paper. Any kind of papers—stock certificates, bills of lading, ship registration—except money.

"You gotta be crazy do money," the paperman said—Hugo Weare his name was—"Money not worth anything anymore."

Framingham used to make cement, which it sold for five times what it was worth to the Midwest cities when they built the Midwest, making the Framinghams very rich. Now instead of cement Framingham made phony deals about nonexistent Philippine cement in phantom ships, which disappeared in phantom oceans, all phantasmagoria. Framingham didn't own Framingham Cement but stole from Framingham industries owned by the Galaxie Conglomerate which was itself infused with Mob figures like Mancuso.

"What we doing in Cleveland?" Hector asked many times.

"We're in a ghost story, trying to get out," Derry said.

The affair was approaching desperation time. All of Derry's nerve ends knew that.

One night he took out the .38 he'd taken off the man back on the Illinois farm and cleaned it, making Hector very nervous.

"What for you doin' that?" Hector asked.

"We're going to need a gun that'll stop a man in his tracks. One shot."

"In a ghost story? A gun?" Hector said.

"You want to get home alive, don't you?"

217

__ CHAPTER __
TWENTY ONE

THE CALL HAD come after dinner. William Framingham had had his dinner alone, as usual, in the great dining room with the colored glass windows, served, as always, by Paddy. Hector and Derry had had their dinner in the kitchen much earlier and were already up in their rooms.

Paddy called them on the brass nineteenth-century speaking tube, which came directly from the pantry to each servant's room. "Harry, Mister Framingham is going out at ten P.M. He requires you to drive him. You there, Harry?" Harry was Hector's Cleveland name.

"I here," Hector said. "Mistah Framingham want me to drive him ten o'clock tonight. Front door?"

"Front door. You'll pick up a Mr. Mancuso at the warehouse."

Hector rolled his eyes around his skull.

"You got that, Harry?"

"I got that." Hector switched off the speaking tube. "That tear it up. That really tear it up. *Mancuso!*"

Derry's mind was on something else. "He ever go out before? Since we been here?"

"Not even once."

"Something's cooking, Hector."

"I can't face Mancuso, Derry. He blow me away sure."

Derry got out the handgun from his bottom drawer underneath the blue jeans and looked at it. It had sex appeal, that big blued .38. "I'll take care of it, Hector. You are going to be sick."

219

Paddy didn't like it a bit, glowering at Derry, who was all dressed up in the 1915 chauffeur's uniform.

"Harry's sick. Real sick," the bearded Derry said gravely. "Threw up three times."

"You got a chauffeur's license?"

Derry showed it. In the name of James Merriweather, his Cleveland name. The paperman had done a fine job, photograph and all. A fortunate thing because the Irish butler took these pieces of paper very seriously. As did everyone.

Imposture was worldwide, the new religion. Derry had read of a Yugoslav women with a fine forged law degree who had become a judge. Very good one. Until they caught her.

Paddy was explaining the situation to William Framingham, who looked as if he were in the wrong century—his feet on the footrail, his hand gripping a silver-headed cane, a black hat on his head. He was seated in the back seat of the twelve-cylinder limousine which had tinted windows you couldn't see into, though you could see out of them. "James knows the way," Paddy was saying. "He's done the route with Harry many times."

"Let's get along then," William Framingham said in his fussy voice. "We mustn't be late."

Later, after Derry had driven up the steep bluff to the heights, Framingham pushed the button that retracted the window between them. "How are the fountains, James?"

"Just fine, Mr. Framingham," Derry said.

"Are you keeping them clean? There's nothing worse than a dirty fountain. I cannot abide a dirty fountain."

"Cleaned it out just today, Mr. Framingham. And every day. It's a very clean fountain."

"I'm happy to hear it."

Mancuso was in a blue Cutlass on the ramp next to Number 2 Warehouse. Two of his men in the front, one of them Mozzi, the head gardener. Mancuso in the back seat alone. Derry held the door for him as he clambered into the limousine. The heavy glance swept over the chauffeur and flicked away without recognition, Derry safely concealed behind his beard.

"Lovely evening," William Framingham said. "This is the time of year when the evenings have the quality of fine champagne."

"Shut the window," Mancuso said in his lead-filled voice.

Framingham pushed the button that closed the window between chauffeur and passengers. With his fingernail Derry turned on the speaking tube. Thus he was able to hear Mancuso tell Framingham, "Tell the man to drive south on I sixty-eight."

"I thought we were driving on the lake front."

"There's been a change. Tell him."

There was no doubt who was in charge here.

Framingham's finger could be heard fumbling with his speaking tube control button. "James, there's been a change. We're to go out I sixty-eight."

"Yes, sir," Derry said, not liking it.

He pulled out onto the empty roadway and turned left. In his mirror he saw the blue Cutlass tailing. He liked that even less. In the speaking tube next to his ear, he heard Framingham clicking the control button, shutting off communication. Except, of course, that it didn't.

Silence had fallen in the back seat. In his mirror, Derry saw the two men, as different as steel and water, settle back into their respective shells. Resentment flowed out of William Framingham, crackling like electricity. Nothing flowed out of Mancuso. He just sat there, impermeable.

After a good ten minutes—Derry headed the limousine toward the interstate leading out into the country—Framingham spoke first. "I wish you'd explain what this is all about, Mr. Mancuso."

Mancuso let it lay there for a very long time, Derry keeping one eye on the blue Cutlass, which was laying well back.

"You been talking to the wrong people," Mancuso said in his lead-bottomed voice.

"No," Framingham said. "Who would I talk to?"

"The attorney general."

"Bill Somers? He's an old friend of the family. I've known him for years."

The chunky figure of the mobster seemed to exude disbelief to such a degree it required no voice.

The limousine was out in the country now. Trees and cows flickered in headlights and disappeared. Derry keeping it at fifty-five.

"We got people in the attorney general's office," Mancuso said. "They tell us things."

"I told him nothing," Framingham said. The voice high and piercing. A little boy's voice, full of strident denial.

"You going to be a witness, our friends say. We don't like witnesses."

"I don't know anything," Framingham shouted angrily. "You know that

221

You tell me nothing. Bill talked to me for two hours. He says there are irregularities in the warehouses. I tell him *everyone's* stealing from warehouses. It's endemic. All over the country. Why pick on me?" The voice high and resentful. A small boy out of his depth.

In the mirror, Derry saw the blue Cutlass getting closer. How would they work it? Mancuso would be the executioner because they couldn't pour fire into a car with Mancuso in it. But they'd have to stop the limousine first because Mancuso couldn't go killing the chauffeur of a speeding car. The Cutlass would get ahead of the limousine and slam on the brakes, forcing him to do the same. Or there'd be stop light up there—lot of gang killing at stop lights. Or there'd be a big truck blocking an intersection. Something like that.

The blue Cutlass in his side mirror was getting closer, at high speed. The time had come. He had to do it to them or they'd do it to him.

Derry felt under the driver's seat and picked up the .38 he'd stashed there. It required a bit of stooping and Mancuso caught him at it. When Derry straightened up, glancing at the rearview mirror, there was Mancuso looking right back at him. It was all there in that heavy gaze. Mancuso had seen the stoop, figured out why, and went for his gun in the side pocket of his jacket.

Derry slammed on the brakes, swiveled in his seat and shot through the partition glass. It made a neat round hole in the glass, a larger hole in Mancuso's forehead.

Outside the Cutlass drew up alongside the limousine, the two gorillas in the front seat, peering at the dark windows they couldn't see through. Expecting that Mancuso had pulled it off somehow and would step out. The near one with the window rolled down.

Derry shot them both through his tinted glass window as they sat in the front seat. The two of them surprised. Not ready for it.

During all this Framingham looked out the side window away from the action. It wasn't happening. Or if it was, not to him. Anyway it was none of his affair. He was off somewhere in his different century as aloof as a mocking bird on the topmost branch of the sycamore tree.

Derry looked at his watch. Eleven P.M. Not so late there might not be a car along the highway. Derry stepped out of his front seat and opened the rear door of the limousine. Mancuso, still upright in the seat, stared back at him, eyes open, mouth open, the round wound in the forehead dribbling blood. Not much. Just a little.

222

Framingham staring out the window in his own private century.

"You'll have to help a bit, Mr. Framingham. I can't manage by myself."

In the end though, he had to. Framingham wasn't much use. Derry pulled the dead Mozzi and the other hood out of the blue Cutlass and piled them on the floor of the limousine. The blue Cutlass he drove off the road, parking it in the emergency lane.

"It's a stolen car," he explained to William Framingham who was in a state of stupefaction. "The police will pick it up."

Driving back to town, William Framingham sat in front with the chauffeur, an inconceivable intimacy. He hadn't yet spoken, which was just as well because things had to be explained.

"It's not over yet," Derry said. "Paddy's their man. We've got to shut up Paddy. Permanently. Otherwise you are in very great danger."

Presently Framingham spoke. "I wanted to get the fountains going again, you see, and there were a lot of other expenses. Keeping the house open and so forth. Anyway, they can't blame me for what was going on because they told me nothing."

The two of them at cross purposes.

"We can't let them find any of these people—Mancuso, Mozzi, Paddy. A lot of money has disappeared—and they've got to disappear with it—or they'll be tracing it back to you, Mr. Framingham."

Framingham was still in a daze of self-apology. "You have no idea how plausible they were. At first. Just getting around government regulations, don't you know. Fooling the bureaucrats. That kind of talk. And I *did* need the money."

"Mr. Framingham, you're going to have to pay attention. You're in much more trouble than you seem to realize. You'll have to get Paddy down the cliff staircase to that room because he won't do anything I say."

That brought Framingham around, the mouth drawn down in disapproval. "What room?" he asked.

"That room on the staircase no one is supposed to know about."

"That's a myth—that room," said Framingham sharply. "There's no such room. Never was. It's a superstition, that room."

Sarah had said the same thing. At first.

"They were going to kill us both," Derry said. "It's not over yet, Mr. Framingham. Until we get Paddy down those stairs. You can call from the garage. Tell him you have a package Mr. Mancuso wants him to carry up to the house. That will do it."

223

William Framingham's face had closed up again. He'd gone back into his century, and when they got back to the huge garage and Derry had pulled down the great double doors with the limousine inside, he had to repeat it all again, had to draw Framingham over to the house telephone and put it in his hand, and repeat the instructions in his ear after he got Paddy on the phone.

"You've got to come to the garage, Mr. Malone," Framingham said. "Mr. Mancuso wants you to take charge of this package."

"I'll be right there, Mr. Framingham."

"I'll wait for you right here."

There was only one way to the garage from the house—down the cliffside staircase. Derry sprinted up the stairs to the point roughly half-way where the room was. The .38 in his hand. The naked light bulbs threw soft yellow light and pools of blackness on the stairwell. A long five minutes after he got to the place, Derry could hear the door opening far above him and Paddy's heavy footfalls on the stone staircase.

He was not one to make a noiseless approach, not Paddy. Derry could hear him every foot of the way, puffing and whiffling. As the footfalls got closer, Derry extended his arm full length and Paddy all but bumped into the gun, rounding the corner, and when it went off, it was not more than an inch and a half from his chest and the impact blew him backward asprawl on the stone steps.

Eyes open. Surprised to death.

The noise resounding up and down the circular staircase like a cannonade.

"You'll have to help me find that room, Sarah," said Derry. "It all looks much alike here."

"It's right there opposite where you're standing." The voice in his ear. No picture. Just voice over.

Derry felt the baseboard near the floor with his fingers and pushed hard. A rectangle of wall disappeared into the base of the stairwell. The room itself was oval of curved oak paneling. Quite a carpentry trick, that. As in the doll's house, it was empty of furniture. Of everything. Derry hauled the dead Irish butler into the room by one arm.

He left the door open and returned to the garage. William Framingham was sitting in the front seat, his black hat on his head, his two hands clutching the cane between his legs, eyes glazed with the pain of it. There was no point in asking his help. He was clearly incapable of it. Derry

224

hunched the bodies, one by one, over his shoulder and carried them up the spiral staircase and into the stairwell room. After the last one, he pushed the baseboard again and the rectangle of wall rose from the floor and filled the space.

That was that.

Well, not quite. Derry had to go down the stairs again and shepherd William Framingham up the stairs into the house and into his room. Walking all the way as if in his sleep.

That still wasn't the end of it. Derry got the Xeroxes of the invoices and brought them down to the room. "Take them to your friend, Bill Somers, the attorney general. Tell him Paddy has disappeared, and you suspect there's been thievery. You found these in his room. Pin it all on *them* as they were about to pin it on you. They can't talk back."

William Framingham roused himself out of his self-absorption. "Why are you doing this?"

"Sarah's peace of mind," Derry said.

"Sarah's dead!" William Framingham said sharply. "She's been declared dead by the courts." Almost stamping his foot like a small boy in temper. Sarah, thought Derry, was much more mature than her Daddy.

He was looking out the great window of the master bedroom down the vista of lawn which led to the fountains.

"She loved you very much," Derry said dryly. "I can't think why."

Framingham was still in the midst of his temper tantrum. "It wasn't rape. You mustn't think that. She was of age—and she did it willingly. She was always a very obedient child. Too obedient for her own good. Or for my good, for that matter. If she'd said no, if she'd put up the least show of resistance, I'd not have . . . and anyway it was only once."

Derry let him run on because what was there to say?

"I don't know what possessed me. I was never much of a one for sex anyway. I think I was getting at her mother, don't you know. It was just a sudden thing, all over just like that. There's quite a lot of it, you know. I'm not the only one. I read an article just the other day. Fathers and daughters. Some even marry them."

"She set the house on fire," Derry said. Self-exculpation was beginning to weary him.

"She set *herself* on fire," William Framingham said. "That's why we had to put her in the tower room." The voice was full of pity now, self-pity. 'I had the best doctors. They said it was the tower room or an institution.

225

What could I do? She was having delusions she was other people. Called herself Mickie."

"How long was she in the tower room?"

"Three years."

That was all he could take. Derry walked out of the master bedroom without glancing back. He walked down the wide corridor with its sixteenth-century paintings of Dutch dragoon guards next to the great sweeping staircase, up the narrow servants' staircase to the third floor.

Hector was sitting on his bed, polishing his shoes.

"Get some sleep," Derry said. "We're leaving in the morning. I'll call you early."

He went to his own room and lay down fully clothed on the thin mattress, and closed his eyes. Somewhere in the early hours of morning, Sarah came and sat on the bed, radiant but dim.

"I'm quite well again," she announced. Very firm tones. For Sarah. "I haven't been Mickie or Vanessa for months now. I'm quite cured. If only I weren't dead . . ."

"It's a great pity," Derry said.

BOOK THREE

__ CHAPTER __
TWENTY TWO

TUMULTUOUS FEELING. MUCH looking. Neither of them saying anything because of the enormity of what there was to say, so much it was unsayable.

I don't know this man. My husband. The beard. The *everything*. A stranger.

The two of them eating breakfast after a night of touching and feeling and a few tears and no explanations. None.

The telephone rang.

Jonathan Glass.

"Milton Ford's been called out of the state on an important case. He left Saturday night."

"*When?*" Jessie asked.

"Saturday night. Right after the deposition."

Liar, Jessie thought. He was in bed with me.

Derry sitting there in his beard eating his scrambled eggs. Listening.

"The deposition is indefinitely postponed," Jonathan Glass said. "This is not usual. I suspect a tactic, Jessie. To delay the trial."

Lawyers, Jessie thought bitterly. And their tactics.

"In its way a confession of weakness," Jonathan Glass was saying.

Weakness? Milton Ford?

"I could move for early trial. Jostle him a bit."

"No, Uncle Jonathan. Don't do anything for a day or two. Let me think." Should I tell Uncle Jonathan Derry is home. No. "I'll call in a couple days. Okay?"

She hung up.

Derry swallowed his eggs, sipped his coffee, and didn't ask questions. Shouldn't he ask questions? So many questions to be asked! Derry asking none of them.

So different from the Attic simplicities of the Greeks. Again and again in *The Odyssey*, Odysseus is greeted by his hosts—Circe, Nausicaa, Penelope—and always, after the overflowing hospitality, the wine poured, the swine killed—there came the story. Great story tellers, the Greeks, and great listeners. Where have you been, resourceful Odysseus? Tell us all, now that your body is bathed and oiled, your belly full of swine. And Odysseus would tell his thievish tales.

I'm sure Derry has thievish tales to tell. After all he'd killed a woman. I have thievish tales of my own to tell. Or not to tell.

Eyeing him all the while like a mother her son. Looking for what was no longer there. What he had been, what she had imagined, in his absence, he had been, what he was now—three quite separate people.

Warren Widdy had left the mail on the kitchen table. On top of the junk mail lay a brown manila envelope, ten by twelve inches, bearing no sender's address. Inside were a batch of Xeroxes—Jessie's applications in her handwriting to the Department of Agriculture, County Committee, County Planning Commission, Environmental Protection Agency, Forestry Service. Underlined on each of these pieces of paper were the little lies and subterfuges she'd used. Most damning of all were Xeroxes of Derry's checks, forged by her. How had he got those? Clipped to all of it a printed memo form: *From the Desk of Milton Ford.*

But Milton Ford hadn't seen the envelope.

She wept. Great uncontrollable sobs, cascades of tears, heart bursting, body shaking, torrential. Derry took her in his arms, and held her tight, the beard tickling her cheek.

"Jake Levin said he was too old for breaking and entering," Jessie sobbed in her husband's arms. "But he knew people who weren't. It was Jake got all this for me, and I got him killed, Derry. I killed him."

"You didn't kill him, Jessie," Derry soothing her like a child. "Somebody else killed him."

Meanwhile, looking over the Xeroxes silently, carefully. The forged checks, the applications with the doctored information. Legend in bold face on one of them: "Full information is mandatory. False information is a felony, punishable by a fine of not more than $10,000 and imprisonment of not more than ten years."

230

"How did he get my checks?" Jessie was outraged by that. An invasion of privacy worse than Harry Sloane marching into her bathroom. "It's against the law!"

Comical. Me invoking the laws I've sidestepped myself when I had to.

"Law is not what's at issue here," Derry said. The new, revised, up-to-date, thoroughly alarming Derry. "That's not what he's got in mind."

"How do you know what he's got in mind?" Jessie whispered, dazzled by this stranger, her husband.

"I got a talent," Derry said. He smiled at her through his beard, charming her, bewildering her. This stranger. But then hadn't Odysseus, too, been a stranger when he got home after twenty years? Indeed he had. Penelope didn't recognize him.

Hector walked in.

"Hector," Derry said abruptly. "You got to go back to Cleveland."

"When?" Hector asked.

"Today." Derry taking Hector's elbow, steering him into the sitting room. Long low conversation in sitting room.

Jessie left out of it.

Ah, woe! Ah, woe! Jessie sipping her coffee, feeling like a Greek heroine, calamitous. I have my special calamities waiting to happen, one after another. And the greatest of these is . . .

The Japanese position.

Somewhere out there were the photographs of herself and Milton Ford in the Japanese position, photographs meant to blow Milton Ford sky high which could instead, blow Jessie Jenkins sky high.

Somebody had to go get those photographs back, but before that happened Jessie would have to explain . . .

The Japanese position.

To her husband.

231

__ CHAPTER __
TWENTY THREE

JESSIE INTRODUCED DERRY to Oscar and Jorvald. My husband, my lovers. In her mind alone, these ironies. My three men. A piquant situation, not contemplated by Homer.

The four of them toured Ski Village from one end to the other. Now almost finished. Painters swarming over the walls of the restaurant, the rental shop, the lounge. Carpenters and plumbers long gone.

Derry said little until they'd inspected the place from top to bottom. He waited until he and Jessie were alone. Then he said, "You got any guards?"

"Night watchman. What's to steal?"

"The cable," Derry said.

"Milton Ford doesn't know about that," quickly.

"Don't count on it!"

"I covered my tracks! Nobody knows about that!" Jessie furious at the implication she was an amateur.

"I'll spend the night out here until Hector gets back," Derry said. "Then Hector can take over until I find some good people."

"You just got home," Jessie wailed. "One night at home, and you're gone again!"

That wasn't it. He was taking charge, and she hated it. It was *her* Ski Village, *her* concept, *her* achievement. She'd prayed to Athena to return this man, her husband, and now she had him back. . . .

Who was it that said answered prayers were the worst? Truman Capote. No, somebody ahead of Truman Capote. It was in all the legends from the

233

beginning of records: the fairies granted your wishes but the wishes always turned into ashes, into mockery.

Jessie drove back to the farm, smoldering. I'll be unfaithful. I'll invite Oscar over! Jorvald! Go to bed with both of them together.

She wouldn't, of course. No more of that. She was in love with this dazzling stranger, her husband.

She wished she knew him.

He wasn't the same person, but then neither was she. Had he noticed? If he had, he hadn't mentioned it. That was his style. Not talking.

But then so is it mine. Have I told him anything? Only what had to be told. Both of us keeping our secrets.

The Japanese position, among them.

On her knees that night to Athena, Jessie said: "How am I going to explain the Japanese position to this . . . stranger."

The Gray-eyed One gleamed through the darkness: "He's been in the jungle of the cities. He's quite ready for the Japanese position."

"Give me courage!" Jessie wailed.

"Haven't I always?" Athena asked.

Later, with the electric blanket on in absence of husband, Jessie thought: I've been tricked by my own capability. We've all been tricked, we capable modern women. The better we get at running our lives, the worse off we are.

Ski Village was now ready for business except for two things—snow for its slopes and cable for its tall towers, my topless towers, thought Jessie, the classicist.

"We've got to get those cables inspected before we can operate," she said to Derry. "You can't put cables up and get them licensed in five minutes. How much longer do you need?"

"Three days," Derry said. "We've got to get the paper in position. That takes specialists, and Hector hasn't found them yet."

The paperman in Cleveland had provided good paper—application forms for grants from the Department of Agriculture, County Committee, County Planning Commission, all the others, complete with signatures, official seals, the works. Getting them into the right files took expertise.

"There's something else," Jessie said diffidently.

They were at the breakfast table, which was where she could pin him

234

down best. Immediately after breakfast he was off doing whatever he did with what he called his talent, which he'd learned in the jungle of the cities. It had to be done at breakfast or not at all.

"What?" Derry asked.

"The Japanese position," Jessie said primly. "It was me Jake Levin was photographing when he got killed. Me and Milton Ford. In the Japanese position."

Derry had been told about the plan to implicate Milton Ford—hadn't been told the rest of it.

"There was no one else we could pin on him. I had to do the work myself."

Watching Derry narrowly to see what he'd do. Or think. Or say.

She could feel the chemistry of him, boiling away, his bearded mouth slightly agape, his eyes gleaming with ferocity. Or perhaps just amusement. He said nothing, but it changed things between them. He's finding out, thought Jessie savagely, I'm not the woman he left behind. It's high time.

"You must show me sometime," Derry said.

"Never!" Jessie said, weeping now because his long silence had been unbearable. "Never again, the Japanese position. I must have vengeance, Derry. For Jake! For the Japanese position!"

"All in good time," Derry said and rose from the breakfast table to go look for Hector.

"I did it for you!" Jessie shouted through her tears. It wasn't strictly true; she'd done it for a lot of reasons. "You leave me alone for months on end! No money! A mortgage to pay! The farm to take care of! While you're off with some woman you killed! Without explanation! No anything! I'm surrounded by these gangsters! You tell me nothing! Force these shameful explanations from me. . . ."

"Who said they were shameful?" Derry said. He kissed her on the top of the head. "I've got to find Hector. We must get those photographs and negatives."

He walked out of the room.

"Sluice was on his ass last night," said Hector. "He thinks maybe he got somethin'." Sluice was the tail. He'd been on Milton Ford's traces for days.

"The matchman?" Derry asked. "He ready?"

"Why we need a matchman?" Hector asked. "Why we can't burn a few photographs ourselves?"

"It won't be a few. It'll be thousands. We need a professional."

Hector grinned. "You never even met the man. Now you readin' his mind."

"I got a talent," said Derry. With Hector he said it in a different tone of voice. It was their private joke. Like all the best jokes, it was true.

"Where is it?" Derry asked.

"Down by the river in Richmond. We back among the warehouses. Like we never left Cleveland."

Derry slipped out of bed at midnight, Jessie sleeping with all her might, as he used to say. Derry picked his clothes off the floor—trousers, shirt, shoes, socks, sweater—and was out the door, soundless.

He dressed in the long upstairs corridor and joined Hector in Jessie's Triumph. They switched on the lights only when they got into the woods out of sight of the house.

"What you tell you wife?" Hector asked.

"Nothing," Derry said.

An hour and a half to Richmond. They talked shop.

"They stumbling over they own feet," Hector said. "Homicide in Folkesbury nevah had a professional shoot in they whole lives. Oney thing they know is one nigger cuttin' another nigger over some trifle. They over they heads."

"They haven't connected to Jessie?"

Hector shook his head. "They just found out what Jake Levin did for a living. He kept records in his head. She paid him cash. No checks. No record."

"The bodies were on Milton Ford's floor."

"They found four floors down. Maybe Homicide can't count."

"There's Mob money in that hotel," Derry said. "They're covering."

They were in Richmond now, driving down the wide, quiet tree-lined boulevards with the handsome houses. An old-fashioned city, Richmond, the kind they don't build any more.

Two A.M.

Derry parked the Triumph two streets away, and the two men walked close to the walls out of the direct glare of the sodium lamps. Swiftly.

The matchman waited for them in an alley directly opposite the warehouse. A Neapolitan named Fozzi. Derry hadn't liked it. "Fozzi smells of olive oil," he complained to Hector. "Which side of the street is he on?"

236

"Whoever pays the bills. He keep his mouth shut, or he catch a bullet in his teeth. He know that. He the best matchman they is."

Fozzi had been there an hour, staying out of sight, keeping the place in view. No night watchman. Nothing. His pickup was parked down the alley in the shadows, the ladder on a rack over its roof. Best to climb in, not cut your way in, he said. It left no marks. Also, it left the Fire Department the problem of fighting their own way through the chain link fence. That delayed matters just enough sometimes for the place to be ashes by the time they got in.

Entry was on the darkest side of the building, the ladder taking them up to the roof, and from there by skylight. Fozzi very swift and capable. He carried the wick on his back. Magnesium. Burned hotter than gasoline, took less space, and left no residue except the smell which, with luck, would be gone by the time the fireflies got there.

Derry didn't care about cover. What he wanted was total incineration. If the insurance people didn't pay, so what? It wasn't his loss.

Derry's flashlight cutting through the blackness.

It was a print shop. Flat presses, three of them widely spaced, lined one wall. In the center were the layout tables with the type faces on them. On the far wall were the hand-cranked binders that turned out the finished product.

There were piles of that, wrapped in bundles in brown paper. There were other piles in brown manila envelopes, already addressed. Derry looked at a few of these addresses. Churches in central Virginia.

Contents designed to give the pastor quite a shock. The magazine was called EROS EROTICA and right on the cover . . .

Jessie in the Japanese position.

In four colors.

Where was Milton Ford? There was a man there all right, but the face was in the shadow, dimmed out altogether. Whereas Jessie—mouth open, as it should never be in the Japanese position—clearly enjoying herself. In four colors. Centered, distinct, unmistakably Jessie.

Derry flipped through the rest of the magazine. Hard-core pornography out of which the Mafia garnered a hundred million a year. Or was it four hundred million? One of those numbers. All sorts of girls in all sorts of positions.

Hector looking over his shoulder.

"Good of her, isn't it?" Derry said.

237

He rustled through the brown envelopes, already addressed. One church after another. The Mafia had very good distribution for its hard-core pornography, but the church group was a little something extra. Featuring a girl on the cover who was clearly unfit to run a ski resort that catered to young people. That was the message to the churches, which carried enormous political clout in central Virginia. It was the churches that had killed horseracing in Virginia, and now they were being lined up to kill Jessie.

"We must find the plates," Derry said. "And the negatives."

Hector found the plate easily on one of the layout tables. The negatives were not so easy. The two men searched the warehouse carefully, going from table to table, while Fozzi lay out his magnesium. There was much pornography there besides EROS EROTICA, and Derry told Fozzi to see to it that EROS EROTICA got special attention. There were four wrapped bundles of EROS EROTICA and they were doused with alcohol from the print shop's own supply, placed on the tables where the draft was fierce.

Meanwhile, Derry and Hector searched for the negatives. They found them in a small office in the top drawer of the foreman's desk. Three shots of the Japanese position, Milton Ford quite visible in these. Derry pocketed them. The plate he poured acid on until the outlines blurred and disappeared. Just for good measure, he broke it in half with a hammer.

"Let's go."

He and Hector were out the skylight, Fozzi last. Ignition was by wire from the roof and Fozzi, meticulous craftsman that he was, watched, his head hanging inside the skylight as the magnesium flared, throwing an explosion of white light through the skylight, illuminating the nearby buildings with almost indecent clarity. After that the secondary whooshes of flame and light, softer orange light.

For a very long time, Fozzi's head hung inside the skylight, making sure everything went according to plan.

When he came down the ladder, he came fast. Within seconds, the ladder was on his back, and they were across the street and into the alley. Three A.M. The best arson time. Flames lighting the empty streets of the deserted warehouse, casting orange light over the James River clear to the opposite bank.

Derry and Hector were in the Triumph cruising at a respectable speed north, out of the warehouse district. It was ten minutes before Derry heard the first sirens screaming across the silent city. Orange flames lit the skyline.

"Look like Fozzi lit up a few more buildings than he planned," Hector said.

Derry was silent, thinking of Chicago. He'd advanced from victim to arsonist. Progress.

Two hours later, Derry crawled back into bed with his sleeping wife. The next day was Jessie's birthday. Derry gave her the negatives for a birthday present.

Jessie's mouth fell open again, just as it was in the Japanese position. She looked at the negatives, all three of them, a very long time. "*Terrible!* Look at my *hair!*"

She kissed her husband, feeling again total surprise and, yes, fear at his terrifying competence. "It's a lovely birthday present."

In a questioning voice. Misery in her face.

"What's the matter, Jessie?"

She blurted it out: "I'm horrified! Arson, my God, Derry."

Derry looked at her unfathomably from behind his beard: "You cut a few corners, too, Jessie."

"I know! I had to! But *arson!* You *killed* a woman. You don't even tell me who or why. Or . . . how many. How many people have you killed, Derry?"

Derry was silent. This thrilling stranger who inhabited her bed, her life, her love. Did she inhabit him to the same degree?

Or at all?

__ CHAPTER __ TWENTY FOUR

THE CABLE WHOSE very existence had been kept secret was being uncoiled by the big winches, Derry and Jessie and Oscar and Jorvald watching every foot. Second-hand cable from a ski resort in Colorado that hadn't made it. The ski resort had gone under fast and the cable had hardly been used. Still there were stringent regulations about ski cables. And there were bureaucrats with their small minds and rigid rules. And vices.

The safety commissioner came himself, lips pursed in a most unpromising way, and as the huge drums rolled out the cable, very slowly, he glowered at the thick steel strands with a ferocity that seemed unnecessary. Jessie didn't like the look of this man, whose name was Morrissey, at all. She'd brought in her own cable expert, R. C. Watkins. Because Derry told her to.

"All right," Morrissey barked. "Hold it right there!"

The drums stopped.

Morrissey put his finger on a bit of cable which looked sturdy enough to hold the *Queen Mary.*

"Unacceptable," Morrissey said, finger on the cable. Eyes glaring. A formidable man.

"What's the matter with it?" asked Watkins, the cable expert.

"It's been tampered with," Morrissey said. "It's unsafe."

"I don't see anything at all," the cable expert said.

"Are you the safety commissioner—or am I?" Morrissey asked. "I tell you it's been tampered with—and that is that. The cable's unsafe."

Derry nodded at Hector, and the two men closed in on Morrissey, one on either side. "I think we better have a little talk."

"There's nothing to talk about," Morrissey said.

That was as far as he got. Derry took one of his arms, Hector the other. The two of them lifted Morrissey right off the ground, up the steps of the lodge, and into Jessie's office.

Jessie following.

"We don't need you," Derry snapped at Jessie.

"I must," Jessie said, fire in her eye.

In Jessie's office, the two men dumped Morrissey down hard in Jessie's office chair. Hector closed the door.

Jessie leaning against it, mouth half open, as it was in the Japanese position.

Because Derry had taken the .38 special from his side pocket, turning it this way and that in his hands, not looking at Morrissey, looking at the weapon which had enormous authority and menace in its gleaming blued steel barrel.

"This is for your protection, you understand," Derry said silkily.

Jessie had her hand on her throat now, as if the menace were directed at her.

Derry was saying, "We think *you've* been tampered with, Mr. Morrissey."

Argument welled up in the Irishman, but he couldn't quite voice it—the weapon choking him off.

"We think you have been got at, Mr. Morrissey, and that would be contrary to law. You could go to jail for ten years if it was discovered you had been bribed or intimidated to misuse the powers of your office."

Derry was sighting down the .38 barrel held in outstretched hands, aimed right at Morrissey's eyes.

"However, we want to protect you from yourself, Mr. Morrissey. We have one cable expert already on the scene, two more on the way. . . ."

A lie, Jessie thought. No more cable experts were on the way.

". . . all ready to testify that cable is sound and you are clearly mistaken— and probably crooked. This could end your career, Mr. Morrissey, and we wouldn't like that, would we? To save you from these career mistakes, we have prepared the authorization forms for you to sign."

242

Hector laid them in front of the Irishman and handed him the pen.

Morrissey didn't sign. Clearly terrified. Not just by Derry. Somebody had got at him earlier, as Derry had said, and now he was faced with two terrors—the terrible consequences of signing when, as Derry guessed, he'd been bribed not to and the terrible consequences of not signing.

Derry had to make that second possibility more terrifying than the first. His voice took on a new and frightful viciousness: "If you don't sign, you'll never be seen alive again by anyone, including Milton Ford, and you can tell Mr. Ford that."

Sighting down the barrel, squinting ferociously.

Scaring Jessie almost out of her wits.

"You've got till I count five. Then I'm going to blow your head off."

He'd do it! Jessie thought, dumbfounded. My husband!

Morrissey signed and, even as he signed, Derry detected the duplicity in the man and moved instantly to quell it. "In case you have any idea of saying you signed this under duress, we will deny it. We will also have on hand the sworn statements of three recognized cable experts that there is nothing the matter with the cable. We'll hang you by the heels in court and shoot your ass off out of court. You can tell Milton Ford that, too."

Derry and Hector walked Morrissey to his car, right past the others— Jorvald, Oscar and Watkins. The gun was out of sight in Derry's pocket, his two fingers giving a good imitation of it in Morrissey's back.

Derry talking all the while, "We're very happy you've changed your mind about that, Mr. Morrissey. Central Virginia needs another ski resort. There are far too many skiers for the few ski places now in operation, and Ski Village will bring much happiness to a great many people. You have done your duty well today, Mr. Morrissey, as a public servant and a citizen, and we will not forget it. I personally will write the Governor to that effect and send you a copy."

And so on and so forth until Morrissey was in his car and had driven off.

A dazzling performance.

It scared the life out of Jessie.

Later when they were alone, she said so.

Derry shrugged. "If he hadn't licensed you, you could have spent a year getting him into court—meanwhile going broke. Now we have his signature, we can go ahead—and he can spend a year trying to get *us* into court. Without his signature we could have screamed he's a liar and a crook—and no one would pay attention. Now he can scream we're liars and crooks—and no one will pay any attention to him. Because we have that piece of paper."

"You can get him killed, Derry," Jessie whispered. "You know that, don't you? If they paid him not to sign and he signed. . . ."

Derry sighed. "It's a jungle out there, Jessie. Kill or be killed."

"I hate it," Jessie said. "Combatting lawlessness with lawlessness. It's getting worse and more vicious each time."

"You did a bit of it yourself, Jessie."

"Yes, and I'm horrified. I wasn't before because I was so . . . busy and so desperate, but now I'm as horrified by my actions as—as, I am by yours. But you, Derry, you're not horrified, and I find that horrifying. You, a simple farm boy I've known all my life, with that gun. . . ."

It fell into a pool of silence, all this eloquence, this passion, this gush of morality that was shaking Jessie to her roots.

"They have all the weapons," Derry said finally. "Do you want Them to win?"

They and Them. The people who tore up cities and ravaged countrysides. The faceless corporations behind which lurked all the Milton Fords and the other lawless lawyers, with their expense accounts and their money and their evil.

Jessie no longer doubted the existence of evil.

What are you going to do about Evil, Jessie Jenkins? Rise above it? Combat it. The two things at the same time. A plan springing full grown in her mind.

_ CHAPTER _
TWENTY FIVE

THE NEXT DAY, Thursday, it snowed all day and all night. A foot of snow on the flatlands, and eighteen inches on Jessie's slopes. There was no skiing in weather like that, but Jessie rushed into the breech with advertising. All day and well into the night the two radio stations WDUH and WMPA hammered away at the message. Ski Village was the *new* place with four brand-new slopes, for all those skiers bored with the familiar slopes at the other places. Ski Village with its restaurants, its ski slopes, ski instructors, ski rental. On Highway 28 just half an hour from Folkesbury. Thirty-five minutes from Martinsville and an hour from this city and that city. Blanketing the air with the message over a radius of 150 miles.

Friday dawned bright blue and cold, lovely skiing weather. By nine A.M. when the lifts opened, there were a hundred people in line on the slopes and scores more in line for the ski rentals and the ski lift tickets. A busy day but not an overwhelming one because it was Friday, and Jessie thanked her special Goddess for that favor because the staff needed a little rehearsal. The lifts and the slopes under Jorvald's direction worked like clockwork. The restaurants didn't. Service was slow and the girls on the cash registers still slower, but getting better every hour.

Just a moderate day for the opening, the slopes busy but not crowded. Total ski tickets sold only 312, and yet Jessie was stunned by the cash receipts. She was still counting the money when they turned on the lights and the night skiing crowd arrived—and there were twice as many as day skiers—more than six hundred of them. Lines for the ski rental wound clear around the building. More than three quarters of the customers didn't

245

own their own skis and were willing to pay ten dollars for ski rental as well as fifteen dollars for a ski ticket. Only six dollars for night skiing lift tickets good only a few hours.

When the people weren't skiing, they flooded the restaurant, paying a dollar-fifty for a hot dog that cost Jessie twelve cents. At ten o'clock they turned off the lights, and the crowd went home. Jessie counted the take which came to twenty-one thousand dollars, not counting sales in the shops.

"I don't believe it!" Jessie muttered. "A license to steal!"

Saturday was a beautiful day, and the roof fell in. Ski Village caused a traffic jam that extended from Skidmore to Battenburg, twelve miles. The skiers got there at eight A.M., an hour before the lifts opened, and Jessie promptly decreed that henceforth the restaurants would serve breakfast on weekends, taking in even more cash. Skiers flooded the slopes jamming all four lifts without let-up until four-thirty when the light got too bad and Jorvald closed them—until nightfall when the night skiers poured in.

Everything was sold out—restaurant, ski rental, ski instruction. Especially ski instruction.

"I have never seen a place in such need of ski instruction," Jorvald shouted. "Even those who don't take ski instruction need it badly. In my whole life I have never seen such terrible skiers!"

As far as Jessie was concerned bad skiers were the best skiers—because they needed instruction at twelve dollars an hour as well as rental skis at ten dollars plus ski tickets—and, of course, food. At the shops they bought sweaters, gloves, boots, trousers—well everything. Nowhere in the world were skiers so ill-equipped as in central Virginia, and there was Jessie providing them goods and services—and food and drink. The beer alone— at the preposterous charge of a dollar-fifty a can—brought in over a thousand dollars. By the end of the weekend, Ski Village had grossed almost a hundred thousand dollars. On its first weekend.

Even better than the flow of cash was the weather. On Monday—Jessie couldn't have scheduled it better if she'd tried—it snowed again—hard. Another eight inches. That meant no skiers, but then Monday was an off day on the slope anyway. Now she had almost two feet of snow as a base, which was better than gold in the bank.

Derry and Hector drove the money to the bank personally—and put it on night deposit. The first night. After that they got Brinks to do the job. "I don't think Milton Ford is so bankrupt of ideas he'd heist it—but I don't want to worry about that. Let Brinks handle it. They're insured. We can worry about other things."

There was plenty to worry about. One slope was too gradual and attracted almost no skiers. One too steep and attracted too many, considering how terrible the Virginia skiers were. They ran into each other with alarming frequency, and the ski patrol was kept busy sorting them out, Jessie praying there'd be no serious accidents, no big lawsuits. The locker room was too small, the restaurant service too glacial. Jessie slashed the menu to the bone—hot dogs and hamburgers and chocolate cake—to make it easy to serve. Skiers were not interested in variety. They wanted food, lots of food. It scarcely mattered what. Nor what she charged—so she charged the earth. The charges in her ski shops were scandalous—twice what they were in Folkesbury for the same sweater. Nobody noticed.

On the main floor, she opened an office to sell condominiums—before she had any. Eighty-five thousand dollars for a one bedroom, one living room, small kitchen, bathroom. Hundred and twenty-five thousand for the big ones with three bedrooms and a southern exposure on the slopes. In two days she signed up six people for six hundred thousand dollars worth of condominiums she didn't own.

"I've got to go to the bank," she announced at breakfast.

"I'll come along," Derry said. Unexpectedly.

Jessie fumbled with her scrambled eggs, sipped her coffee, frowned. She didn't want him along. This was her deal, her play. Ski Village and everything about it was her baby.

"It's banking," Jessie said, not meeting his eye. "I asked for a loan, and they been holding back but now. . . . You'd be bored to death, Derry. Just figures."

Derry looked at his hands. "They are going to throw it at your head the minute you step in that door."

"What they going to throw at my head? I got the figures. The property has gone up two three times in one week. By the end of the year that land is going to be worth ten times what I paid for it. . . ."

"Forged checks," Derry said reluctantly.

"Oh, my God!" Jessie's hand at her throat. She'd forgotten the checks. Her clumsy forgeries!

"What do I say?"

Derry told her, brought her the paperman's skillful work. "It would be highly unlikely you'd have this on hand. What is needed is shocked indignation from you. Can you carry it off?"

Jessie smiled sadly: "I've been telling whoppers—bigger and bigger ones—ever since you went away. I can tell lies with the best of them. What I want to know is when can I resume telling the truth?"

The bank had some nasty surprises. They were kept waiting an hour, though Jessie had an appointment. When they were shown in J. Fred Percy, even more glacial than usual, introduced them to a sandy-haired young man sitting at his desk. Digby Marsh, assistant district attorney. One of the old Folkesbury family of Marshes that went back to pre-Revolution. Very Establishment, very grim.

Allegations had been made. On J. Fred Percy's desk were many pieces of paper. Paper, thought Jessie, exasperated. Now I'm up to my ass in pieces of paper.

It made her angry, which was just what the situation required.

When confronted with her forged checks, she blew sky high. These were the forgeries! The real canceled checks were back at her house in her files. How dare they? etc. etc.

"No accusations have been made," Digby Marsh said, turning on his celebrated Southern charm. "We are simply asking for explanation."

"Where did you get these pieces of paper?" Jessie thundered. Derry laying back, letting her handle it.

Digby Marsh wasn't ready to tell her. Instead he brought forth more paper—Xeroxes for applications for farm assistance, loans, federal grants, changes of land use, all the bureaucratic idiocies—full of Jessie's little prevarications.

"Some of the claims in these applications are clearly fraudulent," Digby Marsh said silkily.

Jessie froze her face into what she devoutly hoped was an expression of total scorn, herself quaking inside, and stepped out of the ring. Derry stepped in, took the pieces of paper out of her hand, looked at each one for a long time, saying "mmm," and "hmmm," pursing his lips, being enfuriating.

"May I see the others?" Derry asked. He could be as frigidly Virginian as Digby Marsh.

Digby Marsh handed him all the Xeroxes, and Derry hmmed and mmed over them for a very long time, letting them wait for it.

248

"Forgeries," he announced. "Every last one."

"They seem to have Mrs. Jenkins' signature on them."

"Have you checked these Xeroxes with the originals which lie in the files of the EPA, the USDA, the County Committee?" Derry asked.

Now Digby Marsh started to hmmm and mmm. Clearly he hadn't.

"I suggest you do—and then apologize, and after you apologize, we'll want the name of the person making these false accusations. We intend to sue, for slander. Come along, Jessie."

Jessie came—mutinously. "I wanted to talk about my loan."

"Later," Derry said.

They were in the car. Derry at the wheel. Doing the driving. Taking charge.

"I hate the duplicity," she whispered, huddled there in her new red coat, her beautiful new expensive clothes.

"We corrected all the duplicity, erased the lies, changed the figures. The figures and the applications are now totally honest—so honest that you wouldn't have got the grants and loans if you had submitted them like that. It's a terrible system, but that's the way things are."

I'm about to change the system, Jessie thought, aflame with her shining resolve. She wasn't about to tell Derry about that for fear he'd take that away too. Instead she said, "What's Milton Ford going to pull on us next, Derry?"

Derry shook his head: "I've had him figured up to now, all the way, but from here on in, I just don't know. All I do know is he's got to make a play, or he's out of the game."

The skiers poured in. January was fair and cold and only occasionally did it snow. At night so the skiers could enjoy the slopes in the daytime.

J. Fred Percy telephoned, stiff with apology, an art form he clearly knew little about. Digby Marsh's apology was in the old Southern tradition—fulsome, witty, thoroughly enjoyable both to Jessie and to Digby Marsh. After an apology like that, thought Jessie, a girl could very easily be bedded by the apologizer. . . .

Musn't have thoughts like that. I've given that all up.

I'm in love with my own husband. Bedded by my own husband. Bewildered by my own husband.

What does he want?

She didn't know.

J. Fred Percy was again on the telephone, this time to say the committee had approved her loan for the condominiums and if she'd like to come in and discuss things. . . .

Everything was going her way. It filled her with foreboding.

Derry was running the farm now full-time because Ski Village was taking all of Jessie's time. He was milking the goats, planning spring planting, getting the pigs impregnated—all the things Jessie so loved doing.

Jessie was raking in money. The good ski weather continued and the skiers poured in, showering Ski Village with gold. She sold twelve condominiums she hadn't yet built for four hundred thousand dollars.

She was rich and powerful.

And unsatisfied.

Ambition gnawing at her.

"I want to shake the tree," she confided to the Gray-eyed Goddess, "until the sky rains rotten apples."

"Don't get hit in the head with your own fury," advised the Gray-eyed One.

"What does he want?" she whispered. "My husband?"

"You wouldn't really like to find out," the Gray-eyed One said. "But unfortunately you will—when the time comes."

One day Hector's wife appeared out of nowhere, and moved in with him in the little shanty in the woods where Hector had been sleeping.

Derry was out cutting wood in the forest, and Jessie told him about it when he got home for supper: "Beautiful girl named Cassandra," Jessie said. "Much too beautiful to be living in that shanty in the woods. And that name, Cassandra. Where you suppose she got a name like that?"

"Her mother said she was bad news," Derry said. "And she is."

At two A.M. the telephone rang. And rang and rang and rang. Jessie slept so soundly she might have slept on but Derry awoke and his movement awoke her. "Hello! Hello! Hello!" she heard him say. "Nobody on here."

Her eyes open now.

"Derry!" she screamed. "Derry!"

Flames licked the sky, red as blood.

"The barn!"

The horror of all farmers, a barn fire in winter, when the animals are

250

locked away. Even as they scrambled into their clothes they heard the first wild whinnying scream, one of the most fearsome noises of the animal world, a horse in terror.

Jessie was faster on her feet than Derry, and she was dressed and out the door, running. He tore after her and, in the barn field, still well back in the blackness, caught her with a football tackle. "No, Jessie, no!" he muttered, holding her down. "The whole thing's rotten."

Jessie lying underneath him, struggling: "The horses are in there!" Jessie screamed. "Wednesday! Saturday! The foals! They're *dying!*"

Derry holding her down, "It's a trap, Jessie. That phone call!"

He could smell the magnesium in the air burning the ancient oak of the barn that would be flameproof to almost anything else. Flames roaring thirty feet up now, throwing white light to the horizon.

Jane and Warren Widdy running up from their cottage.

Then Hector and Cassandra from their place.

"Get down," Derry yelled. "Down in the dirt! Get out of the light."

All stopped, bewildered.

First rule of a farm in case of fire. Get the animals out.

"Down!" Derry howled. "Down!"

Still, struggling with his wailing wife. In the barn the scream of the pigs, loudest of all, louder than the scream of the horses, louder than the Concorde.

Jessie struggling, loving her animals, hating her husband.

Hating him!

The barn blew up with a soft whoosh. A masterful job. It buckled at the very center of the southern wall where it had always bulged outward, the weakest point in the structure. Someone had planted the charge at the exact point where the inspector would attribute it to inherent weakness.

Fozzi. Derry felt no bitterness against the man. Clearly Fozzi didn't know it was Derry's barn, didn't even know Derry's real name.

The barn collapsed inward, the roof beams folding in from the center drawing in the outer walls so that all the beams buckled toward the center in a great shower of flame. One last dissonant scream of agony from eight pigs and four horses, then only the crackle of flame.

"We've got to run for it," Derry said. "Get out of the light. They'll be shooting at us if we don't."

He pulled his sobbing wife back into the protective blackness.

"I could have saved Saturday! I could have saved them all!" Jessie said.

They were in the kitchen—Derry and Jessie, Jane and Warren, Hector and Cassandra.

"It was a trick. The phone call was to wake us up, be sure we knew about the fire. They were over in the cornfield with a remote control firing pin just waiting for us to run into that barn. They'd have brought the whole thing down on our heads. Eventually the flames got to the device and it blew itself up."

Jessie was not comforted. Not comforted at all.

"That his last play?" Hector asked.

"They won't let him make any more," Derry said. "He might bring the roof down on them."

Jessie got the old quilt and wrapped it around her, sitting bolt upright in the big Morris chair in the sitting room where no one ever sat.

"I'm going to sit up a little while and mourn animals," she said primly to Derry. "I brought this down on their heads. I killed them!"

"Oh, for God's sake, Jessie. . . ."

"Go away, Derry."

Long pause.

"All right."

He walked out of the sitting room, out of the house, up the drive. . . .

"You may regret that," the Gray-eyed Goddess said.

"It's over," Jessie said. "My world died out there. I should have known it would end like this in ashes and grief."

"It's the beginning, not the end. You know that, Jessie."

Jessie knew it. She wasn't happy about it.

Two weeks later Milton Ford had an unfortunate accident. His car went off the road and into the Hardware River at one of Virginia's many one-lane wooden bridges, killing the man instantly. And skillfully.

__ CHAPTER __
TWENTY SIX

TWO YEARS LATER.

Brilliant sky-blue October day, the leaves on the Norway maples yellow and scarlet.

The parking problem was massive. There was no way to get so many cars down Jenkins Farm's single-line driveway so all the cars—except those bearing white streamers bearing the big shots—were deflected into Shadow Creek's big field across the road. The voters had to walk a third of a mile up the long driveway, but they didn't mind. It gave them a chance to visit with one another, shout greetings, exchange the news, mostly bad.

Jessie in her white dress. Symbol of purity. "Nobody appreciates purity like the blood-stained," she had said.

Jessie in the barn field greeting the guests and the neighbors, shaking hands with one and all, with a quip and a smile and a kiss, Jessie and her titanic energy.

Jessie Jenkins, Congresswoman. Well, not quite, but on the way.

There was Cousin Agatha from *The Folkesbury Advance,* press card in her hat. "My, Jessie, you do look a candidate! I'm full of admiration. But what you want to be a Congresswoman *for*? Job ain't big enough for you."

"Next time I'll run for Governor," Jessie said with a kiss. "This is just practice. Hi, Jerry. Hello there, Frosty. How's Mandy?" Here they all were again, the Gulf station crowd, her Greek Chorus, Abe Caldwell, Terence Scott, the whole lot of them. Her friends again because her barn burned down. Nothing like a barn burning to weld a community together.

"Dr. Barnes, my goodness! You came thirty miles to hear me talk! You're out of your mind!" Kissing the veterinarian while shaking hands with Humboldt Pickering and then kissing Everlee—all in one motion because a candidate couldn't waste a lot of time and motion.

"Todd Gassett, you're looking well. Todd, why don't you get folks moving over to *that* side of the field. It's getting awfully crowded over here."

In the center of the barn field was the drink stand and the hot dogs and hamburgers. Hector and Derry and Cassandra and Jane and Warren Widdy dishing out the booze, the food, in the Virginia way of politics. Eat first, think later. The speaker's stand was next to the new barn, draped in red, white, and blue with the Commonwealth flag at the four corners.

The new barn was all metal, bolted together in a single afternoon by the company that sold it, all a package deal. It was full of new pigs without names and horses Jessie had no time to ride.

"Harry Sloane!" Jessie was shocked at the change in him. He'd lost thirty pounds, which was probably the best thing that had ever happened to him, but the face was wasted with deep lines in the cheeks and a single deep furrow across the big brow. Still a massive figure, the sardonic gleam in the eye more pronounced than ever.

"You runnin' as the Virgin Queen, Jessie?" Harry asked. "I'd like to run my filthy hands all over that white dress, up and down you backsides."

"Harry!" Jessie giggled. "Where you been hiding? I been asking everywhere."

"We got a place down south. Can't even vote for you because you not in my district. But I thought I come listen."

She led him around the barn. "Let's get out of this mob for a minute. Harry, tell me true. How things with you?"

"Not good. Not bad."

"You want a job? I need a foreman."

Harry Sloane smiled his goatish smile. "You own it all now, don't you, Jessie? Shadow Lawn, Winter Creek Farm. How many farms you own Jessie?"

"Harry, I'm serious. If I get elected, I need a foreman bad. I pay you more money than you ever had."

"What's matter with Derry? Can't he run things?"

Jessie wasn't going to get into that. "Think it over, Harry. I got to go make my manners with the Governor. Give me a ring."

Jessie on the run across the barn field. "Governor, you didn't need to *walk* up the driveway. I left special orders. . . ."

The Governor smiled wryly. "I thought I'd say hello to a few voters, Jessie. Before you steal them all away. The word's out you'll be after my job next."

"Not for a couple of years, Governor." Jessie taking the ball away and dribbling with it. Possession of the ball was the name of the game in politics.

"Hello, Uncle Jonathan and Aunt Tabitha." Kissing them both because, of course, they were with the Governor.

"Digby, could you take the Governor up to the platform and start seating them? I think we better get started."

Digby Marsh, the charm boy from the district attorney's office, now her campaign adviser, his own eye on the district attorney's office. When it wasn't on Jessie herself. He hadn't quite managed to land Jessie.

It was a full hour before the crowd stopped coming, a huge crowd for rural Virginia, almost a thousand. Jessie had worked hard, visited every single farmhouse in her district, every last one.

What she had said to each voter was . . . almost nothing of substance. "My goodness, what beautiful roses! How do you get roses that *pink*?" Throwing the ball to them, letting them talk, show themselves. "I think your wallpaper is marvelous. It shows off the room so well." Or "Oh you're that branch of the Ferguses. My granddaddy used to know your granddaddy." Charm and good manners and an intense interest in what the voter wanted. I'm supposed to be his representative, am I not?

The Governor introduced Jessie with wry courtesy, "I knew her father and her grandfather—and so did many of you out there. Now it looks as if we will know Jessie even better. She is the embodiment of southern determination and gentility and common sense which is becoming very rare in American politics. What sets Jessie apart is the fact she's a woman, which in Virginia politics is still a little unusual and, to me, slightly terrifying."

It got a big laugh, and so the Governor closed with that big laugh and personally escorted Jessie to the rostrum where he led the applause for her. Jessie smiling radiantly, all eyes on her.

Except Derry's. Jessie's glance sweeping the field, acknowledging the applause, stopped at Derry who was whispering something to that black girl, Cassandra, who was laughing fit to kill.

255

Those two!

No time for that.

Her words were simple and powerful.

"My friends, my neighbors, I am a farmer—as are most of you. We are a dwindling band of survivors. American farmers are going broke, moving to the cities, dying and not being replaced, getting out of farming for one reason or another at the rate of eight hundred thousand a year. The newspapers are full of stories about how wonderful we are in agriculture—exporting twenty-five billion dollars worth of food annually while overfeeding our own populace.

"What they don't tell us is that we're losing four billion tons of topsoil a year through water erosion, twice as fast as the soil can be replaced. They don't speak of the five pounds of pesticide and fungicide produced for every single American, destroying our soil biota for generations, giving cancer to Iowa farmers at a rate from fifty to seventy-five percent higher than city dwellers. To say nothing of the proliferation of cancer and birth defects among the people who eat the poisoned food we produce."

Looking out over the silent faces, feeling the power of swaying an audience. "Farming is slipping out of the hands of farmers altogether. Some very curious people are getting into the food business. Greyhound produces turkeys, RCA makes pot pies, and the International Telephone and Telegraph Company bakes doughnuts."

It got a big laugh and while it was subsiding, Jessie glanced over her audience and saw the movement, coming down under the Norway maples. Latecomers, moving swiftly. . . .

"I never thought—and you never thought . . ."

Now the pair had come out of the shadows and moved into the sunlight.

That young freckle-faced Deputy Sheriff Tomlin Perkins. With him that little mouse who worked for the insurance company. What was his name? Garrett. . . .

Jessie not missing a beat. Only a little quaver that no one would notice except Derry. ". . . that we would ever see the day we'd *import* food into this country which has produced so much but I tell you, if we continue on this disastrous course, we will be importing more than half our food by the year 2000 . . ."

Jessie always paused for effect right there. This time she looked at Derry, and this time his eyes were on her. He'd caught that quaver. With the tiniest nod of her head she indicated the insurance man and Tomlin Peters who were, fortunately, on the driveway while the drink and food stand was clear across the barn field, with the crowd in between.

"Our farms are not being run by farmers but by industrialists using industrial methods, and an industrial philosophy wholly unsuited to farmland, to the long term welfare of growing plants, and to our very existence. . . ."

Derry had slung his jacket over his shoulder, and he and Hector and the black girl started walking on the other side of the crowd toward the woods at the end of the barn field. Jessie's eyes swept east, and she saw the insurance man and Tomlin Peters standing by the gate, searching the crowd, looking the wrong way.

Jessie carrying on with the familiar speech, her mind miles away.

"The GAO has reported to Congress that United States cropland has sustained annual soil losses in excess of the limit at which soil productivity can be maintained. And what was done with this report?"

Their backs—Derry's and Hector's and Cassandra's—were to Jessie, coats slung over the men's shoulders. The *jauntiness* of those retreating rears! As if they were *enjoying* this!

"Here is a report that says our nation may *starve,* and it is buried. . ."

Where were they going? And what other alternative was there? If Derry were arrested at this big rally, the publicity would kill not only this candidacy but all others in the future.

"We need a new approach to our soil, to our agriculture, to our food, to our feeding habits. . . ."

When she had first told him she was running for office because she had a need for truth-telling, Derry had said quietly, "You have picked the one profession where truth-telling is almost an indecency."

This whole thing was unnecessary. Jessie had tried again and again to settle the missing tractor-trailer thing, offering to pay for it, kill the thing. Derry wouldn't let her, said he would settle it his own way, clinging to his problem as if it were his identity.

"The Department of Agriculture teems with experts on pesticides," Jessie hoping her voice wasn't becoming too shrill, too passionate, "to such a degree that the USDA is just one great big subsidized salesman for the chemical companies. Yet there is not a single expert in the USDA preaching organic farming. None of our land grant schools teach organic farming or even understand it."

Jessie's mind flooded with bitterness, her eyes on those three jauntily

257

retreating backs. Romantics, all you damned men, she was screaming in her mind. You leave us home to take care of the goats while you're off sacking cities and screwing Circe!

"If I get elected, it will be my sacred duty to call our government to account for a hundred years of neglect and ignorance . . ."

Derry had turned at the edge of the woods and flashed her his gleaming bearded smile.

Homer was full of prune juice about Odysseus coming home and settling down. After they sacked Troy, they never settled down! I could get him back right now! I could run after him, quit this podium. . . .

"We must restore agriculture to farmers, take it out of the hands of huge corporations which are gobbling up America. Today twelve land owners own fifty-two percent of Maine, twenty-five own half of California . . ."

Jessie's eyes glittering with tears.

"He has a talent," the Gray-eyed Goddess said. "He's heard the music of the cities, the siren call."

"Will he be back?" Jessie asked.

"Oh, he'll be back—many times."

"When?"

"When you need him," the Gray-eyed Goddess said. "And you will. You make a lot of mistakes, Jessie."

"I'm entitled," Jessie said fiercely, "to my own mistakes."

She continued with her message.

"Soil conservation is more important than either nuclear research or defense because if we lose our capacity to feed ourselves, we perish . . ."

Derry had long since disappeared into the woods.